Berkley titles by Chanel Cleeton

FLY WITH ME

INTO THE BLUE

ON BROKEN WINGS

NEXT YEAR IN HAVANA

WHEN WE LEFT CUBA

THE LAST TRAIN TO KEY WEST

THE MOST BEAUTIFUL GIRL IN CUBA

The
MOST
BEAUTIFUL
GIRL
in
CUBA

※

CHANEL CLEETON

BERKLEY • NEW YORK

BERKLEY
An imprint of Penguin Random House LLC
penguinrandomhouse.com

Berkley trade paperback ISBN: 9780593197813

The Library of Congress has cataloged the hardcover edition as follows:

Names: Cleeton, Chanel, author.
Title: The most beautiful girl in Cuba / Chanel Cleeton.
Description: New York: Berkley, [2021]
Identifiers: LCCN 2020046449 (print) | LCCN 2020046450 (ebook) |
ISBN 9780593098875 (hardcover) | ISBN 9780593197813 (trade paperback) |
ISBN 9780593098882 (ebook)
Subjects: GSAFD: Historical fiction.
Classification: LCC PS3603.L455445 M67 2021 (print) |
LCC PS3603.L455445 (ebook) | DDC 813/.6—dc23
LC record available at https://lccn.loc.gov/2020046449
LC ebook record available at https://lccn.loc.gov/2020046450

Printed in the United States of America
1st Printing

Book design by Kristin del Rosario

To my editor Kate Seaver and my agent Kevan Lyon.

*Thank you for believing in me
and for making this dream a reality.*

Prologue

I am surrounded by forgotten women.

They rail against their jailers, beat the iron bars with their fists until their knuckles are bloody, sit in the corner of the cells and rock, soft cries from their lips, their arms wrapped tightly around their bodies.

I find myself in prison.

In the damp that escapes the stone walls, the unforgiving cold from the floor that seeps into my pores and settles in my bones. In the cries that fill the silent night, the clanging of metal, the breaking of hearts, the abandonment of hope. It is always dark, and the endless night cloaks me, and that is perhaps the greatest surprise of all, that the darkness can be a comfort. That it can allow me to disappear, to leave this place and the uncertainty of tomorrow until I am left clinging to one thread to hold on to.

I will not let them break me.

I will not let them forget me.

They call this the Casa de Recogidas. It is a place for forgetting women society does not wish to face, for punishing those who have committed perceived slights against the Spanish, for condemning those who have dared to cast off the yoke of societal expectations. For those who fight for Cuba's independence.

We are the abandoned women.

In the evenings, when I cannot sleep, my heart sick with all the unfinished things I have left behind, I imagine they whisper to me, all those women who lived and died here before me. Their stories become part of me; the strength of the women who endured keeps me going.

If only I knew how to escape.

1896

One

GRACE

"I think you'll find, Mr. Pulitzer, that as a woman, I'm able to infiltrate parts of society your other reporters can't access. Why, look what Nellie Bly has done in her reporting . . ."

I clutch a leather folio to my chest, the little speech I've prepared running through my mind once more. As I lean down to right my skirts, I stumble on an uneven piece of wet ground, my shoe slipping, the hem of my dress dropping into nearly an inch of dirty water.

So much for making a good first impression.

"Bad luck," a red-haired newsboy shouts out at me, a mischievous grin on his face and the latest edition of the *World* in his hands.

It's busy today on Park Row, the street that slashes northeast from lower Broadway and houses the major New York newspapers, its proximity to City Hall an attractive proposition for journalists keen to keep up with the inner workings of government. Horse-drawn vehicles form a steady stream of traffic, interspersed by the odd bicycle swerving between them.

I gaze up at the building that houses the *New York World*, number 99 Park Row, the endless stories piled on top of one another. The tallest building in the city, it was originally the site of French's Hotel.

Legend has it that back when Joseph Pulitzer was a penniless veteran he was thrown out of the hotel. Twenty years later he returned, his fortune made, and bought the hotel, demolished it, and constructed this building, topping the new edifice with a four hundred and twenty-five ton gold dome. Two miles of wrought iron columns support the world's largest pressroom, and hopefully, if all goes well—my new place of employment.

"Why, look what Nellie Bly has been able to do," I continue.

I've rehearsed my opening salvo so frequently the words have become rote, but it's done little to calm the nerves inside me. Whereas men go into these interviews needing to be good, I must be better. The crack Miss Bly and others like her have opened for women trying to break into the newspaper industry has made the seemingly impossible possible, but still no easy feat by any measure.

The various articles I've written for smaller papers enclosed in my late father's leather folio represent the last few years of my life. The topics aren't as varied as I'd like: plenty of pieces on women's fashion, some on the care and running of a household from which I borrowed heavily from my mother's example given my lack of a household of my own, the stray piece of relationship advice, which may seem odd from someone who is decidedly—and happily—single. To my readers, my nom de plume A. Markham is a married woman of a respectable age, her children grown, her days spent puttering around her house and dispensing advice when she is not otherwise occupied with her husband's comfort.

I check in with building security, the appointment I made last week the only manner in which I could ensure admittance given the tightly controlled access to Pulitzer's offices. I hurry up to the eighteenth floor, which houses the newsroom.

All of my previous articles for the various small newspapers that have seen A. Markham's advice as fit to print have been sent by post, and so for the first time in my life, I set foot in a newsroom.

I am immediately, irrevocably, in love.

The newsroom feels like a living, breathing entity, the pulse in the air vibrating with excitement. There is shouting and keys tapping, and I've never heard more glorious sounds in all my life. Rolltop desks fill the room. Placards on the walls that say: "Accuracy, Accuracy, Accuracy! Who? What? Where? When? How? The Facts—The Color—The Facts!" surround the perimeter of the newsroom. Peeking out between the placards, windows reveal the city below, and beyond, a view all the way to the East River, New York City in all her muck and glory on proud display.

It's absolutely perfect.

A man approaches me. "Can I help you, miss?"

"I'm here to see Mr. Pulitzer," I reply. "I have an appointment."

Due to his declining health, Pulitzer is reportedly rarely at his office, favoring his private homes or yacht instead, so I seized this rare opportunity for a private meeting.

The man's eyes widen slightly. "And your name?"

"Grace Harrington."

"Follow me, Miss Harrington."

I walk behind him through the newsroom to Mr. Pulitzer's office, struggling to keep from gaping at each new sight that reveals itself. And at the same time, with every step it becomes evident that I am the only woman in the newsroom at the moment, my appearance drawing notice from more than one quarter of the room.

I tried on several outfits before I settled on this one: a sensible white dress with a light blue stripe, fine enough for such a meeting. For all of his success, the rumors that his family in Hungary was wealthy before he arrived in the United States, Pulitzer is a self-made man who understands the divide between rich and poor more than most, considering he's experienced both strata.

The man leads me into Pulitzer's office and announces me before shutting the door behind me, leaving me alone with the newspaperman.

Pulitzer rises from his desk for a moment until I take a seat, and then he follows suit after offering a polite greeting.

Pulitzer is a tall, slim man with a full head of red hair and a matching beard. His career in New York is distinguished—he served as a politician before he began running the *World*. Like my father, he fought with the northern states in the war. Pulitzer had been pulling back from his newspaper's daily operations, but that was before William Randolph Hearst announced his presence on the scene, and the man who was an unmatched Goliath in New York journalism gained a competitor. In the days when Pulitzer anticipated retiring from professional life, he's unexpectedly forced to wage a war for his paper's supremacy.

"Thank you for agreeing to meet with me, Mr. Pulitzer."

"I was most intrigued by your letter. I admired your father a great deal when we served in the war together. I was sorry to hear of his death."

There's a pang at the mention of my father's passing, one that hasn't quite faded in the years since I lost him. I'm not proud that I've used their past friendship to secure this meeting, but the competition for a job as a reporter is fierce—particularly at a paper as popular as the *World*—and since my gender is already a hurdle I must overcome, why not even the odds a bit?

"I confess, I was surprised when you asked for this appointment. While I admired your father when we fought alongside each other, it's been many years. How may I help you, Miss Harrington?"

"I'm here for a job if you have one. As a reporter. I've spent the last few years writing for smaller papers, getting experience where I could." I gesture to the leather folio in my lap. "I've brought samples of my work if you'd like to look at them. They're not necessarily the kinds of stories I want to cover, but they're a start."

"Why do you wish to work here, Miss Harrington?" Pulitzer asks, making no move to take the folio from me.

"Because of the stories you investigate, the impact you have. The *World* has one of the largest circulations in the world."

Indeed, Mr. Pulitzer has just slashed the *World*'s price to one cent, saying he prefers power to profits, circulation the measure by which success is currently judged.

"You have the opportunity to reach readers, to bring about change, to help people who desperately need assistance," I add. "I've admired the work you've done for years. You've long set the tone the rest of the New York newspaper industry follows. You've filled a gap in the news, given a voice to people who wouldn't have otherwise had one. I've read the articles you wrote when you were a reporter yourself in St. Louis, and I admire the manner in which you address society's ills. You've revolutionized the newspaper. I want to be part of that."

"That's all fine and good, but why should I hire you? What would you bring to the *World* that someone else wouldn't?"

"My gender, for one. A woman knows what it's like to be pushed to society's margins. There are some who might argue that a woman cannot do this job as effectively as a man. They would be wrong. Nellie Bly has proven that. You did, too, when you hired her."

"And what do you know of Nellie Bly?"

"You gave her a chance when others wouldn't."

"Cockerill gave her a chance," he replies, referring to his editor.

"With all due respect, Mr. Pulitzer, we both know this is your paper. You saw something in Nellie Bly. And now she's gone, and you need another reporter who can take on the kinds of stories she did and can go places your male journalists can't. What she accomplished at the Women's Lunatic Asylum"—the words "lunatic asylum" fall distastefully from my mouth—"on Blackwell's Island, going undercover like that, was nothing short of extraordinary. Those women's lives have been changed because of Miss Bly's courage and her daring. Those placards out there, the philosophy with which you run your newsroom—I promise to uphold it every single day I work for you."

Pulitzer leans back in his chair. "You're plucky like Bly, I'll give you that."

"I am."

"Your stepfather is Henry Shelton, isn't he?" Pulitzer asks.

"He is."

"And how does he feel about his stepdaughter sullying the family name with something as common as work—as a reporter no less? Considering how the papers are vilified these days, I'd imagine he wants something very different for you."

"He isn't pleased," I admit.

Pulitzer is silent for a beat. "I have to say, I admire your gumption for coming here."

I take a deep breath, hope filling me. This is it. The chance I've been waiting for to prove myself. I've already thought of a list of articles I want to write, can see my name on the byline—

"That said, we already have more stunt girl reporters than we need," Pulitzer adds, sending the hope billowing inside me crashing down. "Nellie Bly is coming back to write a series of articles for us. The move to Chicago didn't work out for her." He shrugs. "Talented as you may be—you're no Nellie."

I bite my tongue, suppressing the desire to point out that they already have more than one male investigative reporter, but that didn't stop them from hiring scores more.

"Everyone wants to be a reporter, but it's not an easy thing. It takes instincts for this business. A nose for the news. It isn't the sort of thing that can be taught. We could use more society reporters, though. Given your familial connections, you'd have an aptitude for that sort of thing. Our readers love learning about the foibles of the Knickerbockers, hearing about the balls, their entertainments."

"With all due respect, Mr. Pulitzer, those aren't the stories I want to write. It has not escaped my notice that the world I occupy—the society my family belongs to—is not what the rest of the city experiences. As a city, as a country, we are at a pivotal moment. We're deciding who we are, what we stand for, *who* we stand for. I want to be part of that discussion."

"I don't disagree with you, and I can't fault your enthusiasm or your convictions. But you're young. And relatively inexperienced. I have a newsroom full of reporters who've been working their beats for a long time. You're not ready."

I was prepared for this. Sometimes it feels like I'm banging my head against all the doors closed to me. I just need one door to crack open a little bit, one shot to prove myself.

"You're right. I'm not as experienced as some of your staff. Although, you've been known to take a chance on cub reporters. I'm just looking for someone to give me a chance. If you do, I promise you, you won't regret it."

"Why do you want this so badly? Why the news? If you're so set on working, why not something more respectable? You could be a teacher or a secretary."

"Because when I read Nellie Bly's report from Blackwell Island, I saw someone standing up for women. Women thrust into that miserable place because they didn't conform with society's expectations. Women who were judged insane by the virtue of being different, with little recourse available to them. What Nellie Bly wrote made a difference in the lives of those women. The grand jury's investigation, inspired by her articles, led to increased funding and an improvement in the quality of care for the women in the asylum. I want to write pieces like that, articles that make the world a better place. There's nothing I'd rather do."

When I finish my speech, I can tell I nearly have him by the expression on his face. After all, Pulitzer has made his fortune in the newspaper business. This is his life. Who else would better understand the passion I feel for this profession?

"Why did you come to me, Miss Harrington? Why the *World* and not one of my competitors? Why not the *Journal*?"

I'm hardly surprised that he invokes the *New York Journal* when he speaks of his competitors. The *Journal*'s owner and publisher, William Randolph Hearst, and Pulitzer have been locked in a fierce battle since Hearst came to New York a year ago. Hearst made a name for himself as the publisher of the successful *San Francisco Examiner*—a newspaper that was floundering when he originally took it over, rebuilding it from scratch—and now he's set his sights on the New York newspaper scene. With his late father's immense wealth behind him, he's a formidable opponent.

"Because the *World* reports on the news," I reply smoothly. "The *Journal* reports on the *World*. It hasn't escaped my notice that you're often the first to break a story only for Hearst to take your work, sensationalize it, and publish the same story in his paper, which he sells at a loss."

Pulitzer's expression darkens. "Hearst has no scruples in the way he runs his newspaper or the manner in which he reports on the news.

It is one thing to use dramatics to highlight important causes or to draw readers' attention. But for Hearst, the dramatics aren't a means to the end; they *are* the end. Months ago, he stole my entire Sunday edition staff. Editor included. When I paid them more money than he did and hired them back, he just stole them again the very next day with the promise of even higher salaries.

"He has spies in my newsroom, Miss Harrington. I doubt his paper can put out an edition without using ours for inspiration. You want to do what the stunt girl reporters do to get the story? You want to be like Nellie Bly? Go undercover and work for Hearst and report back to me on the news the *Journal* is covering. If he has a lead on something, I want to know about it. Let's see how he likes being beaten at his own game, how he enjoys someone else scooping *his* stories. If you do a good job of it, say after a year or so, then I'll give you a position as one of my investigative reporters. It's a better offer than you'll get anywhere else with your inexperience."

Of all the possible outcomes I imagined from this interview, this wasn't one of them.

"Why me?"

"Because Hearst isn't likely to suspect someone like you. And since you haven't worked for me before, there's no reason he would link us together. No one knows you."

I came in here all bluster and confidence, hoping I could sway a man who'd built his fortune through his own ingenuity, but the truth is, I'm more than a little desperate. Ever since I moved out of my mother and stepfather's house, and into my aunt Emma's brownstone, money has been tight. I have a small inheritance from my father, but it will only go so far, and I hopefully have many years of fending for myself ahead of me. Scruples are a luxury I can hardly afford if I am to be truly independent, and more than anything in the world, I want to be one of Pulitzer's famed reporters. Spying isn't that different from other stunt reporting schemes, and if Hearst is doing the same to Pulitzer by placing spies in *his* newsroom . . .

"You want to be an investigative reporter—prove it. Everyone gets their hands dirty from time to time. Do you have what it takes to be a reporter in New York City, Miss Harrington?" Pulitzer makes an impatient noise as if I've squandered too much of his time. "Do we have a deal?"

It's right there in front of me—everything I've been working for, dreaming of, just within my grasp. And if I could do good work, then surely the ends justify the means?

"We have a deal."

What was I thinking?

An hour later, I stand in the newsroom of the *New York Journal* waiting to see if Hearst will meet with me, half hoping he won't. Hearst reportedly runs a more relaxed newspaper than Pulitzer, and while the *World*'s security is notoriously tight, Hearst is said to bring all manner of people into his office, rubbing elbows with his staff as though he is one of them. While I hoped to impress Pulitzer with hard work and gumption, Hearst is drawn to the novel and unusual. Hopefully, a young woman without an appointment showing up at his newspaper in search of employment qualifies enough to catch his attention.

The gamble works, because not a minute later, a man escorts me into Hearst's office, announcing my name as I walk through the door, before closing it behind him.

Two men lounge in the room, cigars dangling from their idle hands. One is big and handsome, his suit dashing and expensive, his angular face punctuated by dark, slashing brows and a nose that looks like it's been broken a time or two. There's a girl standing so close to his hip she might as well be seated on his lap, her stunning features accentuated by her daring dress.

The other man is William Randolph Hearst.

Hearst is younger than I expected him to be; he doesn't look that much older than I am. His light brown hair is parted down the middle, his appearance pleasing, his clothes impeccably tailored, but for the garish color of his suit and tie. Where Pulitzer had a somber look about him, Hearst is the complete opposite. He doesn't have a show-girl at his side, he has *two,* the similarities in their features leading me to the conclusion that they must be related—sisters, perhaps.

Both of the men in Hearst's office have the look of a hard night of drinking stamped all over them, their clothes disheveled, the cuts of their suits not quite as pristine as their tailors likely intended. The pot of coffee sitting on the desk between them and the faint hint of alcohol in the air suggests they're winding down the day rather than starting it.

The big one smiles, sprawled in his chair, his necktie loosened past the point of respectability.

"Can we help you?" he asks.

Most men of my acquaintance would take umbrage at another commandeering their office in such a manner, but Hearst appears unruffled as his friend directs the conversation.

I ignore the dark-haired man, offering a small smile for the women who look more amused by the tableau before them than anything else.

I turn my attention to Hearst. Despite the general sense of debauchery around the room, he's hunched over a stack of papers, a pen in hand. He barely spared me a glance when I walked into the room, but now that the other man has spoken, he lifts his head and his gaze runs over me quickly.

Hearst's reputation precedes him, and considering we once operated in somewhat adjacent circles, I've been privy to the whispers: that he had a pet alligator in his rooms at Harvard, trotting it out at parties on a leash while keeping it drunk on champagne before he was finally kicked out of the school his junior year. Despite his notorious antics, he's known for a desire to eschew most of New York society that's at odds with the flashy showmanship that surrounds him.

"I would like a job." The words come out more clearly, my confidence building now that I've been through this rigmarole once before with Pulitzer.

It seems I have the attention of the room now, the women interested, the dark-haired man eyeing me with greater curiosity.

Hearst rises from his chair, straightening to his full height. I crane my neck to peer up at him.

"What sort of job?" Hearst asks.

"As an investigative reporter. Don't you want your own Nellie Bly?" I add jauntily, capitalizing on his rivalry with Pulitzer.

"Why would I want my own Nellie Bly?" Hearst asks, an unmistakable gleam in his eye.

He might have been up all night, but he's sober and sharp.

"Because she's an advantage for Pulitzer. Nellie Bly is writing a series of articles for the *World*, highlighting women's stories, appealing to their interests. You want to increase your circulation; you need a voice that appeals to women, too. How can you compete with Pulitzer if you don't have the same tools at your disposal?"

"I have money, Miss Harrington," he drawls. "A great deal of it."

"So does Pulitzer. And all that money is only as good as what you can do with it. Why else did you steal his staff?"

"You've done your research, I'll give you that, Miss Harrington. And as it happens, I'm a fan of you girl reporters. Pulitzer isn't the only one who employs them. Are you familiar with Winifred Black's work?"

I shake my head.

"She wrote for me as Annie Laurie when I owned the *San Francisco Examiner* and followed me to New York to work at the *Journal*. You're right, you know. There's an advantage to what women can do, the access they can achieve." He studies me for a moment. "Do you know what we're trying to accomplish here?"

"You want to increase your circulation. You want to dominate the New York newspaper scene."

"We do. But it's more than that. Gone are the days when newspapers simply report on what happens. We must take action. The people depend on us. They look to us. We're not in the business of being concerned with profit. We're courting influence. That's why I'm happy to sell my paper for less than others choose to. I want to reach the greatest number of people possible. I aim to influence policy.

"We're in a position to do something about the ills facing society. We *should* do something; we must shine a spotlight on the struggles they face. But we don't just have to look at what's happening in New York City, or even the United States. When the government fails to do its duty, when it fails to act in defense of the innocent, then the people must compel it to do so, and who is better placed to represent the people than an extension of them—the free press? You could say that is our duty, too."

I'm a little shaken by how close his speech is to the one I delivered before Pulitzer. I'd always written Hearst off as a craven businessman, but the passion contained in his words appears genuine.

His desire to remake the newspaper and its role in society is an ambitious goal, even more daunting than his aim to challenge the *World* for circulation supremacy. When Hearst bought the *Journal* last year, the difference between the two papers was vast, although he's closing the gap.

My gaze shifts to the other occupants of the room, to see if they are as surprised by this version of Hearst as I am. Gone is the languid pose of the man sitting beside Hearst. He's yet to introduce himself, but he sits a bit straighter in his chair, leaning forward, his elbows propped against his knees.

Come to think of it, he doesn't look nearly as debauched as he did earlier, either.

I turn my attention back to Hearst.

"After hearing all that, do you still want to work for me?" he asks.

I could attempt to meet his speech with one of my own, but I'm not sure anything I say could match his fervor, so I don't bother trying.

"I do."

Hearst studies me for a moment longer than is polite, as though he is attempting to take my measure.

Can he tell by looking at me, by my mannerisms, that we unmistakably come from the same place, and yet have turned our backs on society in favor of something new and uniquely our own? Maybe Pulitzer saw those similarities as well when he thought this plan would work.

"We don't offer a salary," Hearst finally replies. "But you'll be paid on space for the articles you write."

My heart thuds.

He plucks a folded newspaper from the stack in front of him and slides it across the desk to me.

It's a copy of Pulitzer's paper, the *New York World*, dated May 1, 1896. The byline is that of Pulitzer's star reporter Sylvester Scovel. On the front page, there is an article about the killing of Cuban civilians by Spanish soldiers in the village of Campo Florida near Havana.

"What do you know about this situation down in Cuba?" Hearst asks me.

Two

꧁ ꧂

EVANGELINA

"They're going to kill my father."

The words pour from me, panic loosening my tongue despite the fact that if this past year of exile with my father fifty miles south of Cuba's mainland on the Isle of Pines has taught me anything, it's that I must be cautious around our Spanish guards.

"Evangelina." My fiancé, Emilio Betancourt, says my name impatiently, his tone low, urgent, filled with none of the romance I'm used to hearing from him. I asked him to meet me at my house, but even here there is no privacy to be had. Emilio glances around us, his gaze resting on the guards standing nearby, watching us, always monitoring our moments as though we are forever plotting insurrection against the Spanish crown. Spain has controlled our fortunes for over four hundred years, since Christopher Columbus first colonized Cuba in 1492, and now as we fight to liberate Cuba, they tighten their hold on us.

"You forget yourself," Emilio hisses, speaking to me as if I am a mere girl and not the woman he has followed around with lovesick gazes, as though eighteen years old is a child's age. He tugs me by the arm and pulls me farther away from the soldiers.

"The Spanish have thrown my father in the jail again," I snap, lowering my voice. "I don't know if he is safe or if he's even alive. I do not forget myself. I know exactly where I am and what I must do. *You* forget yourself."

I lean in to Emilio so we merely look like the engaged couple we are, indulging in the sort of stolen embrace that would normally be frowned upon in polite society. In the distance, one of the Spanish soldiers makes a rude comment to another about my virtue—or lack thereof—but I ignore his cruel words. I might have been born a lady, but we are remade in times of war.

Last year, a small band of revolutionaries—Mambises—under the flag of the Cuban Revolutionary Party declared an insurrection against the Spanish at the town of Baire near Santiago. When we received news of the uprising, I hoped this time would be successful. It is our third attempt to free ourselves from Spanish tyranny in almost thirty years, the first war fought before I was even born.

I grew up dreaming of the independent Cuba my father is willing to risk his life for, listening to his stories as a soldier in the Ten Years' War, and I gave my word that in this new battle for liberation I would fight alongside my father and countrymen. On the night we were to join the Cuban army last year, a spy told the Spanish of our plans and they imprisoned my father for being a revolutionary and sentenced him to death.

"I was the one who visited my father in prison, who cared for him, who begged for his life and saw his sentence commuted to life imprisonment," I add. "I was the one who met with General Weyler and begged for my father to be exiled here to the Isle of Pines rather than sent to the Spanish's penal colony off the coast in Africa. So don't treat me like a child. I may be eighteen, but I've fought for my family and for Cuba."

At least on the Isle of Pines, my sister Carmen and I have been able to accompany our father, to cook for him, do the cleaning, and care for him. Here we have a small store where I can buy food, there is a doctor in town, and many of the other prisoners are old family friends, revolutionaries like my father. We have a little house with a tiled roof and a big piazza. It is hardly paradise, but it could be worse, I suppose.

If not for the new Spanish colonel who controls our fortunes.

"What are you doing about Berriz?" I ask Emilio, glancing furtively around the room to ensure none of the soldiers have heard me. "Ever since the colonel has taken command over the Isle of Pines, he seeks me out. He's thrown my father in the jail. If I am to be your wife, then I need to know you care about me and my family." Disgust fills my voice. "Berriz has told me he loves me."

Emilio pales.

"He toys with us by falsely imprisoning my father and then releasing him, only to jail him again later. I worry about my father's health. I kneeled before Berriz and begged him to return my father to me. And now, after releasing my father, Berriz has arrested my father and thrown him in the jail *again*."

"I've heard that Berriz's wife will be joining him soon," Emilio replies. "Perhaps her presence here will help things."

"And until then? What am I to do?"

Emilio leans closer, running a hand through my long, dark hair. I jerk. Behind us, one of the soldiers says something about a lovers' quarrel.

"Nothing will happen to you or your father, Evangelina," Emilio urges, as though he sees the doubt in my eyes, my disappointment over his powerlessness, the anger filling me. When my father told me war was coming to our island, I was ready to fight, but this waiting around for someone to rescue me is torture.

Emilio offers his reassurances louder than he should, perhaps to convince me or to give himself the confidence he needs to act, and suddenly, before either one of us can move, before we remember that any sign of rebellion is met with force, the soldiers are on him, brandishing their weapons, hitting him with their large guns over and over again until Emilio falls silent, pain etched across his face. Tears rain down my cheeks, anger burning in my chest, but I do not speak a word.

Sometimes it is too easy to forget that we must always fear for our lives. The Isle of Pines might be a beautiful exile on the surface, but no matter how long a leash we are given, it is still a prison.

"Emilio—"

"I'll be fine," he mouths to me.

The soldiers haul Emilio away unceremoniously. His gaze is trained on me as they exit the house, the soldiers laughing and talking among themselves, leaving me standing alone.

Nausea fills me, the urge to retch overwhelming. The scent of the soldiers' sweat lingers in the cramped house, the sight of Emilio's spilled blood on the floor inescapable.

I walk outside, my legs quaking, heart pounding, lungs desperate for fresh air. I can't get used to the violence, to all of the horrible things people do to one another. Nothing in my childhood or after prepared me for the way we live now, for the fear that is my near-constant companion. I didn't appreciate how sheltered I was until the night my father was captured and everything changed.

I lean against the front of my house, my heart rate slowly returning to normal. My gaze sweeps across the landscape, and then a chill trickles down my spine.

Colonel Berriz is several yards away, the sun shining down on his dark hair. His men stand tall under his attention, their chests stuck out like strutting peacocks as they listen to his orders, their uniforms like feathers dragging behind them. The soldiers have become more insufferable with each passing day, their arrogance just one of the indignities we've been forced to suffer.

Berriz stops speaking, his gaze cutting from the men to where I stand beneath the palm tree in front of our house.

To me.

That he makes no effort to hide the gleam in those awful green eyes, the slow unfurling of his smile, that flash of teeth beneath his dark whiskers, is as unsettling as the leisurely look he takes, his gaze starting at the top of my head and working its way down, lingering on the bodice of my gown with hunger, as though he is a wolf and I am an errant sheep that will soon become his evening meal.

I cannot help but wonder if the men acted on his orders earlier, if he told them to look for any opportunity to attack Emilio knowing he's my fiancé.

I see a flash of something that looks a lot like satisfaction in Berriz's eyes.

There is no question about it.

Berriz must go.

AFTER MUCH PLEADING, MY FATHER IS RELEASED FROM PRISON once more, and hope fills me that things will improve, that I can continue to hold Berriz at bay.

But a few days later, the moon bright in the sky, the unthinkable happens.

It must be nearly midnight, but my father has yet to return home.

I walk over to the window for what feels like the hundredth time, parting the curtains, willing the image of my father walking toward our front door to appear.

Surely, I would know if they'd killed him, would feel something in my heart. He's the only parent I have left now after losing my mother when I was a child, and with my other sisters scattered throughout Cuba, there's only me, and Carmen, and our father.

I can't lose him.

I stare out the window, searching for some sign. It's impossible to imagine that my father left this world on a night such as this—still, calm, peaceful—the silver moon shining down on the Isle of Pines.

Surely, I would know if he's dead.

Whispered prayers tumble from my lips, words I learned in childhood that have given me solace throughout my life. God cannot fail me now.

And then I see it—like a divine apparition slipping through the night—

A shadow, moving in and out of darkness.

A man.

I clutch the curtain, my knuckles white, hope beating through my breast.

He is safe. He is home.

Perhaps they questioned him again. Berriz is the sort of man who plays with his food, frightening it to death before he feasts. What better way to strike fear into my heart than to toy with my father's life once more?

The shadow moves again, not with the speed of a desperate man racing for home, but with a languid, feline ease.

A sliver of moonlight illuminates him.

Gold lace adorns his shoulders and the cap on his head, gold stars on his collar, a gold braid on his breast. Between the moon's glow and his golden uniform, it appears as though he has been gilded. The metal on his belt, the hilt of his sword, his spurs all shine.

For a moment, I cannot breathe.

Colonel Berriz.

Berriz walks toward our house, up to the veranda. He pauses, glancing up and down the little street where we live.

For him to visit in the middle of the night, dressed in full uniform . . .

A knock sounds, intruding on the quiet night.

There's a moment of hesitation—a desire to stave off whatever bad news he has likely come to tell me, a fear of being confronted by him once more. But he's an officer, a *Spanish* officer, and in this time, in this place, he might as well be king.

I stare at the latch that holds our door shut, little more than a defense against the wind that threatens to leave it banging against the frame, hardly a comfort or source of security in these times. Wishing I could ignore him altogether, I reach for the latch, but before I can make my fingers do the deed, the door flies open and Berriz stands over the threshold staring at me. I'm unable to gather my bearings, to reconcile the sight of our flimsy wooden door listing drunkenly to the side, when he strides forward, invading my space, closing the distance between us as though he has a right to it, one hand on his sword, the other grazing his mustache, his medals gleaming as though he has groomed himself for some special occasion, the elegant effect at odds with the barbaric manner in which he has broken into our home. I can do little more than gape at him while he stares back at me with a gleam in his eyes that makes the hairs on the back of my neck stand on end.

"You're surprised to see me here," he says.

I blink, the gold on his uniform nearly blinding in its wrongness, his words suggesting I have missed some vital moment that led us to this place.

"Do you—do you have news of my father?"

"I do. There are other matters that stand between us as well."

"Has something happened to my father? Is he safe? Where is he?"

"Evangelina. Honestly. Perhaps the more prudent thing would be to ask if I'm comfortable, to offer me a seat."

The instinct to be polite, to accommodate a guest in my home, is nearly second nature despite the strangeness of this entire evening, despite the urge to bristle at his heavy-handed tone.

"Would you—"

Before I can finish my sentence, Berriz slides into one of the chairs, positioning himself between me and the doorway.

My brain is sluggish, as though I am in a dream, or in this case, a nightmare, worries firing rapidly past me, my worry for my father, the irregularity of Berriz showing up like this, alone, without a care for propriety or my reputation, but each time I try to seize on one of the thoughts, they slip through my fingers like fine granules of sand.

"I wondered what you looked like roused from your bed," Berriz muses.

My cheeks heat, a little gasp escaping my lips.

"Lovely," he croons. "You're so lovely. We will be friends, won't we? It would be a mistake to make an enemy of me. I am a powerful man, and no one is in a better position to grant your father his freedom. Why, without my help he might be sent to Ceuta or Chafarinas, and then who would you have to blame?"

For an instant, relief fills me at the news that my father is still alive. But the words falling from Berriz's lips bring a new wave of horror. The Spanish penal colony off the north coast of Africa is well-known for its harsh conditions. Disease is rampant, hunger prevalent, and the officials treat the prisoners there worse than animals.

"Really, Evangelina. You can't ask me for information about your father, can't expect my assistance, and think I want nothing in return."

I feared we would come to this moment, and now that it's here, I don't know how to manage it—how to manage *him*. I resort to the entreaties that have thus far served me well with the Spanish soldiers I've been forced to beg for mercy. Although, I doubt Berriz has a better nature.

"Please. My father is all we have left. He is a good man. He's a soldier like you. He was doing what he thought was right, fighting for his country, for his friends. Please spare him."

Berriz laughs cruelly. "Why are you wasting my time with such nonsense? Do you think I went to all the trouble to dress myself in this uniform, in a manner befitting a royal reception, to be lectured by a Cuban rebel? You know why I'm here and what I want. It's time we stop this dance and clarify things between us."

Even if I wasn't engaged to Emilio, I could never care for a man who has treated me and my family so abominably. There is no romance to be had between jailer and prisoner, not when Berriz holds my life in his hands with such callous indifference.

"I don't know what you speak of, sir." My voice shakes, but I struggle to get the words out, to convince him that he cannot do this, that he doesn't wish to act in such a dishonorable fashion. "I don't know what you want. I'm only interested in saving my father. I—"

Before I even realize it, Berriz rises from the chair and catches me by the wrist, his big hand encircling my fragile bones. He could break every single one of them with only the slightest effort.

"I love you," he proclaims.

I shudder.

There is no love in his voice, only zeal in his eyes. How do you dissuade a man who believes he is entitled to what you've already told him he cannot have? How do you reason with such a man?

Berriz tugs on my hand, pulling my fingers to his lips.

The feel of his flesh against mine makes my skin crawl.

I struggle past the wave of nausea, his breath hot against my skin, his mouth—

My gaze darts around the room as I search for something to use against him, praying someone will come to my aid. Is Carmen sleeping? The door to her room was closed when I returned to the house after dining with Emilio this evening and I assumed she was already asleep. I open my mouth to call to her, but fear of endangering her, too, stops me.

The door is my best hope of escape, but Berriz moves so quickly, our strength unmatched, the odds of escaping slim.

I jerk my hand from his grasp, panic filling me.

Anger flashes in his eyes. "You don't want to make an enemy of me, Evangelina. I love you more than anything in the world."

What does such a man know of love? What does he know of me? Perhaps he wants me because he cannot have me, but that is not love. Love is something infinitely kinder than this.

He's so close now, crowding my space, and try as I might to escape him, there's no room for me to move. He is everywhere, surrounding me, invading me.

"You're responsible for what happens to your father. Don't forget that." He grips my shoulders, his fingers digging into my skin, shaking me like a broken doll, my head thrown back, the pain from his hands nearly unbearable. "I love you, Evangelina."

He says it over and over again, as though that explains why he's here and attempting this horrible thing, as though his perverted version of "love" forgives all manner of sins.

I hate him.

Sobs escape my lips, but he keeps shaking me, his actions growing rougher with each moment that passes.

Please, someone help me.

Berriz is so big, too strong, and the zeal in his eyes has become explosive, his feelings and wants lashing out at me in an uncontrollable madness. The civilized veneer he adopted when he put on his fine dress uniform has disappeared completely.

He is little more than an animal now, a predator in the jungle.

I scream, the sound ripped from the depths of my soul, a primal terror filling me.

Berriz loosens his grip on me, momentarily startled by the noise, by *me*, and I wrench myself away from him, running toward my bedroom.

My mind is empty save one word running through it over and over again:

Escape.

I throw open the door to my room, another scream torn from me, but he's too fast, at my heels. Berriz catches me by the arm.

It is over. I am doomed.

And then, as if God himself has heard my prayers and answered them—

Suddenly, men pour through my bedroom window, the outer door to our house, shouts and oaths filling the room, the men charging us and separating me from Berriz.

I push through the crowd of men swarming around, the familiar faces filling me with relief. Emilio is there, and so many of our friends, their hands on Berriz, binding him, carrying him from the room, saving me.

There's a commotion outside the house—heavy footsteps and

yells—and Spanish soldiers burst through the door, coming to Berriz's aid as my rescuers shout back at them, my sister Carmen's voice echoing somewhere out there in the entry room.

I close the door to my bedroom, sinking to the floor, my legs shaking.

Where is my father? Is he in jail? Has Berriz harmed him? What will I do? What will Berriz do to me for rejecting him? For drawing attention to his perfidy?

On the other side of the door, men shout, their voices indistinguishable as they argue among themselves, and then finally, all is quiet.

Have they thrown Carmen in jail, too?

I should leave the room, go and see what has happened to my sister, to Emilio, but even as I try to rise from my crouched position on the floor, my limbs are frozen in place.

I struggle to steady my breathing, to keep the panic at bay.

I don't remember my mother, she died when I was so young, but even after such tragedy, the sadness that afflicted our father, we lived a good life in Puerto Príncipe. My sisters, Flor de Maria, Carmen, Clemencia, and I were happy. We had a garden where we would grow flowers. We had some money, and life was as pleasant as we could make it. Perhaps my father might have wished for a son, but he loved all of us and treated us as though we were his equals, never as children.

I would give anything to go back to those days, to be reunited with Flor de Maria and Clemencia. I would give anything to escape these horrors.

I pray my father and sister are safe.

Where is Carmen?

Hours must pass, the walls of the room growing smaller and smaller. Surprisingly, no one comes for me. It's impossible to believe a man like Berriz will let this incident stand, that there won't be some retaliation for me rebuffing his advances. Will he do as he said, and strike at my father to punish me? I have to hope he has merely imprisoned my father; if Berriz's true aim was to seduce me, even he couldn't have been foolish enough to first harm my father.

Finally, I can't take the waiting anymore, the urge to flee overwhelming, and I slip out the door and head toward a little cabin I know from when I used to explore the island with Carmen. It's as good a place as any to hide until I decide what to do next.

I walk toward the hills, each and every sound alerting me to a potential danger. I imagine the beady eyes of animals watching me from the dark, hoping they won't attack me.

At the moment, though, the animals hardly feel like the greatest danger facing me.

What has happened to Carmen?

I trudge on through the dark night, exhaustion seeping into my bones, but the need to find safe shelter for the evening propels me forward.

When I reach the cabin, I slow, the sound of voices reaching me where I hoped I'd find silence instead.

I duck down in the brush and peek out between the foliage.

Soldiers mill about the structure.

They must have come to my house and found me gone, and decided to search the island.

I still, my heart pounding madly in my chest as I watch their movements. As well as I thought I knew this place, the Spanish know it well, too, and they can predict my movements as quickly as I make them. Considering we're on an island, there are limited options available to me. Are there other soldiers out searching for the men who came to my aid when Berriz attacked me? For Emilio and our friends?

I've done nothing wrong in all of this, and yet, while I thought Berriz would be exposed for the villain he is, it seems as though I am the one they seek to punish, my crime that of telling a Spanish soldier the world isn't his for the taking, *I* am not his for the taking.

If they catch me, I'll surely be killed.

I head deeper into the hills, quickening my pace, casting a glance over my shoulder every so often to ensure no one follows me. My feet slip against the ground, and a few times I nearly fall, but I continue on, my body aching, heart heavy.

As I walk on, the sky begins to lighten, daybreak dawning.

Each sound that fills the air around me sends a chill down my spine. Without the cover of darkness, my chances of being caught rise dramatically.

Am I to be thrown in jail? Sentenced to the firing squad?

Up ahead, there's a little ravine, and I quicken my pace as I near it. I crouch in front of it, cupping my hands together, already relishing in the sensation of the cool water sliding down my throat, but when I try to scoop the liquid, it's a dark brown color, too murky to be drinkable.

A sob escapes my lips as I wipe my hand across my face.

My body is covered in mud, my limbs sore from the hills, adrenaline crashing through me.

The sun beats down on me, exhaustion setting in, and I gather some of the nearby branches and brush. If I can't find drinkable water, at least I can build a shelter.

But even as I begin propping up the branches, I know it is for naught. There is nowhere I can hide on this island that the Spanish will not find me. And how long before they punish my family in my absence?

I don't know what awaits me at the house I share with my sister Carmen and my father, but there's nowhere left to try to escape.

THE JOURNEY BACK TO THE HOUSE FEELS AS THOUGH IT TAKES much longer than it should, tears of frustration filling my eyes as I battle exhaustion. I listen for soldiers, but all that greets me are the normal sounds of the island.

As I near the little village that has been our home, it's still early, not a soul in sight. Maybe the soldiers are out searching for me, or perhaps they decided to rest after a long night once they came to the same realization I did—that there's no possibility of me escaping this mess.

Our little house tumbles into view, and for a moment instinct nearly takes over, and I yearn to run away.

I square my shoulders and continue on.

When I reach our home, there are blessedly no soldiers to be found, but Carmen is pacing the length of the bedroom.

"Where have you been?" Carmen exclaims, throwing her arms around me. She looks worried and exhausted.

For a moment, we reverse our roles, and whereas I am normally the one who cares for our family, now I lean into her embrace, drawing strength from her presence, relief filling me at the sight of her unharmed.

"I went to the hills. I thought I might escape the soldiers, but it was so dark, and I was so tired, and there was nowhere to go." A sob escapes, and then another one. "What am I going to do?"

"I don't know. Everyone is upset. The Spanish are very angry."

Dread fills me. "What has happened to Berriz?"

"The soldiers came and rescued him. They rounded up all of our friends who came to your aid, Emilio and the others, and they've thrown them in jail."

I close my eyes, offering a prayer for my fiancé and for all those who helped me. For my father. For myself.

I pull away from Carmen, struggling to maintain calm.

"They're going to throw me in jail, aren't they?"

"I don't know," Carmen replies, but her words are at odds with the tone of her voice and the somber expression in her eyes.

So be it.

Whatever happens next, at least I prefer it to being Berriz's mistress, to accepting his advances.

"Well, I suppose there's nothing to do but wait. I'm going to take a bath and change into clean clothes. Eat some breakfast."

"And if the soldiers come?" Carmen asks.

"Then they come."

MY HAIR IS BARELY DRY WHEN TWO SOLDIERS KNOCK AT OUR door.

There's no opportunity for us to say good-bye to our father, to gather our things, before Carmen and I are shipped out on the *Nuevo Cubano* steamer to the mainland of Cuba with a boat full of other prisoners.

Three

❧

The prison the Spanish send us to, the Casa de Recogidas, makes our living conditions on the Isle of Pines seem like paradise. The prison is located in one of the rougher sections of Havana, surrounded by crooked alleys. The walls are high and thick, topped by stalwart parapets, the windows barred, a military barracks directly behind the structure.

The Catholic Church founded Recogidas over a hundred years ago as a shelter and place to reform women. I'm not one to question the Church, but whatever their original intentions, the reality is a nightmare.

Our journey was an arduous one. On the Isle of Pines we were treated with a measure of respect because we are ladies, but from the moment we boarded the steamer bound for the Cuban mainland, soldiers insulted us and jeered at us. My wrists are still sore from their manacles chafing my skin.

When they boarded us on the train to carry us to Havana, I fervently hoped that revolutionaries would attack the train and rescue us, but we weren't so lucky. Instead, I gazed out the window as immense tobacco plantations, sugar fields, and towering palms passed us by, the countryside decorated by the occasional stone fort.

At night when I dream, it is of my childhood, of our house in Cienfuegos where we all lived as a family—my sisters, father, and I. In the courtyard of our home, there was a great fountain. The water leaped and sparkled in the sun as though it was alive. I used to dance in the courtyard and reach out, as if I could command the water, catching it in my hands, bidding it to stand still and talk to me.

I don't know what has happened to my father, if he is still on the Isle of Pines, if Berriz has taken his anger toward me out on him. I do not know what has happened in the world in my absence, or exactly how much time has passed in this horrible prison. I've heard nothing about Emilio's whereabouts or that of our friends who rescued me; I worry they're imprisoned in an equally foul place.

It feels as though we are waiting to die here, growing mad minute by minute, our bones aging, the life leeching from us.

Carmen takes it the hardest, her tears ringing throughout the night, and I cannot help but feel guilty for the fact that if not for me, she wouldn't be here, that she is being punished for my rejection of Berriz.

I relive the events with Berriz over and over again in my mind, trying to understand how we got to this place, how life could be so unfair to condemn us to this misery.

But then, life is nothing if not unfair.

It is impossible to not feel afraid in this horrible place.

During the day, Carmen and I huddle together like scared sheep, kept in a pen as though we are wild animals.

Our jailers have thrown us into a cave with hundreds of other women. There are bars in front of our cage, and men come in from the street and watch us through the open spaces, speaking of us as though we are unaware of their presence, as though we are not human beings worthy of respect. They blow smoke in our faces and comment on our clothes, our bodies, laughing as they watch us on our hands and knees scrubbing the floors.

It is impossible to not be angry in a place like this.

One day, the clank of metal against metal, the rattle and shake that accompanies the heavy fall of footsteps on dirty, dank stone floors fills the air, and hope springs in my chest at the possibility of a visitor and any news they might bring even as I know such an emotion is futile in this place.

Recogidas has a particular talent for eradicating hope in the women it imprisons.

"The warden would like to speak with you," one of the guards announces, staring at me and Carmen.

Carmen sidles closer to me, clutching my hand in hers.

"Not you," the guard replies, his gaze fixed uncomfortably on Carmen. "Just your sister," he adds, gesturing toward me.

"I'll be fine," I whisper, squeezing Carmen's hand.

Around us, the other women imprisoned here jeer, but I block out their voices.

Recogidas has a particular talent for pitting us against one another, too.

When we first arrived, the women searched us for anything valuable they could use until they realized that despite our appearances, the whispers that we are *ladies*, like them we have nothing. Regardless of how and why we ended up here, we have all been excommunicated from society, abandoned, discarded, and forgotten.

The feel of their hands on my body reminded me so much of Berriz, I was sick afterward.

Behind me, the women laugh as I follow the guard from my cell,

Carmen's anxiety at being left alone a palpable thing that follows me all the way to the warden's office. Will she be safe in my absence?

If they sentence me to death, who will care for my sister?

My family has always been the most important thing in my life, and after all I have done to care for my father and sister, it pains me that Carmen is here, even indirectly, because of me.

The guards parade me through the prison, more women calling out to me. My case has drawn a measure of notoriety thanks to Berriz's stature, heaping more attention on me than I'd like. I can only hope that somewhere outside of Recogidas, there are people working on my behalf, like-minded revolutionaries who are as tired of the Spanish injustices as I am.

I suck in a deep breath as I walk toward the warden's office, trying not to breathe in the air, to keep the odor of the prison at bay. The stench here is an indescribable horror—death, desperation, all sorts of bodily decays mixed together.

I lower my head, careful to keep from making eye contact with anyone. In my mind, I am somewhere else entirely, at home with my family, dancing in the courtyard of our home, the sun shining down and warming my skin. In my mind, I have disappeared, and I am not covered in filth and rags, hunger gnawing at my belly.

The guard stops outside the warden's office.

Nerves fill me as he shows me into the room, and I approach the warden's desk.

"You will need to make a statement about what happened to you," the warden Don Jose announces, all pleasantries abandoned.

I swallow, fear closing my throat. Of all the things I relive at night when the demons come to me, the last I wish to remember is the feel of Berriz's body against mine.

"I will tell you the truth," I say, because there is no point in lying to these people. They will have every part of you whether you wish to give it or not.

I tell him all of it, but when I get to the end of my story, Don Jose looks at me expectantly.

"But not the whole truth," he replies. "You omitted something very important. We want the names of the men who came to your house. The ones who attacked Colonel Berriz. They must be made to answer for their crimes. To attack a Spanish officer is a grave offense. If you do this, you will make things much easier for yourself. We will be more lenient in your sentencing if you show that you are sorry for what you have done, and that you recognize the role others have played in your actions."

It is one thing to discuss what happened, to be forced to remember it, but another entirely to sacrifice my friends, people like Emilio Betancourt whom I love. They've already arrested so many; why must I confirm it for them? Why must I give them my honor, too?

"I cannot give you the names."

Displeasure fills his gaze. "Can't or won't?"

For a moment, I hesitate at the thread of steel in his voice. Perhaps they already have the names and I would only be echoing what they already know. Maybe this is all a test to see how cooperative I will be, how much of a threat I am to them and Berriz's reputation. My friends were already rounded up; but will I be sentencing them to their death, too, if I corroborate what the Spanish suspect?

It would be easy to tell them the whole story in exchange for saving my father or my sister. For pleading for some leniency for myself.

But even as I open my mouth to speak, something holds me back. My father raised me to believe in something more than myself, taught me the honor of sacrificing for my country, and I cannot betray my countrymen.

"The names are not mine to share."

Don Jose's lips tighten into a thin line. "Why do you insist on making this so difficult for yourself? It could be easier, you know, if you were *friendly* with the guards. If you made some attempts to ingratiate yourself to us."

It is impossible to mistake the leer in his gaze or the insinuation in his voice.

I duck my head, my cheeks burning as the indignity of it all rushes through me, that they believe they have some claim to my body. I take a deep breath, and then I look into his eyes, meeting his gaze.

I refuse to be cowed by these men. I refuse to let them shame me.

"What are you charging me with?" I ask him.

"Instigating an uprising against the Spanish military. You lured a Spanish officer—the island's commanding officer, no less—into a deadly trap when your friends accosted him. You will stand trial for your crime."

"I am guilty of no such thing."

Don Jose makes an impatient noise. "You cannot escape this. You can cooperate or you will be punished. Those are your options."

"Is that all?" I ask. "If you are not going to listen to me, then I have nothing else to say."

"No, that is not all. Your sister is being released."

Relief floods me that Carmen will be let go, no longer forced to pay for my sins. But then it hits me—

I will be alone here.

1897

Four

❦

MARINA

They gave us eight days.

Eight days to leave our homes and report to camps in the nearest Spanish-held city or town throughout Cuba. Eight days to leave everything behind—our livestock, our land, our homes, our memories, our dreams. Eight days to make the journey across Cuba's battered countryside, our world on our backs and sorrow in our hearts. They gave you eight days whether you were a babe fresh from your mother's womb or days away from death; they gave you eight days whether you could run, walk, or crawl.

General Weyler reconcentrated the residents of the Havana province on January 8, and the Spanish printed the decree in the government's newspaper, the *Gaceta de la Habana*. Local newspapers carried the news, but for those who could not read or write, the announcement was brought by the Spanish troops who dragged them from their homes and marched them into cities.

We have no home to return to; we are all refugees in our own country.

The Spanish dressed it up prettily enough, claiming their reconcentration camps are a manner of "protecting" us by bringing us into the fortified cities they command, but we know the truth. It's General Weyler's aim to cut off the support for the Cuban revolutionary armies by moving the population from the country to cities controlled by the Spanish to prevent us from supporting the revolutionaries with food and shelter, from enlisting in their ranks as I have dreamed of since my husband Mateo joined the cause.

Weyler is a fool if he thinks separating us will kill the spirit and means of those fighting for a free Cuba. We've come too far now to turn back.

They gave us eight days to leave the countryside and report to a camp before every man, woman, and child would be shot. Then they burned our homes so we would have no shelter, so we would have nothing to return to. They forbade us from bringing food, animals, our treasured possessions.

I didn't want to leave. But what choice did they give us?

Black plumes of smoke fill the sky around us, the charred remains of others' homes. We left before we had to see ours burn, the horses we raised and sold throughout Cuba stolen and slaughtered, all of our hopes and dreams disappearing in a flash. Our home was a far cry from the mansion I grew up in in Havana, but when I think of the life we lived there, the memories we made, the laughter, and hope, and joy, I cannot speak for the lump in my throat at the idea of watching those walls go up in flames.

We walk to Havana, my mother-in-law Luz on one side of me, my daughter Isabella on the other.

The country has essentially been divided between the Spanish and the Cuban army. The Spaniards control the fortified cities and towns throughout the island, the seaports, and the railroad lines. The rural areas are vast and much more difficult for them to administer. The revolutionaries exist in all other spaces, in the countryside, in the plains, and in the mountains. And still, our country has become like a prison, our movements dictated by the Spanish. It's not enough that they've taxed us and legislated us to ruin, but now they've taken our homes away from us, too.

The island has been divided in two from the north in Morón to the south in Júcaro by an immense trocha. Stretching for fifty miles across the width of the island, the trocha is a military defense of barbed wire fencing, armor-clad railroad cars, wire-trapped bombs, fortified structures and more—the materials purchased from American companies despite their pretense of neutrality—held by the Spanish in an attempt to keep the growing momentum in Cuba's eastern provinces from spreading to the western provinces, and strategically, Havana.

My countrymen have liberated enough territory to start a provisional government, but it is difficult to gain control of the entire island when Spain has sent 150,000 troops to defeat us and declared martial law. They're building more and more forts throughout the island, fortifying the ones they already had, so the countryside is filled with Spanish outposts. Still, the Cuban Liberation Army has achieved the impressive feat of crossing the trocha that divides the island and entering the western part of Cuba for the first time since we've begun this battle decades ago.

"What have they done?" Luz whispers, her voice filled with horror as her gaze sweeps across the countryside.

Cuba used to be a tropical paradise. Now, it is a barren wasteland.

Last year, the revolutionaries seized what crops they could to feed themselves and then burned much of the countryside to punish the wealthy plantation owners who sided with the Spaniards and to keep the crops from falling in the hands of the Spanish military. General Weyler seems to have retaliated by burning every single field, large or small, that could be used to feed the revolutionaries. For wealthy land-owners, those loyal to Spain, there have been exceptions: for sugar barons and the like. But for so many of us who work to sustain our-selves, there have been no such provisions. Only reconcentration.

It's not just the land—they have slaughtered every animal they can find.

In the few letters Mateo was able to send me, he spoke of subsisting on a diet of lizards, and eating fruits like mangos for all of his meals. How can you fight one of the greatest armies in the world with so little to sustain you? How will we survive with nothing available to us?

I squeeze Luz's hand, begging her for silence. The sights surrounding us are as horrible as any I could have imagined, but at seven, Isabella hears everything, and she's already been through enough having to leave her home behind for a city she's never visited, a life in one of Weyler's reconcentration camps.

"How much longer, Mami?" Isabella asks me.

"Just a little farther."

This will be her first time seeing Havana. Her childhood has been our little farm, the animals she cared for, our family, and now everything is changing. I've tried to prepare her for what it will be like in the city, but then again, I left in very different circumstances than the ones in which I'm returning.

"Will Papi come visit us?"

"Shh," I whisper, hating that I must deny her this, the link to the man we love. "Remember what we said? Your father has to be a secret for now. He's off doing something important. We can't speak of him until he's back safely with us."

Rumor has it that the Spanish are denying provisions to those with ties to the revolutionaries.

"Will you leave, too?" Isabella asks.

"No, I'll never leave you."

It is a complicated thing to love the man you send off to war, to be filled with an immense pride at his loyalty and his love for his country, the lengths to which he will go to defend what he believes is right. And at the same time, I envy Mateo the ability to take up arms, to leave his family behind to follow his principles. We're forging a new identity for our country, one where we are all united under the banner of Cuba. I want to fight for that, too.

There are those who say a war camp is no place for a woman, but there *are* women in those camps. Women spilling blood for Cuba's future, taking up machetes with the revolutionaries. Perhaps this revolution will finally give us the independence we desire, show men that we can be their equals and are worthy of their respect.

I wish I were beside Mateo.

The cry of "Viva Cuba Libre" sustains me, even if I'm unable to utter it aloud.

"We should have joined the impedimenta," I say to Luz one morning in the camp when there is once again no food to be had.

The Spanish herded more than seventy thousand of us—mainly women and children—into a camp on the outskirts of Havana a few weeks ago at the beginning of January. For the most part, it seems that the men have chosen to join the revolutionary army over suffering this fate. All around Cuba, this same horrible tableau has played out in other towns and cities for many months as they secured us on barren tracts of land inside the fortified cities. There were promises of housing, but that has turned into little more than tents or cots on the ground for the vast majority of us, our bodies crammed together with no care for hygiene or privacy.

We huddle together on our makeshift beds on the muddy ground, while Isabella sleeps beside us.

"Were it not for Isabella, I would have agreed with you," Luz murmurs. "But war is no place for a child."

"I thought that once. But look around us. We don't have the luxury of pretending that is the case anymore. War has come for Cuba's children whether we wish it to or not. What shall we do if we cannot feed Isabella? They've destroyed the countryside and imprisoned all who worked the land. How do they aim to feed the hundreds of thousands in their reconcentration camps? Not to mention the disease that will likely spread when you keep people in such horrible conditions. The Spanish have no plan for us. They do not care whether we are healthy or safe. Perhaps it will be easier for them if we all die from hunger and disease. Maybe *that* is their plan."

"I'm sure it would be easier for them," Luz replies. "But we can't make it too easy for them, now can we? I know how you feel, how frustrating it can be to watch your country embroiled in a seemingly impossible battle, to watch your loved ones go to war, and not be able to do anything about it. I've been through this twice before, and it is hard to feel like this time will be different. But you shouldn't feel helpless. There are things you can do."

I grimace. "And how do you propose we do something about it, stuffed in here like chattel?"

We have a degree of autonomy in Havana now that we have been cut off from the revolutionaries. They tell us we're not prisoners, that this is necessary, even that this is for our own safety, but really the camps are their own kind of prison. We may not be in jail cells, but reconcentration offers an illusory freedom.

If we left the city, where would we go?

The Spanish military patrols outside of the cities, restricting our movements, and even if we could sneak through their lines, what awaits us when the countryside has been utterly destroyed?

A gleam enters Luz's gaze. "I still have some friends back when we fought for independence before. We weren't content to let the men do all the fighting then, either, and women did their part. Look at all the revolutionary clubs that have sprung up, the fundraisers that have been organized by Cuban women in the United States to raise money for weapons. Look at how women are staffing hospitals and supply centers in the countryside. We are not powerless. I know you wanted to be on the front lines with Mateo, but there are other ways that you can be useful, Marina. I was like you once, and I possessed that same anger that sustains you."

My anger is one of the only things sustaining me these days. The Spanish have already broken so many promises to us, the reforms that were dangled before us for most of my life abandoned, that the manner in which they've conducted this shouldn't be surprising to me, and still it is. They've seemingly made no provisions for the care and feeding of the very people they have chosen to imprison. How do you deny people their liberty, their ability to sustain themselves, and then fail to provide for them?

"The soldiers will see us as weak and defeated because we are women and we have been brought low by their treatment of us," Luz adds. "Now that we're here, they think they have us managed, but the reality is there's too many of us, the situation out of their control. There's an opportunity to be had."

"What do you suggest?"

"There are places women can go that men can't. The soldiers might overlook a woman where they wouldn't a man. You could be a courier," Luz continues. "But you must be careful. It's dangerous to be a spy in times like these. I passed messages when we fought in '68. I didn't tell anyone. Not Mateo or his father. They never would have agreed to it; men can have a way of underestimating what we're capable of even when they love us. Sometimes when you hold something too close, you forget that it needs to fly." She reaches out and takes my hand, squeezing it gently. "You're upset that he left."

"I don't know. It's complicated. I wanted him to go. I believe in what he's fighting for." My gaze sweeps around the camp. Everywhere I look, I see desperation. A woman several yards away is hunched over on her side, in pain, writhing on the ground as her children attempt to comfort her. Her neighbors keep their distance, clearly afraid of catching whatever malady befalls her. "We can't live like this. It's hell. I wish I could have gone with him. That I could do my part. I'm tired of the way things are, too."

"Then you'll do something about it now. Years ago, I corresponded with a group of women who secretly supported the war for independence. Some of them lived in Havana. I imagine many of them are still alive and still fighting.

"The townspeople are starting to feel bad for us here. They can't ignore what's going on. I've heard talk in the camp that they're going to start offering jobs in the city to do washing and work to earn a little bit more money, a little bit more food. There aren't enough opportunities for everyone, but if you secure one of these positions, you'll be able to move about the city. There's a network in Havana that is sympathetic to the revolutionaries even if, at first glance, the city is overwhelmingly supportive of the Spanish. You can pass messages to them under the guise of being a laundress. I'll connect you."

Tears fill my eyes. When I married Mateo, I lost the family of my birth, but in Luz I have gained a mother. I couldn't get through this without her love and support.

I want this opportunity so badly I can taste it on the tip of my tongue, the burning need to do something a fire within me. And still—

"And what about Isabella?"

"You will be here for her. And when you cannot be, I will be there in your stead. I am too old for such intrigues; my body doesn't move as stealthily as it once did. You will fight for me. It's a risk, but look around us. What is the alternative?"

Luz is right. I agreed to come to this camp to protect my daughter, but where the battlefield seemed too dangerous, here is a different danger: we are fading away day by day.

I made Mateo a promise that I would keep our daughter safe, but these are extraordinary times, and I can't help but think that if he saw the conditions of the camp, saw all that they've taken from us, he'd want me to do my part to end this horrible suffering and eject Spain from our lands for good.

Five

※

Before

"My parents say this is the last summer I'll spend at the farm."

I try to keep the threatening tears from spilling down my cheeks, struggle to hold back the tremor in my voice.

We sit beside each other on a fallen tree branch, Mateo and I, staring out at the countryside where we would run and play as children, whooping with laughter. My brother was always older and much too serious to be a playmate for me, but from the first moment when Mateo and I met when I was just five years old, we've been inseparable.

But now I am seventeen, and those childish times are behind us.

We both knew, of course, that this was coming. Time has changed, and our bodies have changed, and now when my mother catches sight of me walking around the farm with Mateo or riding a horse beside him, her eyes alight with something other than displeasure that I am playing with a farmer's son.

Fear.

It hasn't escaped me that we've spent less and less time in the country the older I've grown, and now they are sending me to Havana permanently with the hopes that I will find a husband. My time with Mateo has been consigned to stolen hours when my parents are otherwise occupied, our encounters far from their gaze.

Beside me, Mateo shifts, his body grazing mine in a move that sends goose bumps over my forearm. There was a time when I was as comfortable with him as I was in my own skin, but now tension vibrates between us, my cheeks heating when I watch him help his father with the horses.

He has been my best friend for as long as I can remember, but now I wonder what it would be like for him to embrace me as something other than a friend.

A tear trickles down my cheek.

"Don't cry, Marina," he whispers, looping his arm around me and tucking me against his body. I inhale the familiar scents I've come to associate with him—the tang of grass, the smell of horse, a hint of sweat—my heart beating madly in my chest and not just from the fear of being caught together like this.

We've touched so many times throughout our lives, limbs tangling, knees bumping, hands clasping, fingers linking. But the innocence of our touches has been replaced by something burning hot and bright within me, a yearning for something just out of my grasp, a desire to be known as fully as possible by the person I care for most in this world.

For the past several months now, I've wondered what it would be like to press my lips to his.

But the daughter of one of the wealthiest men in Cuba can hardly marry a common farmer. If not for my brother Arturo, I'd likely be married already, my husband destined to take over the family's sugar business. But thanks to my older brother, I am at least relieved of that obligation even if I am expected to marry well, to fulfill the only role expected of me—that of wife.

"We won't see each other again," I say, the words muffled against his skin.

My parents' plan is to keep me in Havana until I am suitably wed. Will our paths cross on vacations with my husband? Will I spend the rest of my life regretting the choices I've made, stuck in a marriage based on society and familial expectations rather than love? A marriage like my parents' marriage?

If I were more daring, if I wasn't so afraid, my heart pounding in my chest, I would press my lips to the spot on his flesh where they hover now.

Mateo doesn't speak, but his grip on me tightens as though he, too, is unable to say good-bye.

How can I be parted from someone who holds my heart?

"You're my best friend," I add, even though that's hardly enough to describe the fact that he has become as vital a part of my life as the air I breathe.

"You'll make new friends," Mateo replies, his voice rough with emotion. "Go to fancy parties in Havana. You might even like it."

I won't and we both know it. Change is coming, and I want no part of the life my family has chosen to lead. I want to be part of this new, free Cuba.

"I don't want any of that. I never have. I can't pretend like this life we live, the privilege I enjoy doesn't come at a cost. If we don't stand up to the Spanish, if we don't fight for change what will become of us? What if the life they have planned for me doesn't include that?"

What if the husband they choose for me, one of my father's friends or their sons, sympathizes with the Spanish as so many do?

It was Mateo who first introduced me to the revolutionary movement, who snuck me to the meetings his father frequented before he died. Mateo's parents supported the revolutionaries in our first war for independence decades ago, and have continued to meet with others who are secretly calling for our liberty from Spanish tyranny. Our mutual dream for Cuba's future is just one of the things I love about him.

"*They wish for you to marry,*" Mateo interjects.

I can't read the meaning behind his words, can't tell if he's merely stating a fact or if there's some emotion lingering there.

"*Yes. They wish for me to marry.*"

Everything about this situation is impossible, but this feels like my only chance to see if he loves me, too.

"*I don't want to marry someone they choose for me. I'd rather marry someone I care for.*" *I take a deep breath and bare my heart.* "*I rather thought I might marry my best friend. If he'll have me.*"

Mateo swears softly. "*You shouldn't think things like that.*"

There's enough despair in his voice, enough of a crack in the facade to make me think I might not be alone in my feelings for him.

"*Mateo, I know what I want. What I don't know, not for sure, is what you want. If you don't feel the same way, if you don't want the same things, I understand. We'll never speak of this again. We can return to being friends and nothing more. But I thought—I thought I might try.*"

Of all the ways I imagined this happening, it was always Mateo on his knees in front of me professing his love rather than me flinging myself at him, but with circumstances as they are, I've come to accept that my fantasy doesn't really matter anymore. I want him, and I'll do whatever it takes, sacrifice my pride, if that means we can be together.

"*I can't offer you this life,*" *Mateo says.* "*You know that. This idea that we could be together is an impossibility. Your family will never allow it.*"

He's right, of course, but even as I fear their disapproval, even as it pains me to sever ties with the family of my birth, if they cannot see past Mateo's background and station in life, if they cannot wish us well, if they don't want what's best for me, then what choice do I have? We have one shot at happiness in this life, and this is mine.

"*I love you. Whatever life has in store for us, I will always love you.*"

Mateo is silent for a beat that stretches on and on, so long in fact that I nearly convince myself I had it all wrong, that I overstepped, that he's never loved me at all.

And then I hear it—

"I love you, Marina. I've always loved you. Always."

I lean forward, pressing myself against him, a sob escaping my lips, feeling the warmth of the sun on his skin, and finally, a deep shudder as though he has come to terms with something he's been wrestling with for a very long time, and he strokes my hair, his lips closing down on mine, and I know without a doubt that I'd give up everything—the gowns, the jewels, the privilege of my life as a Perez—to call him mine.

WEEKS HAVE PASSED SINCE WE FIRST ENTERED THE CAMP, January turning into February, little hope on the horizon. I stare at the house in front of me, the sight of it and the sensation of standing on the familiar street in Havana carrying me back in time. When I eloped with Mateo and my family disowned me, I assumed I would never return, understood that the home where I lived for seventeen years was no longer mine. But now, standing in front of the big iron gates, someone else's washing bundled in my hands, I feel the full weight of how much I have changed even if Havana is seemingly untouched by the weight of war.

The Perez mansion gleams in the sunlight, a bastion of wealth and privilege. The pale pink color looks like the inside of a seashell, the estate dominating nearly the entire block, sweeping palm trees shading the structure. It was built by the earliest Perez ancestor in the mid-eighteenth century, his time at sea likely influencing his desire to settle his family so close to the ocean, seeking privacy for himself and his bride away from the busier—and nosier—parts of the city.

Do my parents still live here? My brother? Or have they all moved on for parts unknown?

My mother frequently boasted of her ability to trace her ancestry back to Spain; we traveled there a few times growing up to visit family. Between their wealth and their sugar interests, I imagine my parents have sided with the Spanish in all of this.

We are a divided island despite our attempts to unify under one Cuban identity, and as I stare out at the landscape, I feel as though I am in a dream—or a nightmare.

In Cuba right now, there are two realities. In Havana, the party continues on. The city's inhabitants have lavish gatherings, attend concerts, and the theater, the women wearing elegant, brightly colored gowns. If not for the Spanish soldiers swaggering around in their uniforms, if not for the American tourists riding bicycles around as they leave the city environs to see where the latest battle has been fought in the countryside, if not for the execution notices in the newspaper, the sound of the firing squads, or the presence of those of us who have been sent to Weyler's reconcentration camps, you wouldn't realize there was a war going on or that the countryside has been destroyed.

In the western provinces, places where there are more Spaniards from the Peninsula than native-born Cubans, revolutionaries are outnumbered by our countrymen who fight under the Spanish flag. Revolution comes from the east and will, hopefully, spread throughout the country. Still—it is an uphill battle. Tens of thousands of Cubans fight for Spain, and Havana is decidedly controlled by Spanish interests, making the threat to revolutionaries that much more dangerous.

This war has shaped our identity, deciding what it means to be Cuban in this new nation we are building. There are those who cling to the past, but there are many of us who look to the future, to a Cuba where those who were enslaved and indentured for centuries and worked the very fields that formed the cornerstone of wealth for families like mine will be truly free and treated as equals.

There are those of us who dream of a better Cuba, one liberated from this colonial system Spain has thrust upon us where from the moment they first reached Cuba's shores, Spain has subjugated, murdered, and enslaved. There are those of us who demand our ability to govern ourselves rather than be exploited to serve another's interests. There are those of us who dream that one day women will have the same rights as men, that we will become the country so many have sacrificed their lives for, that we will all be equal and represented under one Cuban flag.

And there are others who would do anything to retain the power they wield, who would burn the whole island down rather than see it remade into something new, something powerful, something free. There are those who are afraid that the change we seek will leave them pushed to the fringes of a society they have mercilessly dominated for so long. They can't envision a new country of independent Cubans.

It terrifies them.

Given my family's sentiments, I can only imagine the shame they would feel if they saw me now and not just because of the political differences between us.

My hands are rough and calloused, blisters oozing and bleeding from the washing I've been doing for some of the women throughout Havana. I've little contact with the ladies of the house—former friends and companions of mine and their relatives—but instead am left begging to housekeepers. Truly, given life in the camp, it is a blessing to receive the money I do. Women and children are starving. Disease is rampant—cholera, typhoid fever, yellow fever, and dysentery all around us.

Countless have died, and according to reports, whispers spreading around the country, the situation is equally dire in all the reconcentration camps. Death carts come several times a day, emaciated corpses thrown into them unceremoniously like rubbish.

In an act of charity—and no doubt a bit of shame—the towns have organized to distribute to those of us living in the camps a meal of bones and beans per day. I stand in line with Isabella and Luz, miles away from the house where I grew up taking my meals at a lavish table where we wanted for nothing, and we accept their leavings with gratitude. I'd rather trade my portion for milk for Isabella, but milk is impossible to find.

The Spanish have created agricultural zones outside of the cities, controlled by Spanish soldiers and worked by those in the camps, which provide us with limited food options. It's not nearly enough. The ground isn't fertile, the work of growing food challenging, the harvest not stretching enough to feed so many of us. The revolutionaries raid the food in the cultivation zones, in part to rob the Spanish and to feed themselves since there's little in the countryside to sustain them. At least in this instance when there is no food to be had, I can console myself with the hope that the food is being given to men like Mateo who are fighting for our independence.

I adjust the laundry in my arms, the heat beating down on my threadbare black dress that hangs on my gaunt frame. If anyone asks, I am in mourning for a fictitious family member; the truth is, like so many of my fellow revolutionary women, I have been wearing black since General Maceo was killed by the Spanish army.

While we mourned Maceo, church bells rang out in Havana in

celebration as the city's residents hoped his death would bring a swift end to the war and defeat the insurgency. Their reaction is hardly surprising considering the Spanish attempted to assassinate Maceo so many times in his life.

The man the Spanish referred to as the "Greater Lion" and who we lovingly knew as our "Bronze Titan," seemed invincible, and it is nearly impossible to believe that he could be felled by a stray bullet, but sadly, the unthinkable has happened.

Maceo's death is a great loss—his reputation as a military commander unparalleled, his leadership—a blow to us all. We've already lost too many great revolutionaries, and it feels like we're left to our own devices with no one to guide us. Our fate hangs on a thread, Weyler's boot on all of our necks.

I worry that we are so divided, that when this is all over, we will be unable to unite as one country. I worry our allegiances are too fractured between the new Cuban flag we hope to raise over Havana one day and the Spanish one that flies there now. I worry my husband has died fighting for this new, better Cuba and the news has not reached my ears yet, that Isabella will fall ill like so many children in the camps, that I will be thrown in Recogidas with the rest of the women who dared to defy the Spanish.

My heart is a sea of worries.

I cling to the hope that the rumors are true, that Spain is already stretched impossibly thin, their resources shared between the war they're waging here in Cuba and the conflict in the Philippines. I cling to the hope that *this* time will be different.

I walk past my childhood home, my head held high. At the end of the street, I reach my final destination. Rather than approaching the grand entrance at the front of the house, I walk around the property to the rear. Anyone looking at me would merely see a woman in a widow's gown who is down on her luck. In these times, we've become such a common casualty of the war effort that we're everywhere you look.

We might as well be invisible.

After two quick knocks, the housekeeper answers the door.

I hand her the laundry, and she takes it wordlessly, handing me a small pouch wrapped in a handkerchief with her free hand.

There will be coin for the work I've done, and if I'm lucky, she's included a sweet for me to give to Isabella later. It's not nearly enough, of course, and the life my daughter lives sits heavily on my conscience when I lie in bed at night, unable to sleep, missing the weight of my husband beside me, the warmth of his embrace.

When General Maceo fell, I feared I would receive news that Mateo had as well, for they fought alongside each other, Mateo speaking fondly of the beloved general in his letters home.

But God has been good to us for now, and so we continue on.

When I pass by the old house again, I slip into the shadows of one of the walls surrounding the property. I glance around the street, but it is quiet this time of day, no soldiers to be found. Luz's warnings are always with me, the threat of being intercepted by one of the Spanish soldiers patrolling the city and branded as a spy an ever-present danger.

I quickly pull the bundled handkerchief out of my pocket, unfolding the fabric. It's of quality, its owner one of the great denizens of Cuban society. Like Luz, she fought in '68, and when I began doing washing for the citizens of Havana, Luz sent me to her door with a letter of introduction and an invitation—to use me as a courier ferrying messages throughout the city for the network of people sympathetic to the revolutionary cause.

I unwrap the handkerchief gently, a smile tugging at my mouth at the sweet contained there. I can already see the joy in Isabella's eyes.

Beneath the sweet is a folded piece of paper. My fingers tremble as I unravel it, my heart pounding at the words there, the note with my next set of instructions.

There are several women who are sympathetic to our cause imprisoned in Recogidas. Can you get messages to them?

Six

❧

GRACE

I'm going to die.

As I stare down at the New York City street far below me, the rickety ledge that I'm standing on barely wide enough for me to put one foot in front of the other, there's no question about it.

I can hear my mother's voice ringing clearly in my head, lamenting the fact that I couldn't just marry some rich man like her friends' daughters, and questioning why I had the temerity and utter foolishness to pursue a career in journalism. At the moment, I can't disagree with her.

"Isn't she a beauty?" the man shouts at me—at least, that's what I think he says as the wind rushes around me, death a step away.

I nod quickly, trying not to upend my balance and topple to the ground several stories below.

Oh, there's a rope, and they tell you it's perfectly safe, but regardless, standing on the scaffolding of a construction site hardly feels wise.

"It's a beautiful building, Mr. James," I lie, because I've spent half the time up here with my eyes closed. It isn't as much that I am afraid of heights as it is that I'm unsettled by them and would prefer to keep my feet planted firmly on solid ground. But Hearst said to get him a story, and considering this particular building has been plagued by setbacks, and problems, and whispers of more bribery than usual, there's certainly a story to be had here.

It isn't the sort of story I'd normally be drawn to, but if I had to guess, Hearst envisioned an illustration of a girl in a ridiculous dress standing atop a beam overlooking the city to accompany this piece to grab the public's attention, so here I am. A stunt girl reporter's work puts her in all sorts of unusual situations.

"Perhaps we can go down to the ground floor and conduct our interview, Mr. James," I suggest, struggling to keep the utter panic from my voice. A stunt girl never—fine, *rarely*—loses her composure.

"What did you say?" Mr. James, the site's foreman, yells over the noise of the building below.

"Let's get down," I shout back.

The journey back to the street is infinitely easier than the trip up. Only when my feet are firmly planted on the dirt do I feel the color returning to my cheeks, the panic that imbued my veins lessening.

I reflexively reach for my notepad, but since I've been at the *Journal*, I've learned it's a rookie mistake to jot notes during an interview. It takes away from your overall impression of the event, so instead I work to commit everything to memory until I am alone and can transcribe both the things he said and also my impressions of his mannerisms. There are two parts to an interview: what they say and what they don't.

"This building has seen its share of setbacks, Mr. James, but it's clear from talking to you that you run a tight crew. What do you think keeps holding the construction back?"

He scratches his head for a moment, folds his arms over his chest, and then says—

"Well, I suppose it started with the ghost."

Oh my.

Hearst is going to like this even better now.

I smile.

"Tell me more, Mr. James."

I've been typing up my construction site interview for hours now, trying to separate the facts from the specter of the supernatural, which readers will glom on to even if it's far more likely that the crew bribed the wrong people rather than that an angry ghost is haunting their job site. Some days the words come easily, the story pouring out of me, and others it is a struggle to wrangle every single word into a workable sentence.

Despite this morning's excitement, this afternoon is the latter journalistic experience, and I'd do anything to get away from the newsroom for a moment and clear my head.

I'd envisioned a job at a major New York newspaper as a chance to write about the kind of stories I wanted to highlight, to focus on meaningful women's issues. And even as I knew how difficult it would be, I can't lie that I dreamed of reading my byline on a front-page story.

The reality is, as so often is true, far from the fantasy.

The newspaper business is more work and less glory than I imagined. The hours are long, my average day clocking in around twelve hours and thousands of words written, my hands cramping by five o'clock from the effort of writing longhand. The competition is fierce, more newspapers and reporters than the demand calls for. We're all vying for attention with so many newspapers to choose from, all reaching for the scoop that could make or break our careers.

As cub reporters, we learn our trade by doing, so there's nothing to do but jump in and hope for the best. There are very few of us women in the newsroom, and even fewer assigned front-page stories. We receive half the pay the men do for the same pieces.

And still, there are those women I aspire to be, whose work I look up to, their greatness an inspiration to keep going in the days when the work feels insurmountable.

Recently, Pulitzer's *World* printed a report that Nellie Bly was going to fight for Cuba and was recruiting women volunteers for her first regiment. From elephant trainer to crossing the globe in a balloon to military genius, it seems there's nothing Bly can't do in her stunt reporting. I keep a notebook filled with clippings of the stories she's written, an homage to the daring work she's done to get the story.

One day.

The rest of us who aren't highfliers are paid by the column size, our salaries barely clearing ten dollars a week. It's a far cry from the wealth I grew up around, from the millions men like Hearst earn. I am fortunate for my living situation with Aunt Emma, because otherwise I shudder to imagine how I'd support myself.

I've gleaned little intelligence of note to share with Pulitzer, added few writing credits. The circulation battle between Pulitzer and Hearst has hardly subsided, though. In a major coup, Hearst managed to steal Pulitzer's prized managing editor, the legendary Arthur Brisbane.

Brisbane is one of the hardest working editors, waking hours earlier than others to get the news out before they do. Hearst wooed him away from Pulitzer after a dispute over the editorial freedom and direction of the *World*. Hearst and Brisbane are more than just publisher and editor; they've also become roommates and friends.

In an industry where editorial personalities set the tone for the newsroom, Brisbane is a fair and energetic employer, and his assistant editor, Elizabeth Garver Jordan, has become another inspiration to me.

"Harrington," Hearst calls from his office interrupting my struggles describing an imaginary ghost.

I pick up my pad and pen from the desk, scurrying over to where he stands in the doorway with another man.

"Yes, Mr. Hearst?"

"This is my friend Rafael Harden." He gestures toward the man beside him.

It takes me a moment to place him. It's the same man from that first day in Hearst's office. The one with the showgirl nearly on his lap.

Rafael Harden inclines his head ever so faintly in greeting, hardly enough to be considered polite.

"It's nice to meet you, Mr. Harden," I murmur as I study him, trying to discern why Hearst has introduced us.

Rafael Harden's clothes appear expensive, his entire manner giving the impression that he is someone accustomed to having his way. He looks like one of those new-money men who have built palatial mansions on Fifth Avenue, and given the rumors that Hearst eschews most of proper society, I imagine he is.

"His sister belongs to one of the Cuban revolutionary women's clubs in the city," Hearst continues. "They're having a meeting today at her apartment. Rafael will take you there. I want you to see what information you can glean from them and bring your findings back here. We've done quite a bit with the revolutionary party in the city, but we haven't offered our readers much perspective from inside one of these women's clubs, and I think you'd be the perfect person to speak with them and tell their side to *Journal* readers. Can you handle that?"

In the past several months, both the *Journal* and the *World* have reported at length about the conflict in Cuba, each trying to outdo the other in their battle for newspaper supremacy. When he first hired

me, Hearst dangled Cuba before me, but up until now, I haven't had
a chance to work on one of the *Journal*'s more high-profile stories.
Maybe this is a sign that he's appreciated the stunt work I've done and
thinks I'm ready for more substantial material.

Cuba is on everyone's minds. The Republican William McKinley
was elected president after a contentious election, ensuring the mon-
eyed classes have a friend in the White House. His views on Cuba
remain to be seen, but after his own military experiences, he is said to
be opposed to war in principle. And still, he supports the Monroe
Doctrine and firm foreign policy, and his political party favors intervention and foreign investment opportunities. He's rumored to be a
man concerned with courting public opinion, and therein lies Mr.
Hearst's opportunity. Conflict seems imminent, and we are all on
tenterhooks to see what McKinley will do. The stock market has been
particularly volatile, plunging considerably, and the number of people
joining militia groups has risen substantially.

The stories coming from our correspondents in Cuba are grim.
Hearst has moved beyond his desire for the United States to formally
recognize the revolutionary movement and is demanding that the
American government restore order in Cuba, protecting American
citizens and their investments on the island, and bringing an end to
Spain's suppression of the rebellion and the suffering of the Cuban
people. For a country like the United States founded on a desire for
liberation from a foreign power, the conflict in Cuba certainly reso-
nates with our American audience. Not to mention, the close proximity to our shores makes Cuba a more compelling issue for our readers
than so many other places around the world where horrible things
happen on a regular basis.

The Spanish have made it harder to get news and correspondents
in and out of the country, so Hearst has commissioned a new dispatch

boat to travel down to the region, a yacht that is considered to be the fastest in New York, the *Vamoose*. Still, censors monitor everything, and Hearst's correspondents' movements are closely tracked, the Spanish careful to keep our reporters from getting too close to the fighting and to the revolutionaries. The end result is that most of our impressions of the war come from Cuban sources outside of the country—groups like these women's clubs and their male counterparts. There are estimated to be well over one hundred such clubs in the United States.

"Bring me something good," Hearst says before dismissing me.

"Yes, of course. Thank you for the opportunity, sir."

I lengthen my strides in an attempt to keep up with Mr. Harden as I follow him, curious gazes being cast our way. As usual, the newsroom is a flurry of activity, and everyone is eager to get the scoop on breaking news—including the sight of me with one of Hearst's personal friends.

We exit the newsroom and walk through the building. Mr. Harden glances back at me a few times, but he doesn't slow down until we reach the street where an ostentatious carriage waits at the curb.

Rafael gestures for me to enter the vehicle ahead of him, and I climb in and seat myself on the bench.

"How did your sister become involved with the revolutionary women's club?" I ask him once he has settled across from me. Rafael crosses his legs, shifting to accommodate his size. For as big as the carriage is, he must be several inches over six feet, and much of it is leg.

"Our mother was born in Cuba. She came here in 1868 during the start of the first war for independence with the intent to return when her country was free. She met my father, and they married. Our mother never returned home. There are quite a few Cubans living in the United States, particularly on the East Coast and in New York. It's as good a place as any to settle. My sister Elena has taken an interest in the island and kept abreast of the situation there. We still have family in Cuba. Elena has been an active member of the club since the fighting broke out again."

"Was your father born in Cuba as well?"

"No, he was from New York."

I note the past tense. "I'm sorry for your loss."

"It was a long time ago. I was just a boy."

"I was twelve when my father passed. It's a difficult thing to lose a parent."

He turns away from me and glances out the carriage window.

"Are you involved with the revolutionaries as well?" I ask.

"I'm not. My sister has enough enthusiasm for the both of us."

"And what do you do?"

He laughs, the sound surprisingly full and rich. "I am not the story, Miss Harrington. I am merely doing a favor for Will. And my sister."

"I realize you're not the story. I'm only trying to get some background. I confess I don't know much about these groups. This is the first time I've been assigned a story on Cuba."

He turns his attention back to me. "They're probably not that different from the reformer meetings you likely attend. My sister believes she can improve the situation in Cuba. She and her friends meet and discuss how they can do so. They raise money for the cause and send it back to the revolutionaries for supplies and equipment. There are similar groups all over the country. Las Dos Banderas is arguably the most well-known in New York."

"And do you believe in the revolutionaries' cause?"

"Do you, Miss Harrington?"

"I don't know much about it beyond what I've read in the papers, certainly not as much as you do, but I'd like to learn. Hearst has taken a great interest in Cuba. He believes it is our duty as journalists to inform readers about the horrific living conditions under Spanish rule."

"Yes, Will's interest is the primary reason you're invited to this gathering. Newspapers could play an important role in drawing the United States into war with Spain, or at least garner support for the revolutionaries. Everyone wants to win public opinion."

"It is our job to keep the public apprised of the news," I counter, not entirely comfortable with the picture he paints of our role in the conflict. As much as Hearst aims for us to shape the news, I haven't quite acclimated to my publisher's manner of doing things.

"Is that what you call it, 'keeping the public apprised'? I thought your job was making a spectacle of the news."

I have to remind myself that I am supposed to be a disciple of Hearst's and keep from making my true feelings known; in my personal time, I still read the *World* to stay informed.

"I wouldn't call it 'making a spectacle,' merely bringing important causes to the public's attention in whatever manner is most likely to draw their notice. People are busy. You have to get to the heart of the matter and entertain them," I say, parroting Hearst.

"How nicely put," Rafael drawls.

How much does his opinion on the role of the newspaper differ from that of his friend Hearst?

"And what is it you do, Mr. Harden?" I ask again. If he believes I'll be so easily fobbed off, he's sorely mistaken. "Since you've so clearly expressed your disdain for the newspaper business, I assume you're not a newspaperman like Mr. Hearst."

"I'm not. I'm a businessman."

When he doesn't elaborate, I try again.

"What sort of business?"

"Stocks, railroads, buildings."

So he's one of the new-money industrialists buying up and building the city.

"And how did you get into such a line of work?"

"*I* am not the subject of your article, Miss Harrington. I assure you, very little of my life would be fit to print."

"Too scandalous?"

"I suppose it depends on a matter of perspective." He grins, his expression softening as he leans into me, as though we're sharing a secret, his change in manner catching me completely off guard. "But in a word—yes."

WE ARRIVE AT A FASHIONABLE BUILDING SEVERAL MINUTES LATER, and I follow Rafael up to his sister's apartment. He enters without knocking and leads me into a formal sitting room where well-dressed women speak animatedly in Spanish. When Rafael and I walk in, all conversation ceases, and a tall brunette rises from an elegantly appointed silk settee to greet us.

Rafael takes her outstretched hands in his, leaning forward and pressing kisses to each cheek before stepping back and presenting her to me.

"Miss Harrington, this is my sister Elena Santiago."

Standing next to each other, the similarities between the siblings are clear. They're both tall, dark haired, and striking.

"Thank you for including me in your meeting today," I reply. "You have a lovely home."

She smiles, hooking her arm through mine and drawing me to the couch. "It's my pleasure."

Rafael hovers in the doorway for a moment before turning away with an, "I'll be back for you in an hour, Miss Harrington," thrown over his shoulder before he disappears entirely.

"Off to smoke cigars and discuss business with my husband," Elena mutters. "My brother has little tolerance for politics. We are so happy to have you join us. I've been pestering Rafael for months to impress upon his good friend Mr. Hearst the importance of our cause." She frowns. "The newspapers attend the press conferences the Junta holds daily, but they've yet to give our meetings the full attention they deserve." She lowers her voice to a comical whisper. "Because we are women, and surely, can't have any insight into politics. No matter that so many of our countrywomen are involved in the conflict in Cuba at this very moment."

"Are there women fighting?" I ask. Hearst's correspondents carry tales of beautiful, long-haired women waving machetes, but one never knows quite what to believe, especially given the correspondents' limited access to the conflict. The line between fact and fiction can be razor-thin.

"Of course, there are women fighting in Cuba. There are women treating the wounded troops and providing medical assistance, women working as couriers and passing information back and forth. In some ways, the couriers are under even greater danger than those on the front lines. The punishment for spies if they are caught—particularly spies with access to important information—is severe."

"And what would you like the *Journal*'s readers to know about the conflict? About your efforts there?"

"That the situation is very desperate," another woman chimes in. "The Spanish are a formidable foe that we've been battling for a very long time. The revolutionaries need money, arms, and assistance. Cuba cannot remain a colony any longer. We've suffered for centuries under Spanish rule. We want the ability to unite under one flag, to be able to govern ourselves. We hope the Americans will support our cause in every way they can."

At the moment, I cannot think of a place I'd rather be than sitting among a group of women plotting revolution.

"How was the meeting?" Rafael asks when we are once again ensconced in his lavish carriage, driving away from his sister's apartment.

A hint of cigar smoke lingers on his clothes.

"Informative. Very informative. I liked your sister a great deal," I add.

"I had a feeling you might. Elena isn't content to let things stand as they are. When we were young, she was always rescuing something—small animals, other children, sometimes me. I figured someone who barged into Hearst's office asking for a job would be a kindred soul. Next you'll be asking me for introductions to the Junta."

The Junta, the revolutionary organization run by exiled Cubans in New York that was once helmed by José Martí, was a popular topic of conversation in the meeting today. Comprised of Cubans and those sympathetic to the revolutionary cause, the Junta's primary goal is to raise money and garner support for independence.

"Are you friends with those men?" I ask.

There are already reporters who regularly attend Junta meetings and work closely with them, but it wouldn't hurt for me to have a connection there, too.

"In my line of work, you learn to be friends with everyone," Rafael replies. "You don't know when someone will be useful."

THE MOST BEAUTIFUL GIRL IN CUBA

"And you never thought to join your sister in her efforts?"

"I'm not one for meetings," he drawls, infuriatingly deflecting my questions once more.

You're not getting away so easily, Mr. Harden.

"Which one of you is the elder?" I ask, changing tack.

"I am. By three minutes, at least."

"I didn't realize you're twins, although now that you say it, I suppose the resemblance is clear."

"Hmm. So they tell me. Where should I have my driver drop you?" he asks, ignoring my conversational rejoinder.

I give him my aunt's address, and his brow rises.

"I would have thought you would live with your mother and stepfather over in Gramercy Park."

And now it's my turn to be surprised. He's clearly done some research into my family and their background, although I can't imagine when—or why—he would have accomplished it.

"I live with my aunt Emma. My mother's sister. I am my own woman," I feel compelled to add. "My life is separate from that of my family."

"I thought you debutantes were kept under tight wraps away from men with questionable reputations and the like."

"If I weren't allowed in the company of men with questionable reputations, I could hardly expect to find myself in this carriage with *you*."

He grins, faint crinkles showing around his eyes.

"Besides, I'm hardly a debutante anymore," I reply.

My debut was far from a splash, more like a slow drizzle, and now at twenty-five, unmarried and living with my mother's eccentric sister, I am hardly marriage material. Not that I have any complaints. A husband in my social circle would hardly indulge a woman working, particularly in a field as salacious as journalism. Certainly not with the hours we keep and the stories I cover.

I've seen enough of my mother's marriage to my stepfather, how she tiptoes around him and the money he controls, to value independence over all else.

"You aren't that old," Rafael adds almost as an afterthought.

I snort. "I will expire from such flattery."

He laughs. "I doubt you're the sort who would tolerate flattery. You seem like a woman who wants to cut to the heart of things."

"And you deduced this from what, an hour or so in my company?"

"You forget, I also witnessed your little speech with Will. You know what you want, and you clearly aren't afraid to go after it. If you were the sort of woman who wanted to play by society's rules, you'd be married to some impoverished British lord like so many of your set. But you're not—you're sitting in the carriage across from me, and your fingers look like they're just itching to pick up that notepad beside you. I don't like people wasting my time. I'll do you the same courtesy of not wasting yours."

Well.

The carriage comes to a stop.

"Good day, Miss Harrington."

I can't muster a response beyond a quick nod, and then I'm standing on the curb outside my home, watching his elegant black carriage trundle down the street.

Seven

⁂

Anyone who is anyone in New York society—plus several hundred others who would never make Caroline Astor's guest list—is crammed into the ballroom of the Waldorf-Astoria on Fifth Avenue and Thirty-Third Street, which for the evening has been transformed into the Palace of Versailles. When Hearst called me into his office earlier today to ask if I was planning on attending and if I could cover the ball for the *Journal*, I agreed with great reluctance. After all, I hated society when I was part of it; writing about the society beat seems even less interesting. But considering the expense Mrs. Cornelia Bradley-Martin reportedly undertook for the fete this February evening—four hundred thousand dollars spent on eight hundred guests—and the more than three years of economic depression the country has experienced leading up to this culmination of excess, the more I glance around the room, the more I see a story demanding to be told.

I can hardly fault the Bradley-Martins for doing what so many others have done—throwing around their immense wealth in an attempt to buy their way into New York society—but this is another level of extravagance.

The guests were instructed to come in costume dressed as royalty from the sixteenth, seventeenth, or eighteenth century, and the normal absurdity of these events is only magnified by the occasional—and inevitable—wigged Marie Antoinette gliding past. For her own part, Mrs. Astor has chosen to dress as Mary, Queen of Scots.

I've no doubt that tomorrow the papers will report this to be the most opulent ball New York society has ever seen. After all, where do you go from here?

I was raised among privilege, but this display could best be described as gauche by my mother. And still—she and my stepfather are somewhere in this crush. After all, the only thing worse than throwing a party filled with such vulgarity is missing out on the opportunity to judge and condemn it.

What will the *Journal* readers say when they open the newspaper and read this story? The ones working twelve hours a day, six days a week, their children holding down jobs as well. I think of the young newsboys standing on street corners, many of them orphans, selling the very papers that will cover this story to support themselves and their families. How angry will this party make the people, considering the wealthiest one percent of Americans hold as much money as the bottom fifty percent?

Mrs. Bradley-Martin has reportedly said that the ball would help stimulate the economy by giving so little notice that everyone was forced to have their costumes designed locally rather than having them made in Paris, but I think the city's residents would have rather had the four hundred thousand dollars instead. More likely, Mrs. Bradley-Martin wishes to dethrone Alva Vanderbilt from the position she's held for over a decade as reigning queen of the most famous ball New York City has ever seen. It looks like she'll succeed, too. The papers have spoken of little else for weeks now, the impending party gaining national attention and notoriety.

I take a turn around the room, writing down a few notes before slipping the pad into my reticule. There's an advantage to attending these sorts of functions as a journalist rather than as a young girl expected to make a good match, freedom in the ability to see without needing to be seen.

In truth, I lacked the beauty and the fortune to make a splash at an event such as this one. My features have never been particularly fine, nor have I embraced the love of fashion as so many in this set have. The dowry my father left for me before he died was adequate, my stepfather's addition to it satisfactory, but neither my pale blue eyes, blond hair that could never be described as golden, nor my purse were fine enough to draw the notice of a prime catch. And truthfully, having lived on my own with my aunt for a few years now, I can't quite countenance why women are so eager to put up with men and all of their peccadilloes.

"Grace."

I whirl around at the sound of my name in a tone I've heard since childhood.

My mother and stepfather stand before me, dressed in elegant costumes. We last saw one another at Christmas, and I wait for a rush of emotion, but am as always left with the sensation of crossing paths with an acquaintance I have not seen for several months.

"Hello, Mother."

She leans forward, kissing my cheeks in greeting, the familiar scent of her perfume wafting over me, and my stepfather follows suit.

Her eyes widen slightly as her gaze runs over me. "I confess, this is the last place I ever imagined to see you, Grace."

I smile wryly. "I don't doubt it. I'm here for work."

Her mouth parts in a little "o," but she says nothing, my stepfather silent beside her.

My desire to be a journalist has been a bone of contention between us, but my mother is too well-mannered to comment on it, particularly in public. Whatever hand-wringing has been done, it has been conducted in the privacy of their home.

Truthfully, I'm not sure my mother occupies herself too much with such things. When she married my stepfather, she jettisoned her old life and her memories of my father. I didn't fit into her new world, her child from a previous marriage, so she paid me as little attention as possible, hiring nannies and governesses to care for me. My lackluster debut into society and lack of marital offers ultimately gave me the one thing I craved—independence.

My living situation with my aunt benefits both of us in a way, and our relationship is mostly conducted in a few holidays spent together, and occasions such as these when we exchange pleasantries and little else.

We speak for a few more minutes, and then they're off to visit an acquaintance from their social set, leaving me to my own devices once more.

I jot down a few additional observations, struggling to find the particular turn of phrase I'd like to use to capture the scene before me, when—

"I'm gratified to see your notepad in attendance this evening," a voice murmurs beside me.

I nearly jump, so caught up in the story I was drafting in my mind and the difficulty of translating the images before me, the utter decadence of them, into something passable.

Rafael Harden stands beside me, dressed in a costume of some vague European origin, so generic it feels as though he's thumbing his nose at the whole business.

He arches his brow at me. "Queen Elizabeth?"

"Short-notice costume. Hearst sorted it out for me." I have the feeling Hearst borrowed it from some theater production. "Besides, I'm working," I add, gesturing with the aforementioned notepad in my hand. "And you are?"

"Wondering why the hell I came."

His deadpan response elicits a smile from me.

"Why did you come? I wouldn't have guessed this would be your usual fare."

He shrugs. "Business. Same reason as you." He casts a derisive look at the rest of the crowd. "Some of us do work for a living." He glances down at my notepad from atop his tall perch. "Get anything good?"

"I'm not entirely sure. Maybe. The society beat isn't my usual."

"Then why'd you take this assignment?"

"Mr. Hearst asked me. I think he hoped I would have special insight given my former entrées into society."

I didn't want to disappoint Hearst with the truth that I hardly possess salacious gossip to pass on to his readers. I also couldn't afford to say no to an opportunity to impress my boss.

I wait for Rafael to move on, but he doesn't, his feet firmly planted on the extravagant floor. I turn my body away from his, searching the crowd once more so I can beg off. Whatever his game, I wish he wouldn't play it with me. He's too plainspoken for polite society, too handsome, too bold, his reputation too scandalous.

"You don't like me very much, do you?" he asks, his tone mild.

"I hardly know you well enough to dislike you. I'm sure that'll take another month of acquaintance, at least," I joke.

A smile tugs at his lips. "You surprise me, you know."

"How so?"

"I can only guess why you don't approve of me, but I would have thought your derision would extend to Will. Doesn't most of your set look down their noses at him? Why would someone like you want to write for the *Journal*?"

Hearst's exploits are notorious, his reputation for being far more at home with the common man than the Four Hundred an anomaly on an otherwise distinguished pedigree. And still, I have to admit whatever my impression of him prior to working at the *Journal*, Hearst has surprised me. Despite his reputation, and the trouble he might get up to in his extracurricular time, he is professional and fair with his staff.

"Mr. Hearst is not what I expected," I admit, sidestepping his latter question about my motives for joining the *Journal*.

"True. Will is nothing if not unique."

The genuine affection in his voice catches me off guard. I had assumed their friendship was limited to similar interests—whiskey, and women, and general debauchery, and perhaps a shared utility when it comes to Cuba. The protective note in his words suggests something else altogether.

"And how do you like working for Will?" Rafael asks. "He's a force to be reckoned with, that's for sure. Some people admire that about him. Others fear it."

"We come from the same place, and yet, I heard what everyone said about him—that he eschewed society for hanging out with the people—and figured it must be part of his persona, a way to endear himself to the masses, to increase his circulation. But he seems to genuinely embrace change. Is that why you're friends? Because you're both looking to shake things up?"

He laughs. "You have a delightful way of deflecting questions and turning them right back around so the focus is on the questioner and not yourself. Is that a prerequisite to becoming a journalist or a particular skill you've cultivated?"

"I suppose I could ask you the same thing, considering you do it as often as I do."

"Touché. I wasn't born with the same advantages Will was. I'm not sure polite society would have me if they truly knew where I come from. My money—now that's another matter entirely."

"I'm surprised you say that. In my experience, money gives people the ability to reshape the world as they see fit."

"The world perhaps. Not Caroline Astor and her Four Hundred."

"I wouldn't think you'd give a fig about all that." I lean in closer to him, my voice dropping to a whisper, not quite unconvinced Caroline Astor doesn't have ears in every corner of New York. "They're not that fun, really. The parties, I mean." I pause for a moment, anticipating a bolt of lightning to come down from the heavens. In this insular world, Mrs. Astor might as well be a god.

"I'm beginning to see that." His gaze sweeps across the ballroom once more. "Although, I suppose it's more a matter of wanting what you cannot have."

"It can be frustrating to have doors closed to you, to always have to prove yourself, to never have a chance to be judged on your own merits," I agree.

"I thought you might be able to understand, given the way you handled yourself in Will's office. You aren't afraid to push the doors open." He smiles. "See, you're already an excellent journalist. You've mastered the skill of getting your interview subject to spill their secrets."

"The sort of secrets you possess would likely make a lady blush."

"Perhaps. I'd imagine it depends on the lady, though. You don't seem one for blushing. Not in a job like this."

"You do realize, when you say 'job like this,' you sound positively like Mrs. Astor."

His laugh fills the air. "You've got me. I've never been one for reporters."

"And yet you're friends with a publisher. And not just *any* publisher, the most notorious one in the city."

"True. I suppose there is an exception to every rule. And if you're going to break a rule, you really should do so thoroughly."

"Why the aversion to newspapers?"

"It seems a bit like vultures picking over the bones of people's lives. Think about the stories that litter the front page. They're hardly testaments to the best and brightest parts of people's affairs."

"'Best and brightest'? Now you sound like a romantic."

"Whereas you are what, a cynic?"

"You think someone so young—and let me guess, female—shouldn't be a cynic?"

"I don't actually. I've seen plenty of women—young and old—carrying their families on their backs. That's the difference between people like you and people like me. Maybe your people shelter women as the 'fairer sex,' but on the dirty streets of New York and in the tenements piled on top of one another like the layers of human sweat that fill the air, the working class in this country doesn't have that luxury."

My gaze narrows speculatively. It's another facet to him that I wouldn't have predicted. Despite his wealth, he wears his disdain for money as well as his impeccably tailored clothes.

"Is it odd being part of a society that you hate?" I ask.

Now it's his turn to look surprised. "Pardon me?"

"You're one of the wealthiest men in New York."

I've done my research, too.

"Perhaps your origins aren't up to Mrs. Astor's standards," I add, "but you cannot pretend you don't rub elbows with some of the same people you decry in the same breath."

"Yes, but rubbing elbows with them is not the same as being part of their little world."

"So, you seek to create change from within?"

"Is that a note of censure I hear, Miss Harrington? You have this delightfully prim way of making one feel entirely put in their place when you open your lips."

I flush at the intimate description. It's not so much that he lacks the manners necessary to navigate polite society, for there are certainly moments when his bearing is flawless; it is more that he sometimes clearly doesn't give a fig about deploying them.

"I'm sure I don't know what you're talking about."

"Don't you? You remind me of a schoolmistress. I half expect you to take a ruler in hand. How did you end up in the newspaper business, anyway?"

For some reason, giving him the same explanation I shared with Pulitzer in his office—about Nellie Bly and feeling as though I was seen in her writing—feels too intimate, as though I am providing him with a deep insight into my personality I'd rather he not have. He's already too perceptive by half.

"I suppose I just saw enough around me that made me angry, that made me want to do something to make things better. My father was like that. It annoyed my mother tremendously. He could never let things go like she wanted. He believed if you saw something you didn't like in the world, you should do what you could to change it."

"He would be very proud of you, then."

"I hope so."

"How did he die, if you don't mind me asking?"

"Pneumonia. After all he'd been through, fighting in the war—they said it changed him, all that he'd seen, the men he'd killed. He didn't come back the same. He had health problems. Sometimes he would be quiet for long periods of time. He told me once that when I was born it felt like he got a new start at life. He was a good man. I never imagined I'd lose him at such a young age. And then one winter when I was a little girl, he got sick. He was gone a few weeks later."

"You must miss him very much."

The kindness in his voice catches me off guard.

"I do miss him." I clear my throat discreetly, past the emotion there. "He was my best friend. I looked up to him quite a bit."

I can't bear to meet Rafael's gaze after sharing something so personal, so I turn my attention to the crowd before us, only to be surprised by how many people are staring back at us. Our conversation has drawn its share of notice, and I know I'm hardly the cause of them. I've been out of society so long, I'm quite sure I've been forgotten. But the glances our way are coming from the feminine quarters of the room.

Suddenly, he leans in closer to me, his lips an indecorous distance from my ear. "Do you want to get out of here?"

I lurch backward. "Mr. Harden, if I have given you the impression that I am interested in you in any way, I do apologize. I am not one of your women, nor am I—"

Rafael lets out a sharp bark of laughter. "Good God, I wasn't asking you to come with me so I could have my way with you."

My cheeks must be flaming red.

"I very much doubt we would suit. But, since you do have your notepad with you, there's an event you just might be interested in. Some members of the Junta are meeting tonight. There's news out of Cuba. Care to join me?"

I hesitate for a moment, staring out at the sea of royalty, but it's no contest. The lure of a Junta meeting is no match for high society.

"Lead the way."

IF ANYONE IN THE MEETING IS SURPRISED TO SEE RAFAEL STROLL in dressed dubiously as royalty, a poor imitation of Elizabeth I in tow, they give no indication. We spoke little on the carriage ride here, and when he led me into the closed law office on Broadway where the meeting was taking place, no introductions were made. The men are already deep in conversation when we arrive, so with a nod from Rafael, I pull out my notepad and get to work.

The Cuban Revolutionary Party has spent a great deal of time and money highlighting their cause, from the rallies they organize, to the chapters that have sprung up all over the country, and the newspapers they publish. They're notorious for feeding stories to reporters, and I can't help but wonder if this invitation was as spur-of-the-moment as it appeared at the time Rafael asked me to come or if he somehow finagled this whole endeavor in advance.

"We must do something about the situation in the camps," one of the men says. "Women and children are suffering. The Spanish cut off their means of support with the destruction they've wrought in the countryside. If this doesn't garner the attention of the Americans, I don't know what will."

Rafael adjusts beside me in his chair.

"Look at what happened to the Armenians," someone else adds. "You would think the Americans would have learned by now and won't want another situation like they had with Turkey."

"Do Americans care about dead Cubans? Truly?"

One of the men lifts up a folded newspaper, and from my vantage point I can make out the article's headline.

Just last month, Hearst sent Richard Harding Davis and Frederic Remington down to Cuba, putting the full force of the *Journal* behind the endeavor and paying them an exorbitant sum. The article in the newspaper is the one Richard Harding Davis wrote for the *Journal* about the death of Cuban nineteen-year-old Adolfo Rodríguez. An illustration of Rodríguez's face in his final moments before the Spanish firing squad killed him takes up nearly the entire front page. The grotesque details have increased circulation and angered our readership, and Davis's reporting leaps off the page, but it's done little in terms of advocating for meaningful involvement in Cuba.

"Rodríguez was a boy," the man continues. "He was a farmer. Civilians are waging this battle. They don't stand a chance without help."

"What will it take for the United States to intervene?" another man calls out. "They don't care about the death of a boy."

"A woman, maybe," another man says. "Or a child."

"Then they should go to the camps. Plenty of dead children there."

My hand cramps from how quickly I write, their conversations flowing from one topic to the next. No one so much as turns our way, but I can feel the weight of Rafael's regard on me even though he doesn't speak throughout the meeting.

When the meeting is over, we exit the building and climb back into Rafael's carriage. Despite the late hour, I've no doubt the Bradley-Martin ball is still going in full force at the Waldorf-Astoria hotel. After everything I heard about the situation in Cuba, it's even more difficult to imagine going back to the room filled with thousands of flower petals.

"Where to?" Rafael asks me once we settle into the carriage.

"Home, I think. It's just off—"

"I remember," he replies, giving the instructions to his driver, his gaze on me.

"Why did you bring me here tonight?" I ask.

"You were looking for a story, one that would do something to distinguish you with Hearst." His lips twitch slightly for a moment. "It can't all be haunted buildings."

"How did you—" I wrote the haunted construction piece under a nom de plume lest having my name out there make it more difficult for me to do investigative stories in the future. How did he know it was mine?

He ignores my question, and his expression sobers. "Given everything the Spanish are doing, the Junta could use the coverage."

"Do you really think the press can sway McKinley to act?"

"I don't know. I'm not even sure American intervention is a good thing."

"Why not?" I ask, surprised that his view differs so greatly from that of the Junta who spent the last hour calling for that very thing.

"Let's say the Americans get rid of the Spanish. Fine. Good riddance. But now America is looking at Cuba. Don't forget that the United States has tried to buy Cuba several times. No one does anything in this world out of the goodness of their hearts. The question we have to ask ourselves is whether we're prepared to give the Americans whatever they want in exchange for their support."

"What do you think the Americans want with Cuba?"

"What does everyone want? Money. After all, the Spanish cancellation of the trade pact between Cuba and the United States in '94, and imposition of higher taxes and trade restrictions, led to much of the unrest. The vast majority of Cuba's exports go to the United States. A fair bit of Cuba's imports come from the United States. No country has as great of a trade relationship with Cuba, not even Spain. The Spanish know it, too, and that's making them nervous. After the recent economic troubles in the United States, the price of sugar isn't what it once was. Look at how many American corporations have taken over sugar plantations in Cuba. The United States isn't going to lose such a valuable connection. The Spanish might have political authority, but the economic power is invested in the United States, and when it comes down to it, money wins every time. No wonder there's such a push for American intervention."

"But that's such a cynical perspective to take. Perhaps we would intervene because it is the right thing to do. Because women and children are starving in those camps. You speak as though there is not a set of higher ideals we all aspire to, a force that shapes us as a nation."

His mouth twists in a sardonic smile. "That's a pretty thought after the spectacle we just witnessed at the Bradley-Martin ball tonight. America rides to Cuba's rescue, but what about her own people? The tiniest fraction of this city controls nearly all of its wealth. People are starving and dying all over the world, and no one is coming to their rescue. People act out of their own interests. Nothing more. Nothing less. If you want to romanticize it with a patina of shining ideals, you can do so, but beneath this gilded city is a whole lot of rot."

I study him for a moment, all of my potential responses tangled up in my throat. Whereas I once thought him to be a bounder and a cad, I now recognize that he is a *smart* bounder and cad, and a formidable sparring partner, indeed.

"You're right, of course," I say. "There is much work to be done."

"Be careful with the Junta. They are one voice in all of this, and they are one of the loudest considering the excellent campaign they've launched to court public opinion. But there are other voices here, and most Cubans living in the United States don't feel as they do, don't encourage the armed conflict the Junta advocates for."

"And where do you lie in all of this?" I ask him. "You speak about both groups as though they are separate from you, but you are both Cuban and American. Where do your loyalties lie?"

"Maybe with the one who needs me the most at the moment." He shrugs. "Maybe I'm waiting to see how it all plays out."

Debauchery aside, it's hard to imagine how Hearst, the seeming romantic, and Rafael, the seeming realist, are friends, but if my short acquaintance with my employer has taught me anything, it is that people are a remarkable study in contradictions, and that it is possible to be both the playboy and the tireless advocate for a different, better future.

I just wonder whose interests motivate Rafael.

Eight

After the night of the Bradley-Martin ball, there are no more visits from Rafael, no trips to the Cuban Revolutionary Party's meetings.

My mother is fairly appalled when my byline is run on an article critical of the excess of the Bradley-Martin ball, but then the public backlash against the Bradley-Martins swells beyond any criticism I levied their way, and my column is all but forgotten. Still, I received high praise on the piece from my editor Arthur Brisbane.

My notes from the Junta meeting that night are incorporated into several different stories, the conditions in the camps confirmed by the correspondents on the ground in Havana who see firsthand the devastation that General Weyler's policies are causing. Although, what would one expect from a man who claims that the only job men have in war is to kill?

Even though I do not see him again, I cannot get Rafael's words out of my mind, and I confess, everywhere I look now I feel as though I am seeing the city with new eyes. I knew we needed to do better, wanted to be a part of those reforms, but I am beginning to wonder if Hearst is somewhat right. Maybe it's not simply enough to report on the news. Maybe we are called to act as well.

In late February, I travel to the corner of Beaver and William Streets for a rare meeting with Pulitzer in one of the private rooms on the second floor at Delmonico's.

It's nearly been a year since Pulitzer hired me to begin spying on Hearst, and I fear that I've unearthed little information of use to him. I'm hardly privy to the sort of stories Pulitzer would likely be interested in. Hearst's correspondents are off doing the real reporting in far-flung places. I can relay the goings-on in a ballroom or dangle myself on a building scaffolding, but I've yet to find my foothold in the world, the story that will make me respected among my colleagues. My reporting vacillates between the mundane and the stunt—scaffold walking and the like—with little meaningful journalism in between, the stories about women I'd hoped to write unpublished.

And the more time I spend at the *Journal*, the more I find myself questioning my loyalties while the deadline Pulitzer originally gave me weighs heavily on my mind.

Still, I dress carefully for the occasion, choosing an elegant navy dress from my wardrobe and a matching hat, bundling up in an attempt to ward off the elements. It's been a bitterly cold winter, and many have struggled throughout the city to stay warm.

Around the newsroom, I dress as plainly as possible, but in a nod to Mr. Pulitzer's position in society and the locale, I spent more time on my appearance than I normally would.

When Pulitzer requested this meeting at such a public place, I felt a pang of nerves. The *World* newspaper offices are, of course, out of the question considering the frequent staff turnover between the two men and the likelihood of discovery, but still. At least Delmonico's isn't the complete crush it once was with so many of our set moving uptown to the Waldorf-Astoria and its environs. If I'm lucky, it'll be a quick meeting between us.

I walk through the Beaver Street entrance, keeping my head ducked as I make my way to the second floor.

Delmonico's has long been a favorite of mine. It is perhaps the personification of the disparity between the wealthy and the poor that this city does to such an extreme, but as much as it represents excess, it is also filled with fond memories. My father used to bring me to the restaurant when I was a little girl. We celebrated birthdays and other momentous occasions here, and in the rare times when I dine at Delmonico's now and look across the table, over the flawless place setting, I glimpse my father staring back at me.

As I turn a corner, I run straight into a hard object.

"Pardon me, I didn't see anyo—"

I stare up into Rafael Harden's eyes.

"Fancy meeting you here," Rafael drawls. He glances behind me to the private dining room's open door for a beat, and then his gaze returns to me, his brow rising. "A private dining room? How decadent."

Of all the people to encounter, today of all days. I hope Mr. Pulitzer is already waiting for me and not en route.

Rafael leans down slightly, closing the distance between us so we are nearly eye level.

"And in the afternoon? I didn't think you were after such assignations."

My cheeks burn under his knowing gaze.

For a moment, I can't decide which is worse: the implication that I'm meeting a lover here or the truth.

Definitely the truth.

"And if I am meeting someone, what of it?" I bluff. "I notice you're here in the same place, for what, a similar purpose?"

He grins. "Well done, Grace. I didn't know you had it in you."

It doesn't go unnoticed that the "Miss Harrington" has been dropped between us.

"As it happens, I'm not meeting a woman here. I had business. Not all of the men I work with want their *affairs* conducted in public drawing rooms."

My eyes narrow at the emphasis he puts on the word "affairs." I have to admit, part of me is curious about his business interests, but the desire to see him gone far outweighs any curiosity I might have.

"Well, it was lovely to see you again, Mr. Harden," I lie.

"Oh, I think we're far past this 'Mr. Harden' business. Call me Rafael. All my friends do."

"I wouldn't describe us as friends."

"No? How about this. In the spirit of our budding friendship, I'll give you something you want."

"I don't think we're well enough acquainted for you to know what I want."

There's that devilish grin again. "Well, now you've piqued my interest. I was talking about business, but you've just opened my mind up to a whole other host of delicious possibilities." He leans against the wall, settling in, and it takes everything in my power to keep from looking over my shoulder to see if Pulitzer is in the room waiting for me. Would Rafael tell Hearst if he saw us together? I can't imagine he wouldn't, considering they're friends. And still, despite the urgency, the word "business" reels me in.

"What business? Cuba?"

He nods, and before I can fully register the movement, he's pushed off from the wall and leans into me, his lips inches from my ear.

"You need to tell Will to be careful with this Clemencia Arango story."

It takes a moment for the name to come to mind with him standing so near to me.

The *Journal* recently ran a front-page piece on Clemencia Arango, a Cuban woman who was expelled from Cuba on suspicion of working as a courier and delivering letters to the revolutionaries. Richard Harding Davis heard that Arango and two other women were on the *Olivette,* an American ship in the Havana Harbor, when they were strip-searched by Spanish detectives three separate times. Frederic Remington provided an illustration of a naked young woman being examined by three male detectives, which Hearst printed prominently in the paper. He was sure the article would spur public interest, and it has, arousing much public condemnation of the Spanish.

"What's wrong with the Clemencia Arango story?" I ask. "The idea that a woman was violated like that—and on a ship flying the American flag."

Rafael grimaces. "Well, I don't know what information Davis and Remington received, but what I heard is that the women weren't searched by men at all, but by a Spanish policewoman. Clemencia Arango is in Tampa now, and she's telling a different story than the one Will splashed on the front page of his paper."

If that's true, it will certainly damage the *Journal*'s credibility. Already, the paper has been criticized by the *New York Press* for partaking in "yellow journalism" and sensationalizing the news. At the same time, I was outside Hearst's office when he first learned of the women's predicament, and we were all horrified by the story.

"I'll tell him."

"I know Will is eager to help and to sway public opinion toward the revolutionaries' cause, but he needs to be careful. One wrong step and he'll lose the public for good."

I agree, although "careful" is certainly not the word that comes to mind when I think of Hearst.

"If he's looking for a story, though," Rafael adds, "I have one that will definitely fit the bill."

"Why are you telling me this? You hardly need me to serve as a conduit to Hearst. Why not just give him the information directly?"

"I could tell him. But despite your claims to the contrary, you and I are friends, too. If the information both helps Will and helps you garner credibility with him, why wouldn't I give it to you? Still looking for your shot?"

"Every day."

His mouth quirks as I pull out my notepad, and then his expression turns serious.

"There's a Cuban-American dentist who wound up dead in a Spanish jail," Rafael says. "His name is Ricardo Ruiz. He's an American citizen. He was born in Cuba and fought in the Ten Years' War before he fled to the United States and received American citizenship. When the situation in Cuba calmed down a bit, he went back, set up a dentistry practice, married, started a family. He was recently arrested and imprisoned by the Spanish because the revolutionaries robbed a train carrying Spanish government officials and they thought Ruiz was involved in the robbery. The police rounded him and others up. The governor of the jail claims Ruiz killed himself while he was incarcerated. But, that's not the story I've heard."

"What have you heard?"

"Ruiz's body is battered as though he was beaten. Prisoners in the surrounding cells heard him screaming and crying the night of his death. His body is being kept at the jail in Guanabacoa outside of Havana. As the top-ranking American in Havana, Consul General

Lee has the power to investigate this further, to order an autopsy to determine the cause of death. If Ruiz was murdered, this could be just the thing to push for General Weyler's recall."

"And what's your interest in this? I thought you said you weren't involved with the Cuban cause."

"I told you my motives. Just trying to help a friend. There's no need to be so suspicious. Give that story to Will, and it might open some doors for you."

"And see Mr. Ruiz avenged, of course."

"That, too." A gleam enters his gaze. "Weyler is a problem. He is hell-bent on destroying the island to win this war, and he's doing a damned good job of it. He needs to be recalled to Spain. Maybe this is what it will take to do it. You and I both know the press needs a good story. Give Will this one."

"You're a terrible cynic, aren't you?"

"No, Grace, just a realist." He looks at me for one long moment, and then with an incongruously jaunty, "Enjoy your date," leaves me standing in front of Delmonico's private dining room, staring at his retreating back.

JOSEPH PULITZER IS ALREADY WAITING FOR ME WHEN I FINALLY enter the private dining room, and he frowns for a moment while I offer a poorly mangled apology for my tardiness.

"What news do you have for me?" he asks without preamble.

For as much as I know this is normal practice in the newsrooms, and Hearst certainly wouldn't hesitate to use me in the same manner, the subterfuge of this arrangement with Pulitzer feels wrong. At the same time, an opportunity to be taken seriously at the *World* isn't a chance I'm likely to get again. Despite Hearst's attempts to close the gap between them—their circulation battle continues with Pulitzer nearing an audience of a million Americans, and Hearst not too far behind him—there are many, including me, who hold the *World*'s journalistic standards in higher regard than Hearst's more dubious ones at the *Journal*.

I offer Pulitzer some tidbits, stories we're working on, a few that I have a feeling are pilfered pieces from Hearst's spies in the *World*'s newsroom.

"And what about Cuba?" Pulitzer asks. "What has Hearst learned about the situation down there? They've arrested one of my correspondents—Sylvester Scovel—for communicating with the insurgents. He's being held in a prison in Cuba. He's in grave danger."

I've read the *World*'s stories on Scovel's imprisonment; the degree to which General Weyler seems ready and eager to punish American journalists in the country has become alarming, highlighting the importance of an independent press. And if what Rafael just told me about Ricardo Ruiz is true, it sounds like the Spanish have no problem killing American citizens they deem to be a threat.

"Mr. Hearst is concerned about the safety of his correspondents as well," I reply.

Ricardo Ruiz is exactly the sort of story I imagine Pulitzer would love for his paper, and yet, I can't bring it upon myself to share the information with him. Seeing the story in the *World* would make Rafael suspicious, and I can't square the violation of his trust.

Not to mention, I want it for myself.

"We've also heard troubling things of Weyler's treatment of the press," I add.

It's a bland statement, and an obvious one considering the number of journalists Weyler has expelled from the country and the lock he's kept on outgoing wires, but it seems to satisfy Pulitzer, who does indeed look concerned about his reporter's fate.

"Is that all then, Miss Harrington?" he asks, the displeasure in his voice clear.

The feeling that I've disappointed him again is overwhelming. It's been drilled in me since I started working at the *Journal:* you do what it takes to get the story, to get ahead. For all that Hearst has given me a job on his staff, I've yet to truly be taken seriously as a journalist, to have the chance for my writing to stand on its own merit rather than whatever "stunt" angle Hearst can exploit. Now it feels like I'm losing my chance with Pulitzer, too.

"I confess, I thought I saw a bit of myself in you when we met that day in my office," Pulitzer says. "When you told me how badly you wanted to be a journalist, when you gave me the impression you were up to the task, I believed in you. This is a dirty business. Arthur Brisbane was my editor, a man I trusted, and Hearst stole him right out from under me. There's no loyalty in this business if that's what's giving you pause. You said you wanted to be taken seriously in this line of work. That means making difficult choices. I gave you a year to prove yourself, Miss Harrington, and so far you've shown me you aren't the investigative reporter you professed to be. You're certainly no Nellie Bly. Maybe you're meant to write advice pieces and the like. Maybe you don't belong at the *World* after all."

There's only one thing I have to offer. After all, Rafael said Clemencia Arango is already disputing the *Journal's* account. It's likely only a matter of time before the story breaks, and if I lead Pulitzer to it, the repercussions can't be that bad.

That's what I tell myself at least, as I take a deep breath, feeling like I'm sacrificing a piece of my integrity with each word that falls from my lips.

"The *Journal's* story about Clemencia Arango is wrong."

Nine

EVANGELINA

After Carmen is released from Recogidas, 1896 turning to 1897, it feels as though all hope is lost. But when hope fails me, anger sustains me through my days in prison. In the evenings, when the sounds of wails fill the night, I pray, although I fear no one answers me, because when the sun comes up, I am still here. They tell me I am to be shipped to a penal colony in Africa, and I wait for that unknown moment, the specter of it hanging over me and my endless days.

I think of my father constantly, not knowing whether he is even alive. I pray for my sisters. Emilio Betancourt similarly occupies my thoughts, and I wonder what has become of him, what punishment he has received for his part in helping me. Has he been released from prison and moved on from his life now, or is he withering away in the same conditions as me?

The past few nights, I've dreamed of him, of when we first met. It feels like a lifetime ago, like it happened to a different woman. In the beginning, Emilio used to walk back and forth in front of our house. I didn't notice him right away, but when I did after a few weeks, I was initially struck by the fact that he was the handsomest man I'd ever seen. Now when I attempt to remember the way he made me feel, what he looked like, I am left with the sensation that those were a girl's memories. So much has changed in such a short time. I am no longer the girl I used to be.

Life here is very different from what I knew on the Isle of Pines. There we were allowed to roam the island, were given adequate food so there was no gnawing hunger in our bellies. Now I am jailed in a vast common cell and am forced to scrub floors. My clothes are in tatters hanging from my body, my cheeks gaunt. We are kept in an immense courtyard, a gate with ironwork containing us. Visitors still come every day to leer at us through the bars, taunting us for our predicament. Many of my fellow prisoners beg for money, reaching their hands through the bars and pleading for someone on the other side to help them. There are spies in the prison who report back on our movements, and perhaps that is the hardest part of all. We live side by side, yet it is impossible to speak freely, to know who you can trust, even more so now that I am alone, my sister Carmen lost to me.

And still, even in this horrible place, there are those whom I love: Señoras Agramonte and Sotolongo, Miss Aguilar, the wives of generals Recio and Rodriguez. They're all fine women imprisoned alongside me because they're related to revolutionaries.

One day I stand in the cage, surrounded by my fellow prisoners. There are about a hundred of us here, from different backgrounds, fate dealing us all the unforgiving hand that brought us to this miserable place. Our jailer is holding court, two well-dressed men beside him. They speak of us as though we cannot hear them, as though we've lost our humanity in this horrid prison. Maybe we have. The more time that passes, the more I feel as though someone else has taken control of my body. When you strip away the things you love, the things that make you whole, what is left?

Sometimes, I think there's hardly enough to sustain me. Other times, I'm fueled solely by the desire to keep my captors from seeing me fall apart.

And then, I hear the men's conversation shift from the women surrounding me, to me.

I steel myself, turning my attention their way, making sure they know I hear every word out of that odious jailer's mouth, his filthy suggestions that I should ingratiate myself to the guards by handing my body over to them. If I can't have respect in this place, then at least I will evoke their shame.

But the leer on the jailer's face isn't matched by his two companions.

No, on their faces I see a combination of horror and pity, which in its own way might just be worse.

I duck my head, hurrying back inside the enclosed portion of the common cell. The courtyard affords fresh air of sorts despite the horrendous stench, but the prying eyes make it nearly unbearable.

With each day that passes, I slowly go mad.

ONE AFTERNOON, THE WARDEN SENDS FOR ME AGAIN.

"You have visitors," a guard announces. "Americans."

I cannot think of any American friends who would come to see me. Still, better to have a visitor than to spend the day closed up in this cell. Tuesdays, Thursdays, and Saturdays from noon to four in the afternoon are visiting days at the jail. On those days, the waiting room is filled with people who have come to share in our sadness and to carry news of the outside world to us.

Each visiting day I dream that my father, my sisters, Emilio will come see me, but I'm always left with disappointment instead. Even though I am surrounded by people, privacy an impossibility in a place like this, I am lonelier than I have ever been in my entire life.

I follow the guard through the prison, ignoring the noises surrounding me, the ever-present taunts. I trip down the stairs, righting myself quickly, and walk across the end of the courtyard, and through the gate into the reception room, ironically named the "Salon of Justice," as though such a virtue exists here.

The Salon of Justice is a small, unforgiving room with a stone floor, its name painted on one of the walls, the words mocking me.

Today the room is occupied by two men who at first glance look vaguely familiar, although I can't imagine where I would have come across them before.

They both rise as I walk in, the gentlemanly gesture surprising me. It's been so long since someone treated me like a lady. They wait until I am seated and then follow suit.

"My name is George Bryson," the first man says. He lowers his voice slightly. "I am a reporter for one of the American newspapers. The *New York Journal.*" He says this proudly, as though I would somehow be familiar with his work and that of his paper. "This is George Musgrave," he adds, gesturing to the man beside him.

And then, I recognize them. They were here a few days ago meeting with Don Jose, the warden who runs the prison. Embarrassment floods me as I remember the way he spoke about me in front of these men, the conditions in which they saw me: in a cage like an animal, sunk in mire and desperation.

I sit up straight, trying to make my ancestors proud and doing my family justice rather than letting these men see me brought low.

"You shouldn't be here," George Bryson says. "We were alerted to your plight by some of your fellow countrymen, and my employers and

I would very much like to right the wrong that has been done to you. We spoke with the warden, and he told us you were imprisoned because you were involved in an insurrection plot against the colonel in charge of the Isle of Pines."

Anger fills me at the warden's characterization of that night, the way in which the Spanish have smeared my good reputation by erasing Berriz's villainy and making me the guilty party in his attack on me. I long to speak, to clarify Don Jose's twisted version of events, but if prison has taught me anything, it's that silence can be an armor of sorts, the need to guard your innermost thoughts paramount.

"Seeing you in person, well, we could hardly reconcile the elegant lady before us with the role the warden described you playing in such an affair."

Musgrave nods in agreement with his friend's words.

"I doubt someone as angelic and young as you could be involved in such perfidy," Bryson adds. "We would like to hear your story."

Their manners are impeccable, the solicitous way in which they speak to me a welcome change from the guards here. But at the same time, I have quickly learned that drawing attention to myself only hurts my case. That Berriz is the nephew of the Spanish minister of war and a close personal friend of General Weyler has certainly brought a great deal of attention to my alleged crimes, and Weyler himself has taken a keen interest in my future. After all, it wouldn't do for my story to inspire others to rise up against the Spanish and their cruelties.

"I cannot give you an official statement," I caution, even as hope blooms.

What if this is the answer to all I have prayed for?

"You must understand that the charges before me are quite delicate," I add. "The Spanish are quick to anger, and I cannot take the chance that they will retaliate against me for speaking with you."

"That is understood," Bryson replies. "We are here because we are genuinely concerned about the travesty that has been done to you. We promise you discretion. We will do everything in our power to see you liberated from this hellish place."

Tears well in my eyes, falling down my cheeks. I've never cried so much as I have in Recogidas, not even over the loss of my mother, and their simple kindness undoes me.

Or maybe it's the fact that in the face of all I stand to lose, this chance to fight for my freedom feels like one of the most important moments of my life.

I can do this. I can be strong. I have to be.

I square my shoulders and meet their gaze. "What would you like to know?"

MY THROAT IS SORE AFTER MY MEETING WITH GEORGE BRYSON and George Musgrave. I think I spoke more to them in one sitting than I have since I came to Recogidas. I'm not sure what it is about the two men that has made me trust them so much, but at this point, I have little to lose. I can die in Recogidas, or in a penal colony at Ceuta, or I can cautiously take my chances with the Americans.

Soon enough, they prove their loyalty to me.

The warden corners me one day, the stench of his putrid breath inches from my face making me gag. "You're being moved, Evangelina."

My heart pounds. It isn't the first time they've told me such a thing; they regularly taunt me with all sorts of possibilities dangled before me.

"To Ceuta?" I ask, referring to their penal colony in Africa.

"No, not Ceuta. Yet. Apparently, the American consul general

Fitzhugh Lee has taken an interest in your case. You clearly have some fine benefactors. Consul General Lee personally came by to look at your accommodations and that of the other political prisoners. He protested over the fact that you and your friends are forced to share quarters with common criminals.

"You'll sleep elsewhere from now on. Hopefully, it's up to your elevated standards," he says mockingly. "If you have any complaints about the care you receive during your stay here, please let us know."

There's enough innuendo injected in his voice, coupled with the earlier comments he's made about me, to leave me with no doubt as to where his thoughts lie and what he thinks I should do in order to secure better accommodations myself.

I can barely suppress a shudder.

He grips my arm, his fingers digging into my skin, leading me toward my new home, and despite the horrible feel of his body against mine, the stench of his odor, the moisture of the sweat wetting his palm, my heart is light.

Perhaps there will be a different future for me.

THEY MOVE ME FROM THE MASS HALL WITH THE OTHER PRISONers to a smaller cell of my own. I am allowed to read books and to cook my own food, and even though I'm alone, it's almost like it used to be when we lived on the Isle of Pines when I was able to make a home for myself and my family, even in a difficult situation.

I still miss my family and friends, but I cling to the hope that I will be freed.

In a stroke of immense good fortune, the wife and daughter of Consul General Lee visit me in Recogidas, showing me kindness I'd nearly forgotten. Mrs. Lee speaks to me as I imagine a mother would, and I am awed by her gentle nature. I did not know my mother well since she died when I was young, but it is in times like these, when I miss her most, when I wish I had someone I could lean upon, someone who would care for me and help me be strong. It's exhausting carrying the weight of all that has happened on my own.

I see more of George Bryson and George Musgrave, and I am able to thank them for their benevolence in person under the suspicious eyes of my jailers. It is a delicate balance my captors are forced to maintain. They cannot risk angering the Americans entirely, for the worst possible thing would be for the United States to throw their full military might behind the revolutionaries. At the same time, it is clear the Spanish bristle at the Americans' influence.

Each time I see George Bryson, I am cheered as he tells me I have friends who want to help me, who are advocating on my behalf. Bryson is working on securing my release, trying to bribe a military judge to let me go. I am also visited by Donnell Rockwell, a clerk with the American consulate staff in Havana who occasionally visits the Americans who are imprisoned here. Suddenly, I have a new host of American friends who are concerned for my welfare.

Finally, I beg George Bryson to get word of my father.

He slips me a note at our next meeting.

When I am back in private, I take the note from my pocket and unfurl the piece of paper, reading the words contained there with a sharp burst of joy followed by immense pain.

My father is alive.

He is imprisoned in La Cabaña.

Ten

꧁꧂

GRACE

"Grace!" Hearst shouts from his office.

I rise from my seat, grabbing my pad and pen off my desk.

Hearst's newsroom is a modern one, filled with banks of typewriters, and in his printing presses and in his use of photograph, he's embraced the newest technology, too. Like many, though, I've yet to fully embrace the typewriter, the loud noise too jarring, preferring instead to write my articles by longhand. There's something intimate about putting a pen to paper that lets me express my thoughts more clearly. Besides, even with the allowance I receive from my family, the expense of such a machine hardly seems reasonable given how infrequently I'm able to put it to use. For Hearst's star reporters, the typewriter's speed can't be denied, particularly when they're working on a tight deadline.

The scoop Rafael gave me on Ricardo Ruiz made a good impression, but since the initial coup of delivering the news to Hearst has faded, the story passed on to more senior—and male—colleagues, I am back where I started: desperate to prove myself and looking for a story that could make my career. It's a difficult time to be a journalist in the city. It seems there are more of us than the demand calls for, and all of the major newsrooms have been rife with layoffs. Each day,

I walk into work wondering if it'll be my last. It's hard to stand out among the likes of writers like Mark Twain and Stephen Crane.

Hearst is standing just over the threshold with Arthur Brisbane when I walk into his office.

"We need someone to go to the Peanut Club and listen to the press briefing," Brisbane announces. "Everyone else is tied up on stories right now and can't make it. Besides, you did good reporting on Ruiz earlier. It seems fair to give you a shake at the story."

Nicknamed the "Peanut Club" for the large boxes of peanuts provided for all who gather there, reporters meet daily each afternoon at the Junta offices on Broadway. The office where Rafael took me the night of the Bradley-Martin ball is the office of Horatio Rubens, a local lawyer who is sympathetic to the Cuban cause. It's the primary place for the dissemination of news about Cuba, and is our own sort of wire service, offering details of life on the island we would otherwise be unable to glean, particularly useful considering Pulitzer has blocked all possibility of Hearst ever having an Associated Press wire service.

"Can you handle it?" Hearst asks me.

"Absolutely."

THE STREET IS TEEMING WITH PEOPLE WHEN I WALK OUTSIDE. These are the moments when I love the city most, when everything feels so alive, the air electric. Some of the *Journal*'s newsboys stand out on the street, hawking our latest edition to pedestrians. Without them, Hearst, Pulitzer, and the rest wouldn't be able to reach the circulation numbers they dream of with their afternoon editions. The young boys buy the papers and then turn around and sell them in the afternoons and evenings at a half a cent profit for each paper, the money going to support themselves, and for some, their families. Many of them are orphans and runaways.

"How's it going, Johnny?" I ask, recognizing my favorite of the bunch.

He's a tall boy, about eleven, with a full head of red hair and a big personality. He smiles when he sees me.

"Good news day." He gestures to the nearly empty satchel bag next to him. "You write any of these articles on the front page?"

I shake my head. "Maybe next time."

He grins. "Can't wait for opportunities to come your way, you know. You gotta make 'em on your own."

This city. It makes children grow up in an instant.

I reach into the pocket of my dress and hand him a bag of the saltwater taffy he favors. I make a point of keeping them handy should our paths cross when I leave the office.

Johnny's eyes light up at the familiar sweet.

I've often wondered where he stays when he leaves for the day. Some days, the newsboys who don't sell enough papers are simply gone. If they don't sell enough of their inventory, then they don't have money to buy papers to sell the next day. It's a hard, risky business.

"Working on a story?" he asks me.

"Hopefully."

We say a quick good-bye when a customer approaches him, and I hurry down the street toward the Junta meeting. I follow the line of reporters into the Junta offices, unsurprised to find that I am the only woman in the group.

Today, the president of the Junta, Tomás Estrada Palma, stands at the front of the room, addressing the growing crowd of journalists. Estrada Palma came to New York after the Ten Years' War and worked closely with José Martí, the famous writer and poet who spent most of his life fighting for Cuban independence. Since Martí's death two years ago, Estrada Palma has become the Junta's leader, and there has been speculation that Martí had privately tapped Estrada Palma as his successor in the event of his death due to the close friendship between the two.

The more time I spend around the Junta, the more I'm not sure what to make of them. There is no question that they're passionate and devoted to their cause, nor is there doubt that at times the stories they give to the press are exaggerated beyond belief. Rafael's earlier warning to be careful forever rings in my ears. And yet, we come to these meetings, because thanks to the Spanish censors and their reluctance to allow an independent international press, the Junta is all we have. While the stories might be a mythologized version of actual events, the unvarnished truth is that something horrible is going on in Cuba.

The Spanish in all of their ire and eagerness to cast blame at the American newspapers have failed in one important lesson. The Junta has harnessed the power of the press to sway public opinion, so we hear very little of the other side of the violence.

War is not only waged on the battlefield.

Even the Junta's critics have to acknowledge their impressive reach. Their petitions in support of the revolutionaries secure hundreds of thousands of signatures. They publish over a dozen exile newspapers. They've organized to advocate for their interests in a way that is certainly powerful, and with good reason.

It turns out, Rafael was right about the Clemencia Arango story, and Joseph Pulitzer pounced on the information I gave him, sending reporters from the *World* to interview Arango and her friends when their ship docked in New York. Davis was left embarrassed over the journalistic mistake, but from what I can tell, Hearst is hardly fazed.

But today we're here for the other piece of information Rafael fed me:

Ricardo Ruiz.

The American consul general Fitzhugh Lee, a nephew of Robert E. Lee and former governor of Virginia, visited the jail where Ruiz was held prisoner, as did the *Journal*'s correspondent, George Eugene Bryson, and both men found Ruiz's death to be highly suspicious. It's unclear, though, if Ruiz's death is enough to prompt the American government to action. Congress has passed a resolution asking for more information on the case and voted to demand the release of other American prisoners in Cuba.

Hearst has arranged for Mrs. Ruiz and her five children to come to Washington D.C. to meet with President McKinley and Secretary of State Sherman. Hearst is pressing for our stories to lead the public to the decision that war is inevitable, demanding we report on the news and shape it in a way I'm not entirely comfortable with, even if the urgency of the situation demands action.

And still, when the government fails to act, who should fill that void? Is it the people? And are we truly, as Hearst says, the voice of the people? Or are we too motivated by our need to boost circulation, by the agenda we all intrinsically possess?

The estimated death count in Cuba has reached three hundred thousand, and the fear is that if Spain continues on this trajectory, they might eliminate the island's entire population.

I take notes on the meeting; there's nothing really new on the Ricardo Ruiz situation, although some of the Junta's talking points are nearly identical to the articles we've published on the subject, and it's clear that in this we are merely regurgitating the facts they have given us.

I turn to leave, and I collide with a warm body and a familiar voice says—

"Fancy seeing you here."

Rafael walks beside me as we exit the Junta meeting, and when I turn to say my good-byes, he tells me he's headed to the *Journal* offices to see Will and doesn't mind accompanying me on the journey.

"So, what did you think of the meeting today?" he asks. "You're becoming quite the regular."

It's impossible to miss the hint of teasing in his voice, and I realize that to him I must very much seem as though I am playing at the Cuba issue, as are so many of us. After all, no matter how much we speak of war or condemn the Spanish, it isn't really our struggle, is it? There's a difference between writing about atrocities happening to other people and experiencing them ourselves.

"I wouldn't count a few meetings as making me a regular," I reply. "I'm still trying to learn as much as I can about the conflict."

"Considering the misinformation that gets published on a daily basis, you're in good company. The need to learn more about the conflict hasn't stopped many of your colleagues from covering it."

I can't argue with him there.

"Interesting how we should run into each other again at a Junta meeting," I reply. "For someone who claims to not be a revolutionary, you participate in enough of their meetings."

"I told you—my sister is the one with the revolutionary aims. I'm merely protecting my interests."

"Oh, I believe you're protecting your interests, just not that they're as pecuniary as you pretend them to be." I pause. "I haven't seen you around since we ran into each other at Delmonico's. Where have you been?"

He grins. "Why? Did you miss me?"

"Hardly."

"I was in Florida." He says it carefully, his usual devil-may-care attitude suspiciously absent.

And then it clicks into place, the conversations surrounding the Junta, the articles we've worked on.

"You're involved with the filibusters, aren't you?"

The filibusters are private shipping expeditions that bring arms and recruits to the revolutionaries, frequently leaving out of ports in Florida. According to the Neutrality Act of 1895, military aid to the revolutionaries is illegal. Many of the filibusters sink or are intercepted, although the United States has been criticized for quickly releasing detained men and not enforcing the Act as stringently as they should.

"Are we off the record?" Rafael asks.

"Yes."

His gaze is searching, and then, surprising us both, I think, he says, "Then, yes, I am."

"I can understand why you would support the filibusters, but why do you go to Florida yourself?"

"My boats, my business."

"Does Hearst know?"

"No."

I'm surprised he would share this information with me and not with his friend, and I can't help but feel a stab of guilt at the realization that he's taking me into his confidence whereas I betrayed his by telling Pulitzer about the Arango story.

"The risk you take—"

"Isn't so bad. You shouldn't believe everything you read in the newspapers. The Spanish navy might say they control the waters surrounding Cuba, but it's surprisingly easy to evade them if necessary. The most dangerous part is the landing," he admits. "The revolutionaries try to intercept the boats first, but the Spanish do everything they can to prevent the filibusters from making landfall. After all, considering how much both sides are struggling to adequately supply their forces, having ammunition can make all the difference in the world."

It's a new facet of his personality, one I never would have guessed at. But then again, it explains so much about his friendship with Will Hearst. They are both men with streaks of idealism you never would imagine given their outward appearance.

"How long have you been sending arms and aid to Cuba?"

"Two years. I'm not sure how much of a difference it makes, but I can spare the boats."

I don't know why he's downplaying his role in all of this, but I doubt it's a very small thing.

"There's money to be made in smuggling," he adds.

I stop walking and study him for a moment. He's entrusting me with something important about himself, and I feel a need to respect his honesty and return it with some candor of my own.

"It's not just that. You're not a reckless man, and there must be far easier ways for you to make money. Not that you likely need all that much, anyway. You do it because you care."

He looks momentarily embarrassed. "Can you ever have enough money? I'm not sure that's possible."

"I don't believe that's your motivation. Try as you may, you're not going to convince me you're that mercenary."

"Why do you care so much about my motivations?"

I open my mouth to reply, and then close it again, no good answer coming to mind.

"I suppose you can call it my sentimentality, then," Rafael finally replies. "I am Cuban even if I don't live on the island, and it's impossible to not hear of the atrocities they're suffering and not feel some desire to help out, even if I'm not entirely convinced it isn't all for naught."

His gaze lingers on me, and I duck my head, my cheeks heating at the intensity of his stare. With each moment that passes, it feels as though the conversation grows more intimate, and I realize we are standing uncomfortably close together on the crowded street.

"Who were you meeting at Delmonico's that day?" he murmurs. "I confess I've thought about it a great deal."

Embarrassment floods me as I remember the impression I gave him, how he teased me over whether I was meeting a lover there. Except there's nothing joking in his demeanor, now.

"Not a lover."

He quirks a brow at me in question.

I take a deep breath, the words rushing out. "I was meeting Joseph Pulitzer."

"Pulitzer? Don't tell me he's trying to steal you away from the *Journal*."

Maybe it's my guilt over betraying his confidence with the Clemencia Arango story. Or the fact that he trusted me with his secrets, and I can't help but share something about myself with him. Or maybe I suppose I consider him to be a friend after all, too. All I know is I surprise us both, I think, by telling him the truth.

"I've been spying on Hearst. For Pulitzer."

He gapes at me. "You've—"

"That day we met in Hearst's office, I had gone to see Pulitzer first about a job at the *World*. But Pulitzer wasn't interested in hiring me unless I proved myself. I was too inexperienced, but he saw an opportunity to use me. He knew Hearst had spies in his newsroom, and he wanted me to do the same for him at the *Journal*. He didn't think Hearst would suspect someone like me."

He doesn't speak for a beat that stretches on longer than I'd like and then—

"What have you given Pulitzer?"

I can't decipher the tone of his voice, and I don't look him in the eyes, for I don't think I could bear to see disappointment in me reflected there.

"Little things here and there. When you told me there were problems with the Clemencia Arango story, I shared that information with Pulitzer. I'm sorry. Truly. I do regret that. Maybe most of all."

"Why did you do it then?"

"I'd given Pulitzer so little information since I started working for him. He offered me a year to prove myself, and it's almost up, and he was clearly growing frustrated with me. I didn't want to lose my chance, but I also didn't want to tell him about Ricardo Ruiz. I figured since the Clemencia Arango story was already beginning to leak, it wouldn't matter so much, he'd learn the truth eventually. I suppose that's how I justified what I did.

"I'm not the person you thought I was. I'm not—I'm not the person I thought I was, either. I know it's the business—you do what it takes to get the story—but this feels different. Dishonest. Hearst has given me opportunities others haven't, and I've repaid his chances by spying on him. I need to come clean, need to confess what I've done. I want to be a reporter, but not like this."

"Don't be too hard on yourself. You're ambitious. I've always admired that about you, from the first moment you marched into Will's office and proposed he hire you. And as for the deceptive part of your endeavor, well, it is possible to be good and still make mistakes, to put your ambition before others."

"Would you have done what I did?"

"Would I have scraped and clawed my way to get ahead? Of course. I can't say I haven't done worse. Same with Will. You wanted to write for the New York newspapers. This is the business. There's a war raging on Park Row. Eventually, though, you're going to have to pick a side. If it's the *World*, then go take your shot there. If it's the *Journal*, then come clean with Will before he finds out from someone else."

We stop in front of the *Journal* offices. I scan the newsboys sitting out front, but Johnny is nowhere to be seen.

"This is where I leave you," Rafael says.

"I thought you wanted to speak with Will."

"Maybe I just wanted a chance to walk you back. I'll be gone for a bit again." He says it casually, but now that he's told me about the filibusters, I imagine there's nothing casual about it.

"Running guns to Cuba?"

"It almost sounds romantic when you put it like that." He grins. "It'll be okay. However dirty you think your hands are, I promise Will has done worse. Good-bye, Grace."

"Good-bye, Rafael." I hesitate, wanting to say more, but the words eluding me until I settle on, "Be safe."

I watch him walk away, more than a little confused by the entire encounter and my desire to call after him and continue our conversation.

Eleven

MARINA
Before

"*What news do you bring us?*" one of the women sitting next to me asks the speaker. Beside me, Mateo leans forward, his elbows resting on his knees, his body tense.

There are twenty of us gathered together in this hut in the countryside. It's dark out, the hour late, the danger of meeting high. The Spanish monitor our movements, so it is rare that we are able to come together like this to discuss our dreams for Cuba's future.

We all come from different backgrounds, a testament to how unified we are in our desire for independence. It fills me with hope, that our anger and our conviction can be harnessed into something powerful that the Spanish will be unable to match.

"There was an uprising in the village of Baire, near Santiago de Cuba on the twenty-fourth of February," the man answers, his voice low, urgent.

It's hardly surprising considering revolution has been building in Cuba, our list of grievances against the Spanish only growing.

"Some think this might be the impetus we need to defeat the Spanish," he adds. "There's talk that many who are in exile are planning a return, and they're organizing an invasion of Cuba. We must be ready to fight when we are called to do so."

"Do you think we'll be successful?" another man asks.

"Do we have a choice?" the woman interjects. "Look what Spain has done to us. They tax us to death. They control what we say and what we do, keep us from speaking out, from advocating for ourselves for a better future. They don't give us a chance to govern ourselves, and we exist solely to serve the Spanish crown. For centuries, they have taken from Cuba to serve Spain. They'll never give us our independence. We'll have to take it."

"What will be different this time?" I interject. "We cannot afford to fight another war we will not win. We cannot afford for them to weaken us if we don't assure victory."

"We have been preparing for this for decades now," Mateo answers. "We've learned from all the time we've spent fighting them. We have exiles placed all over the world who have garnered international support for our cause, who can harness the power of the international press and the diplomatic relations they've established. Our leaders are ready for this. It is time for us to show Spain that Cuba is ready to govern itself, that we no longer accept their interference in our affairs. It is time for independence."

MATEO AND I WALK HOME FROM THE MEETING, HIS ARM SLUNG AROUND my shoulders.

Our daughter Isabella is back with his mother Luz at the little house we built. I can't remember the last time it was just the two of us. It almost feels like it used to be before we were married, before we had Isabella, when we used to sit beside each other and discuss the writings of José Martí, reciting the lines from Versos Sencillos from memory.

It has made our love easier, certainly, that we both have the same wishes *for Cuba, that we see the world the same way. I cannot imagine loving someone who disagreed with me on the fundamental character of our nation and our selves. There are some things that are too important to be ignored, and in this fight, we must all do our part.*

"Do you think what they said tonight is true—that we are to have war once more?" I ask him.

I was a small child when Spain defeated us in the Little War, the year-long conflict organized by the veterans of the prior fight for independence. This is to be our third attempt, and if we are not successful, I fear we will only embolden the Spanish to forever see us as their property.

"I think everyone is ready. Martí, Maceo, Gómez, and the others have been in exile. I'm sure they're eager to return to Cuba and conclude this fight, to see our Cuban flag fly proudly. Aren't we all desperate to be free?"

"Will you join them if they fight?" I ask Mateo.

"How can I not? I can't stand by and watch my countrymen sacrifice their lives for something I believe in, too."

"If you go to war, then I want to go with you."

"Marina. No."

"You said it yourself. How can I stand by and watch my countrymen sacrifice their lives for something I believe in and do nothing? They will need nurses in the camps. There will be roles for women to fill; there has to be. It's our Cuba, too, and we deserve to represent her as much as you do. If we are to fight under a united flag, if we are to stand a chance of defeating the Spanish, then we must all work together to do so. We are stronger if we are united, if we do not allow the Spanish to divide us."

"And Isabella? My mother cannot care for her on her own. Your family doesn't even know she exists. Marina, I know how you feel about Cuba. But we both cannot leave her."

I cannot imagine watching others fight this war for me, for other women to sacrifice and struggle while I stay home in our little farm. There has to be some good I can do for Cuba while still caring for Isabella, some change I can make within the life I have chosen, that I may be of service somehow.

"When will you leave?" I ask him.

"When the revolutionaries cross over into our province. It may be some time before I can join them, for them to make their way to the western side of the island, but when they do, I will be ready. I don't want to leave you. But I promise, when this is all over we will be together again."

I close my eyes for a moment, listening to the sounds of the countryside at night, the animals creating their own melody. When I open them again, the starlit sky shines down on us, Cuba in all of her splendid glory.

"Then I pray it shall be a quick war," I reply.

"WHERE IS PAPI?" ISABELLA ASKS ME AS WE WALK NEAR THE HA-vana harbor together one morning in May.

She keeps her voice low, as she's already learned the valuable lesson of discretion in the camp. We speak little of her father, a fact that pains me greatly. Before reconcentration, I attempted to keep him alive for her by telling her stories about our life together, trying to remind her of better times when we were all a family. I worry that she's so young that she's struggling to remember him, that if—when—he comes home, it will be difficult for us to resume our lives together, to slip into the roles we've played for so long. This war has changed so much that it's nearly impossible to believe we will come out the other side as the same people we were when it began.

"I don't know," I admit, loath to lie to her. "Somewhere in the country, I imagine. Although, I suppose he could be anywhere."

"I miss him so much," she whispers.

I was never particularly close to my father. What little time was spent at home was dedicated to raising my brother Arturo, to ensuring that he was fit to take over the family legacy. He had little use for me as a girl, leaving me instead to my mother's care.

Mateo's relationship with Isabella has been different from the beginning, a fact I'm eternally grateful for. He was the one who set her upon the back of a horse for the first time when she couldn't yet walk, who beamed and cheered her on when she took her first steps, and she loved nothing more than running after him as he worked on our farm, helping with the care and feeding of the horses, listening to his stories about growing up in the country. My childhood was so different and staid in comparison, that the joy and adventure that infused hers before our world fell apart always filled me with immense pride that I had set my daughter on a different course than the one I chafed against. She will be able to love freely one day, to follow her heart rather than her family's expectations. I hope she will be able to pursue her interests, her passions without being denied the same opportunities afforded to a man.

I fight for a new Cuba for myself, but also for my daughter, for her children, for all of us who deserve better than what we have been given.

"Do you think he misses us?" Isabella asks.

I'm not quite sure how to convey the depth of a parent's love to her, to put into words the pain and longing I know with certainty Mateo feels for his family, and even as I begin to, a wave of emotion takes hold and so I seize on the happy memories rather than lingering over the stab of pain in my breast.

"I know he misses us. Do you know what he said when you were born?"

Isabella shakes her head.

"I was lying in bed just after having you. I was so tired, and so full of love for you, and he took you from me for the first time, bundled you up in his arms, and looked down at your beautiful little face. And I saw the emotion come over his expression, it just swept across him, and I watched the moment when he fell in love with you. He reached out and he touched your cheek, and he had this look of wonder in his eyes, just absolutely beaming with joy. And then he turned to me and said he'd never seen anything so extraordinary in his life."

Tears threaten again, but this time it is the promise of that memory that fills me, the knowledge that once we carved out an immense amount of happiness despite the troubled circumstances surrounding us, and the hope and surety that one day we will do so again.

"I know without a doubt in my mind, that wherever your father is at this moment, he is thinking about you and missing you desperately, and doing everything in his power to fight his way back to us. I promise you that. So we must do everything we can to be strong, to survive this.

"When you're sad, or when you miss your father, think of those happy moments we spent, think of how much we love each other, and know that no one can take that away from you. Whatever the Spanish do to us, however difficult things become, we must always keep a part of ourselves safe, filled with hope. We must keep them from destroying our spirit. That is how we will win this war."

"I miss him," she whispers, tears swimming in her eyes.

I wrap my arms around her, enfolding her in a tight hug.

"I know you do. I miss him, too. I know how hard this has been for you. How much you have lost in such a short time. I am so sorry for it. But know this—there will come a better time than this moment we are living. A time when we are all together, when there is food to be had, when we are happy and healthy, and when we are *free*. We fight for that moment, we sacrifice for that future. The one of us whole and happy in Cuba together."

"Viva Cuba Libre," she whispers, echoing the call sung by the revolutionaries.

"Viva Cuba Libre," I say, pride bursting through me, my voice low for now, waiting for the day when I can shout it throughout Havana and the rest of Cuba.

Twelve

GRACE

After I confess my secret to Rafael, the need to end this spying business weighs heavily on me. Now that I have proved my utility to Pulitzer with the intelligence I offered him on the Clemencia Arango story, he demands more and more information as though I am suddenly part of Hearst's inner circle. Most of our correspondence is conducted by hectoring letters Pulitzer sends me—addressing me by one of the many code names he employs for Hearst and everyone in his sphere, the *Journal* itself referred to simply as "Geranium." Pulitzer complains about my lack of results when I tell him I have nothing left to offer him, railing against the *Journal*'s shockingly low prices, growing circulation, and Hearst's unflagging arrogance.

For all of his wealth and his negative reputation, working with Hearst has certainly made me view him in a different light. There's a shyness about him that is so incongruous with the man who loves a spectacle, and I assume people easily mistake his reserve for standoffishness. But, what people fail to understand is that for all Hearst loves celebrating his paper, for all of his determination and drive, he is a man happiest on the sidelines, surrounded by those who are familiar to him and with whom he can be at ease, be it a man like Rafael, a chorus girl, or one of his editors.

No one would describe Pulitzer as shy, and even though he comes from a much more unassuming background, he is a man who demands respect from those who work for him, his temper best described as irascible. While the *World* presents a professional front to the public, since I've begun working among other journalists with former ties to Pulitzer, I've heard he's a difficult man to please, the atmosphere in his newsroom often more chaotic than what is ordinary in our business, his disposition creating a stressful environment for his employees.

With each letter he sends me, it becomes clear that the situation cannot continue on, the year we agreed to coming to its close, and I finally agree to meet with Pulitzer on one of the rare occasions when he is at his home in the city.

That afternoon, I leave the office in a hurry, late for our meeting and filled with nerves.

When I arrive at Pulitzer's immense mansion at 10 East 55th Street, I'm immediately shown into his office by his butler, who announces me with little fanfare before shutting the door firmly behind me.

Once I'm seated, the barest of pleasantries exchanged between me and Pulitzer, he asks me, "What do you have for me?"

"I received your last letter asking me for information on our reporting on Cuba, but I didn't come here for that."

He frowns. "Then why did you come here?"

For a moment, I can't believe I'm letting the dream that was within my grasp slip between my fingers, even as I know it's what I must do. For better or worse, I've decided to cast my lot with Hearst and the *Journal*.

"It's been a year since we made our agreement, and I came to thank you for meeting with me that day in your office and for giving me the impetus that sent me to the *Journal*. I didn't realize it at the time, but it was the right place for me to learn how to be a journalist. I've gotten the experience I needed, even if the stories I covered weren't the ones I envisioned working on.

"I can't keep spying for you. I don't feel right about it. Hearst has given me a chance and I can't repay that by passing information to you."

"I thought you wanted to be a journalist, Miss Harrington. It seems like my initial concerns were correct and you don't have what it takes."

Considering how long I've admired his paper and career, the words sting more than I'd care to admit.

"I am a journalist. At the *Journal*."

"We'll see how much longer that proves to be true. Are you going to tell Hearst what you did?"

"I am. It seems only fair."

"Surely, you cannot be so naïve to believe that. Do you think Hearst cares about fair?" Pulitzer scoffs. "He professes to advocate for the common man, but how can you do that if you've only ever been seeped in privilege? That man cares about himself and little else."

"He cares," I reply. "People don't understand that about him, but you can't miss it when you work beside him."

Hearst might have started his business with inherited money, but it's easy to forget that when he started the *San Francisco Examiner* the paper was failing or that while he did replicate much of Pulitzer's success, he also exceeded Pulitzer's accomplishments. There's no doubt that Hearst has set the new standard all other newspapers aim to emulate.

"So this is it. The end to our little arrangement."

"Yes. I'm sorry I haven't been more helpful."

He waves me off without another word.

AFTER I LEAVE THE MEETING WITH PULITZER, I HEAD BACK TO
the *Journal* office. I walk through the newsroom, nerves filling me,
heading toward Hearst's office. I square my shoulders, raising my
hand to knock on Hearst's office door, a tremor sliding through my
body.

I try to remember what Rafael told me, trust that Hearst will appreciate me coming here and confessing to spying for Pulitzer, that
he'll repay my honesty with forgiveness. All I can do is hope he won't
fire me.

"Come in," Hearst calls out from the other side of his office.

I walk inside, closing the door gently behind me.

"May I have a word?" I ask him.

"Of course."

"I need to talk to you about something. I—I haven't been honest
with you from the beginning."

"I'm surprised to hear that. How have you been dishonest?"

"When I originally came to you asking for a job as a journalist, it
was at Mr. Pulitzer's behest. He wanted a spy in your newsroom and
he proposed that I attempt to secure a job here and report back to him
on the inner workings of the *Journal*."

"I see. And what did you give him?"

"Details about the stories we were working on here and there. The
fact that the Clemencia Arango story was wrong, for one."

"What did he offer you in exchange for the information? Money?"

"A job when it was all over. I originally wanted to work for Pulitzer. I've admired the work he has done at the *World* for some time. I

secured a meeting with him, but he wasn't looking for another girl reporter, at least not one with my lack of experience. I knew it would be difficult to get a job in New York, but this is the center of journalism, and if I'm going to make a name for myself, it's here.

"When he offered me a job, only if I was able to get work at the *Journal,* I thought about telling him no, but honestly, I wanted the opportunity he offered me too badly. So, I took it. I'm sorry. So sorry. You've given me chances when no one else did. I shouldn't have betrayed that."

Hearst is silent for a moment.

"You've done good reporting here, Grace," he finally says. "You've grown as a writer. I don't like that you were spying for Pulitzer. I figured there were *World* plants here—it's inevitable with how many staff we have rotating out between our two papers and I certainly have my own at his newspaper—but I never imagined one of them was you."

The rivalry between Hearst and Pulitzer has always seemed to be something Hearst takes in stride. Where Pulitzer is genuinely angry about Hearst's challenge, Hearst treats the whole thing like a game he can win. Perhaps that's the difference with growing up with wealth behind you, cushioning your every daring move, and having to make your own way in the world.

"I understand if you want me to clean out my things and leave. I understand if you can't have a spy in your newsroom."

"I don't know that it needs to come to that. Have you told Pulitzer you're done spying for him?"

"I have."

"And will you be loyal from here on out? I'm willing to give you one more chance, but you need to devote yourself to the *Journal.* I need to know that I can trust you. That when you're assigned a story or privy to sensitive information, you will guard it. If you're going to write for the *Journal*, then I will accept nothing less now than your absolute loyalty. Do we have a deal?"

Relief fills me. From here on out, I will be a model employee for the *Journal*. I vow it.

"We have a deal."

I FOLLOW UP MY PIECE ON THE JUNTA MEETING WITH AN UNDER-cover stint as a maid at one of the hotels on Fifth Avenue, my stunt reporting days never behind me. I'm hunched over a typewriter putting the finishing touches on the story—and detailing the moment when one of the odious male guests got a little friendlier than appropriate—when a shout emerges from Hearst's office, sounding through the newsroom.

"We have Spain, now!" Hearst exclaims, drawing the notice of all the staff.

I rise from my desk and edge closer toward his office door.

"Get me Chamberlain," he says, calling for one of his editors. "Send a telegraph to our correspondent in Havana. Have him wire every detail he has about this case. Notify our correspondents all over the United States that it's their job to get signatures from the women of America. We want the important ones to sign first. Then send the signed petition along with the names of the signatories to the queen regent demanding this girl's pardon. Alert our minister in Madrid. The Spanish minister wants to go after our correspondents? Let's see how he does when faced with the women of America. We must bring as much attention to this as we can. *This* is how we open the country's eyes to what's really happening in Cuba. Much more effective than editorials and political speeches. We'll save this girl no matter what it takes."

"What's going on?" I ask Michael, one of Pulitzer's former reporters who has since jumped ship for the *Journal,* as he emerges from
Hearst's office. "I haven't seen Hearst this excited since the *Journal*
solved the East River murder mystery last month."

Michael grins. "Hearst just received a cable from Havana. There's
a girl being imprisoned in the Casa de Recogidas. George Eugene
Bryson and George Clarke Musgrave went down to the prison themselves to investigate. She's Cuban. She's a lady, and she has no business
being in Recogidas. She's been there over a year awaiting trial. She's
only nineteen years old. Bryson's been sitting on this story, afraid
international scrutiny will make her situation more precarious. But
he's finally decided to file it under the byline of Marion Kendrick.
Hopefully, that'll leave his name out of it and keep him from being
expelled from the country while still raising the attention we need for
the situation."

That this woman has reached Hearst's notice seems a bit unusual
given how many women are likely in the prison down there. For a
while, I thought Hearst's attention was diverted to the troubles in
Greece, but now it seems he's back with his original instincts that the
revolution coverage will set the *Journal*'s future.

"Who is she?"

"Evangelina Cisneros," Michael replies. "She's reportedly the
niece of the former president of the Cuban Republic. Bryson says she's
beautiful. Like no woman he's ever seen. He's half in love with her
already. They're referring to her as a Cuban Joan of Arc."

With each fact he dispenses about her, his voice rises in triumph,
a crescendo building until his cheeks are reddened with excitement.

"So that's the story?" I ask. "A beautiful woman is imprisoned in
Cuba?"

What about all the other women imprisoned there who don't have the benefit of fine eyes?

"Hearst thinks she's the perfect person to compel the American people to push for intervention."

It's a page right out of Pulitzer's own newspaper, a similar tactic that Pulitzer used when he rallied support for Sylvester Scovel's imprisonment. Still, the public isn't the one Hearst needs to worry about swaying. Despite his party's aggressive stance toward armed conflict, President McKinley is reluctant to thrust us into war with Spain.

"How has she ended up in such a notoriously foul place?" I ask.

Michael grins, the near glee on his face at odds with the predicament of a young girl in prison.

"That's where the story gets even more interesting," Michael answers. "She was living on a penal colony on the Isle of Pines with her father, who was exiled for his role in the Cuban insurrection."

"They imprisoned her along with her father?"

"No, she and her sister volunteered to accompany him. Readers are going to love *that* fact. Her father was originally sentenced to death for raising a rebel cavalry unit. Reportedly, she negotiated with Captain-General Arsenio Martínez Campos and later General Weyler to have his sentence reduced to life imprisonment."

"I didn't think Weyler was so easy to persuade."

General Valeriano Weyler, the Spanish crown's military governor in Cuba aptly known as a butcher, has a nasty reputation that precedes him.

"He's not. But then again, everyone who comes in contact with Evangelina remarks on the girl's beauty and grace. She's an angel."

I struggle to keep from retorting that it was likely her persuasive intellect and not divine beauty that saved her father.

"It depends on who you believe," Michael adds, "but some say the Spanish governor Berriz took a liking to her and forced himself upon her. She defended herself, others came to her aid, and they were able to take Berriz prisoner. To hear the Spanish tell it, she was complicit in an uprising and lured him to her rooms one evening with the express wish of imprisoning him."

"And what does Evangelina say?"

That seems to be the most important piece of the puzzle.

"That she is innocent, of course." He shrugs as though guilt or innocence is of little import to him. "They're threatening to transport her from Recogidas to a penal colony in Africa."

"Why this woman? The atrocities have touched women before. Where was the outrage then?"

"Have you seen her?" He pulls a picture out of his pocket. "That face is the story."

The image staring back at me shows a young girl with long, dark hair, fair skin, and dark eyes filled with a defiant stare. She is indeed lovely, and still, it seems insulting almost in the face of all she has endured to remark upon her beauty as though it is her defining characteristic, to consign her to hues and angles rather than the strength of her character and spirit.

"What do we know about her life in Recogidas?" I ask.

As much as I can't agree with their take on things, if this is what Hearst wants, then I'll become an expert on Evangelina Cisneros. After all, it's the type of story he should want me to cover by virtue of my gender, and I did just promise him my loyalty.

"Our man in Havana spoke with some of her prison companions who said the conditions are harsh. She is surrounded by awful women—criminals, women of loose morals and character, and the like."

"'Awful women'?"

"Recogidas was built for women like that. Not women like Evangelina."

His dismissive tone toward her compatriots sends a sleek arrow of fury through me.

"It seems like the problem is with Recogidas, then. Not the women," I retort.

Maybe the story here isn't just one woman, but a prison where women are treated so abominably and discarded. It's Nellie Bly's reporting at Blackwell's Asylum all over again. Regardless of the country, there are always places where women are suffering.

"And the other women with Evangelina?" I ask. "What is their story?"

"One of the women is elderly. In her seventies, perhaps."

"If the conditions are as bad as they say, I imagine she's more in danger there than Evangelina. How did she end up in such a place?"

"Her sons have high-ranking positions in the Cuban Revolutionary Army."

"And the other women?" I ask, incredulous. "What grave crime did they commit? Are their neighbors members of the Cuban Revolutionary Army?"

"No, their brothers."

"And for that these women were imprisoned in Recogidas? Surely, there's a bigger story here than simply Evangelina."

"Grace, stop overthinking it. Evangelina is the story. Hearst has already said it. She is the perfect rallying cry to galvanize people to push for American intervention against Spain."

It remains unspoken between us, but I can hear the words, as distasteful as they are:

Just think of all the newspapers we'll sell.

"She's one woman. There's more here than that."

"The women of America, the upstanding women whose husbands will listen to them, they will relate to this girl. They don't care about a prison filled with criminals and the lowest women of society. They'll see themselves in Evangelina, and they'll want to help her. In doing so, maybe we can change this whole situation with Spain."

That he condemns a group of women in the same breath that he seeks to save one clearly escapes his notice. Or the fact that despite everyone's great admiration of her beauty, their intentions are hardly noble. She is a means to an end to sell more papers, to force the United States to act.

"Do you really believe that's possible?" I ask. "Do you truly believe the stories we write will be enough to bring about a war?"

I started writing because I wanted to do something that mattered, because I wanted my life to serve a purpose, to illuminate the people and places society overlooked. And still—there is a difference between shining a light on the darkest corners of this society and daring to bring about a war that will change the world as we know it.

Michael grins at me. "Let's hope so."

"I've got it," Hearst shouts from his office once more, interrupting our conversation. "We'll call her 'the Most Beautiful Girl in Cuba.'"

Thirteen

EVANGELINA

One by one, my friends leave me as they are released from prison or sent on to other places. Unfortunately, this war creates a never-ending supply of women to punish for others' deeds, so newcomers replenish their ranks—the wives or sisters of Mambises whose only crime is loving one of Cuba's proud patriots. When they are gone, others come, and so the cycle continues, and still, I remain. My final friend, Señora Sotolongo, is with me a bit longer, but eventually she's taken to a prison hospital.

There are others who visit me: Donnell Rockwell who works at the American consulate and has become a great friend of mine, and Karl Decker, a new friend who says he will be working at the *Journal* in Havana.

And then one day, I am called to see the warden once more.

The Marquis of Cervera is seated in the warden's office.

The warden places a newspaper on his desk, and shock fills me at the sight of my face staring back at me. I read the name of the newspaper: *The New York Journal.*

"It would appear that you have some fine friends," Don Jose accuses.

I never imagined my case would draw the interest of the Americans in such a fashion, that my story and face would be plastered across their papers, that the world would see me brought so low. All along, Bryson promised me he would keep me out of the press to avoid further angering the Spanish. The last time he visited me, he told me that the judge he'd attempted to bribe in order to secure my release was trying to force his hand by threatening a harsh sentence for me. Perhaps once Bryson's plans went awry, he had to come up with another option, but I wish he had warned me that this news was breaking. If the Spanish were determined to make me pay for embarrassing Berriz before, this can only make things worse.

"George Bryson has been expelled from Cuba on the orders of General Weyler," Don Jose announces.

Horror fills me.

"Because of you," he adds, a gleam in his eyes as he delivers the crushing news. "The queen regent of Spain herself has directed General Weyler in this matter."

As the warden speaks, the Marquis of Cervera sits there silently, watching me.

I should have known Bryson's promises were too good to be true, should have realized the Spanish wouldn't give up so easily. The more attention the situation draws, the more likely it is to prompt Spain to retaliate against American interference. After all, more than anything, right now they need to appear strong.

"You must wonder what will become of you," Don Jose says.

I have been wondering that every minute of every hour of every day that I have spent in this horrible place for the last fifteen months, but if my past interactions with my jailers have taught me anything, it's that whatever they tell me, it won't be the truth.

I lift my chin slightly, keeping my mouth shut. I can't bear the thought of asking him, of giving him the satisfaction of seeing me desperate and dejected.

"You will be sent to Spain," he continues. "You will serve twenty years in a convent."

Originally, I was to be sent to a penal colony in Africa, then led out into the square and shot like a spy, or imprisoned for life in Cuba, and now they plan to throw me into a prison of sorts in Spain. It seems like each day they throw a different horror my way. I bite the inside of my cheek as hard as I can to keep from crying out, my anger a living, palpable thing unfurling inside me.

"There will be no more visits from your friends," Don Jose tells me. "You will be held incommunicado for the rest of your days here."

The Marquis of Cervera leans forward in his seat, speaking for the first time since I walked into the room. "There is one thing you could do to help yourself."

He says it idly, as though it is little more than an afterthought, when I've no doubt this was his true intention all along. Why else would he go to all the trouble to come here?

"If you were to withdraw your accusation against Berriz then we might be able to work something out."

"No. I will not lie. He is guilty of assaulting me. I will never change my story. That is the truth."

"Don't be so hasty, Miss Cisneros. Think of what we've just told you. Is that really how you want to spend the rest of your life? There are consequences to your actions. A much better future could await you if you would confess that Berriz came to your room that night at your invitation, that you sought to entrap him. A word from you and this could all be over. You could go home to your family. To your friends."

For a moment, I imagine what my future would look like if I went along with this plan they've concocted. Would I go home to my family, would I have a chance to marry Emilio? Could I be happy? Could I live with myself knowing the truth was buried?

"Some of your compatriots, those men who came to your rescue so valiantly that night, will testify against you," the Marquis of Cervera adds. "They've been released from La Cabaña. They're prepared to say that you lured Colonel Berriz to meet you. That you conspired to have him killed."

A sinking feeling hits my stomach. I can't entirely blame my friends for changing their stories in favor of leniency, but it is another reminder that I am truly alone.

"Emilio Betancourt is among those willing to testify against you."

I bite down on the inside of my cheek to keep from crying out in hurt and fury as a piece of my heart breaks at the sound of his name. After all the times I've thought about him in prison, the affection I felt for him, for him to betray me like this—

If you are willing to sacrifice the woman you professed to love, the country that has your heart in order to save your own skin, what sort of person are you? That is not a man, nor is it the action of a man I could ever care for.

The dream I had of a life for us in Cuba is lost forever.

"See what we can do for you if you cooperate with us? We could grant you a pardon as well. Wouldn't you rather have us as friends instead of enemies?"

His words are so close to the ones Berriz said to me that night; they are etched in my memory, sneaking into my dreams when I am asleep at night, and a tremor racks my body as I am transported back to that night for one awful moment.

These fifteen months in prison have been the hardest of my life. And if it is as they say, all hope of escape is behind me. I have lost my

friends—both the Americans who said they'd help me and my rescuers on the Isle of Pines. My family is gone, my fiancé a traitor. And
now, my future hangs on the goodwill of people who hate me.

All is lost.

There's no choice to be had.

I look the Marquis of Cervera in the eyes.

"I would rather die in Recogidas."

Fourteen

GRACE

Bryson files his first story about Evangelina on August 17 under the byline of Marion Kendrick. The piece is filled with glowing adjectives describing her beauty and equally damning ones decrying the conditions of Recogidas.

For two weeks, the *Journal* is filled with Evangelina Cisneros.

Our attempt to secure signatures calling for Evangelina's release has resulted in more than ten thousand names, including such prominent figures as Clara Barton, President McKinley's own mother, and the wife of Secretary of State Sherman. The author of the "Battle Hymn of the Republic" has written to Pope Leo XIII asking him to intervene with the queen regent on Evangelina's behalf. I'm not sure I've ever seen so many support a previously unknown figure. Regardless of how this ends up, in making Evangelina a celebrity, Hearst has undoubtedly succeeded.

It must infuriate Pulitzer that Hearst has scooped him on this story, using Evangelina to stir up such public fervor. George Eugene Bryson, who brought the story to Hearst, once worked for Pulitzer at the *World* before jumping ship to write for his rival.

Hearst has done so much to shake up the newspaper business recently that Pulitzer's newspaper looks sedate and outdated in comparison. It's difficult to remember that a little over a decade ago, Pulitzer was the newspaperman revolutionizing journalism in New York amid a lightning rod of controversy. But the higher Hearst climbs, the more others set their sights on taking him down.

When Consul General Lee arrived in New York on leave a few days ago, he was bombarded with questions about Evangelina Cisneros and made a point of claiming that the stories about her were falsehoods, stating that she wasn't related to the former president of the Cuban republic, that she was well-fed in Recogidas, her days spent in leisure rather than scrubbing floors. It's a strange turn of events, considering how much he's worked with the *Journal* and its staffers in the past. Hearst is, once again, unbothered by Lee's public comments, but I can't tell if there are more forces at play here—nervousness on the part of the American administration that Evangelina Cisneros is the story that will finally push public sentiment calling for an entry into the war to a point of no return.

Our competitors have begun publishing stories undermining Evangelina's credibility and the *Journal*'s reporting on her case.

Reportedly, the queen regent has requested that Weyler treat Evangelina as a distinguished prisoner and move her to a convent while the legal proceedings are happening, but Weyler has instead cut off access to her at Recogidas, and now no one knows anything of the girl's fate. There are rumors of a growing political power struggle within Spain, and given the international attention as a result of Evangelina's celebrity, Weyler's future may be in jeopardy.

Rafael has been absent from the city, but his sister Elena has been an invaluable source on Evangelina, corresponding with some of her contacts in Cuba about the girl's background. I've written a few of the *Journal*'s pieces about Evangelina, and even though I have my doubts surrounding the angle we've taken as a paper, after confessing my spying to Hearst, I promised him that he would have my loyalty, and so I've thrown myself into this story with gusto despite my misgivings.

Michael gestures to me one morning while I'm working on a story in the newsroom. "Hearst's office now."

I grab my pad and pen and follow him into the office. Hearst is seated behind his desk, looking as though he hasn't been to bed yet, his editor Chamberlain beside him, and two other reporters I know vaguely. I'm the only woman in the room.

Michael shuts the door behind us.

"We're sending Karl Decker from the Washington bureau to Cuba. We're setting him up as our man in Havana," Hearst says, skipping any formalities, his voice filled with excitement. "Since Bryson's been expelled from the country for his reporting, we'll say Decker is his replacement."

Hearst gestures toward Chamberlain. "Sam just went through the plan with him. Decker's been there before, speaks Spanish, knows his way about town. If anyone's going to break her out, he has the connections and daring to do so."

My jaw drops at the words "break her out." Surely, he doesn't mean to send a reporter to *break Evangelina Cisneros out of prison.*

I've done my share of dangerous things to get a story, but this violates all sorts of international norms and principles, and if Decker is caught—

"We have the support of the American consulate in Havana," Hearst continues. "One of the consular clerks, Donnell Rockwell, has taken an interest in Evangelina's case. He's met with her on several occasions now. He knows Decker and reached out to him. It's a good plan, and if it's successful, well, we'll make history."

And if it isn't successful, people will likely die.

"What about the rest of the consulate?" one of the reporters asks. "What about Consul General Lee?"

"Fitzhugh likes his intrigues," Hearst replies. "After all, the man runs his own network of spies throughout the country, and let's just say I'm not sure how much he does after checking with Washington and how much of it is a result of him being left to his own devices. Lee won't be a problem. He's not one for all of the State Department's protocols and restrictions. The biggest issue is getting the girl out of Recogidas. But we'll leave that to Decker to solve."

"And if the plan fails?" I murmur to Michael.

I haven't the courage to voice my fears in the face of Hearst's enthusiasm, but it seems like a very real concern given Weyler's anger and subsequent retaliation over a few news articles about Evangelina. What will he do in the face of an attempted jailbreak? If we fail, Evangelina's life will hang in the balance, her movement to a penal colony in Ceuta or somewhere similar a near certainty.

If we succeed, how will Weyler retaliate to reassert his authority in Cuba?

Fifteen

❦

MARINA

Throughout the summer of 1897, the war continues on. What we lack in numbers facing a military force five times our size, we make up in ingenuity and resourcefulness, exploiting the weak areas of Spain's defenses. Cuba's terrain has proven useful, and the revolutionaries shelter in the mountains, making raids down into the countryside. All sorts of ailments and maladies plague the Spanish, thinning their numbers as they're unused to the hostile elements we've grown accustomed to. We may be unable to defeat them in a single battle, but there's no denying Spain is growing weary with each attack.

At the same time, so are we.

The situation in the camps has grown dire. Sewage fills the streets, people sleeping nearly on top of one another in cramped quarters, using threadbare blankets for cover against the elements. Disease is everywhere, and it seems that not a day goes by when someone hasn't succumbed to their illness, death a constant companion. Yellow fever, cholera, and smallpox plague us, many of the camps' inhabitants walking around with sores over their bodies. The dead are no longer buried; their numbers are simply too great. They are left on the ground, their flesh devoured by dogs and birds; they are eventually tossed in roving death carts to be ferried away.

I've been fortunate to stay mostly healthy, although I fear for Luz and Isabella given their ages and their more delicate constitutions.

It is mostly women and children here, and we are the casualties of war, the ones who stand the greatest chance of losing our lives, while the men in the mountains are protected by the island's natural defenses.

I am more determined than ever to do my part to see this war to its natural conclusion, with the stakes for independence higher than ever. The Spanish have demonstrated what they will do if they're given unfettered reign on the island, and the Americans have certainly been hesitant to intervene on our behalf.

Washing clothes for the city's elite has turned out to be both the difference between us going hungry and being able to sustain ourselves, and has also provided the perfect opportunity to pass intelligence throughout the city. Through a referral from one of the women in the network Luz was acquainted with, I've begun laundering linens for some of the American diplomatic staff in their private quarters, and today I received a note folded in some sheets from one of the consular officers, asking me to meet an American who has a job for me.

The American is staying at the Hotel Inglaterra on the Paseo del Prado, in front of the Parque Central, the lodging reportedly frequented by the likes of Maceo and Martí when they were alive. The hotel's café is a popular gathering place for artists and intellectuals who meet to discuss the war and Cuba's future.

I travel to the hotel's guest rooms on the second floor, following the instructions my contacts gave me.

I knock twice on the door, gazing around the empty hallway. In my current attire, everyone makes a concerted effort *not* to make eye contact with me as I pass by them. My appearance provides the perfect opportunity to work as a courier because no one, least of all the wealthy and privileged citizens of Havana, wants to confront the human face of this war.

When the door to the room opens, I am greeted by my past.

The man on the other side isn't the American I expected, but the very familiar face of Carlos Carbonell, my father's old friend and a banker in the city. I haven't seen him since my marriage to Mateo all those years ago, and I certainly never would have envisioned him working as an intermediary between the revolutionaries and the Americans.

He smiles at me. "Marina. It's been a long time. It's good to see you."

"It's good to see you, too," I say cautiously, recovering from my initial surprise.

It's clear he was prepared to see me again, but the connection to my past makes me nervous, stripping away some of the anonymity I clung to for safety. The stakes are high, the punishment for spying severe, and I cannot bear the thought that something might happen to my daughter because of my efforts with the revolutionaries, or the possibility that something will happen to me and Isabella will be left without both parents.

Carlos Carbonell is a complication I didn't see coming. With his connections, he's well-placed to pass information around, but I never took him for a revolutionary. My parents and their friends are far more concerned with keeping things as they are so as to not affect their wealth and power than they are with upending the system to make the world a better place.

Carlos moves away from the doorway, allowing me to enter the room.

My cheeks heat as our gazes connect. I've never been overly concerned with my appearance, but I'm uncomfortably aware of how much has changed in my physical appearance, manner of dress, and toilette since he last saw me. A rush of gratitude fills me at the respect he affords me and the lack of pity he allows to slip through his expression—he treats me as though I am the same person I was, as though he understands my pride.

Whatever Carlos's involvement in this, it must be important, since clearly, he's better informed on what to expect than I am.

I cross the threshold and wait while Carlos shuts the door behind me.

Another man sits in the room quietly, his gaze trained on me.

The American.

Carlos makes the introductions as I settle into one of the chairs in the room, and then the American man whom he introduces as Karl Decker takes over. There's no time for pleasantries; meeting like this is already risky enough as it is. If we are caught together—

"I've heard you're able to get messages to prisoners in Recogidas," Decker says. "That you're familiar with the prison."

I nod. Doing some of the jail's laundry has given me access to the women imprisoned there, and I've carried messages back and forth for a few of the political prisoners.

"Does this look correct?" Decker asks me, sliding a plan of the prison in front of me.

I scan the diagram contained there.

"Bryson got it a few months ago," Decker adds. "He also has a list of the guards and the schedule for when they do their rounds."

Is this Bryson another American? What's their interest in Recogidas? I can't think of an American prisoner there at the moment, but I don't know everyone.

"From what I remember, this looks correct to me," I reply.

"There is a girl in Recogidas—her name is Evangelina Cisneros," Carlos says.

The name is familiar. I've heard the whispers about her, although I've never met her myself. They say her father was imprisoned as a revolutionary.

"We need to break her out of Recogidas," Decker adds.

I gape at him. "That's why you're here?"

This has escalated from dangerous to deadly. Recogidas is a fortress.

For a moment, I contemplate getting up and walking out of the room. It is one thing to take risks when Cuba's future is on the line, but I don't see how breaking this woman out of prison serves Cuba.

"What's the Americans' interest in all of this?" I ask Decker. "Why do you care about a Cuban woman in a Cuban prison?"

"I'm a reporter for an American newspaper in New York City. My employer has taken an interest in Miss Cisneros's plight. We've tried to free her through diplomatic means to no avail. We now believe it's time to act outside of normal channels. I've met with Miss Cisneros, but now we have a problem—Weyler has cut off our access to her."

I turn toward Carlos. "And you? What is your interest in her? Is she a friend of yours?"

Given Carlos's reputation as a bachelor, and Evangelina Cisneros's reported beauty, I can't help but wonder if she's more than just a friend.

"I've never met her," Carlos answers.

"Then why?"

"Because we aren't winning this war. And we need something to tip the odds in our favor. I've seen the articles the Americans have written about Evangelina. I've spoken with others who have been following the public response to her case. She might be what we need to prompt the Americans to throw their support behind us."

Women and children are dying in the camps; it's hard to believe that in the face of all that suffering, it will only take one woman to inspire the Americans to act. Where was their outrage when the Spanish put us in reconcentration camps? Where was their anger over dead Cubans? Why is Evangelina's life worth more than others? Why does she merit rescuing while the rest of us don't?

"And it's just the two of you attempting this?" I ask.

Decker is hesitant for a moment. "There are others concerned with her situation."

They must have some diplomatic help from the American consulate to even attempt this. The Spanish check documents for people entering and leaving the country, so getting her out of Cuba will certainly be a challenge.

"What will you do if you break her out of Recogidas successfully?"

"We've found someone who can forge a passport for her to get her out of the country and take her to the United States," Decker answers. "We've looked at the available transport options, and we can ferry her out of Havana on a steamer."

If they can get her out of the prison, and that's an extraordinary *if*, considering the prison and how notorious Evangelina is becoming, there are so many things that can go wrong with this plan.

"Our problem is Recogidas," Decker adds. "A daylight raid is out of the question. Too dangerous. We've thought about using dynamite to break her out, but the rest of the plan hinges on a modicum of discretion, and we're not likely to find it with a loud explosion. We have the other pieces in place; we just need to figure out the most important one."

"Have you asked Evangelina? For as much time as she's spent in the prison, I would think she might have some ideas on how to escape."

Both men look momentarily flummoxed by the idea of asking her what she thinks.

"Weyler's made sure all of our communication with her has been cut off," Decker answers.

It's not the normal sort of effort I would be involved in, and it's a difficult pill to swallow that her life is the one that will inspire America to act considering the tremendous amount of suffering throughout Cuba, but given the situation we find ourselves in, I'm desperate to do anything I can to end this horrible war and see Cuba liberated.

"I can get a note to her."

"Thank you," Carlos replies, the relief on his face surprising me. "When you hear from Evangelina, come to me."

I nod, somewhat comforted by the fact that he is to be my liaison in this rather than the American. Hopefully, our shared history will keep Carlos from double-crossing me down the road should this all blow up in our faces.

I say good-bye to both men with the promise that I will be in contact with any news from Evangelina. Decker walks me to the door, and I pull it open, peeking into the hallway to make sure it is empty. I cross the threshold, shutting the door to the hotel room behind me quickly, my heart pounding.

I walk down the hallway, heading for the exit when one of the doors to the neighboring rooms opens and a man steps out.

I duck my head to keep him from seeing my face, but as I do, something catches in my peripheral vision—a slash of dark hair, a familiar profile, a set of full lips I know as intimately as my own.

I stop in my tracks and come face-to-face with my husband.

Sixteen

Before

I wake to the sound of rustling in my bedroom, the spot next to me in bed where my husband Mateo normally lies, empty.

I sit up, my heart pounding as my gaze sweeps across the room.

It's still dark out, but with the sliver of moonlight cast into our bedroom, I can just make out the silhouette of Mateo getting dressed, a sack at his feet. His sword, the one that was his father's when he fought in the failed attempt for Cuba's independence in the Ten Years' War, rests beside it.

I've known this day was coming, revolution a whisper on our breath. The hope, the possibility of freedom sustains us after centuries of Spanish rule.

And now that the army is close to our home in the countryside, it's time for Mateo to join them.

I've known this day was coming, and now that it's here, the ache inside me is nearly unbearable. We fell asleep last night with our limbs entwined, the curve of Mateo's body wrapped around mine. I stayed awake long after he fell asleep, listening to the sound of his breathing, feeling his heartbeat against my back, wondering how I was going to endure this coming separation.

I pray this revolution will be over quickly. That we will be independent. That my husband will come back to me.

I watch Mateo finish dressing as I have done thousands of mornings before, when he would go work on our small farm, early before the sun would come up. I know every inch of his body as well as my own, have seen his transformation from the boy I fell in love with in my youth to a man I have built a life with. We've grown up together, Mateo and I, navigating each of life's transitions with our love and friendship to see us through any difficult times.

When we married, we vowed to never be parted.

How long will he be gone fighting for Cuba's future?

Will he come home to me and our daughter or am I to join the ranks of so many who have lost their loved ones in this fight for independence?

"Marina."

Mateo stops dressing, and moves to the edge of the bed. He reaches out and takes my hand, interlacing our fingers.

"Were you going to leave without saying good-bye?" I ask.

He squeezes my hand. "It's hard enough leaving you and Isabella. I don't know how to say good-bye."

The emotion in his voice threatens the gossamer thin hold I have on my emotions. My tears, my pain will only make a difficult moment more unbearable.

Mateo leans in to me, resting his forehead against mine. We stay like that for a moment, our breath mingling, a heartbeat between us.

There's so much I want to say, as though I could force the lifetime we were promised into this moment, as if I could account for the coming absence by filling this yawning space of grief.

What I fear most is the unknown—the life we will both lead in these ensuing days, weeks, months, years? And far at the end of this journey we must travel alone, there is the terror I cannot face, for the possibility of it is too horrible to even contemplate—

How will I exist in a world without him in it?

"I could go with you," I say, the thought my constant companion. "I could join the impedimenta."

The impedimenta, a noncombatant army, follows the revolutionaries and cares for their necessities; there are women among its ranks, most notably with General Maceo's army, which my husband hopes to join. Maceo's mother, Mariana Grajales, whose family was dedicated to Cuban independence, followed her son in combat during the Ten Years' War at the age of sixty-three.

"And Isabella?" Mateo asks. "Would our daughter join the war, too?"

Even as he says it, I know my joining the fight is an impossible thing. Our daughter is still a child, and someone must stay behind to care for her, even if I yearn to do my part, too. Even as I hate being left behind. Even as I wish to fight for the free Cuba I believe in.

We've had this argument many times, my desire to do more in this war, to help my fellow countrymen a source of mild friction between us. As much as Mateo says he understands the fire burning within me, as much as we share the common goal of seeing the Spanish defeated, I'm not sure he can understand the sensation of feeling trapped by virtue of your gender. Nor can he understand the pulls between a mother's love for her child and her desire to fight for what she believes in.

But this morning is not the time for such a discussion, our good-bye imminent, so instead I say, "I love you," leaving the rest unsaid between us.

"I love you, too," he replies. "Always."

There's power in his words, and in the knowledge that in this world where so much is uncertain, our love is the constant that I can rely upon.

"I have to go," Mateo whispers, regret threading through his voice.

He leans up and presses a kiss to my forehead, and somewhere in the middle I meet him halfway, our lips connecting.

I hold on to him, savoring the moment, keeping him close to me for as long as I can.

Mateo releases me slowly, and I sit up in the bed where we've made love *countless times, the bed where Mateo held my hand as I brought our daughter into this world. I draw the blanket over me, watching him as he continues to dress, his movements quick and silent.*

The penalty for insurrection is imprisonment or death, and these days, it's hard to know who you can trust. We've spoken of Mateo's plan to leave to no one but his mother, Luz, but I'm still afraid someone will see him sneaking out, terrified that he will not be able to evade the Spanish soldiers as he crosses by the forts they've established in his attempt to join the revolutionaries. Spain has long considered Cuba to be the pearl of their empire, and they're desperate to retain control over our fortunes, their military on the island monitoring our movements for any sign of rebellion.

Mateo leans down and picks up the sack from the floor. "I looked in on Isabella. Gave her a kiss while she slept. Will you tell her . . ."

His voice trails off; he has to know it is no easy task he gives me. How do I explain to our six-year-old daughter that her father is gone and might not return?

I nod, not trusting myself to speak.

In all the sadness filling me, there's also a dart of anger that he is the one leaving—however noble the cause—and I am left to pick up the pieces after he is gone. I am the one who will be forced to break our daughter's heart and tell her she won't see him for a while. It will be my responsibility to hold her when she misses him, to assure her that he will come home even when I don't believe it myself. I will be both mother and father, be the one to keep our home going while he is away fighting.

Over the near decade since we first wed, I've learned what it means to be a farmer's wife, traded the wealth and privilege of my family's life in Havana to something all my own. And still, the task he leaves me with, the responsibility for providing food, safety, and shelter for me, Isabella, and Mateo's mother Luz who lives in the house beside us, feels daunting when it is to be undertaken alone, particularly in these difficult times.

How will I keep us safe in a time of war?

When Mateo's sword is fastened, he leans over the bed once more, and I clasp his face, drawing him down to me.

I cannot unravel the emotions coursing through me—fear, pride, anger, grief, love—so once again I say the only thing I know how to, which seems to encapsulate all of them perfectly.

"I love you."

The words come out on a sob.

"You are my heart," he whispers, and I know that even as this is true, Cuba is his blood, and for now she will have all of him.

I wish he didn't have to leave. I wish I could go with him. I wish everything was different and that the cost of our freedom wasn't so high. What would it be to live in a world where your energy is reserved for things other than liberation?

Mateo holds me against him tightly before releasing me, gazing at me as though he is attempting to memorize my features even as I do the same to him.

Will I ever see him again? What chance do we have of winning a war where farmers become soldiers in an attempt to defeat one of the most powerful militaries the world has ever known? Even in decline, Spain is a formidable foe.

Are they all simply marching to their death?

"Viva Cuba Libre," I whisper to him, the cry for a free Cuba forever in my heart.

"Viva Cuba Libre," he echoes fiercely.

Mateo releases me, and I sink down to the bed, watching him walk away, until he is gone and I am alone in the house where we were to spend our lives together, the house that is now mine to care for.

A cry breaks out in the middle of the night. Then another.

*The sound of the door closing when Mateo left must have woken Isa-
bella, because I hear her calling for me—*

"Mami, mami, mami."

I rise from the bed and walk into my daughter's room, my heart heavy.

"I had a bad dream," she whispers, her eyes wide.

*I go to her, revolution momentarily forgotten, and I wrap my arms
around her, stroking her hair and rocking her, singing a song my mother
sang to me when I was her age as my tears begin to fall.*

FOR A MOMENT, I THINK I MIGHT FAINT.

My husband stands a few steps away from me in the hallway of
the Hotel Inglaterra.

He's alive.

"What are you doing here?" I ask as my knees buckle, and I sag
against the wall for support.

A door opens at the end of the hallway.

Mateo takes a step forward, and then he freezes in place, his gaze
darting from me to the open door, and back again, and I can see that
he's working out the precariousness of the situation, favoring discretion where I cannot summon mine.

My husband. My love.

He is alive.

Mateo looks nothing like I've envisioned. He's clean-shaven, his
hair recently shorn. His clothes are laundered and well mended. It's
obvious, though, that he's lost a great deal of weight since we last saw
each other. While his clothes fit him, albeit a bit loosely, his body is
slighter than I remember.

"Are you well?" he asks me, worry in his eyes. I know what I must look like, all the changes that have occurred since he left. I nod jerkily, words still failing me, and out of the corner of my eye I catch sight of Carbonell and Decker standing outside the open door.

Decker and Carbonell hesitate, before looking to me, and I offer them another quick nod to let them know all is well and to be on their way. They file past us, their heads ducked, hats pulled low, not making eye contact with Mateo.

The hallway is once again empty now that they're gone, and Mateo takes a step toward me, and then another, stopping when we are close enough that the skirt of my ragged dress brushes against his serviceable trousers.

He tugs on my hand, leading me to the door nearest him, the room he originally stepped out of, and it is the most natural thing in the world for me to do as I have since we were children.

I follow him.

MATEO CLOSES THE DOOR TO HIS HOTEL ROOM.

I can't resist the urge to reach out, placing my palm against his cheek, the beard he's grown since he's been gone scratchy beneath my fingertips. My fingers drift to his mouth, tracing the shape of his lips.

"Marina," he breathes.

Tears fill my eyes.

I've been holding it together for so long, trying to do my part, to take care of our daughter, his mother, to be strong as the world around me falls apart, but now the sight of him before me is my undoing.

"Is everyone else well?" he asks me urgently, his voice low. We are alone, but in Havana and throughout Cuba now, the walls have ears, and neither one of us can forget the precariousness of our positions.

"Yes. They're both well."

Relief fills Mateo's expression. "And you, Marina? How are you?"

What is there to say? I can't add to his worries by telling him the truth, how we are hanging on by a thread in the camp.

"I am healthy," I reply. "I have been fortunate. We all have."

"You don't know how many nights I've wondered if you were all safe," he says.

"We're safe."

He squeezes my hip reassuringly, leaning forward so his forehead rests against mine. His hand drifts lower, his touch instantly shifting to something else entirely, his fingers stroking my hip, clasping the folds of my dress.

The time apart has created a distance between us we've never experienced before. I've changed in these past years, too, life in the camp altering me, making my bones more pronounced, my cheeks gaunt, my skin sallow. Vanity hardly seems to matter, though, considering the most salient point:

We are both alive when so many are not.

Not a moment has gone by when I haven't felt the absence of him acutely.

We reach for each other in a frenzied tangle of limbs, pretense abandoned.

Mateo's mouth is at my neck, his teeth scraping over my skin, my back hitting the wall as he reaches between us, hiking up my skirts as I grapple with his trousers.

His lips find mine, and I reach up, threading my fingers through his hair, pulling his head down toward me, giving me better access to deepen the kiss, the fire inside me that has been dormant for so long suddenly awakening.

I thought I'd lost the ability to feel passion, another casualty of this war, but there's something powerful about the two of us here, together, and for a moment, it's as though we were never parted.

I would know him anywhere.

Mateo moans against my mouth, his body hardening against mine, whispered endearments breaking through between our kisses. His hands roam the planes of my body, and I am too far gone to care that the curves he once knew and loved have disappeared. I have become someone stronger than I imagined since he left, and it feels as though he is learning this new part of me as I am doing the same to him.

"Marina."

Tears prick at the sound of my name falling from his lips, the familiarity of it taking me back to a different time even as his hands and mouth on my body hold me firmly to the present.

Mateo grips my hips, lifting my leg up, bracing me against the wall.

There's some fumbling between us, hands brushing, a frenzy taking over, and then he thrusts inside me, our bodies one.

When we both find our release, he sags against me, letting me down gently. My legs are limp beneath me, and I slide down to the floor, my limbs boneless. Mateo joins me, leaning against the wall and wrapping his arm around me, resting my head against his chest.

His hand finds mine, and our fingers intertwine.

Neither one of us speaks, the force of our joining startling both of us, I think. There is a quiet desperation I have kept at bay in the face of the circumstances surrounding us, and there is a sense of immediate relief in letting go, even for a moment.

I have never felt safer or more myself than I do with Mateo.

I tilt my head, studying him. Some of his tension appears to be gone, but his expression is still filled with worry.

"What are you doing here?" I ask again, realizing he never answered me to begin with.

"I'm here trying to get some intelligence. What are you doing here? Those men in the hallway. Were you meeting with them? What have you gotten involved with?"

"I've been passing information," I say reluctantly. "As a courier."

A blistering oath falls from his lips.

"At this point, you'd be safer on the battlefield. Of all the jobs you could do, that has to be one of the most dangerous ones you could have chosen. Do you know what will happen if you are caught? Do you want to live out the rest of your days in Recogidas? For Isabella to grow up without both her parents? Marina, you have to be careful."

"Of course I don't want that. I've been keeping everyone safe, but that doesn't mean I don't want to do my part as well. This isn't just a man's war. You went off to fight, but the war came to us. We were forced from our home and sent to Havana. What was I supposed to do? Nothing?"

"You were doing something. You were taking care of our daughter. Our home."

"Our home is gone. All we worked for, all we built. The Spanish have taken that away from us. We can't come out of all of this having lost so much with nothing to show for it. We must defeat them, and I won't rest until I've done my part. This war—there's no room for anyone to not take a side, to not join and fight. We're outmatched enough as it is. Did you really think I wouldn't do what I could to help you? To help myself? The longer this war drags on, the worse it is. I want to see it finished as much as you do."

"I know that. I know it's been hard for you. When we heard that Weyler had reconcentrated the Havana province, I was sick with worry."

He doesn't know how hard it has been. Not really. He can guess at what we've endured, but it's not the same as living it.

He runs a hand through his hair. "I can't lose you. I am fighting for Cuba, yes, but never think I'm not also fighting for you and for our daughter. If anything were to happen to you—"

"Nothing will happen," I interject, even if we both know it's not a promise I can make. "I'm being careful. Your mother is watching Isabella when I am gone. It was her idea, actually."

"Why am I not surprised?" Mateo says, a trace of affection in his voice. "I miss them both terribly. Isabella must have grown so much."

Not as much as she should given how we struggle to find good food for her, but I don't tell him that.

"She's wonderful. You'd be so proud of her. She misses you and can't wait until we are all together again. And your mother is so proud of you."

"And how are all of you?" Mateo asks. "Truly. You don't have to pretend with me. You don't have to protect me, too. They say things in Weyler's camps are bad."

I can't bring myself to tell him the truth. I can't bring myself to worry him. If this time together is all we have, I don't want to spend it dwelling on our troubles.

"We're fine. I promise. We'll all be together soon."

"I wish I could see Isabella." He swallows. "Does she ask about me?"

For a moment, I picture sneaking him into the camp, letting him see his daughter, even as it's a dangerous impossibility. Still, the force of the image of the two of them together rocks me. I hate that this war has denied them the relationship I hoped they'd have.

"Every night."

"Thank you."

A tear trickles down his cheek. And then another.

We hold on to each other tightly, our grief consuming as I mourn all that we have lost, all that has been taken from us.

"What's it like out there?" I ask, wanting to understand how these years have been for him, wanting to give him a moment to unburden himself, to share in this, too, as we have shared everything else between us.

"We live our life on the run. It's harder than I imagined. More waiting around than I imagined, too. I suppose I thought we'd meet them head-on, but with their numbers—it's more skirmishes than anything else, stealing supplies from their trains when we can, sabotaging what we can."

"Do you think we will win?"

He's silent for far too long. "I don't know. It's hard to feel like we are truly doing enough, like these encounters will make a difference. When we lost Maceo—I doubt we'll see another like him leading us. I can only hope that this war will end soon and that we will be victorious. That all of the good men we have lost, that their deaths will mean something." He sighs. "I can't—I can't stay much longer, Marina. I wish I could stay with you forever, but I must take the information I gathered back to my men. They're depending on me."

I nod, because I've learned by now that being a soldier's wife means the war always comes first.

We dress quickly, setting our clothes to rights.

We pause at the threshold of the room, our gazes on each other.

"Promise me," I say.

It's a game we used to play when we were children—*promise me you'll wait for me, promise me you won't go to the river without me, promise you'll meet me here tomorrow, promise me . . .*

"Promise you'll be safe," I say. "Promise me you'll come back to me. To all of us."

"I promise," he replies, even as we both know it just might be the one promise he's ever made me that he can't keep.

"I love you," he tells me.

I reach out and press my palm against his cheek, reveling in the feel of him for one more moment before he's gone again.

"I love you, too," I reply.

Mateo leaves the room first, saying good-bye with a quick kiss, leaving me to wait a few minutes to clean myself up and make my own careful exit.

For a moment I close my eyes, tears threatening, the urge to fall to my knees and sob, to rail against this war, overwhelming. Instead, I take a deep breath and square my shoulders.

If anything, this moment with Mateo has filled me with resolve. I will do anything and everything I can to end this war.

I need to formulate a plan to get a message to Evangelina.

Seventeen

EVANGELINA

Time creeps by slowly now that I am cut off from my American friends. There are no more hugs from Mrs. Lee, no more promises that I will be freed, no more hope to be had. The world has forgotten me, and perhaps that's what the Spanish wished for all along. The American papers have likely moved on to other stories. Thanks to General Weyler, there are plenty of atrocities for them to report on. I am merely one woman wronged, one human tragedy, in an endless string of them.

On the days when I'm not working in Recogidas, scrubbing floors and doing the other chores they assign us, I write letters for the women who cannot write themselves. There's comfort to be had in their friendship. We all have more in common than I ever imagined regardless of why we've ended up here.

We're all just trying to survive.

One day, a new woman sits across from me.

"I have heard you are willing to pen letters to family members for those of us who cannot write," she says.

"I am."

She carries herself as though someone has drilled into her the importance of maintaining proper posture, her back ramrod straight, her head tilted in such a manner that I can almost envision an elegant hat angled atop her mass of dark brown hair despite the rags she wears. Her hands tell a different tale, however, her skin red and calloused much as mine is now.

She looks like a lady who has fallen on hard times. Perhaps she is a political prisoner or the wife of a Cuban revolutionary officer.

I remember how I felt when I first came here, how scared I was, how alone. Even though Recogidas isn't a place that lends itself to friendship, I've found that we all crave some form of companionship.

I smile. "I'm Evangelina."

"Marina. I've heard of you," she adds, her voice low.

I pause. My notoriety certainly hasn't made it easier for me here. "And what have you heard?"

"Your friends have not abandoned you," she whispers, and then, louder—

"I would like to write a letter to my husband."

"Of course," I say smoothly, struggling to keep the emotion from my face.

My heart pounds madly as I put my pen to paper. I barely hear the words she dictates to me, my mind racing the longer we keep up this fiction. It's clear from the way she speaks that she's learned, and this is all a giant ruse, but to what end, I do not know. I yearn to come out and ask her how she knows my friends, what her purpose is in being here, but we are too exposed, and even though at the moment, no one appears to be paying us much attention, the truth is you never know who is listening and what they will do in order to ingratiate themselves to our jailers. This place thrives on secrets, bribes, and subterfuge.

When I've finished the letter, I hand it back to her wordlessly.

She takes it from my hands, our fingers grazing, and with her free hand she grips me tightly.

"I'll be back tomorrow," she whispers.

A crumpled piece of paper rests between my fingers.

THERE IS LITTLE TO NO PRIVACY TO BE HAD IN PRISON. THERE ARE always people around: guards, other prisoners—some are so caught up in their own intrigues and problems that they couldn't care less about yours; others are eagle-eyed, waiting for any slipup that they may use against you in order to further their own interests.

In prison, information is power.

I unfold the note the woman—Marina—pressed in my palm, reading the elegant script there.

Your friends have not forgotten you. We will help you escape the prison. We vow it. We're working on a plan now. Can you assist us?

As quickly as I unfolded the paper, I crumple it back up, pressing my fist to my mouth and swallowing the words written there even as I wish I could keep them close to my breast and reread them in my moments of doubt. In my moments of weakness.

Can I help them with a plan?

I've only envisioned my escape from this place hundreds, thousands of times.

A calmness like none other I have experienced settles over me. For the first time since I arrived, there is something for me to do, a purpose beyond sitting here, waiting to die.

I select one of the pens I use for my letter writing and a blank sheaf of paper. Many of my fellow prisoners can't read or write, but some of the guards can, so it's best not to take any chances.

I begin writing.

"What are you doing?" a woman asks me.

I smile, trying to still the pounding in my heart, and think of one of the most boring things I can say to send her away.

"Studying my English grammar."

I can't tell if she believes me or doesn't care, but she walks away, leaving me alone with my thoughts once more.

My brow furrows as I consider the options available to me, the pitfalls of attempting to escape Recogidas.

I put the pen to paper once more.

The best chance of escape is from the roof. You should bring a rope to use to climb down from the roof and also acid to destroy the bars of the windows.

I pause, my gaze sweeping over the room at the women surrounding me. Our paths might not have crossed but for life bringing us to this horrible place, but I feel a kinship I never imagined would exist. Guilt pricks me at what I must do, but I continue writing:

I will also require opium or morphine to put my companions to sleep so that I may escape. I can use sweets in order to feed it to them. If three of you guard the various corners of the roof, we can use a lighted cigar as the signal to raise an alarm and a white handkerchief to let me know that it is safe for me to climb down. I will tie my clothes around my waist, so I have what is necessary for after I am gone. This is my best idea for escape. Let me know if this is convenient for you.

I add a diagram to the note should they need further explanation.

Surely, they can manage this plan. I'll pass the directions to Marina when she returns to the jail.

When I am done, I pray.

Eighteen

True to her word, Marina returns a day later, laundry in hand. As she walks past me, she drops a blanket on the ground, and I reach down to pick it up for her, slipping the note I've written inside the linens.

The next afternoon, she sits down across from me and asks me to write another letter for her.

"Tomorrow night," she whispers. "But I can't get you the laudanum. They search us when we come in here to bring the laundry. The note was dangerous enough."

Disappointment fills me. Now that my circumstances have changed, I'm no longer in a cell by myself, and there's no chance I'll be able to escape without drawing the notice of others who might raise the alarm.

"I'll think of something," I reply.

"Thank you for writing the letter for me," she says more loudly, and then—"Good luck."

When she's gone, I write letters for a few more people, and then I grip the side of my face, complaining of pain in my tooth.

The jailer gives me leave to visit the prison doctor, a man I've seen a handful of times since I've been in Recogidas.

"What's bothering you?" he asks when I'm seated in the infirmary.

"My tooth has been aching for some time now." I try valiantly to summon tears, thinking of all the things that have been weighing on my mind. "I can't bear it anymore."

A tear falls down my cheek.

"Open your mouth and let me see what's wrong."

I do as he says and let him examine my "hurt tooth."

He pulls back after a few seconds. "I don't see anything. It'll probably feel better in a day or two."

I grab his arm before he can turn away. "Please, sir. I can't take the pain anymore. I wish I were stronger, but it keeps me up at night, and I cannot sleep. If I could just have something for the pain, to ease my suffering. Please."

"I can't just give you pain medication," he sputters.

I flutter my eyelashes through the tears, staring up at his craggy face, imploring him to take pity on me.

"Please. I have prayed for relief, and God has not answered my prayers. If you could help me, I would be eternally grateful."

It's not normal practice to give medication to the inmates, but I've also learned by now that there isn't much men won't do for a pretty face. In Recogidas, rules can be bent if you have the right currencies to trade.

"Please."

If I have to get down on my knees and beg, I will, pride forgotten. I have no shame. Nothing matters in this moment other than the chance of escape.

He sighs. "It pains me to see you suffering so. I will give you some laudanum, but you must be very careful to not let anyone else know that you have it. You must also be cautious when you take it. This is a serious medicine. It can kill someone."

My eyes widen. "I didn't realize it was so dangerous. How many drops would it take to kill a person? I wouldn't want to make a mistake and accidentally do myself harm."

"Oh, you shouldn't have to worry about that. Your dosage will be nowhere near deadly. It would take twenty drops to be lethal."

I smile. "Thank you so much. You've saved my life, doctor."

THAT AFTERNOON, I MAKE THE COFFEE AS I REGULARLY DO FOR the rest of the women who share the dormitory space with me.

The laudanum is clutched in my hand.

I glance over my shoulder, making sure no one is watching me.

I drop the laudanum in the coffee, trying to measure out the drops as quickly as possible, counting them to make sure I stay under the doctor's recommended dose to keep from administering a fatal one.

I've grown to like the women here, and as desperate as I am to escape, I can't bear the thought of harming them.

When it's done, I turn, fixing a smile on my face, and offer the coffee to the other women.

Now I wait.

THAT NIGHT, I LIE AS STILL AS I CAN IN MY BED, HOPING THE DOCtor was right about the laudanum dosage, that it is enough to induce sleep, and not death. It feels as though an eternity passes, my heart beating unnaturally quickly, but after thirty minutes, an hour, the only sound in our dormitory room is of the other women's rhythmic breathing and soft snoring.

I push back the blanket and rise from the cot, careful to keep my movements quiet, wincing as the bed creaks beneath me. I dress quickly in a dark gown that blends into the night, and move toward the window, waiting for my rescuers to arrive.

The second-story window, invisible from the street, looks out over a flat roof that covers the lower rooms of the building.

The moon seems nearly as bright as the midday sun. A large gas-lighted lamp illuminates the street below.

A sound startles me, and I whirl around, half expecting to see my jailers enter the room, to learn that this was all a ruse to further entrap me, punishment for the Americans' attention and the notoriety I have attracted.

Instead, I am greeted by the sight of one of my fellow prisoners, Rosa, turning over in her cot. Her breaths have changed, prolonged as though she is about to speak, but she doesn't.

I turn back to the window, my heart pounding as I wait.

Every few minutes, Rosa tosses and turns in her cot again, and I wonder if she is dreaming about the baby she sometimes pretends she is holding in her arms, if she is as haunted in her dreams as I am.

Each time she moves, a chill slides down my spine.

Suddenly, Rosa sits up and stares straight at me, and my heart nearly stops.

She opens her mouth to speak, the words tumbling out nearly indecipherable.

I walk toward her to ask her to be quiet, but before I can reach her, she lies back down, silent once more.

I turn back to the window, the urge to scream rising within me, panic bearing down on me. It's been at least two hours now, and I've yet to see a sign of my rescuers. I pray to God, count numbers in my mind, anything and everything I can do to distract myself from this situation I have found myself in, from the fear of being caught. And then I see it—rising over the roof of the house next to the prison.

The shadow of a man.

I blink to assure myself that I am not dreaming, but when I open my eyes once more, he is still there, walking toward me along the roof.

Karl Decker.

We only met once, but he introduced himself before the guards cut off contact between me and my friends.

Karl crosses the distance between us quickly and puts his hand through the bars, taking mine. In a sliver of moonlight, I spy a bearded man behind him, and another man behind them.

I can't contain the little cry that escapes my lips at the sight of them.

"Don't be afraid. We'll have you out of here soon," Karl whispers, squeezing my hand in his.

I want to speak, to thank him for coming for me, but there are no words, so I release him and watch as he pulls out a saw and sets upon the bars, his friends joining him.

It's louder than I imagined it would be when I first devised the plan, the sound of metal clashing enough to wake the dead. The acid I suggested would have been much faster and more efficient. I don't know why they didn't bring it, but without it, the saw's work is unbearably slow even with both of them working as hard as possible.

For an hour, loud noises fill the room as the two men attack the bars. If they continue like this much longer, there's no doubt someone will wake up. It's a miracle no one has heard them so far.

I pivot from the window and walk over to my cot, grabbing a sheet and wrapping it around my body to cover myself so that if any of the other women do wake, they won't wonder why I am dressed in my daytime clothes rather than my nightgown.

As I am about to return to the window to check my rescuers' progress, a cough sounds behind me.

I whirl around just as Rosa rises from her bed, alert once more.

"My head hurts," she complains.

This is it. I open my mouth to speak to her, but no sound escapes. If she spots the men behind me, if she yells for the guards—

But even as I anticipate her cry of alarm, I am greeted by silence.

Blessedly, the sawing has stopped behind me, the dormitory quiet. I yearn to look and see if my rescuers are still at the window waiting for me, but I can't take my gaze off Rosa.

One shout from her is enough to bring the guards running.

"Who is at the window?" she asks.

"N-No one," I sputter. "I am feeling poorly and came to the window for air."

Rosa stares at me for a beat, and I can't tell if she believes me or not. There are moments when it feels as though she is here with us, and others when she is somewhere else entirely, an altogether different sort of prison.

She doesn't respond, but she lies back on her side, curling her body as though leaving space for another to fit inside the curve.

The low hum of a familiar nursery rhyme my older sisters once sang to me fills the room as she sings to the baby she lost as she so often does.

Tears prick my eyes.

I approach the window once more to tell the men it's too risky tonight, that the laudanum clearly hasn't done its job sufficiently. If I'm caught trying to escape, they'll kill me.

I return to the window, but it's clear that the men have already figured the same thing out for themselves, because their tools are gone, the bars intact, my hope of escape this evening shattered.

Karl hovers on the side of the building.

"Promise me you'll return tomorrow night," I whisper, tears

threatening. "Please. Promise me. I cannot spend another night in this place, I cannot—"

"We'll be back. I promise." Karl reaches through the bars and squeezes my hand again before he pulls away, leaving me to stare after his retreating back as the men return to the house across the street.

There's nothing to do but lie down in my bed like the others, even though I doubt sleep will come with the nerves and fear rattling around inside me. To have freedom so close I can taste it and then yanked from me so quickly feels like a cruel thing indeed.

But despite the events of the evening, my eyes eventually close, my body sinking into sleep.

When I dream, I am back home, in the house with the courtyard and the dancing fountain, and in the precious hours when I am asleep, I am free.

THE NEXT DAY BEGINS AS ORDINARILY AS ALL THE ONES BEFORE it, and as much as I worry Rosa will speak of the unusual goings-on last night, she keeps to herself, occasionally cradling her imaginary baby and crooning to it, her thoughts on the past and not on me.

I watch her carefully, waiting to see if there is a moment when she will give me away, and then finally, I ask the question I never thought to ask before.

"Your baby? What is its name?"

Rosa stares through me, and just when I think she isn't going to answer me, she replies—

"Her name was Maria."

She walks past me before I can say another word.

Did she lose her daughter before she came here? Or is her body buried somewhere in this place?

How could you move past a thing such as that?

As the day wears on, I do everything I can to keep from arousing suspicion, guilt over drugging my cellmates with laudanum again plaguing me.

Later in the day, I go to make the coffee, the laudanum clutched in my hand, my back to the other women.

Behind me someone calls out—

"I've been feeling terribly all day. Perhaps Evangelina used some of that famous beauty and bewitched the coffee."

My cheeks heat, but before I can turn around and deny it, peals of laughter greet me.

I join in, my shoulders shaking with feigned mirth as I pour the drug into their coffee.

Nineteen

The moon burns bright in the sky, illuminating far more of the night than I'd prefer. The temperature is hot, the air still, the heat bearing down on me.

My room is on the second story of the prison on the Sigua Street side. There is a small window that looks out to the city and opens up to a flat roof that must be about twenty feet wide, hidden from the sight of the street by a high parapet along the front of the building.

Behind me, the women in the dormitory sleep, dreaming laudanum-laced dreams. I increased the dosage from the night before to ensure there would be no repeats of Rosa or any of the others waking, but hopefully not so much as the doctor cautioned would bring about death.

The rhythmic sounds of their breathing are a balm to the nerves inside me.

I stare out at the sky, at the clouds surrounding the moon. There is a movement across the street, and I think I see three figures walking toward me once more, but then they are gone.

Have they given up entirely?

"Evangelina."

At the sound of my name, I glance down from the sky to where a man stands on the roof. He walks toward me, and I recognize him instantly from last night's attempted escape.

"Are you ready?" Karl whispers.

"I am."

His friends, who introduced themselves as William MacDonald and Francisco De Besche, join him and they immediately set to work on the window bars again, using a wrench on the one they already began sawing last night, and even though I now know how loud it can be, my heart still pounds with fear that we will be discovered.

What sort of people risk their lives to save someone like me? If they're caught aiding in my escape, they'll end up behind bars as well. I am immensely grateful that they are willing to risk their freedom for someone they've never even met.

And then, as though I dreamed it, the bar in front of me breaks with a clear ringing sound that could wake the dead.

But miraculously, no one stirs behind me.

I lean forward, dropping to my knees, and try to pull the bar even farther apart, as though I could escape through my own force of will, but Decker pushes me away. He catches the bar and pulls it toward him in a "V" motion, creating an opening.

I can hardly contain the sound of relief that escapes my lips.

"Is the opening big enough for you?" Decker asks.

It hardly seems as though it could be so, but I stick my head between the bars, relieved to see that it does indeed fit. My body follows, and I realize I can easily slip through the gap.

Decker reaches for me.

"Don't try to climb all the way out," he hisses. "They'll hear you. Let me lift you out."

"It's easy to be still when you haven't been locked up for over a year," I whisper back, but I force myself to keep from moving, my body hanging limp as he lifts me out of the gap created by the broken bar.

Decker grabs me around the waist and slides me fully through the bars.

The moment my feet hit the solid ground of the roof beneath me, I think my legs might give out at my first taste of freedom.

By some miracle, I stay upright, my escape by no means a foregone conclusion.

There is still much to be done.

A cry escapes born of relief and exhaustion, and all the emotions crashing through me now. Decker puts his hand over my mouth and picks me up in his arms and carries me quickly to where a ladder lies, urgency in all of our movements.

What if the guards decide to check the dormitory and see the broken bars? What if they notice I'm not in my bed as I should be?

MacDonald waits for us to follow him, crossing first. A spindly ladder that sags in the middle runs from the wall to the roof of the house across the street.

"Let me carry you across the ladder," Karl whispers. "It was the best we could find on such short notice, but the ladder's old and it's not particularly sturdy."

"It's too risky," I protest. "I'll do better on my own. Trust me."

He sets me down on my feet.

They seem to want to treat me as though I am as breakable as glass, but they don't realize that I couldn't have survived this time in Recogidas if I wasn't made of sturdier stuff.

I take a deep breath and put my foot on the first rung over the ladder. Decker reaches out and steadies me for a beat before he lets me go. I take the first step, relief filling me when the ladder doesn't collapse beneath my weight. I take another step. Then another, focusing on putting one foot down at a time, counting as I go. It takes a dozen steps to cross from the jail to the house they've rented across the alleyway, but I run quickly as I go, bending forward, my arms outstretched to keep me from falling off the narrow crossing. It feels like I'm flying over Havana.

Behind me, Decker stumbles over the rungs, and more than a few times I worry that the noise he's making will be enough to raise the alarm that I've escaped, but for me the ladder is the easiest part of the journey. After all I've been through, to be this close to safety, well— my feet carry me home.

When I reach the parapet of the house, MacDonald catches me in his arms and lifts me to the roof.

Once Decker has finished crossing, the men remove the ladder quickly.

We all climb down from the roof into the patio of a little house across the street from Recogidas. It takes everything in me to keep from looking over my shoulder as though the guards might follow us out of the prison window.

We race through the house to the entrance where Karl takes my hand and leads me quickly into a waiting carriage. MacDonald settles in the driver's seat, Decker and De Besche lingering behind us once I am safely ensconced in the vehicle. No sooner am I seated than the horses begin to move with a lurch and a jolt.

I listen for soldiers' cries and the pounding of horses' hooves surrounding us, but I only hear revelry and the usual sounds of the city.

THE STREET IS QUIET WHEN WE FINALLY STOP IN FRONT OF A beautiful home.

Despite the late hour, it looks as though the owners of the house have recently hosted a party, because guests still linger when our carriage arrives. As nerve-wracking as it is to be among others, it is easy enough for my conveyance to blend in with those of the party guests, to give the impression that I am one of them.

I exit the carriage and turn toward the building MacDonald pointed out to me.

I am nearly at the door that my rescuer has left ajar for me when I stop in my tracks. Two policemen walk toward me, deep in conversation.

My heart pounds.

Have I been given up already?

One of the policemen looks my way, his gaze resting on me.

I gather the skirt of my gown in my hand, ready to return to the security of the waiting carriage, but the policeman merely inclines his head in greeting, stepping aside to let me pass by.

I wait for his friend to say something, to sound the alarm, but miraculously neither one of them appears to recognize me.

Quickly, I walk into the house through a door left open just as my rescuers said it would be. I follow the instructions I was given by Decker and MacDonald, and press myself against a wall, peering around the corner as the last of the guests depart. I can almost make out the shape of a dark-haired man standing near the front door in elegant evening dress.

I try to steady my breath, drawing back so none of the crowd can see me.

Finally, I hear the sound of the door shutting, and then there's a light touch on my arm.

I look up into the dark eyes of the man I saw glimpses of before, and his image swims before me, exhaustion overtaking me.

"Come," he says gently, and he leads me quickly to a suite of apartments for my exclusive use.

He leaves me alone with two women who will look after me, and after I am bathed and tucked into bed, I fall asleep.

Twenty

When I wake the next day, I can scarcely believe the change in my fortunes, my accommodations the furthest cry from my cell in Recogidas. The suite of rooms is spacious, the furnishing elegant and lavish, certainly nicer than any I knew even in my father's care. Whoever my protectors are, they must be well connected.

The staff says little, but they bring me a large breakfast, and despite my hunger, I can't eat, my stomach unused to having so much food, my nerves shattered. My clothes hang off me, my body changed so much since I entered the prison.

How long will it take for my body to go back to the way it was before this nightmare began? How long will it take for me to go back to who I was? Will I ever, or is the loss of the girl I once was another thing Berriz and the Spanish have taken from me?

After I am settled in the room, I ask for a newspaper to be brought to me.

Do the staff know who I am? Do they fear retribution for their part in this? Can I trust them?

When the maid returns with a newspaper, I can't resist asking—

"I would very much like to thank the people who own this house. Will I see them today?"

"I will ask," she replies, taking her leave with a quick bob before shutting the door behind herself entirely.

The newspaper she brought me is spread out before me, the details of my escape laid bare for all of Havana to see.

With each word I read, my fear builds.

The newspaper reports that my cellmates say that I drugged them. My jailer and four workers who were on duty have already been arrested. It feels as though the Spanish are on my heels, their determination to see me recaptured laid out in black-and-white before me.

Will I ever truly be free?

I would prefer death at my own hand over surrender.

Suddenly, there's a knock at the door to my room.

"My name is Carlos Carbonell. We met last night," a voice calls out. "This is my house. I was told you wished to speak with me. May I come in?"

"Yes, please do," I say, straightening the papers.

The door opens, and Carlos enters with smooth strides, dressed more casually than last night, but no less elegantly. He shuts the door behind him, his gaze appraising. He looks to be my father's age, in his late forties perhaps, and carries himself with a distinguished bearing.

He smiles. "It's a pleasure to finally meet you considering how much you have occupied my thoughts and concerns of late. Are you well? I confess it is much better to see you here, comfortably settled as you should be, than in that awful place."

I nod, words momentarily escaping me, and then I take a deep breath, steadying myself. It is a strange thing to go from living in a dark, dank cell to suddenly finding yourself free—even more so when that freedom is potentially temporary.

"Thank you for taking me into your home," I reply. "I don't know what I would have done without your assistance, only that I would like to thank your wife as well for her kindness."

"There's no need to thank me. Any patriot would have done the same. You are a credit to our country, and it is my pleasure to serve you in whatever manner I may." His smile deepens. "Besides, given all the Spanish have done to us, it isn't exactly a hardship to thwart their plans.

"As for your other thanks, I have no wife for you to meet, unfortunately."

"I'm sorry. I shouldn't have presumed. You are a widower, then?"

"No, I've never had the pleasure of finding someone to spend my life with."

I never imagined that they would take me to a bachelor's house, and suddenly, it occurs to me that I am alone with a strange man, and after my experience with Berriz—

He must read the unease in my expression, because he says to me, "In this house, you will be treated with nothing but the utmost respect. I can't imagine what you have been through, and I understand how it would cause you to distrust the actions of men around you, but I promise you I will treat you with the same level of love and respect that I would accord to my own mother."

There's something so earnest in his voice and courtly in his manner that despite my misgivings, I relax somewhat. It is good to be reminded that all men are not Berriz, that there are kind men in this world.

"If all goes as planned, you will leave tomorrow on the passenger ship *Seneca*, which is bound for New York City."

New York City.

"That seems an impossible wish," I confess.

"Not so impossible. Not for those of us who have dedicated our-selves to your cause. I have connections with the Havana agent for the Ward Line that owns the *Seneca*, which has certainly helped. Besides, you have influential friends, and importantly, you have friends among the Americans. Consul General Lee himself has taken an interest in your case."

"Are they searching for me?"

"They're going house to house. But you have nothing to fear. I keep cash on hand, and if I need to bribe any of the authorities to look the other way, I have no qualms about doing so. I don't want you to worry about your safety. I won't let anything happen to you. We haven't come this far to taste defeat so soon. Besides, if the cash doesn't work, I have a revolver on hand that will."

There's something about him that reminds me a bit of my father. He seems to be a man of his word, who despite his elegant appearance isn't afraid to dirty his hands and fight for what he believes in.

It gives me peace where there otherwise would be none. After years spent caring for my family and languishing in prison, this sensa-tion that there is someone else looking out for me is entirely welcome.

"If for some reason you do need to escape," Carlos adds, "I have rented the house next door. We've broken the windows between the two houses in case you have to climb between them."

I smile in amazement. "You've thought of everything, haven't you?"

"Not everything. I must confess, we were quite stymied on how to get you out of Recogidas. I can't tell you the relief we all felt when we saw your careful instructions. And the diagrams." He laughs. "I think we all fell a bit in love with you then. Decker, certainly."

My cheeks heat at the casual way in which he says the word "love" and the gleam in his eyes.

"I have had a great deal of time to contemplate escape."

His expression darkens. "Yes, I imagine you have."

"Why did you help rescue me?"

I am used to fighting for myself, for the dreams of an independent Cuba that I and others around me believe in, but I am shocked by their willingness to risk so much for someone they have never met.

"Because it was the right thing to do. It is difficult to live in these times and not feel helpless. I am fortunate that my wealth has kept me somewhat protected, but we all have a responsibility to do something when called to it. I love my country. This was my attempt at serving her in the manner I knew best." His expression gentles. "And how could I not? I saw you in Recogidas. I went by one day, and while I didn't want to raise suspicions by formally requesting to meet with you, I had heard talk that you were there, and I wanted to see the woman who had spurred the Spanish myself. Maybe I fell in love with you myself that day," he says, his tone and expression suggesting he is in jest, although I can't deny the warmth that fills me at his attention.

"Thank you for all of your help. I don't know what I would have done without you. For you to risk your life like this—"

"It is no risk. It is my pleasure to do what I can to right the injustice that has been done to you."

Expressing my gratitude seems hollow, no words I can offer enough for the magnitude of what he has done for me. How do you properly show your appreciation for someone who saves your life?

WE SPEND MOST OF OUR WAKING MOMENTS TOGETHER WHILE WE wait for the ship that is to carry me from Cuba. Carlos is an excellent host—solicitous and considerate—and I am fascinated by the stories he tells of his career in banking, his American friends, the years he spent studying in the United States. I absorb his every word as he speaks of the country that is to be my new temporary home, as he gives me advice on acclimating to my life there. More than anything, I am drawn to how he listens, the interest he takes in me. I tell him about my sisters, my life before my father was arrested. Berriz is the subject we avoid, and we both dance around my time in Recogidas as though through some silent agreement to ban all unpleasantness from this sanctuary we have created.

Every so often, he excuses himself to go check on details for my eventual escape, and I find that I miss his company even during the short intervals when he is gone.

"I brought you some clothes to wear," Carlos announces as he enters my room Saturday evening. "This will go much easier if you are dressed as a boy."

"They're still out there looking for me, aren't they?"

He nods.

I doubt they'll give up until they've recaptured me.

Carlos's presence has done much to distract me from the danger of my situation, but he hasn't been able to fully eradicate the fear inside me.

"What if they catch me?"

"I won't let that happen."

"I can't go back there. I'd rather die."

I don't regret the choices I've made so far, or the fact that I never recanted my story about Berriz, but now that I know what awaits me in prison, now that I've tasted even this small amount of freedom, I know with every part of my soul that I would choose death over returning to that hell.

Carlos reaches out and takes my hand, lacing his fingers through mine, squeezing gently. "I know. I promise you. I won't let anything happen to you. I will do everything in my power to keep you safe."

He steps forward, wrapping his arms around me, fitting me against his body. There is nothing untoward in his embrace even as I know how wholly inappropriate it is for me to be with a man like this, but given the fact that my reputation lies in tatters already, I don't care. It feels good to lean against another after being on my own for so long, and at the moment, I'm not sure there's anyone I trust more in the world, given all he's risked for me.

Carlos strokes my hair while he holds me, whispering to me that all will be well, that he won't let anything happen to me, that I will be safe, that I have escaped, that I will be free.

He releases me and stands before me for a moment, studying me. And then—

"I'll leave you alone to get changed. We need to depart soon."

The clothes he originally brought me sit bundled together on the couch.

Once he's gone, I undress quickly, changing into the items he brought.

I look like a young sailor in the blue shirt, trousers, and flowing tie. Carlos thoughtfully supplied a large slouch hat for me as well. It takes several tries and the use of pomade to plaster down my hair so it fits under the hat.

If I don't succeed in altering my appearance, then I'm sure I'll be recognized, given how much my image has been splashed all over the newspaper.

"Will this do?" I ask Carlos when he reenters the room.

A smile tugs at his mouth. "Almost. Here, this might help." He reaches into a humidor in the sitting room, drawing out a fat cigar. "May I?"

I nod as he hands it to me. Our fingers brush as I take it from his hands and lift it to my mouth. My fingers tremble slightly as I inhale the familiar tobacco scent that lingers faintly on him.

"Better," he replies. "Are you ready?"

"As ready as I suppose you can ever be for this sort of thing."

"I'll be with you every step of the way," he promises.

"But not on the boat."

"No."

I think I hear a note of sadness in his voice, and I can't help but wonder if he's grown as fond of me as I have of him in the short time we've spent together. For so long, I was friendless in the world, and in the hours we've shared together, the friendship that has sprung up in such difficult circumstances has meant a great deal.

I give an embarrassed little laugh. "You must think me foolish, but I will miss you."

"Not foolish at all. I will miss you, too. Your presence here has brightened the house considerably. If you could be safe here, I wouldn't want you to leave."

My cheeks heat, and I stare down at my feet, unable to conjure up a suitable response, until the words escape as if of their own volition—

"If things were different, I imagine this is the sort of place where I could be very happy."

We're both silent as we leave the room together, and as eager as I am to leave Cuba and the threat surrounding me, there is a part of me that wishes I could stay ensconced in this room forever.

Carlos takes my hand, leading me through his home, and I commit all the little details to memory—the paintings hanging on the wall, the settee, the polished wood floors—so that when there is an ocean between us and I have occasion to think of him, it's here, safe in this home he clearly loves.

He stops before the front door and releases my hand. For a moment we stand still, and then Carlos leans forward and presses a soft kiss to my cheek.

My skin tingles in his wake.

"All will be well," he promises, and he opens the front door, the sights and sounds of the city intruding on this refuge we have created.

I take a deep breath as we walk outside, steadying myself, my cheeks flushed from the innocent kiss he gave me.

A gust of wind comes, lifting the hat from my head and sending it fluttering to the ground.

Beside me, Carlos tenses.

Heart pounding, I reach down and pick it up, settling it back over my dark hair.

I wait for someone to call my name, to recognize me, but no one does.

From the corner of my eye, I spy Karl Decker nearby, his hand near his hip where a gun is seated. The other men who have helped me occupy various positions on the road, their bodies alert and tense.

I loosen my gait, trying to imitate the walk of the men of my acquaintance, striving for nonchalance even as my body yearns to run.

Carlos's house is two blocks away from the wharf, and we walk down Obispo Street together, Karl and the other men trailing behind us, their guns swinging loose from their hands now, ready for trouble. A little farther behind them is a carriage, and I've been urged to run to its safety if someone recognizes me and sounds the alarm.

It's evening now, that in-between time when twilight crosses over into darkness. Every so often we pass by someone on the street, but for the most part people are in their houses eating dinner. The real danger will come at the Machina Wharf where my friends tell me the Spanish officers often loiter. With each step, my nerves grow, but when we near the wharf, there are only a few people in sight. Passengers have gathered near the landing stage for the *Seneca*.

The lights in Regla reflect on the water. The dark sky is illuminated with stars, and for a moment, I break character and cast my face upward, taking in all I've missed since I've been in prison.

I can feel Carlos's gaze on me. Tears prick my eyes as I am overcome by the beauty of the night.

When will I see Cuba again?

Beside me, Carlos clears his throat, and I am returned to myself once more.

Off in the distance, the steamer lies in the harbor, plumes of smoke drifting from her funnels as she readies to set sail.

We hurry on.

There is a flurry of motion on the docks as the propellers of the launch carrying passengers to the *Seneca* start up with a whirl. I stand still, Carlos a hairbreadth away from me, watching the passengers board the launch. From the corner of my eye, I spy Decker and his friends heading toward a café that overlooks the harbor, a Spanish policeman in their company.

"This is it," Carlos murmurs. "Karl and the others will distract the policeman. The quartermaster will help get you on board."

"This is good-bye, then," I say, sadness filling me.

"It is. You'll be fine. The Americans will love you. How could they not?" He smiles. "I don't think I'll ever forget you."

There is so much more I wish to say, but there is no time for it, so I turn away from him and climb into the little boat with the other passengers, my gaze on the docks. I can barely make out Carlos's silhouette, and then he disappears from view entirely.

We arrive at the *Seneca,* and as I climb on board, a sailor walks toward me and instructs me to follow him.

My friends told me there would be people around helping me along the way, but the sailor's presence still surprises me, and for a moment, I almost don't follow him, afraid this is a trap.

A few policemen including the chief of police mill around.

I keep my gaze trained to the ground, following the sailor to another part of the boarding area.

An officer requests my passport, and I produce the one Carlos gave me that proclaims me to be Juan Sola, an eighteen-year-old sailor.

My heart pounds as I wait to see if my papers arouse suspicion, but the officer waves me on without another glance.

The sailor leads me to a small cabin on deck. He opens the door and tells me to enter, before closing it behind me quickly, and I am alone once more.

I crawl onto the lowest berth, staring up at the bunk above me. The room is dark, and even though I am alone, I lie as still as possible to avoid attracting any attention. Time passes slowly, and every so often there is a noise that sends a chill down my spine.

To have come so far, only to be sent back—

The boat rocks slightly, but I can't tell if we're moving or not, if we've cast off, and then suddenly, my stateroom door swings open.

Heavy footsteps fill the room.

I can't see the intruder, but by the rustling noises filling the room it is clear that they are searching for something—or someone—in the cabin.

Have my friends been captured as well?

I press my body closer to the wall, holding my breath and stilling my limbs as much as possible in the hopes that the intruder will think the cabin is empty and leave immediately.

The sound of a match being struck fills the room, followed by the glow of a little flame.

This is it.

Tears of frustration and anger fill my eyes.

When they take me onto the deck, I'll look for the first opportunity I can to jump overboard.

"Evangelina," a man's voice calls out.

I don't dare respond.

"Miss Cisneros—I'm Walter B. Barker. Where are you?"

I recognize the name instantly from my conversations with Carlos. If my memory serves, Mr. Barker is an American diplomatic staff member who was posted in Havana and is a confidant of Consul General Lee's.

He is a friend.

I crawl out from the berth, relief filling me.

Walter smiles at me. "We've been at sea for about an hour now. We're far enough away from Havana that no one can hurt you. Why don't you come up on deck with me?"

Tears spill down my cheeks.

As much as I want to, the events of the past few days crash into me over and over again, until I can do nothing but cry, unable to believe my good fortune—

I am really and truly free.

Twenty-One

❧

GRACE

On October 8, 1897, the *Journal* reports "the Most Beautiful Girl in Cuba," Evangelina Cisneros, has escaped from Recogidas. There's no mention of the paper's role in the story, only that she never appeared for the prison's roll call in the morning and they launched a search for her, only to find one of the bars in her room had been filed and bent outward, several prison employees arrested for allegedly aiding in her escape. The article is remarkably succinct for Hearst's usual style, absent the flourishes and dramatization that has characterized the entire proceeding up until this point.

The next day the newspaper tells a new tale:

General Weyler has resigned from his post.

His legacy has left half a million Cubans in reconcentration camps.

Weyler's political fortunes have been tenuous for months now. The Conservative Spanish prime minister Antonio Cánovas del Castillo was assassinated by an anarchist back in August, and the new Liberal leader Práxedes Sagasta is said to be looking for a more conciliatory policy toward Cuba. Recalling Weyler is an excellent first step, but there is still much to be done. Evangelina's escape must have been the final nail in Weyler's coffin.

On October 10, Karl Decker's six-column headline filed under his pen name, Charles Duval, shouts the truth from the rooftops:

The *Journal* has rescued Evangelina Cisneros.

It's all anyone can talk about as Hearst crows of his paper's accomplishment:

While Others Talk, The Journal *Acts*

Hearst has us interview prominent political figures, private citizens, anyone and everyone who can praise his paper for doing the impossible and rescuing Evangelina from prison. Many of the newspapers who have viewed Hearst's journalism with scorn in the past are now quick to celebrate the *Journal*'s success.

The *World* is doing their own reporting as quickly as they can, attempting to poke holes in Hearst's story, but the wave of praise for the *Journal*'s accomplishment is overwhelming.

Hearst calls me into his office one morning, as I'm finishing up yet another article on Evangelina. These days, it seems like the entire newsroom is writing about Evangelina, covering any and all angles about her life.

Arthur Brisbane stands beside Hearst's desk as they look over copy for the next edition.

"Grace. Just who I wanted to see," Hearst announces. "Evangelina Cisneros is nearly in New York, and it occurred to me that it would be helpful for the *Journal* to have a woman as part of the contingent to greet her. She might be more likely to open up to one of our reporters who is a woman, especially after everything she's been through."

"Of course."

I turn to leave, and he says—

"There's something else. We're going to publish a book. The story of

Evangelina Cisneros, in her own words. We'll include a section from Decker where he can talk about his role in the escape, and then we'll have Evangelina discuss her life, the situation in Cuba, her version of events. She'll need someone to help her write it. I think a feminine touch would be nice. Of course, your name won't be on the story, and there will be others working on it, but it'll be good practice for you. It'll give you the kind of experience that will prove helpful to your journalism career."

It's a far cry to go from writing articles to a full book about someone's life. I've never taken on such a project, and for all Hearst isn't afraid to stretch the bounds of comfort, this feels like too ambitious of a project for me, but if my career has taught me anything, it's to say yes to the opportunity and figure it out as I go along.

"I'm flattered, Mr. Hearst. I would love to."

"I'm sure you'll do a fine job," he says. "We'll make sure you have a chance to look over Karl's piece so you can write hers in a similar style. And you'll want to read over all of the pieces we've published on her so that you can maintain a similar style and tone. Miss Cisneros is a national treasure, and she should be treated as such.

"It will be a delicate matter," Hearst continues. "Some of the men involved in getting Evangelina out of prison must remain anonymous. They're still embroiled in schemes in Cuba, and it wouldn't do for their identities to be revealed. Same for any diplomatic assistance she received. We'll have to use code names for some of them to protect their identities."

Despite my reservations, my fears that I am no biographer, it feels like an opportunity to distinguish myself in a crowded field, in the hopes that perhaps one day I can move beyond these stunt articles.

It feels like a chance to make my career.

"You can count on me," I reply.

"I hope so. This is war."

Twenty-Two

EVANGELINA

The next day at sea, I change out of the boys' clothes and into a red dress. I finally feel rested enough that I venture up on deck, and the passengers gather around me, news of my ordeal clearly having spread throughout the ship. The women encircle me, hugging and kissing me, the men telling me I am brave to have survived all that I have.

When I was in Recogidas, I didn't think of what it would be like to be out of the prison, didn't realize how difficult it would be to re-enter society after spending so much time in such harsh conditions. In prison, we were constantly watched and spied upon, people reporting on our movements, mine more than anyone else's given the notoriety surrounding my case. It makes the attention everyone pays to me now even more uncomfortable.

While they mill around me, I sit on the deck listening to the glorious sound of the water rushing past the ship, admiring the expanse of sea before me and all the possibilities there. My body may be on the *Seneca*, but my mind is elsewhere. Even with the future before me, I can't help but think of my friends back in Havana, of the men who risked their lives to help me.

Is Carlos safe in his home near the wharf, smoking one of those cigars that reminds me of him like the one he gave me that rests in my cabin below deck now with the folded-up boys' clothes? And the other men? The woman Marina who passed me the notes? What of all of them?

Decker had planned to board a separate steamer to the United States, but I worry that he was caught, that he might be facing the ramifications of helping me escape from Recogidas.

As much as I wish to enjoy the boat ride, I can't quiet my thoughts enough to concentrate on all of the conversations around me. Everyone wishes to know the details of what has happened to me, but the desire to be alone with my thoughts is greater than I imagined, the weight of all I have endured hitting me at unexpected times. How do you explain life in a prison like Recogidas?

I alternate between resting in my cabin and allowing myself these little entrées into society. My journey is largely uneventful, most of it spent in Walter's esteemed company and that of the ship's purser.

I try to imagine what my life will be like when I arrive in New York, but I can't quite envision it when so much of what I love is back in Cuba. I've had no word of what has happened to my father, if he is alive or dead, nor of my sisters. I hope they will not be punished for my escape.

Will I ever see them again? Will I ever return home?

I suppose it is better to not worry about such things, to content myself in all I have accomplished, the miraculous fact that I have escaped from Recogidas, that the Spanish have no claim over me. After living my whole life under their authority, it is a glorious thing to be free.

As we near the end of our journey, I walk out on deck and take in my surroundings, enjoying the fresh air on my skin, the crisp, clean scents surrounding me a welcome change from the filth of prison.

Off in the distance, I spy a light. It is so bright; it must be a star.

I don't realize I've said the thought aloud until the man next to me answers, "It's the Cape Hatteras light. It's on top of a lighthouse off one of the islands in North Carolina."

"Oh." I breathe the word, the light conjuring more wonder in me than I imagined.

Cuba and all of my family and friends are truly behind me now.

I am torn between the urge to weep tears of joy and tears of sorrow.

We continue on our journey and sail up the bay to New York, and my excitement overwhelms me, emotions ricocheting through my body. Suddenly, the boat stops and a small steamer comes up alongside the *Seneca*. There's a crowd of smiling passengers in the boat, and at once, I see him, the first American to visit me in prison, the man who brought my case to international attention—

Mr. Bryson.

Emotion fills me, and for a moment, I am back at Recogidas staring at him through the metal bars, and it truly hits me how far I've come. Without him, I'd probably be facing the rest of my days spent in prison.

With help from some of the others, I board the steamer where I am engulfed in hugs and well-wishes, my welcome to this new country great indeed.

After a short ride in the little boat, I am ferried in a carriage up a seemingly never-ending street that is so illuminated that it feels like a fairyland. I am surrounded by journalists from the *New York Journal*, the newspaper that first brought attention to my plight, their pens and papers poised. Every so often, one of them scribbles something down on a pad of paper, their eyes seemingly taking in everything I say and do, as though I am performing on a stage.

"How do you feel?" one gentleman asks me.

I answer as honestly as I can, stringing the words together in some fashion—

"Like I am in a dream."

Twenty-Three

My new friends settle me into the Waldorf-Astoria, a grand hotel the likes of which I have never seen, the building towering some thirteen stories over the city. While my accommodations on the *Seneca* were fine, the hotel is opulent beyond measure. There is electricity throughout, private bathrooms in the suites. They tell me to get comfortable in the new rooms and rest, treating me as though I am a delicate creature.

And still—despite all I have endured, I cannot deny that for all of my strength, Recogidas has left its mark on me whether I wished it to or not.

In spite of the splendor of my surroundings, the soft bed and cool sheets, I wake in the middle of the night, my body covered in sweat.

I lurch up in the bed, the darkness of the room disorienting me. For a moment, I can't remember where I am, if I am in our little house on the Isle of Pines, or in Recogidas, but the bed and sheets feel too fine to be either place. In sleep, in my dreams, I am back in Recogidas, the familiar sounds and smells of the prison assaulting me. It takes me a moment to acclimate to my surroundings, to realize that I am in a suite at the Waldorf-Astoria, that I am in New York, that I am safe.

It takes me hours to fall back asleep, and when I do, I sleep fit-fully, thinking of everyone I left back home, wondering if Carlos knows I have arrived here successfully, if he is aware that all he risked for me was successful, if he is safe.

At half past six in the morning the day after I have arrived in the city, there's a knock at my door, reporters from the *New York Journal* standing over the threshold. Among them is a woman who introduces herself as Grace, and I recognize her from the contingent that greeted me upon my arrival in the city. Thanks to the *Journal*, my room is filled to the brim with boxes of dresses, lingerie, hats, accessories, all the things I could ever hope to need.

How do you thank people for such generosity? Words hardly seem enough.

After I am dressed and made presentable, an hour later, I go down to breakfast with the newspaper staff. The newspaper has thoughtfully provided a chaperone in the widow of General John A. Logan. I'm told she writes on women's issues for the *Journal*, and her excitement and energy are infectious. Grace and the others trail behind us, noting my reactions to everything.

I dressed carefully for the morning in head-to-toe black. The somber color feels like a balm, the simplicity of it calming.

The reporters pepper me with questions, their pens and pads at the ready. The woman—Grace—says little, but she has the sort of eyes that seem to take in everything. She must see the nerves in my face, because she offers me a smile that puts me a little more at ease.

After breakfast, the *Journal* staff takes me on a tour of the city. Everything in America is done on a grand scale: the wide streets, the elegant carriages, the soaring buildings that tower over us. Even the brass buttons on the policemen's uniforms gleam. The people who aren't in carriages zip along on bicycles, and I find myself longing to try one, watching with envy the serene countenances of the many women navigating them.

I could get used to a life such as this one.

Every reaction to the sights appears to be catalogued by the *Journal* staff, from the words I say to the sketches of my face as I'm presented with some new and exciting thing. It's a bit odd to feel as though your entire life is on display. Before Berriz attacked me, I lived a perfectly ordinary life. It's a bit overwhelming to go from that to this strange celebrity that has been thrust upon me. At the same time, considering how they saved me and the debt I owe them, it seems a small thing to let them sketch my picture and to answer their questions.

When I remain still while they capture my image, I seek out the female reporter—Grace—my gaze settling on hers. I imagine I see understanding in her eyes; no doubt in her line of work as a journalist she's used to being an oddity.

I am once again a novelty to be stared at, but at least I am no longer behind the bars of Recogidas, men jeering at me on the other side of a cage.

I am free, and if this is the price, so be it.

AFTER A FEW DAYS IN NEW YORK, I ASK MY NEW FRIENDS TO TAKE me to the Naturalization Bureau in the Supreme Court of the State of New York where I swear on a Bible my intention to become an American citizen.

"You will have to renounce the sovereignty of any foreign powers, including the queen regent of Spain," the clerk cautions me, as though this is a difficult endeavor, when what started all of this trouble was my reluctance to accept Spanish rule.

A laugh bubbles up inside me. "That will be the easiest part of all," I assure the man, struggling to maintain a straight face in keeping with the solemnity of my surroundings.

They tell me it will take five years before I am a full-fledged American citizen, but with one hand on the Bible and the other stroking the red, white, and blue of the American flag, I feel protected.

Let Spain try and come for me now.

When we are finished in the courthouse, a mob descends upon us as we walk down the stairs. My face has been on the cover of the New York papers for so long now that I am recognized everywhere I go in the city, yet another part of my new life that will take some getting used to. The American public has known me for months, but this is still novel for me, and it's a bit overwhelming to navigate this change with all eyes upon me.

To that end, Mr. Hearst, the editor of the newspaper that has secured my release, has suggested I write a book telling my story, so I can share it with the rest of the country.

That afternoon, I sit with Grace and a woman from one of the Cuban relief societies in the living area of my suite at the Waldorf-Astoria.

"Mr. Hearst would like me to help you write about your experiences," Grace says. "He thought you might be more comfortable talking to a woman considering what happened to you."

"At this point, it hardly seems there is anyone who hasn't heard the terrible details of Berriz's attack."

"True. We thought this might be an opportunity for you to tell your story since so much has been written about you, but nothing written *by* you. Mr. Hearst also thought the proceeds of the book sales should go to you. The money might help you in your new life here."

Truthfully, everything about the past few years of my life has felt

so insurmountable that I've done little more than look to my daily
needs and challenges. The notion of starting over here now that I have
nothing is a terrifying one. Money is certainly a pressing concern, but
it is hardly the only one.

Where will I live? When will I return home? This book seems like
a godsend if it will give me the financial means to support myself, and
still, I can't help but wonder—

"Do you really think people will be interested in reading a book
about me? Even after all of the pieces that have been written about
me? Isn't everyone tired of me by now?"

"I do think they're interested," Grace answers. "The public has
truly related to your story in a way that I admit, even I didn't anticipate. But I think there are many people who know what it feels like to
be terribly abused, to be put in an unfair and desperate situation, and
in you and your story they see hope."

Does it fill them with hope? What a strange thought. Given all I
have lost, I suppose it's a bit difficult to see that side of the story. Even
harder when I've spent so long defending myself. It's hard to know if
I am truly among friends, if I am to be believed. I asked the hotel staff
for copies of the other newspapers, and I've seen what they're writing
about me, the articles questioning what happened to me.

Does Grace believe that Berriz attacked me, that I am the victim
in all of this, or is she simply acting at the behest of her employer,
writing this story because she has been directed to do so?

I wish I knew who I could trust.

"I wish I could be the heroine the people seem to want me to be.
I wish I could have done more for Cuba. For my family."

"You must miss them very much."

I open my mouth to say something, but a sob escapes instead, the
force of the emotion surprising me. For so long, I've been focused on

surviving, my strength reserved for enduring Recogidas, that now I am overwhelmed by all of the emotions I haven't dared face since this all began.

"I'm sorry—I—"

I don't know how to explain to her what it's like to have to pretend to be what everyone expects you to be when your insides are eaten with fear or worry. I am happy to be free, but there is so much uncertainty before me.

"My father—" I try again. "I miss him. And my sisters. Terribly."

Grace reaches out, taking my hand and squeezing it gently.

"You must feel very alone at times. Having come all this way, being so far from home, away from your friends and those you love. Especially after all you've been through."

"I can't help but wonder if I'll ever see them again," I admit. "My greatest fear is that after all of this, to have come this far, I won't be able to go home, to see the people I love."

"I heard you left your fiancé back in Cuba. Is that true?"

"Emilio Betancourt. Yes. We were engaged shortly after I arrived at the Isle of Pines."

"You must miss him a great deal."

"I did. Once. Now I can't remember what he looks like—It's such a small thing, but I loved him for so long, and now it's almost like he's a stranger. I remember pieces of his face—his mustache, his eyes. I remember the butterflies I used to feel in my stomach when he would walk in front of the house where I lived with my father and Carmen. We used to talk through the window gratings of our homes when he was courting me on the Isle of Pines."

"Was he a prisoner there, too?"

"He was. He hoped that he would be pardoned, and when he was free, we would be able to marry."

"What happened to him?"

"He was there that night I was attacked by Berriz. He was among the group that tried to save me. He was punished and arrested like all of my rescuers."

The hurt is still there, when I speak of his betrayal. "I learned later from the Marquis de Cervera that Emilio was among the men who agreed to cooperate with the Spanish and testify against me in exchange for their freedom. I understand why the other men would do so, but it was hard to forgive Emilio for his betrayal. We were supposed to love each other for all of our lives. How do I reconcile such a loss of fidelity? He is not the patriot I thought he was. That part of my life is over now."

"He sounds like he didn't deserve you."

"No, I don't think he did."

"We've heard stories, but I can't imagine what it's like in Cuba now, what it was like for you in Recogidas."

"No, you couldn't. I had no idea before they threw me in that cell how difficult it would be. Nothing in my life had prepared me for it. I think about the women I left behind, the ones I drugged so I could escape. Who will rescue them? Who will put their stories on the front page of the paper? Why was I saved when so many others aren't?"

"I can understand how you would feel that way. The conditions those women are living in, the reports we've heard are abominable. Clearly, something needs to be done to end the suffering in Cuba. Mr. Hearst and others hoped that your story would incite the people of America to push harder for intervention against Spain."

"It's hard to believe my story could move America to act against the Spanish. I haven't quite gotten used to the attention, to the sensation that people care about me. It's a heady thing to have everyone looking to you. It's a scary thing to make your way in this world alone,"

I confess. "Being here is difficult. Everyone has been so kind, and done so much for me, but it is a terrifying thing to have an uncertain future," I add. Even though she's a reporter, there's something in her manner, perhaps the fact that she is a woman left to her own devices to make it in this world, that makes me trust her where I otherwise would exercise caution. Or maybe I'm just too homesick to be prudent anymore. "I never imagined my life would end up like this. I never envisioned myself leaving Cuba, never wanted to. And then Berriz changed everything."

She swears softly under her breath in a most unladylike manner that is oddly somewhat reassuring.

"You were treated horribly," she says.

"I was. So many are in Cuba. Things are bad there. I don't know how to explain it to people who have never known what it is to struggle like this. So many of the things we suffer must seem unbelievable to you and your countrymen."

She squeezes my hand once more. "Tell me about Cuba, then, so that you can show them what it's like. What would you like the women of America to know about you, about Cuba? You've had others tell your story for so long now. What do you want to say?"

Besides Carlos, she's the first person who has really listened to me for so long, who has been curious about my thoughts and feelings rather than treating me like someone to be protected, that I can't resist the urge to be honest.

"First off, the name they have given me—I'm not a 'girl.' I'm twenty years old and I am a woman. I am not a child who needs to be cared for. I have been caring for my family for a long time now.

"I was born in Puerto Príncipe, which is the capital of the province of Camagüey. I was raised by my father. My mother died when I was a very young girl. I don't remember her, really, but everyone says she was very beautiful. When she died, it was like a piece of my father died as well. He was restless, morose. But in her absence, he relied a great deal on me and my sisters, and we cared for him, cooking and keeping the house. And in turn, he never treated me like a child, as though I needed to be sheltered from the world. We used to stay up late in the evening and he would talk to me about all sorts of things: Cuba, politics, his time spent as a soldier in the first war for independence. He loves Cuba very much, and I always admired him for his willingness to sacrifice his life for his country. I can think of no greater love for a proud patriot."

Tears swim in Grace's eyes, the force of the emotion staring back at me catching me off guard.

"I lost my father when I was young," she replies. "But he was proud of his country as well, and he was ready to sacrifice everything for her. He raised me to believe I had a duty to defend what I believed in."

"You understand then. Sometimes the love you feel for your country and the love you feel for your family become one in the same, until your family becomes your country and your country your family, and the two are inextricably linked in your heart. I love Cuba as I love my own father, the memory of my mother. I would die for Cuba. When my father said he was going to go join the revolutionary movement, I was prepared to go with him."

"What happened?"

"There were fifteen of us who were planning to join the revolutionaries. My sister Carmen and I met with them. We were constantly being watched by the Spanish, but we pretended we were loyal to them, all while we planned revolution. My father hid weapons and ammunition around the neighborhood in preparation. But the day before we were going to join the front, one of the men in our group betrayed us. Soldiers detained my father and when they searched him, they found incriminating papers on him. So they jailed him in our town."

"You must have been terrified."

I can still remember how helpless I felt comforting Carmen as she cried. "I was. I bribed the prison guard with a meal of eggs and meat that I made that morning to pass a message to my father letting him know I was worried about him. After the first time, we had an arrangement where I would give the guard food and he would pass some along to my father and eventually he let me see him."

"I heard that after your father was transferred a few times, you pled his case before Weyler himself."

"I did."

It's strange to think that I met with Weyler so long ago to beg for my father to be sent to the Isle of Pines, at the time not realizing what an important role he would play in my life, how much his specter would haunt me.

For hours, we talk as I tell her about my life, our exile on the Isle of Pines, that terrifying night with Berriz. I share some of my experiences in prison with her, and I'm beginning the tale of my escape from Recogidas when there's a knock on the door to my hotel room.

I rise and excuse myself to answer it.

I open the door and immediately freeze.

Karl Decker stands across the threshold.

I haven't seen him since that fateful walk to the *Seneca*, and now that I am here, the sight of his face takes me back to that night in the prison, to waiting behind bars, hope coursing through me.

A cry escapes my lips, and I move forward, throwing my arms around him in a fierce embrace as though we are old friends.

Twenty-Four

GRACE

Now that Evangelina Cisneros has landed in New York, our stories about her have only increased, the hours I spend at the *Journal* growing longer each day. There was little opportunity to speak with her on the day she landed, and given their prior history, George Bryson certainly had the claim to her. It was obvious, though, how nervous she was by the whole thing, and where I told myself I would be objective about the story, it's impossible to not feel sympathetic toward her plight.

Once she settled at the Waldorf-Astoria, there have been ample opportunities to interview her, and after spending hours speaking with her about her years in Cuba, she's given me a glimpse of the turmoil she's experiencing.

Tonight, though, I've slipped away from work to join my aunt Emma for our annual evening at the opera.

The Metropolitan Opera House is the new-money solution to a society problem. Located at Broadway and Thirty-Ninth Street, the opera house is more opulent and elegant than the Academy of Music favored by old Knickerbocker families like mine. When the new wealthy elites in the city couldn't secure private boxes at the Academy, they built this opera house that could seat over three thousand opera lovers with seventy private boxes to see and be seen, simultaneously creating a place for themselves in New York society and upstaging the old Academy, thus rendering its exclusivity void.

I like the opera well enough, but I come more for Aunt Emma. These outings serve as an opportunity for her to get her fill before she says that she's exhausted of the whole business and much prefers her brownstone apartments and friends who aren't part of Mrs. Astor's Four Hundred.

We dress for the opera, the occasion calling for me to wear one of the Worth gowns from my old life when my mother hoped I would marry well. The pink color suits a girl far younger than I am now, but the fabric is fine, and no one is really looking at me, anyway.

"Don't look now, Grace, but it appears you have an admirer," Aunt Emma whispers in my ear.

I only half pay attention, my focus on the opera and the soprano's soaring voice. "What are you talking about?"

"There's a man in one of the boxes across from us, and he cannot keep his eyes off of you. I don't think he's turned his attention to the stage once."

"He's probably someone who knew me before and is surprised to see me here considering how infrequently I come to these things," I whisper back, my attention on the stage. "Or he thinks I am someone else and is mistaken. You're missing the opera."

Aunt Emma waves me off. "The show taking place in front of me is far more interesting, I assure you. Besides, the performer they had in the role last week was much better."

A woman in the box next to us turns quite noisily and fixes us with a stare and an unspoken admonition to quiet down.

I wrench my attention back to the stage, the music swelling over me. I lean forward, tears filling my eyes.

I've never been particularly musical, as several piano teachers and one particularly beleaguered choral master can attest to, but there's something about the passion and emotion of the opera that draws me in every time. Perhaps it's the way human stories play out on a different stage from the one I live and work in.

Aunt Emma leans in to me once more. "He's very handsome, Grace."

I stifle the urge to roll my eyes. She means well, and I love her dearly, but I've never shared her interest in social intrigues—particularly when they're aimed at me.

"Perhaps he's looking at the next box over. The Davenport girl is the talk of the season."

"He's not looking at the Davenport girl."

She lifts her fan to wave to whatever man she's describing.

I turn my gaze to offer a silent apology to the poor gentleman she's decided to torment, who's probably just hoping to enjoy his night at the opera.

I nearly drop my opera glasses instead.

Rafael Harden is seated at the box across from ours.

I haven't seen him for months, not since that day at the Junta meeting, and Aunt Emma wasn't wrong—he isn't looking at the stage at all, but instead is studying me with his lips quirked in that smile of his that makes it hard to tell if he's laughing at me or not.

I incline my head in a nod of acknowledgment, my cheeks heating under his gaze. It feels strange seeing him out in society like this, his presence more suited to work and Junta meetings. This is a vestige of my old life, and one I'm not entirely used to sharing. I feel silly in the formal gown; the innocent pink color and floral pattern makes me feel more like a debutante than a journalist.

And then my gaze shifts, and I realize he isn't alone; a stunning blonde is seated beside him.

I duck my head, embarrassed to be caught staring.

Then again, I suppose he was staring first.

"Do you know who that is?" Aunt Emma whispers.

I nod, hoping Rafael's gaze is directed back to the stage and no longer trained on our box.

"They say he's richer than Croesus," she adds. "How did you meet?"

"He's a friend of Hearst's. He's at the office sometimes. He's given me information on a few stories."

"And here I worried you'd bury yourself in your work and not have time to meet a man. Is he a friend of yours?"

"We're acquaintances. Occasional friends," I add belatedly, feeling a bit uncharitable not acknowledging the strange friendship that has sprung up between us.

"We'll see him at intermission," she predicts.

"I doubt it. It's quite the crush tonight, and I'm sure others will want his company."

"Oh, he'll come," Aunt Emma replies. "No man looks at a woman like that unless he's set her in his sights."

"I hardly think . . ."

The words trail off as my eyes connect with Rafael's across the opera boxes.

He isn't looking at the stage at all; he's looking at me, and there's a faint smile on his lips as though he knows every single thing Aunt Emma and I were just saying about him.

DESPITE MY NUMEROUS ATTEMPTS TO CONVINCE AUNT EMMA that I'd really rather stay in my seat for the intermission, she won't take no for an answer, and we mill around with the other guests while she says hello to the odd acquaintance and friend. I asked her once why she only comes out in society a few times a year considering she seems to enjoy it so much when she does, and she told me society was best enjoyed in small doses, an axiom I can't help but agree with.

"Grace."

I whirl around at the familiar sound of my name and come face-to-face with Rafael.

He stands in front of me, alone, impeccably attired in evening dress.

"Hello," I reply, feeling my cheeks flush slightly.

He doesn't respond immediately, but instead, his gaze completes a lazy perusal of my person, from the top of my head to the bottom of my shoes, which I belatedly remember are nearly a size too small, a relic from my former life.

"I like the dress," he says by way of greeting, and I feel my flush deepening. "You look nice," he adds.

"You flatter me," I murmur, and he laughs at the hint of sarcasm in my voice.

But really, what woman wants to hear she looks "nice"? I doubt I could think of a more banal compliment, even if the dress hardly merits rhapsodies on how pleasing it is.

"How are you enjoying the opera?" I ask, trying not to glance over his shoulder, to get a better look at his companion.

He shrugs. "Well enough. I don't have to ask you how you're enjoying it, though. You wore your emotions on your face throughout the first act."

I can't think of a suitable response to *that*, so instead I say—

"I haven't seen you in months. Have you been in the city?"

Now that some of the initial surprise in seeing him here has passed, I take the opportunity to study him, much as he did me. He looks well, and his skin is definitely tanner than the last time I saw him, giving the impression that he has spent some time in the sun, in a more tropical climate.

"I've been in the city only rarely. I've spent some time in other climes."

So he continues running arms to Cuba.

"I stopped by the *Journal* offices between one of my trips," he adds. "I thought I might see you, but I didn't."

"I must have been out on a story. No one told me—"

"No. I didn't imagine they would." He takes a step closer to me. "Speaking of stories—are you here undercover? Should I have addressed you by another name?"

"No, the secrets of the opera house are safe—for now. There's little chance of me taking to the stage for some undercover assignment."

He laughs. "I think I'd pay to see that. If anyone could get to the heart of the opera house's secrets, it would be you."

Pleasure fills me even as I protest the veracity of his words. "You give me too much credit."

"Hardly. Is there such a thing as too much? I must admit, your exposés are the highlight of my day." He leans closer, a hint of brandy on his breath, his voice dropping to a stage whisper. "Don't tell Will, but I was a *Times* man until you started writing for the *Journal*."

I gape at him.

"I—"

"Aren't you going to introduce me?" Aunt Emma interjects, walking up beside me.

I close my eyes for a moment, hoping she doesn't embarrass me overly much. I love her dearly, and I know she means well, but she's comfortable in her own skin in a manner I aspire to yet haven't fully achieved, and I think it's difficult for her to understand that when you're still finding your place in the world, any attention drawn to you can often feel like too much.

"Rafael Harden, this is my aunt, Emma Van Housen."

"A pleasure," Rafael says smoothly, taking the outstretched hand she bestows to him like a queen before a courtier. Aunt Emma has an uncanny way of slipping on her position in society like an elegant cloak and then casting it off when she chooses to run with the artistic set.

Her eyes gleam. "So you're the gentleman who has been escorting Grace home at all hours of the night in that enormous black carriage of yours."

"Guilty as charged," Rafael answers smoothly. "I enjoy your niece's company very much."

"And just what exactly are your intentions toward her?" she asks, a teasing note in her voice.

Horror fills me. "Aunt Emma. Please."

Rafael's smile widens. "I believe we're embarrassing Grace."

He doesn't sound the least bit sorry about it, the bounder.

"We're friends," he adds, his tone mild.

Aunt Emma shoots me a sly look. "Hmph. That's what she said, too. You'll forgive me for not quite believing it. In my day, a man didn't look at a woman like you were staring at her throughout the opera if he didn't have a good reason."

Now, it seems it's Rafael's turn to look embarrassed, and as mortified as I am by the entire encounter, I'm at least mollified by the fact that he can't meet my gaze.

"Don't hurt her," she adds before swirling away in a cloud of her expensive perfume.

An uncomfortable silence surrounds us in her wake.

"My aunt has a vivid imagination," I say, struggling to fill the void. The last thing I want is for him to get the wrong idea about all of this, to think that I have designs on him. "She can be eccentric, too. I think she gets bored sometimes, and she can't resist stirring up a bit of trouble. She means well; she simply—"

"Grace. It's fine." Rafael leans down, taking my hand and pressing the faintest of kisses there. "It was nice to see you again."

He walks away, heading back to the blonde, leaving me staring after him, unraveling the encounter in my mind, not sure what just happened.

Twenty-Five

❧

MARINA

The summer of 1897 turns into fall, Weyler recalled to Spain. There are no more sightings of Mateo, and I assume he is back with the other revolutionaries. Luz and Isabella are relieved to hear that he is well and alive, but as the months pass, our relief dulls as this war seems no closer to ending. Whatever triumph I might feel in my part in the successful rescue of Evangelina is dampened by the conditions in Cuba. The death toll in the reconcentration camps keeps rising, the food supplies nearly nonexistent, my hope dwindling with each day my despair increases. In Havana, there have been demonstrations and protests decrying the United States in the wake of Evangelina Cisneros's escape from Recogidas. Some twenty thousand citizens have taken to the streets, professing their support for Spain.

It's difficult to understand how my countrymen can support Spain after all they've done to us. I often feel as though I must inhabit a different version of Cuba than they do, one where I see suffering and injustice everywhere I look and they turn their gaze away, eagerly supporting our oppressor. The Spanish have certainly done their part to stoke fear and division; when you control the news and regulate speech in a country you can shape reality however you see fit. And yet, are the camps not enough proof that Spain does not have our best interests at heart, that they are literally killing Cubans at an alarming rate with their cruel policies? How are we still so divided? How can two people look at something like Spain's absolute and cruel dominion over Cuba and see it so differently?

I was coming back from passing a message to a household sympathetic to the revolutionaries when one of the protests in favor of the Spanish passed me by, and I felt a wave of fury unlike any I've ever experienced before. The Spanish have burned my home to the ground, killed or seized the animals we raised for their own purposes, and forced so many Cubans into reconcentration camps. Do our lives, our loss, mean nothing to our countrymen who have not suffered a similar fate? What will it take for them to support us?

One afternoon, I return to the Hotel Inglaterra for another meeting with Carlos Carbonell. He's waiting for me in the same room as before, but this time he is alone.

"We were successful," Carlos says in greeting.

I've seen the newspapers strewn about Havana that carried the news of Evangelina's escape from Recogidas, but I've heard little about the fate of the rest of the men involved in her rescue.

"We were. Is everyone else safe?"

"They are. Decker is back in the United States."

"And Weyler is in Spain where he belongs," I reply, although in truth, given all he has done, the death that constantly surrounds me in the camp, I'd rather see him in hell.

"He is. Hopefully, it is the first step to bringing about change in Cuba." Carlos motions to a velvet bag beside him. "I brought you something—a thank-you for helping us."

"I can't—"

"You can," he replies, his voice gentle. "It is only right. We couldn't

have gotten her out of prison without your help. We all owe her freedom to you. You risked a great deal."

"It's no different than what you did."

"I have less to lose," Carlos replies. "You have a family?"

"I do."

"I thought you might. I remember the scandal awhile back. Your
parents said little about it, but the rumor was that you had married."

"I did."

"Are you happy in your marriage?"

"Very much."

"I'm happy to hear that for you. That man the last time we met
here—the one you were standing with in the hall—there was something between you. Love in your eyes and his. Was that your husband?"

"It was."

"And he is fine with you working as a courier?"

"It's complicated. But we're all doing our part for Cuba now, aren't
we?" I hesitate, and then I ask the question I have wondered about
since our paths crossed again. "Have you—did you tell my parents
that you saw me?"

"I didn't. Would you like me to?"

"No, I can't imagine that they would understand. We haven't seen
each other in many years, but from what I remember, their sympathies
were always with the Spanish."

"I think their sympathies are with whomever helps them retain
the life they are accustomed to. They'll have to adjust wherever the
tide turns in Cuba or they will be left behind in this new world we are
creating."

I don't disagree with his assessment of my family. My parents have
never been overly political, but then again, supporting the status quo
is a choice in and of itself.

"Is that why you fight for Cuba?" I ask him. "Because you think the world is changing and you want to move with it?"

"Perhaps. Is that why you do this? The courier work? You have to know how dangerous it is; they expelled Clemencia Arango from the country for it. Other women are in Recogidas."

"We're all risking something in Cuba at the moment. The reconcentrados are dying in the camp. The risk is worth it, if it means ending our suffering. Some days it feels like death breathes down my neck, whether it be from the disease and hunger in the camps or the risk of the Spanish branding me a spy. If I'm going to leave this world, I'd rather do it fighting for what I believe in."

"Your parents would help you if they knew you were among the reconcentrados. Your brother has grown into a fine man. I can't imagine he would want to see his sister brought so low."

"I made my choice a long time ago. There's no place for me in the life they live. As you said, Cuba is changing, and I must change with her. I can't pretend as they do that everything is fine. I want more for myself. For my family, for my daughter. For all of us. We deserve better than this country we have been given by the Spanish, deserve more than this life we're forced to lead."

"This money will help then. If you want to continue passing messages for me, I have work for you. As long as you're sure that this is what you want, that you understand the chance you're taking."

"I've been doing this for over a year now. I understand the dangers."

He holds the bag out to me.

I take it from him, pride be damned. We need it. I'll open it later and count the money, but every little bit will help.

"Why Evangelina?" I ask, the question sticking with me since the day they asked me to ferry a message to her. "Truly?"

"I told you before. I'd hoped it would get the Americans involved."

"It's frustrating though, because besides Weyler's recall, it feels like it achieved so little."

While I can't deny a personal sense of satisfaction that the architect of the reconcentration camps that have brought us so much misfortune is gone, this war has grown so much bigger than one man's cruelty.

"We saved an innocent woman's life," Carlos replies.

"We did. And I am grateful for that. I just wish we could do more, when there are so many innocents—children, no less—dying in the camps. No one is coming to save them."

No one is coming to save us.

"I can't argue with you. We must seem very mercenary in our interests to you. We wage a war with politics, and ideology, and strategy at the forefront, and it is easy to forget that ordinary people have been caught in the crossfire, that they're suffering on a scale the rest of us simply aren't. Most of us in Havana are shielded from the things you see on a daily basis, from what you are living. I can only hope that one day we will all be free, that Evangelina is just the beginning. She shares our passion for independence. She has sacrificed a great deal for Cuba's future, too."

"You admire her."

The emotion in his voice when he speaks of Evangelina is clear, the affection contained there evident.

"It is difficult not to admire her. She's smart, she's passionate, she's brave, and she's loyal."

Growing up, my father was close friends with Carlos Carbonell; as far as I know except for one near miss with marriage, he's always appeared to be the consummate bachelor. Now he looks like a man in love. That Evangelina Cisneros was able to capture his heart in such a short amount of time is quite the feat.

———————

ON MY WAY BACK TO THE CAMP, I STOP AT A MARKET AND USE the money Carlos gave me to buy extra food for Isabella and Luz.

There is little to be had, the destruction of the countryside affecting the food supply in the cities now, but I am able to find a bit of dried meat even if I pay dearly for it. It's been so long since my daughter has eaten meat; it's hard to believe that once we lived off the land we farmed and the animals we raised.

It's hard to believe that once we were happy.

I return to the camp, seeking out Luz and Isabella to share the good news of the food with them, but when I arrive another danger awaits me.

Twenty-Six

❧

EVANGELINA

On Saturday morning after I arrive in New York City, I dress in a long white gown that makes me feel like a princess. Karl Decker meets me at the Waldorf-Astoria and escorts me to a waiting carriage along with a woman from the Ladies' Cuban Relief Association of New York. Karl has visited me a few times since he first appeared on my doorstep, and I am reassured by his presence today. Throughout our journey, he turns and checks on me, asking me if I am all right and squeezing my hand.

A guard of soldiers and naval cadets in gleaming uniforms flanks me as I am paraded through the streets of New York City. Thousands line the streets cheering my name; I've never seen anything like it in all my life.

We stop at a large banquet room in an elegant restaurant called Delmonico's where I am asked to give a little speech in front of the august gathered crowd of Cuban patriots, American dignitaries, and *Journal* newspaper staff. The crowd rises to their feet when I walk into the room, their applause thunderous. As much as I struggle to find the right words to say, I fear I don't do justice to their kindness.

"You were wonderful," Karl says when I have finished speaking, and then he looks past me, his gaze settling on someone in the crowd, his smile deepening. "Ah, the man we all have to thank for your rescue." Karl waves the man over, and he walks toward us.

"Miss Cisneros," he says, introducing himself to me. "I'm Will Hearst."

For a moment, I am unable to speak. I have spent so much time in the company of *Journal* reporters, but this is the first time I've had the pleasure of meeting the man who did so much to secure my release. He is younger than I imagined, and handsome to boot.

Mr. Hearst extends his hand to me.

Emotion fills me. "Sir. I cannot thank you enough for all you have done for me, for saving my life."

He doesn't speak, but he nods in response, taking my hand and shaking it.

Before I can open my mouth to speak again, he has taken his leave from us and is gone as quickly as he came, leaving me staring after his retreating back.

"I wish I could have said more to him," I whisper to Karl. "He must think me ungrateful for all of his efforts on my behalf."

"No, that's just Will. He's happy to take the glory for his paper, but he hates being in the limelight." Karl clasps my hand. "Come on, we'll be late for the event at Madison Square."

A group of soldiers, sailors, and policemen in uniform escort me up on the stage at Madison Square where a large crowd has been gathering for quite some time now.

I've never had so many people staring back at me in all my life.

A cheer rises through the crowd as I walk up on the stage, and I feel the rumble of it in my bones as I look out at the sea of faces. There must be thousands of people here—tens of thousands. I knew when I saw my face on the New York papers that many people would hear my story, but seeing this is a different thing altogether. How much power must Mr. Hearst have, that he can draw such a crowd from the stories he publishes? And what could that power do for Cuba to have all of these voices united in her defense?

I wave my handkerchief in the air, the cheers growing impossibly louder.

How did I go from dancing in a simple courtyard with my sisters to this? I'm not sure I'll ever understand what it is about my story that's garnered so much attention. There are so many who are fighting for their freedom that it seems a bit wrong that I am being celebrated for doing so little in comparison, but hopefully this mobilizes the Americans to support us. It is hard to not look out at this sea of people and dream that this enthusiasm might carry us to independence.

Karl stands beside me onstage looking handsome and strong, and then he gives me a little push forward as though eschewing the attention for himself and centering it all on me.

Fireworks explode in the air, their bright colors dazzling. The band plays the Cuban national anthem, the sound bringing tears to my eyes.

When will the Cuban flag fly over Havana? When will we be free?

Twenty-Seven

GRACE

All of New York City is enthralled by Evangelina Cisneros. For her part, she seems a little dazed by it all.

She has become a unifying force for the Cuban exile communities in the United States. There are rallies and parades in her honor all over the country; women's clubs are renamed to pay tribute to her. This celebration at Madison Square is the largest outdoor public reception since the end of the Civil War. There must be seventy-five thousand people in the crowd this evening, an impressive number even if it is short of Hearst's goal of one hundred thousand attendees.

The park is the perfect location for this gathering, surrounded by stately buildings, its proximity close to the theater district, Madison Square Garden, the headquarters of the Democrats and the Republicans, and Delmonico's.

Above the Worth monument, the *Journal* has erected an enormous electric sign with a message of welcome for Evangelina.

Hearst organized this celebration with the precision and passion of a mother marrying her daughter off to a supreme catch. Then again, who would expect less from a man who loves and appreciates the theater as much as Hearst does?

I hang back in the crowd watching as Evangelina stands onstage next to her noble rescuer, Karl Decker, who has been firmly cemented as the hero of the tale, his bravery and daring lauded in terms as though he is a courtly knight avenging a fair maiden. Beyond the tales of chivalry printed in black ink, there are rumors that Karl and Evangelina are more than appearances seem, and from what I saw the day he visited her at the Waldorf-Astoria, it's clear they are close. I can't help but wonder what his long-suffering wife thinks of the whole business, if she is worried they are carrying on the torrid affair critics hint at, if it pains her to see her husband standing beside such a beautiful young woman while the world heaps praise upon them, adding insult to injury.

And what woman could compare to the paragon we have created in Evangelina? Can the real Evangelina even measure up to this caricature of herself?

The *Journal* gushes about her poise, her beauty, the fact that she's familiar with the works of Victor Hugo. One hundred thousand coins have been minted with her profile and the Cuban coat of arms. Who could live up to such a lofty standard?

While Evangelina is celebrated in New York, in Cuba, they now estimate that half a million people have perished at the hands of the Spanish.

The Spanish prime minister gave a scathing interview about Evangelina's rescue, deriding the American government for being less powerful than the newspapers. It was likely intended to be a criticism, but for Hearst, I'm not sure there is higher praise one can give.

I stand near the back of the crowd, pen and paper in hand, jotting down my observations of her for both the book we're working on together and one of the many articles I'm sure I will write commemorating the occasion.

Despite all of the conversations we've had now, I still haven't figured out what to make of Evangelina. I like her; I think it is impossible not to with her easy manner, but there are layers that leave me feeling as though I've merely scratched the surface. She is both the ingenue others imagine her to be and someone who has shown immense political savvy.

I wouldn't call us friends, yet. Despite the moments when we speak, my role as a journalist too often invites her to put up her guard. If things were different between us, would we be friends in another life?

Perhaps.

The sound of footsteps comes up behind me, and then I am greeted by a familiar hint of cologne.

I stiffen, the memory of that mortifying night at the Metropolitan Opera House rushing back to me.

He settles beside me, without a greeting, his gaze like mine fixed on the stage in front of us.

"So this is the face Will hopes will launch a thousand ships," Rafael muses.

I smile at the apt comparison. "Something like that."

"She's not quite what I expected. Will's paper makes her sound like a delicate flower, but there's some steel in that spine."

"There would have to be, wouldn't there? To survive what she's been through. Decker says she came up with the plan for her escape entirely on her own," I murmur to Rafael, careful to keep from speaking too loudly lest anyone overhear us. "They couldn't figure out how to get her out, so apparently they sent her a note with the hope they'd get some ideas. Instead, she sent them a detailed plan and a diagram."

Rafael laughs. "I'd have liked to see their faces when they opened that. Well, she'd better be ready for the fuss that's being drummed up.

Every reporter in the city is digging into her past right now, trying to find something to discredit her story."

Pulitzer already sent me two notes at my aunt's house asking for a meeting, which I promptly ignored. For better or worse, my loyalties now lie with the *Journal*.

"That's the problem with putting someone on a pedestal," Rafael adds. "No one can live up to those expectations."

I study Evangelina carefully onstage. As closely as she and Karl stand together and given the obvious intimacy between them, the rumors about the true nature of their relationship likely won't be put to bed. I can't help but feel badly for her, for how much of her life has been defined by others' actions, for the fact that she must now pretend to be the version of herself that we all have created.

"She's young," I say. "She's alone. Her father's been imprisoned for years, her family torn apart by this war. The conditions of the prison where she was held are indisputably wretched. Her story is interesting enough without all of this." I wave my hands around me, gesturing at the spectacle.

"Will does like his fireworks."

"He does. But sometimes I worry that we lose sight of the subject of our stories when we sensationalize them. I don't think any publisher works as hard as he does. He's passionate about the news, about the stories we cover. I know there are those who say he's just in it for the money or to increase the paper's circulation, but I don't know if I believe that anymore. There's something quixotic about him. But that can be dangerous, too."

"As it happens, I agree with you. Will's going to change the world or die trying."

"I rather thought that was a politician's job," I say dryly. "Perhaps if he is so intent on reshaping the world order, he misses seeing things

as they are rather than as he would make them. Evangelina is smart.
She wouldn't have escaped the prison if she wasn't. If you listen to her
story—there were multiple times when she convinced the Spanish to
be lenient with her father throughout his imprisonment. It was her
desire to ask for American citizenship when she came here because she
understood that it would offer her some protection. Why don't we
celebrate that as opposed to presenting her as this helpless victim in
need of rescue when she's clearly able to rescue herself?"

"Will is very good at understanding what the public wants and
giving it to them. They're drawn to the salacious stories; to the dramatic rescues and the damsels in distress. People might want to be
informed when they read the news, but they also want to be enter-
tained. You don't know what it's like to spend twelve hours working
in a factory somewhere, body aching, worrying about every damn
thing. When you read the news, you don't want to read about every
arcane policy disagreement. You want to *feel*. That's how you win the
people." He gestures toward Evangelina. "I have a feeling she understands that, too."

There is something in the manner in which she plays to the crowd
even as she seems overwhelmed by the attention, the different versions
of her that don't quite seem to line up.

"People like you and me," Rafael continues. "We see things for
what they are, and we appreciate the simplicity of them. We're realists.
She and Will are made for this in a way.

"For you, truth is the end. You have a firmly seated sense of justice
that I imagine is very difficult to shake." He shrugs. "Problem with
that is justice means different things to different people. Same with
truth. Will's learned that and how to use it to his advantage. You're
still grappling with which side of things you want to be on."

I gape at him, unsure of how to respond. It's easy to view him through a shallow lens, but I recognize how false that is when he hits on something I hadn't quite worked out myself.

"The right side, of course," I reply.

He smiles, and for a moment, I wonder if he's one of the first people in a long time to truly see me.

"Speaking of—has Will dashed off already?" Rafael asks me, changing subjects. "I thought his French motorcar was out front at Delmonico's."

The first of its kind in New York, Hearst's motorcar is legendary in a city where everyone flaunts their wealth and status for all the world to see.

"He has. Everyone looked a little bewildered by the fact. I think they expected the man who demands fireworks to make a little more of a spectacle of himself."

Rafael laughs. "Not his style. It's a shame, though. I was hoping I'd run into him."

He's silent for a beat, and then almost as an aside, he says—

"You look beautiful tonight."

Now I'm quite simply gobsmacked. He's never paid me such an extravagant compliment before, and considering this dress isn't particularly fine, I wouldn't have expected this to be the moment he chose to do it.

"Thank you." And then because I can't help myself, I add—"That's quite a step up from 'nice.'"

He laughs. "If I'd told you you're the most stunning thing I've ever seen, you would have accused me of flattery and dismissed the compliment. Maybe I'm working up to the truth."

"I thought the truth means different things to different people," I say, feeling more than a bit faint.

What is happening to me? Why am I flirting with Rafael?

"Are you going to the reception after this?" he asks me, his gaze once again trained to the stage so all I can make out is his profile.

Hearst has reserved the grand ballroom at Delmonico's at Fifth Avenue and Twenty-Sixth Street for a more intimate and formal event celebrating Evangelina.

"Of course. I'm to document all of this," I reply, gesturing to my notepad and pen. "Hearst has me working on her life story as well."

"He told me."

I never imagined they would talk about me.

"He likes you," Rafael adds, leaving me further caught off guard in a conversation where I largely feel out to sea. "Says you're ambitious, that you aren't afraid to go after what you want. He thinks you're talented, too. A natural."

"I never realized. He's never said."

Rafael shrugs. "Will isn't like the rest of us. Sometimes I think he forgets what it feels like to be a mere mortal."

He's silent for a moment. "It's a hard business, isn't it?"

I nod, beyond mortified by the lump forming in my throat. The fact that Hearst thinks I'm talented, those few words delivered by Rafael, mean more than he can probably ever know. When I first envisioned becoming a reporter, I had glamorous visions of exposing society's ills for the world to see. The reality is that I exist on tenterhooks, waiting to see if this will be the story that gives me a chance to make a name for myself, or if today is the day I'll be called into the editor's office and let go.

For each story that one of Hearst's star reporters gets, the thousands of dollars they are paid to dash off to Cuba or the like, the more this jealousy that I am hardly proud of grows; the fear that it will never be my name on everyone's lips is overwhelming. It's not supposed to be about the fame or the glory; it's supposed to be about the stories we write and the public's interest to be informed, but it is impossible to walk this tightrope of a career and not fear obscurity for that is our death knell. The truth is, as much as we work together in close quarters, the competition is fierce, and there's a thread of desperation in all of us that pushes us to take whatever risks necessary to get the story.

"I admire you for doing what you do," Rafael says without a hint of teasing in his voice. He leans down, closing the distance between us. "I particularly liked your exposé of the landlord," he whispers.

The story I wrote about a thieving landlord ran in the paper a month or so ago and was another stunt job I took on at Hearst's behest.

"How did you—"

Rafael is gone before I can finish asking him how on earth he figured out that it was my story when I used a pen name on the byline.

Twenty-Eight

✦

EVANGELINA

After the whirlwind that is the reception at the Waldorf-Astoria, I travel from New York City to Washington D.C., for a special reception for me and Karl where I am to meet President McKinley.

I am excited to see the town where Karl is from, considering all he has done for me, and am more than a bit nervous to meet the American president. I've practiced over and over again what I want to say if I'm given the opportunity. I am here because of my story, but I am also Cuban, and my people desperately need my help.

We drive onto the beautiful grounds of the White House, and the closer we get, the more my nerves grow.

I remember the conversations my father had with me growing up, the legacy of revolution that runs through my veins. I am representing my family and my country, and it feels as though this is too big of an opportunity for me to squander. What if America could intervene against Spain as they have for me? If they directed the support they've given me to the Cuban people, then I can't imagine Spain would stand a chance.

"The president is very excited to meet you," Mrs. Logan whispers, squeezing my hand. She's become my frequent companion and also a wonderful friend. "There's no need to be nervous; despite his position, he really is an unassuming man. And very kind."

Grace sits across from us in the carriage.

"There's truly nothing to be nervous about," Grace reassures me. "After all, you've faced off against the Spanish. President McKinley should be tame in comparison."

I smile at the teasing note in her voice. We've struck up a friendship of sorts in the weeks we've spent together. I will truly miss her companionship when I leave to tour the country to tell my story, and hopefully raise funds and awareness for the fight for independence.

I've finished my part of the book over the course of a few conversations with Grace, and now she's writing it all down, including events like this one and the reception at Madison Square. It feels strange that a story of my life should end at twenty years old, as though I will forever be defined by this one part of my life. I wish I could have ended the story with something inspiring, a grand triumph, me returning home to a free Cuba, but there is so much that is uncertain right now.

This is to be a smaller reception than the one Hearst had for me in New York, but I think the very intimacy of it almost makes it more frightening. There's anonymity to be had in a crowd of people, at least. Still, perhaps it will give me a greater opportunity to advocate for American assistance for Cuba.

The carriage pulls up in front of the White House, and we are escorted to one of the reception rooms where we are to meet President McKinley. Everything is so grand in this country—at least to me. Grace and Mrs. Logan seem perfectly at home despite the formal circumstances.

"You'll wait here for the president," the usher tells us.

I try to remember my lessons on comportment that now feel like they were a lifetime ago, keeping my back straight and head held high. I still my hands, the desire to fidget running through me. I have become so many different versions of myself these last few months, years even, that I scarcely recognize which one is truly me: the young girl who stayed up late speaking to her father about politics, the woman who cared for him, who fought for his freedom, the woman who was loved by Emilio Betancourt, the notorious prisoner, the saint, the Most Beautiful Girl in Cuba.

All I know is that I have certainly come a long way from Recogidas.

Karl moves up beside me, his presence instantly calming me. I can't imagine what I would do without his friendship. In addition to being my rescuer, he is one of the few people in this country who truly understands what I have been through. He saw the prison and the conditions we lived in. Without him, I might be halfway to Ceuta by now.

"Are you nervous?" he whispers.

I nod.

He flashes me a devastating smile. He certainly looks handsome today.

"Just be your wonderful self and you'll capture their hearts as you have the rest of America," he says.

I flush. "You're too kind to me."

"Just being honest."

I've heard the whispers about us, the insinuation that there is something more between me and Karl than mere friendship, even though he is a married man. Maybe there's affection in his eyes when he looks at me, but when you've been through an experience like we have, you'll always have a special connection. I count myself lucky to be his friend.

The whispers, though, are dangerous to my future. The American people love me now because they see me as some paragon of virtue, but should my reputation become besmirched, I doubt they would support me as they have.

As much as I am grateful to be free, I wish nothing more than to return home, to the life I had with my father and sisters, when we were happy and I knew nothing of the things one hears in the dark moments of night in a place like Recogidas.

I am not the girl they want me to be. You cannot see the things I have seen or live them and be the innocent they all toast.

It is an elaborate fairy tale, and everyone looks to me to play my part.

Karl reaches out and surreptitiously takes my hand, the folds of the skirt of my gown hiding the motion from view. He links our fingers for a moment and squeezes, as though he can transfer some of his strength to me.

He releases me as quickly as he clasped my hand.

An announcement fills the reception room—

"The president!"

President McKinley walks into the room.

His demeanor seems kind, and something about his manner puts me at ease. He looks every inch the gentleman.

Mrs. Logan takes my hand and, amazingly, presents me to the president as though there is some honor in making my acquaintance.

I open my mouth to thank him for all his country has done for me, to tell him of how dire the situation is in Cuba, and how much we could use the Americans' help against Spain, but the moment overwhelms me, the words rushing through my head. I feel as though I am floating, hovering above my body, watching someone else take my place.

"On behalf of the women and children of Cuba, who are helpless

at the moment, I implore the government of the United States to protect them. The men are left to their own devices as they wage war in
the fields, but the women and children are the victims of the horrible
atrocities going on. The women and children in Cuba are on their
hands and knees begging you to help them."

The president gives a faint nod at my words and moves on with a
smile, Grace behind me, scribbling down more notes on her pad.
Sometimes the more I talk, the more I think she sees through the
mask I have cultivated, that she understands in a way maybe no one
else does, not even Karl. For he wears the role of protector with joy, as
though it is a mantle he adopts proudly. But for us women, everything
is more complicated. We choose the faces we must wear out of necessity, and I have a feeling Grace, who keeps her head down living in
other people's lives, knows a thing or two about that.

After my official presentation to President McKinley, we are led
to yet another reception—the first of many in my future. Mr. Hearst
plans for me to travel the country, speaking to the different groups
who have supported my cause.

When George Eugene Bryson told me that his employer had
taken an interest in my cause, that they were going to see me released
from prison, I never envisioned this being the outcome—me touring
the country, telling my story, reliving that night with Berriz. He has
made me famous, a rallying cry, and the part of this that sees me cast
as a victim hasn't settled well with me. Sometimes I wonder if I will
ever truly be free of what Berriz did to me that night if I am constantly
having to perform my pain for others.

After I meet the president, I am presented to another crowd who
cheers as Karl introduces me, and I'm not sure I'll ever get used to the
sound, or the way they look at me as though they expect something
profound to escape from my lips. My English has improved since I

first landed in New York, but I lack the ability to speak without re-serve, or maybe given the unusual circumstances, I'd feel the same in Spanish.

I am a performer on a stage, playing the role of a lifetime: as myself.

All I can hope is that the affection and goodwill that they show me will also extend to Cuba.

Twenty-Nine

MARINA

"We must talk about Isabella," Luz says to me one night in the fall as I lie on my pallet on the ground beside her, watching my daughter sleep. Every so often Isabella coughs, her body rattling with the effort, and it takes everything inside me to keep from screaming in frustration at the sense of helplessness that her sickness has been plaguing her for weeks now, and it's not getting better.

"She's ill," Luz says.

"I know," I reply, not taking my eyes off my sleeping daughter's form. "I've been saving some of the money I've made to see if I can get her medicine."

Everything is expensive in Cuba now, the effects of the destruction of so much of our agricultural capability being felt even in the city. I've done as much as I can with the money Carlos gave me as thanks for doing my part to help Evangelina, but it only stretches so far, and we need more.

"I know you have. I've seen how little you're eating to make up the difference, but you must know by now that it's not enough. She's not getting better, and with all of the disease in this camp, the dead bodies, she doesn't have a chance of it, either."

I squeeze my eyes shut, trying to hold back tears. I told Mateo I would keep our daughter safe, and I've already failed her. I'm supposed to be her mother, supposed to protect her, and no matter what I do, it doesn't feel like it's enough. She deserves so much better than the horrible conditions in which we are living. We all do. But this war continues on, and we are still not free.

"I can't lose her," I whisper, reaching out to stroke Isabella's hair. She looks so much like her father. "I can't."

"We need to get her out of here," Luz replies. "She needs to be somewhere safe where she can receive proper medical treatment and where she has a hope of recovery. Her odds of survival in these conditions are too low."

She doesn't say the rest of it, but then again, she doesn't have to. In my most desperate moments, I've considered going to my family and asking them to take my daughter. The war has barely touched them, and they have the power and money to take care of Isabella.

I can't imagine being parted from her.

I can't imagine going back to that house and asking for help after I left with such finality years ago.

I can't lose her.

"I don't know that they would be willing to help. When I chose to marry Mateo, they said that I was dead to them. They've never met her. They don't even know I have a daughter. What am I to do, show up on their doorstep and ask them to care for her?"

"It is the best chance she has," Luz replies. "I don't know them as well as you, of course, but I was always under the impression that for all of their faults, family was everything to them. Many things were said in anger when you made the choice to marry my son, but I cannot imagine they would abandon their only granddaughter. Especially if they knew she was living in these conditions."

She's right, of course. It is the best chance Isabella has. Even if I am afraid to risk them rejecting me once more. Even as my pride balks at the idea of returning to my family home and begging for them to acknowledge and care for my child. I don't regret the decision I made to marry Mateo and abandon the life I had as a Perez, nor do I wish for things to go back to the way they were. But as a mother, I cannot fathom not doing everything in my power to save my child's life.

And still—

"What if Isabella thinks I'm abandoning her?"

Our daughter has only me now. How will she feel if I leave her, too?

"One day, she will understand that you are doing the best you can to give her a better life. One where she will be healthy and safe. And whenever this nightmare ends, you will be there for her, to start over. These are impossible times, Marina. We're all doing the best we can. She'll understand that when the time comes."

Will she?

I look over at my daughter's sleeping form, the shallow rise and fall of her chest.

"They might not take her in."

"You won't know until you ask." Luz is silent for a moment. "I will miss her, too."

She reaches out and takes my hand once more, and I realize it's not just our love of Mateo and our family that unites us. We both know what it's like to have to give up a child in this war.

I stay up all night, long after Luz has gone to bed, watching Isabella sleep, praying she will survive.

THE NEXT MORNING, I DRESS ISABELLA CAREFULLY, MY HANDS trembling as I comb her hair, a memory filling me of my mother doing the same to me when I was Isabella's age. Her clothes are threadbare, her body slight from her illness and the lack of nutrition in the camp.

We catch a ride in a horse-drawn cart for most of the journey, and at the end of the block walk together to the big house, Isabella's hand clutched tightly in mine.

I haven't told her what we're doing, but she's a smart girl, and she must realize something is different about today. No doubt she registered the manner in which Luz hugged her a bit more tightly this morning, her fingers trembling as she caressed Isabella's cheek. All that has been forgotten, though, as Isabella gawks at her surroundings, the grand Perez mansion that is nothing like the simple houses near us in the country. It's easy to forget that she has not grown up as I have.

"They're just houses," I whisper. "It's all right."

"Who do you know who lives here? Who are we going to see?" Isabella asks me.

There's no privacy to be had in the camp, and I didn't dare speak of this to Isabella back there when all manner of people might be listening. For as quickly as she's had to grow up, she's still a child, and I've been loath to put the burden of subterfuge on her.

"We're going to see your grandmother," I whisper back. "Your other grandmother. My mother."

Isabella's eyes widen.

I've told her a bit about my background, but I suppose it's a different thing seeing the splendor for yourself.

We stop outside the enormous mansion, and I crouch so we are eye level.

"You have been so brave, Isabella. I wish you didn't have to face the things that you have, wish your father was with us, but I can't change the circumstances we live in. The camp is full of disease and death. I didn't think we had a choice when we came here, but I never imagined the conditions would be as bad as they are. So I want you to stay with my family for a while until everything gets better."

"No. I want to be with you. We're a family. We should stay together."

There's something about the stubborn tilt of her head that reminds me so much of me. When did that happen? It's as though somewhere along the way she went from a child to a young girl.

"I know." I struggle to keep my voice steady, to hold the tears at bay, to be strong for my child. "I want nothing more, either. But it's not safe in the camp. And you haven't been feeling well for a while. Your cough is getting worse. They'll take care of you."

I don't tell her my deepest fear—

You could die.

Tears fill her beautiful brown eyes, fear swimming there. I have asked her to endure so much, and now I worry I am breaking her heart by sending her away.

"Mami."

The sound of my name falling from her lips calls to something deep inside me, a yearning to take the pain threaded through her voice and bear it for her so she doesn't need to suffer.

I would give anything to take her hurt away.

I fight back the tears threatening to spill over my cheeks, summoning whatever strength I have left to make the unendurable somewhat easier for her. "I'll come see you when I can. We can write each other letters. It won't be long, I promise."

I reach out and wrap my arms around her, clasping her tight against me, smelling her scent, holding on to her for one last time.

In that scent, in her embrace, I am transported back in time to so many memories: the first time I felt her kick in my stomach, the movement catching me wholly off guard and filling me with an unspeakable joy; the first time I held her in my arms after she was born when I looked at her face and knew my heart was irrevocably hers; watching her first steps; drying her tears; the times when we were a family filled with laughter and happiness; these last few days when I have prayed and begged and watched over each sleep-filled breath and cough, willing to make any sacrifice, any concession to keep my daughter alive.

"I need you to be brave for me, Isabella. Just for a little bit longer. Things will be better soon. Do you remember what I told you that day by the Harbor when you asked about your father? If you feel afraid or if you miss us, I want you to pick a good memory and I want you to hold on to that."

She nods, tears spilling down her cheeks.

"I love you," I whisper.

"I love you, too."

"Did I ever tell you where your name comes from?" I ask her.

Isabella shakes her head, a cough rattling in her chest.

"In my parents' house, there's a painting of one of your ancestors. Her name was Isabella like you. When she was not that much older than you, she was shipped from a convent in Spain to come to Cuba and marry a man who was a stranger at the time. She arrived here alone, cut off from her family, her homeland, and she set out to make a new life for herself. She was brave, and she was strong, and she fought for what she believed in. She and her husband built the house my parents live in. They had children and lived happily together for many years. I always admired her story—her strength and courage. I named you after her. No matter what happens, never forget that her blood runs through your veins. Never forget that you are strong, and that you can face anything that comes your way. Whenever you doubt yourself, whenever you are alone, remember who you are."

When Isabella was born and I held her in my arms the first time, staring down at her little face, at the miracle Mateo and I made, I couldn't imagine ever being parted from her. I swore I wouldn't make the same mistakes my parents had made, that I would love her and protect her no matter what. And even as I know this is the right thing to do, the best thing for her, it is impossible to not feel as though I am responsible for her tears.

Have I failed her?

Isabella pulls back first, wiping at the tears on her cheeks. Her skin is splotchy from crying, her eyes red, and the expression on her face haunts me. She looks so alone in this moment. She has been forced to grow up so quickly.

What sort of childhood is this?

We have lost so many children in the camps, their little bodies dumped in the death carts. Such a loss has become a common occurrence now, grief clouding our daily lives. There's no denying I am fortunate to have this opportunity to save my daughter that many others don't.

With one last hug and a kiss on the cheek, I rise and walk with her through the enormous entry gates to the estate, grateful they are open and I am spared having to ask to be let in.

Some of the gardeners are out working, and they cast a few curious glances our way, but I keep walking, Isabella's hand clutched in mine as we near the front entrance.

We stop when we arrive at the house, and I take a deep breath before reaching out and knocking on the door, Isabella coughing beside me.

A minute later, it opens, and our longtime housekeeper, Carmela, stands on the other end.

For a moment, she looks through me as though she doesn't recognize me, her mouth open as though she is about to send me away or redirect me to the servants' entrance, and then her eyes widen with awareness.

"Marina!"

"Carmela."

I step forward and wrap my arms around her, the familiar weight of her body a comfort. She looked after me when I was a little girl, provided sanctuary in a house where there was often disharmony between my parents. She raised me and my brother Arturo as much as my mother or father did, likely more so, and I've thought of her often through the years, missing her dearly.

When I finally pull back, her gaze shifts from me to Isabella.

A little gasp escapes Carmela's mouth.

"And who is this?" she asks, her voice gentle.

"This is my daughter, Isabella."

Carmela's eyes fill with tears. "She looks just like you did when you were a little girl. She's beautiful."

Isabella steps forward and greets her as I've taught her, and I can't miss the flash of worry in Carmela's eyes as she takes in the sight of my daughter. I've grown so used to life in the camps that our appearances don't shock me anymore, but the contrast between the way we've been living and the enclave of wealth this house and my parents' position provides is stark.

"I'd like to see my mother," I say. "Is she home?"

CARMELA LEADS US NOT TO THE GRAND SITTING ROOM WHERE MY parents entertain guests, but rather to the smaller, more private salon we've always used for family gatherings. We've celebrated many a Christmas in this room, and for a moment, the memories of all of our special occasions flood me, and it is as if I have been transported back in time.

Isabella appears dazed by the furnishings, and I squeeze her shoulder reassuringly. "You'll be fine.

"Is my brother here?" I ask.

Arturo and I were never particularly close, but I've missed him over the years, and often wondered if he has married or had children of his own. It's strange to be so disconnected from one's family, to share blood with them and yet know so little about them. Have they thought of me over the years or when I left to marry Mateo was I simply written off, my name stricken from the family Bible?

"Your brother and your father are at work," Carmela replies, her gaze understanding. She's a trusted family member, and she's privy to all of the goings-on of the house, including the details of my estrangement from my family. "Arturo will be sad that he missed you, I think."

She opens her mouth as though there is more she wants to say, but all she offers is a—

"Let me tell your mother you're here."

Isabella and I sit beside each other on the green silk settee after Carmela leaves.

Nerves fill me, but between my mother and father, my mother is the easier, more sympathetic choice.

I hear her before I see her, the sound of her heels clicking against the floor a familiar noise from my childhood.

I rise slowly, steeling myself for the moment I've imagined, and then she's standing in front of me.

She's still as beautiful as she always was, and despite the years since we've seen each other, she looks so much as I remember. I see pieces of myself and Isabella in her—our eyes, the shape of our face, our mouths.

Her eyes widen slightly as they rest on me, drifting to Isabella seated behind me.

I can only imagine her impressions of me. The daughter who left home at seventeen is now twenty-seven years old, and yet, I'm sure I look worn-out and tired, far older than I should.

My mother looks and smells like wealth and security, whereas I wear all of my losses like a badge of honor I couldn't remove even if I wanted to.

I didn't expect a dramatic reunion. My mother isn't the type to descend into theatrics. Rather, her fingers drift to the ostentatious pearl necklace that was her mother's as they always do when she's nervous. The familiar gesture brings a wave of emotion I hardly expected.

"Marina. What a surprise." Her gaze settles on Isabella once more.

"This is my daughter, Isabella. She's eight."

My mother simply nods, her fingers stroking the pearls, her gaze on Isabella, and I feel a pang of guilt at having sprung this on her and not having had the opportunity to prepare her properly.

"We've been living in a reconcentration camp," I continue. "We were forced out of our home by Weyler's edict."

My mother flinches.

"Isabella's sick," I add. "The situation there is dire. Please take her in. I am afraid for what will happen if she stays there."

My mother is silent for a beat, and then she nods smoothly as though I have given her a simple request like adding another guest to her dinner party.

"Of course. She can stay in your room. I'll have Carmela prepare it for her right now."

Tears fill my eyes. As a mother, the desire to be strong for Isabella is paramount. But standing before the woman who gave birth to me, for a moment, I'm a child again, and the sensation undoes me.

"Thank you," I reply.

"Is there anything else you need?" my mother asks, and in the silence that follows, I wonder if she's hinting that there's a path home for me, too.

I shake my head.

She hesitates, as though she might say something else, but in the end she merely nods. "Let me tell Carmela she'll be joining us. She'll be back in a moment to escort Isabella upstairs."

I turn to Isabella, who looks so small and alone in this room. Her eyes are wide as she struggles to process each change being thrown her way.

I give her another hug, pressing a kiss to her brow. "You'll be fine," I whisper. "Your grandparents will be kind to you, and Carmela will love you. She raised me when I was a little girl. You can meet my brother, your uncle. And I'll be back for you when I can. I promise."

Carmela reenters the room a moment later and takes Isabella by the hand, a kind smile on her face.

"Your mother's room is lovely. Just as she left it. You'll have the best view of the garden, too." She puts her arm around Isabella's shoulders, and with my daughter's back to me, Carmela hands me a bundle, which I take from her wordlessly.

After Carmela has led Isabella away, after I've walked out of the house I grew up in, my head held high, a bundle of food in my hands that I don't know whether she or my mother thought to have sent to me from the kitchen, the tears begin to fall until my body is wracked with sobs.

As difficult as it was turning my back on my family years ago, as much pain as I felt when I sent Mateo off to war, this is something else entirely.

My heart is broken.

Thirty

❦

GRACE

At the *Journal,* we celebrate the extraordinary successes of 1897 in our own exuberant fashion.

They say no one throws a party like Hearst, and based on the spectacle before me, I'm inclined to agree.

Tonight we ring in the new year of 1898 as well as celebrate Brooklyn, Staten Island, and sections of Queens and the Bronx becoming incorporated into Greater New York, nearly doubling the population to almost three and a half million people, and making New York the second-largest city in the world after London.

I bundle deeper into my coat, the vicious chill battering me as the wind burns my cheeks. And still, despite the elements, I wouldn't have missed this for anything.

Once again, Hearst has proven that the *Journal* acts. The celebration itself had been a point of contention between all of the city's interested parties, until Hearst swooped in in his own inimitable fashion and proposed the *Journal* fund and organize the event in addition to the Christmas dinner we hosted for five thousand of the *Journal*'s newsboys. After all, it's been quite the year. Our paper is cited by members of Congress when they speak on the floor regarding the situation in Cuba. Evangelina Cisneros's saga has launched the paper in a new direction, her face immortalized on the cover of our paper standing next to President McKinley. Hearst has taken every opportunity to capitalize on her story as she tours the United States speaking to various groups, rallies, and parades thrown in her honor in an attempt to garner support for Cuban independence.

He published the book of her account of her life and rescue that I helped write. My name was never mentioned as a contributor, and the woman on the pages is more identifiable as a saint than a human being, the words I wrote with her eventually rewritten and altered by numerous other editors and authors until I hardly recognized them myself. Just as much of her life has been co-opted by the press, the words contained there were no longer hers or mine, but a carefully and elaborately curated attempt to shape public opinion. I was angry about it at first and sent a letter with my apologies to Evangelina, but in her response she seemed resigned to the whole affair. If working for Hearst has taught me anything, it's to give the people what they want.

Tonight is no exception.

For the past few weeks, we've raided the coffers of the city's most influential men asking for donations for the New Year's event and we've solicited the participation of every marching band and civic group in the city for a parade from Union Square to City Hall, where the celebration culminates in the spectacle before me. There were prizes for the best floats, more fireworks than I can count, and the parade itself was billed as celebrating the unity and diversity of New York City. The *Journal* offices are ablaze with colored lights and illuminations and an oblong square arranged in stars and stripes.

Everything has been choreographed to perfection, except, of course, the one thing that even Hearst could not bend to his will:

The weather.

Rain falls heavily, the cold converting it into the occasional snowfall.

We briefly considered postponing but decided against it. It was the right call.

The weather hasn't affected the crowds one bit. They came early and in droves. There must be a hundred thousand people here.

Mr. Hearst has taken this city, and all of its dirt and grime and misery and defeat, and transformed it with a flick of his elegant wrist.

And, of course, because he *is* Hearst, advertisements encouraging people to read the *Journal* are everywhere you turn.

The air pulses with magic, a heady excitement that spreads like contagion throughout the crowd as if for one night the entire city is on tenterhooks to discover what possibility awaits them in the new year. In this spectacle, this absurd, overly indulgent, perfect night, Hearst has given the people the essence of what the Four Hundred tried so desperately to manufacture in their drafty ballrooms. Tonight, out here beneath the exploding lights, is the beating heart of New York City, and I doubt there is a person among us who at this moment isn't imagining all that could be if fortune would just turn its favor upon them.

Children laugh around me, their legs pumping as they run past to see whatever singular amusement is up ahead. Their parents call behind them, their voices laced with good-natured humor, the glee and wonder contagious. We exist in a sea of umbrellas, the elements be damned.

My fingers reach instinctively in my coat pocket for the pad of paper and pencil I keep there, the desire—need—to etch these moments into memory too powerful a lure to resist. I don't trust my own ability to recall them, the champagne I've drunk altering my senses and loosening my limbs.

"I think I'd give up my entire fortune just to hear your thoughts right now."

I whirl around at the familiar voice, at the confidence injected in each syllable that seems intrinsic to breathing.

Rafael stands before me wearing another impeccably tailored coat, his hands shoved in his pockets.

"Your entire fortune? I find that very hard to believe. I assure you my thoughts aren't worth nearly that much."

"I suppose we'll have to agree to disagree. After all, it's entirely in the eye of the beholder."

Despite the cold, warmth seeps into my bones.

He takes a quick, sure step, and suddenly, we are no more than a breath apart. Rafael lowers his voice as though we are coconspirators sharing a secret. "Perhaps half, then. You're right—I'm entirely too mercenary to give up everything."

It takes everything in me to keep from retreating. He's the sort of man that, if you cede an inch, will try for a mile.

And yet, he's the one who ultimately takes a step back, putting distance between us once more even as his gaze turns speculative.

"Why does it feel like every time I see you, whatever progress we've made has been erased?" he asks.

"Progress?" I echo.

I haven't seen him since Evangelina Cisneros's reception at Madison Square.

He smiles. "Our friendship, Grace."

"I didn't realize we were making progress," I lie.

"You wound me."

I barely stifle a snort. "I find that very unlikely."

"And yet, true."

I can't quite formulate a proper retort to that one.

"Would you like to walk together?" he asks. "Moving is probably our best ward against the cold."

I nod, surprising myself.

As we walk, the weather hardly registers, the atmosphere far too magical for such sensibilities. Even though I was privy to much of the planning for tonight's event, I still can't help but be a little dazzled by it as everyone else is.

City Hall Plaza is lit up with magnesium lights.

A firework fills the night sky. You can barely hear the choral singers over the sound of the other entertainments.

"What if I told you I wished to be something other than your friend?" Rafael asks unexpectedly, stopping me in my tracks.

I gaze up at him, waiting for the witty rejoinder, or a teasing note to fill the air, but his expression is hooded, and I can't decipher if it's amusement or something else in his eyes.

"You're joking."

"I'm not joking."

It takes far longer than it should for me to formulate a response.

"I'm flattered," I say carefully. "I am sure you are quite the catch."

His lips curve, amusement filling his gaze.

"But I doubt we would suit," I add.

He shifts, and I can no longer see his face. "You don't think so?"

"I like you, as a friend, of course. But the other—No."

"Why not?"

"I—I don't have time for such things. Or the patience for them."

A man would no doubt object to my choice of career, would rather me see to his needs instead of fulfilling my own. What's romance if not a precursor to marriage, and I've yet to see the marriage that didn't require a woman to sacrifice far more than she should.

I sneak a peek at him, trying to read his expression, a pang in my chest at the idea that I might have hurt his feelings.

"You've thought about this a great deal, I see," he replies.

"I've always known I didn't wish to marry."

"Always?"

"Well, I suppose since I was old enough to start thinking of such things. I saw the marriage my mother and stepfather have, and I couldn't imagine myself in such a situation."

"You like your independence."

"Of course."

"And you think that if you love someone else, you won't be able to maintain it?"

The word "love" enters the conversation with as much subtlety as one of the fireworks exploding overhead.

Rafael lets out a sharp bark of laughter. "You should see your face. I said 'love.' I didn't utter profanity." He shakes his head. "It would figure, wouldn't it? And I thought I was the most marriage-averse person in the city."

I wrap my arms around me, wishing I'd worn a slightly thicker coat.

Wordlessly, Rafael reaches into the pocket of his coat and hands me a flask, his initials engraved on the exterior.

"What's in it?"

"Whiskey. It'll warm you up."

I hesitate.

"Otherwise, I'll have to do the gentlemanly thing and offer you *my* coat, and if I stand out here in this damn weather in my jacket and shirtsleeves, I've no doubt I'll catch the death of a cold."

His lips twitch as though he injected the "damn" just to prove his point about the word "love" evoking a strong reaction from me.

I take the flask from him, lifting the cold metal to my lips. Belatedly, it occurs to me how intimate such an act is, that his mouth once

261261261

grazed the same place, but I take a swig, the liquid sending a heat of fire down my belly.

"My grandfather was a cigar maker in Cuba. Did I ever tell you that?"

I shake my head.

"My mother worked as a seamstress."

His gaze slides to my outfit; even though it isn't flashy, my coat is finely made, though hardly on the same level as his.

"And now you're one of the kings of New York," I reply.

He smiles just a touch ironically. "The American Dream."

"It's not your—your background," I say, lest he think I care which ship from Europe his family hailed from over a century ago or whether they're descended from Dutch settlers like mine.

I wait for a quip or one of his usual dry remarks, but he's strangely silent, inviting me to fill the space with an explanation I'm not sure I know how to give.

"Even if I were interested in a romantic entanglement—"

His lips twitch.

"—our temperaments are too different," I add.

"And you should like to be with someone exactly like you?"

"I would like to be with someone who shares my view of the world, if I would like to be with anyone at all. I'm quite content on my own, though. Truly."

"Content sounds awfully boring. As does your idea of the perfect relationship."

"I didn't say it was 'perfect,'" I protest. "Simply that if I *had* to entangle myself with another, it would be nice to be with someone who shares my interests."

"Interests like politics? Current affairs? And what was it you said about the word 'nice' when you complained of me using it to compliment you at the opera?"

"You delight in mocking me, don't you?"

He laughs again, the sound having a little more bite than it did earlier. "Believe me, if anyone is the subject of mockery here, I believe it is me. Divine mockery, to be sure. Why wouldn't you want to be with someone who challenges you? I've never known you to choose safety over adventure."

He turns from me, walking on, and for a moment I am torn between the urge to stay exactly where I am and to follow him.

It is one thing to pursue professional advancement, to put it all on the line for my career, and another thing entirely to do so with my personal life.

I lengthen my strides to catch up with him.

Once we are side by side once more, Rafael slows a bit, matching his pace to mine, the knot in my chest loosening somewhat.

We walk in silence as the party carries on around us, and then I can't help asking him the question that has filled my head many times since that night at the opera.

"That woman you were with. At the Metropolitan Opera House. She is very beautiful," I say carefully.

"She is."

I open my mouth to ask him more but close it again almost as quickly. It doesn't feel as though I have a right to his answer, to ask him anything about his private affairs with women.

"Is there a question you'd like to ask me, Grace?" His tone becomes silky. "You can ask me anything."

"No—I—Is she . . ."

I can't make myself form the word.

"Are we lovers?"

I flush, tearing my gaze away from him, and nod.

"It's none of my business," I blurt out.

"Considering the conversation we just had, I'd disagree with you. We were lovers. Once."

I can envision her in his arms, can see—

"We haven't been for some time," he adds. "But she's a friend and she likes the opera so she uses my box occasionally."

I'm afraid to acknowledge the emotion that accompanies his words, for it almost feels a lot like—

Relief.

The music around us changes to the familiar strands of "Auld Lang Syne."

A lump forms in my throat.

"This song always makes me so sad," I say, feeling a little silly for confessing such a thing to Rafael, even as tears fill my eyes, the lyrics swelling within me, the singers' voices joining in unison.

"Why?"

"It always feels like the end of something."

"Or the beginning."

I stop walking and look up at him.

Behind us, the crowd is chanting now, the new year upon us. And still, even with Hearst's amazing feat as an electrical impulse sends the flag of Greater New York up the staff of the flagpole on City Hall playing out for the crowd, the hundred-gun salute, the skyrockets, and cheers of one hundred thousand spectators, I don't tear my gaze away from Rafael as he bends down, a question in his eyes, and I offer him a jerky nod, an answer I didn't know I was going to give, and his lips swoop down on mine, ringing in the New Year with a kiss that stretches on longer than is proper, longer than the tradition calls for.

Instead, my mouth opens to his, my arms leaving my sides, moving as of their own volition, wrapping around his neck, pulling him down to me, my body coming alive with his touch. He groans against my mouth, leaving me no question of the force of his desire, his hands running over my curves, pulling me up against the hard length of his body.

When I finally pull back, I cannot speak, my heart racing, an ache settling in my bones, my first kiss nothing short of extraordinary.

We square off across from each other while all around us the city rejoices the new year.

What have I done?

Rafael recovers first, leaning into me, the lips that I just feasted on hovering near my ear. His mouth grazes my skin, and a tremor racks my body.

"I'll tell you a secret," he whispers.

I shudder as his mouth brushes against me once more, and my knees nearly buckle as I reach out, grabbing on to the only steady thing I can find for purchase—Rafael's arms.

"When someone tells me I can't have something I desperately want, I do everything in my power to make it mine. I won't kiss you again if you don't want it, but I'm going to try my damnedest to make sure you do."

Well.

"I'm not interested," I say, even as a part of me very much wishes to pick up where we left off.

He smiles. "Of course you aren't. Happy New Year, Grace."

With those parting words, he leaves me staring after him in the crowd once more, thinking 1898 just got off to a very unexpected start.

1898

Thirty-One

❦

MARINA

While we were unified in our hatred for Weyler, now that he is gone and the more moderate Blanco is in his place, the promise of autonomy dangling before us, many Cubans have deserted to the Spanish side. While a great number of my countrymen are willing to flock to the Spaniards now, I cannot move past my anger at what they have done to our country and my belief that if we do not assert our independence, they will destroy us.

In November of 1897, after I sent Isabella away, Weyler's replacement, Ramón Blanco, offered an end to reconcentration and an opportunity for farmers and other classes of workers to return to their homes. On paper, Blanco's order put an end to reconcentration, but the reality has proven to be much different. Most of the reconcentrados are too sick or unwell to make the journey to their homes, little to nothing waiting for them when they do. Instead, many, including myself and Luz, have stayed in Havana, waiting out the end of this horrible war.

The Spanish have tried giving credit to the provinces and providing military support to the reconcentrados when they return to their homes in the countryside, but everything the Spanish offer is far too little, far too late. They cannot undo the piles and mounds of corpses that have plagued us since Weyler sent us to these godforsaken camps.

Besides, how can I leave, when I am needed in Havana.

In my more desperate moments, I try to remind myself that things are different now, that the Spain we fought during the Ten Years' War is not the Spain we face now. They are weaker, and running out of resources, and surely the longer this continues on, the better chance we have. Or so I hope. They're not just fighting a war in Cuba, but also an insurgency in the Philippines, and the Spanish public must grow weary of the toil of waging war on two fronts.

Unfortunately, we are worn down by the war effort, too. Isabella's cough has improved, and she is flourishing at my parents' home, but the toll of being away from her has certainly made my days harder, and as desperately as I wish I could have her back with me, she's better off with the comfort and security they can provide her. I've only seen her a handful of times in person, mostly when she is playing in the backyard. A few times I've gone by the house and as I'm leaving discovered food left for me near the entrance.

Months after he is recalled to Spain, Weyler's specter continues to loom over our island. For as grateful as I and others like me were to see him go, many of those loyal to Spain have viewed his dismissal as a harbinger of awful things to come. In the wake of international condemnation, political changes at home, and the ongoing war, the Spanish have offered colonial reforms and a degree of home rule for Cuba. Those loyal to Spain view any autonomy we are granted from Spain as a closer move toward independence, and they fear their reduced position under such circumstances. To that end, there have been riots in Havana, and the Americans have sent a great warship down to protect American interests on the island. Things have largely calmed down since the unrest last month, but the *Maine* lies in wait in the harbor. Its presence is a tricky thing—Blanco has made an effort to downplay it so as to not increase the tensions or to stoke the unease in the Habaneros. At the same time, it has been a source of great interest, with many touring the mighty American ship—including some Spaniards.

I hurry past the harbor and the *Maine*, headed toward one of the meetinghouses Carlos Carbonell has taken to renting for his own purposes.

I carry a bundle of laundry in my arms. In the past few months, I've gained a reputation for doing good, reliable work, and the extra money we've taken in has been a lifesaver when it comes to ensuring Luz and I have food to eat.

I knock on the door, glancing around as I wait on the threshold for Carlos to answer it. Even with Weyler gone, this is still a dangerous business.

Carlos opens the door quickly, moving back so I can walk inside. He immediately closes the door behind him.

"Are you well?" he asks me, and I nod, for I suppose I am as well as I can be considering everything going on around us.

He hands me a note. "I need you to deliver this message to the American consulate at once. It's extremely important that you do so."

"Why do you need my help? I thought you had close ties to the consulate."

"I do, but I've had to be more careful since the business with Evangelina. The Spanish watch me more closely than they used to. No one has proof, but there are enough suspicions, too many people who saw me in the company of Karl Decker when he was in Havana."

"I can get the letter to the consulate. I've delivered their laundry before, so no one should think anything of it."

"This letter is extremely important. This could be what we need to end the war once and for all."

He's not a man prone to exaggeration, but I find the claim a little hard to believe. "What could possibly be that important?"

"Dupuy de Lôme, the Spanish minister in Washington, wrote a letter to a friend of his, José Canalejas. Canalejas is the editor of the Madrid *Heraldo* and frequently travels to Havana," Carlos adds. "He also has dealings with the New York City Junta."

"What does the letter say?"

"It's critical of President McKinley."

"How so?"

"De Lôme calls McKinley weak and a low politician. Says he caters to the masses. If the American newspapers had such a letter in their possession and printed it, the embarrassment for the president would be too great to ignore. It might be the push we need for him to act."

"How did you find out about the letter? Surely, Canalejas couldn't have been so indiscreet as to share the contents."

"No, but when he came to Cuba he brought the letter with him. He hired a man who is sympathetic to our cause to be his secretary here. His name is Gustavo Escoto. He saw the letter and realized its value immediately."

"Where is the letter now?"

"Escoto has the letter. He's on the next boat for New York. He's going to deliver it to Tomás Estrada Palma and the Junta with the hopes that they can give it to the New York newspapers to publish. If we can anger the Americans—perhaps this is the shot across the bow we need."

"Do you really think the Americans will support independence if they get involved?"

When things were as desperate as they were under Weyler, it seemed like the Americans were our best hope. But now I can't help but worry that the interest they have always shown in Cuba, the multiple attempts to buy the island, will drive their actions. After years of armed conflict between us, neither Spain nor Cuba is in much of a position to face off against the United States.

José Martí warned us about the Americans, was concerned that if we weren't careful, Cuba would change hands from Spanish ones to American ones.

"I believe so," Carlos replies. "Look how much they have championed our cause."

I can't tell if he believes it or if it's what he must tell himself considering how much he has reportedly aligned himself with Consul General Fitzhugh Lee. My father used to say that Carlos always had a way of taking care of his own interests before anyone else.

"Will you take the letter to the consulate?" he asks me. "We've copied out the contents here. It's not as good as the original, but if something happens to Escoto, it's the best chance we have."

I'm in too deep to turn back now. If this will bring my husband and daughter home to me, then what choice do I have?

"I'll deliver it to them."

I HURRY THROUGH THE STREETS OF HAVANA, THE COPIED LETTER Carlos gave to me wrapped in the laundry I carry in my arms. It's late in the day, the sun setting over the city, people milling about, and Spanish soldiers all over the place. Of all the things I've done, all the messages I've ferried between loyal patriots, this is without question the most dangerous.

Even as fear fills me, adrenaline rushes through me.

After all we've fought for and lost, for as much as I've railed against my ability to act, *this* is the moment when it feels like I can truly serve my country in my own way. War isn't just waged on the battlefield, and if this letter has the power to end the bloodshed, then I hope it will do so swiftly.

I slow as I near Consul General Fitzhugh Lee's residence. Carlos told me to leave the linens and note with his staff, that they would pass them on to the consul.

A group of Spanish soldiers stands near the neighboring street, their hands on their weapons, their gazes surveying the crowd.

My heart pounds.

I slip down one of the side streets and flatten myself against the wall. A woman hurries past me, but she doesn't spare me a glance.

I wait a beat, and then two, but no one else comes down the street.

Quickly, I go through the linens, safeguarding the letter, my palms damp as a line of sweat forms on my brow.

If I am caught . . .

I peek around the corner of the street, hoping the soldiers have moved on.

They're still there.

The longer I stand here, the more I risk drawing someone's notice when they pass by. And if something happens to Escoto on his way to New York City with the original letter, then this is our best chance at undermining the Spanish.

I walk out into the street.

This time, I don't duck my head, and when the soldiers' gazes settle on me, I meet their eyes. Better to look as though I have nothing to hide. The fear I can't quite strike from my expression hopefully adds to the impression that I am just a woman, struggling, intimidated by the soldiers and their weapons.

I walk past them, my shoulders squared, a chill sliding down my spine.

Please don't stop me. Please don't stop me.

"What do you have there?" one of the soldiers calls out to me.

My heart sinks.

I turn slowly and face him.

I've no doubt the blood has rushed from my face.

"Linens, sir. I do some extra washing for those who need it." I bite down on my lip. "I'm in the camp, you see, and the good citizens of Havana have given us jobs to earn a bit of extra money."

He doubtless knows all of this, but the reminder of our plight, of the toll the war has taken on women seems to shame him slightly, and he nods and gestures for me to pass him by.

I take another step, when—

"Let us have a look at those linens," one of the other soldiers calls out.

He strides toward me, none of the sympathy I saw in the first soldier's expression on him.

I hand him the linens wordlessly, tears welling in my eyes.

I offer a prayer to God that he will see me through this.

The soldier searches through the linens I meticulously folded, sullying them with his dirty hands.

Dread fills me.

He thrusts the linens back at me.

"You can go now."

I nod meekly and move away from him, struggling to keep my pace steady, to refrain from breaking into a run as my body desperately wishes.

When I reach the consul's residence, I quickly reach into my dress and pull out the folded letter, nestled between my breasts.

I shove it back between the linens.

The housekeeper opens the door, and I hand the laundry to her. "See that it goes to Consul General Lee."

IN THE DAYS THAT FOLLOW, THE DE LÔME LETTER MAKES THE international stir Carlos craved. In the end, the message I delivered to the American consulate in Havana wasn't needed, as Gustavo Escoto made it to New York safely and delivered the original letter to the Junta there, who immediately did what they do best and passed it on to the New York newspapers for publication.

Despite the outrage, there still hasn't been an official declaration of war from the Americans.

I walk back from Carlos's residence once more after delivering another message to him. In the aftermath of the publication of the de Lôme letter, he's only become more intent in his desire to force a war between the United States and Spain.

It's a warm night as I stroll along the water, the air still and heavy, the sky overcast.

Havana is the city of my childhood, and being here has brought back so many memories of what it was like before Mateo. While I have no regrets for the choices I've made, I can't deny a sense of nostalgia.

It's the second day of Carnival in the city, and even though it is nearly ten o'clock in the evening, there's a festive energy in the air, so different from life in the camp.

I walk along the harbor, gazing at the giant American warship resting there. The *Maine* is the largest ship in the water, its presence a stark reminder of America's might and their complicated relationship with Cuba.

Suddenly, an impossibly loud noise rings out over the city, followed by a bright light shining over the harbor, and then the light disappears, and there is only darkness, and the sound of men's screams and cries, dust and materials raining from the sky.

Bells ring out over the city, whistles blowing, an alarm sounding. I run toward the water.

Thirty-Two

GRACE

I sit hunched over the typewriter in the newsroom, begging the words to come. The story needs to be filed within the next hour, and for as short of a piece as it is, I shouldn't be struggling this much. Still, with our comprehensive coverage, sometimes it's difficult to not feel as though I am simply rehashing a story that has been told over and over again many times.

The de Lôme letter has been a gift to Hearst presented not by the head of the Junta, but by Horatio Rubens, their lawyer. In this matter, it's clear Tomás Estrada Palma wants to keep his hands as clean as possible. The entirety of the front page of the *Journal* was devoted to de Lôme's letter and a call for his dismissal from Washington. While the Junta's lawyer gave us the facsimile of the original letter, the story is too big for the other newspapers to not run with it as well, and almost instantly, de Lôme resigned from his post and headed back to Spain.

The story has dominated newspapers and public conversation for over a week, spurred on by the unearthing of a book de Lôme published decades ago where he was critical of American women and our American customs.

President McKinley has yet to act, but he has to realize public opinion—including that of Congress—is pushing heavily for war with Spain, and he is a man who cares very much for what the people think.

Whether de Lôme's letter proves to be the tipping point that thrusts us into war remains to be seen, but at the moment, it's done much to fire up support for the revolutionaries, and once the letter's authenticity was confirmed by de Lôme, even the most cautious couldn't ignore its damning nature.

And while it is de Lôme's harsh criticism of the president that has drawn the most ire, his letter to Canalejas and the private words contained there have also made it clear that despite Spain extending a limited degree of autonomy and home rule to Cuba in an attempt to end the war, they have no real intention of granting independence, and that the Spanish will cling to their last vestiges of empire until someone wrests them away from them.

"How's the article going?" Brisbane asks me, gesturing to the typewriter before me.

"Well enough."

"You've done good work lately. Your writing has been particularly sharp after working on the Evangelina story."

"Thank you." I can't help but ask the question that's been plaguing me for so long now. "Where do you think the end is in all of this? We publish these articles, and people become angry, but little truly changes. It's been years since the war for independence began."

"Weyler's gone, at least. I imagine we have Miss Cisneros partly to thank for that."

"What have you heard of Weyler's successor, General Blanco?"

I'd hoped to ask Rafael about his impressions of Blanco, but I haven't seen him since New Year's Eve.

"Blanco seems interested in keeping friendly ties with the American press," Brisbane answers. "I imagine he saw what happened to Weyler and how damaging public opinion was to his career and hoped to learn from his predecessor's imbroglios. He had Scovel and the wife round for dinner a few months ago." He winks at me. "Maybe we'll send you down to Cuba."

My heart pounds at the possibility there. Hearst's foreign war correspondents are becoming legends. I would give anything to join their ranks.

"Is that story almost ready?" he asks.

"Almost."

I bend over the typewriter and get to work.

THE QUIETEST MOMENT IN THE NEWSROOM IS RIGHT BEFORE dawn, when the editors have put the early edition to bed. I've been assigned the long watch, a great way to get a little bit of extra money as I stay in the newsroom after my story has gone to print, waiting for any last-minute information to come in.

Suddenly, one of the other editors bursts into the room.

"We just received an Associated Press bulletin. The USS *Maine* has blown up in the Havana Harbor."

My jaw drops. "Call Hearst."

Thirty-Three

MARINA

Bodies float in the water, the immense *Maine* nearly destroyed. Pieces of her remain above the sea—the mast and some of her forward parts—but the majority of her and the over two hundred and fifty souls on board rest at the bottom of the harbor. The American sailors have taken to hanging wreaths from the ship's mainmast, which sticks out from the water, the American flag flying at half-mast on the *Maine* and other American ships.

People come by to pay their respects to the dead and to gawk at the scene before them. It's as though the entire city holds its breath waiting to see what the Americans will do in response. Some think the Americans bombed their own warship as an excuse to insert themselves into our war with Spain, others blame the Spanish, and some don't care what caused the explosion as they hope that this will soon be the solution we desperately need: the hope that the Americans will defeat Spain and free Cuba once and for all.

I don't know what I believe in this strange world filled with never-ending tragedies.

The Spanish seem to realize how dangerous the situation has become. Spain has already stopped feeding and paying many of their soldiers, and the men now desert to the countryside by the hundreds, and then thousands, switching sides and joining the revolutionaries after likely realizing their country has abandoned them.

The *Maine* is all anyone talks about in the city, and as much as I struggle to glean any information about what will happen next, who is responsible for the explosion, and how it will affect the Cuban cause, I have dire concerns of my own to worry about.

Since I took her to my parents' home, Isabella is much improved, but Luz has become ill now.

I return to the camp from dropping off some laundering to check on Luz. She's sleeping in one of the beds they've made her, her skin pale.

"How is she?" I ask one of the nurses.

The American Red Cross has sent workers, led by their founder seventy-six-year-old Clara Barton, to care for the ill and infirm in the camps, and to distribute aid and relief throughout the island.

"She isn't doing well," the nurse says. "Her fever has gotten worse."

"It's yellow fever, isn't it?"

I haven't missed how her skin has yellowed over the past few days, and we've certainly seen enough of it in the camps to recognize the symptoms ourselves. There's no point in worrying if I'll catch it; it's everywhere, unavoidable in these conditions.

She nods. "I'm sorry."

"Do you—" The words stick in my throat.

For so long, Luz has been like a mother to me. I can't imagine the world without her in it. How will I tell Isabella her grandmother is gone? Or tell Mateo he has lost his mother? How will I carry on without her? How much do we have to lose in this war?

"Do you think she'll survive?" I ask.

"I don't know. We're doing everything we can right now to keep her comfortable, but her immune system was already compromised. She's malnourished, and—"

Tears fill my eyes, a wave of guilt hitting me. I should have worked more, tried harder to get us food. I should have gotten us out of the camps, shouldn't have brought us here to begin with. I should have tried to convince my family to take her in alongside Isabella, I should have—

The nurse lays her hand on my arm. "There is nothing you could have done. Yellow fever has ravaged these camps. If it wasn't that, it would have been something else. In all my years of caring for others, I've never seen anything like this place. No one should live like this. No one should have to."

I SPEND THE EVENING BY LUZ'S SIDE, HOLDING HER HAND AS SHE drifts in and out of consciousness. It's clear that the disease is ravaging her body now, just as it is obvious that she isn't going to get better, and despite my fear and grief, I pray she will find a respite from this suffering.

I speak to her the entire time, telling her stories about Mateo, remembering the day Isabella was born, happier memories on our little farm in the country, when the world was an easier place. I have no idea how much she hears or is even aware of, but every so often she'll squeeze my hand, or I think I see a hint of a smile on her lips before it fades away again.

The nurses are kind to her, stopping by to check on her and wipe her brow, and they seem like angels in their uniforms, ministering to us in our darkest hour. I try to thank them for the extraordinary gift they have given us, leaving their homes to come here and lend us aid, at the risk of catching disease in a place that feels like if you lit a match the whole thing would simply explode.

The more suffering I see, the angrier I become. Blanco's attempts at reconciliation are for naught. The Spanish have already done their damage to us and to our island. They can't just expect us to say all will be forgiven because they've tossed some crumbs our way. We've come too far and lost too much to settle for anything other than unfettered independence.

As the sun rises in the morning, Luz begins to fade.

Death has become such an ordinary occurrence around us that there's little shock when it happens, but right now, it feels all-consuming.

I wish she'd had a chance to see Mateo again. He should be here beside her, too.

She shouldn't die like this.

There's no peace around us, the normal noise of the camp intruding on her final moments, the cries of others suffering, the sounds of the nurses rustling around, trying to ease their pain.

And then she's gone, the finality of her death hitting me like a lead ball.

I lean over her body, closing her eyes, tears falling down my cheeks.

There will be no funeral, no chance for her family and friends to wish her a final good-bye. Her body will be gathered with those of the other dead and burned, the final indignity for all who have perished in this wretched place.

After they take her away, I gather my things, the little money I've made doing laundry and errands for others, and stagger from the camp. I've worried her death was coming for days now, but I am unprepared for the grief that takes hold of me and doesn't let me go.

I walk down the streets, one goal in mind.

I'M EXHAUSTED BY THE TIME I MAKE IT TO MY FAMILY HOME, BUT I traverse the familiar path, stopping just out of view of the house, peering through one of the small holes in the stone wall that my brother and I used when we were children to watch people passing by on the street.

My heart pounds as I peek in the backyard.

I hear her before I see her, the sound of Isabella's laughter a familiar one that's been largely absent for many months now.

For a moment, I close my eyes and listen to it, reveling in how *alive* she sounds—

I open my eyes and peek through the hole.

It takes a minute before she dashes into view, chasing another girl I don't recognize, her lacy white gown flowing around her. Her skin has lost its pallor, her body fuller and healthier. I remember the rich meals we dined on throughout my childhood that I took for granted. She looks like she is well cared for.

I want nothing more than to go around to the front door, to walk through the grand house and out into the backyard, and to take my daughter into my arms and hug her and kiss her, and hold her close. For a moment, I imagine going inside the house and begging my family to take me in, too. I can almost taste the rich food on my tongue, can feel the warm water of a bath the likes of which I haven't had in over a year. But if I give up now, then what was this all for? So many deaths were in vain if we don't see this through to the only conclusion that is acceptable—a free Cuba.

I stand there a few minutes longer than is wise, drinking in the sight of Isabella, and then I turn and walk away, the scent of death and disease clinging to my worn clothes.

She is safer here than any home that I can give her now, and as desperately as I want her with me, as much as it *hurts,* sometimes the best thing you can do is send those you love away.

Thirty-Four

GRACE

The front page of the February 16 *New York Journal* is consumed by the *Maine*. The other stories we were previously working on have been abandoned or pushed to other parts of the newspaper. In Hearst's mind this is the only story that matters. This is the biggest event since President Lincoln's assassination.

A day after the explosion, Teddy Roosevelt proclaims the Spanish to be guilty as details pour in from our correspondents who have seen the scene, but the situation is chaotic at best. Hearst offers a hefty reward for information solving the mystery of who sank the ship.

Hundreds of American sailors are dead, and no one knows why. Many think it's an act of Spanish aggression, even though Consul General Lee has stated it was likely an accident. Still, there is no consensus on the *Maine* explosion, but what does it matter, really? An American warship has blown up in waters controlled by the Spanish, and regardless of the cause, *this* is the shot across the bow Hearst has been waiting for, and there's no doubt he means to make the most of it. Day after day, we cover the *Maine*, using conjecture where there are still more questions than answers, even if our best guesses are presented more as facts. It's a dangerous kind of reporting given what is at stake if we do go to war. How can we ask men to risk their lives if we lie to them about what they're fighting for?

We've been covering the Spanish as villains for so long that the public can see them in no other role. They are guilty of so many crimes—both things we have accused them of that may or may not be true and then matters like the de Lôme letter where their guilt is spelled out in black newsprint—that for them there is no redemption. They are the de facto villains whether they are guilty of blowing up the *Maine* or not.

Hearst sends one of his yachts down to Cuba filled with his star correspondents—Karl Decker, James Creelman, Frederic Remington, and more—and a delegation of politicians. He offers his personal services and the use of his yacht to the navy as war fever spreads through the *Journal* newsroom.

The other newspapers have no choice but to follow Hearst's lead, and even Pulitzer has dived into the coverage with gusto.

"Remember the *Maine*" has become a rallying cry for all.

Where Hearst took an incendiary approach with the *Maine*, Pulitzer's coverage has been more measured, publishing President McKinley's early comments that he believes the explosion to be accidental. While Scovel's initial coverage on the *Maine* was praised, and Pulitzer tried to send a crew of divers to the wreck to inspect the damage only to be denied access at the scene, his initial forays haven't been enough to sustain the same volume and magnitude of Hearst's efforts. Since Pulitzer's *World* hasn't fared as well against the *Journal* in the circulation race, rumors have begun to spread that he's facing financial problems.

Bulletin boards have been erected on Park Row and at strategic points throughout the city, the competition between the newspapers growing more and more fierce, accusations of newspapers stealing stories from one another growing.

We might not have war in Cuba yet, but we certainly have it on Park Row.

Thirty-Five

MARINA
Before

"What have you done?"

The shock in my mother's voice is one thing, but the hurt contained there, her eyes wide, skin pale, creates a knot in my stomach.

"I've told Mateo I will marry him."

I've always strived to please my parents, to be the daughter they wanted me to be, to cause little trouble and to draw as little negative attention to myself as possible. There was enough disharmony in my family because of their marital disagreements that I strove to keep the peace. To keep them both happy.

But despite what my mother may think, this marriage is not some rebellion against my parents' authority or how I was raised.

I have loved Mateo all my life.

"You have not," she snaps.

"I have. He's a good man. He cares for me very much. I haven't done anything wrong. We love each other."

I could have dealt with anger, but the sadness in her eyes nearly undoes me.

"Oh, Marina. He may be a good man, but what kind of life will he offer you? Living in a little hut in the country somewhere while you work in the fields? What sort of life will your children have? He seemed like a nice

enough boy, which is why I never objected to you playing with him when you were too young to know better and there were no other playmates to be had in the country. But he's not for you."

"That's not true. He's everything to me."

"Then you would choose him over your family?"

"I would rather I didn't have to choose at all. Why can't I love you both? Why can't he be part of our family, too? Why does it have to be like this?"

"Your father would never accept him. You know that. The shame that would fall on this family would destroy our position in society, everything we have worked for."

"There's no shame." I lift my head an inch. "There's no shame in love."

But even as I hoped, wished, they would stand by me, she speaks the truth. We live in a rigid society that assigns people to certain strata based on various details of their birth and economic station, and there is little to be done to change those circumstances.

I was foolish to hope things would be different.

"Your father had another husband in mind for you," she says.

It's common for marriages to be arranged in our circle, but this is the first I've ever heard of it.

"Who is it?"

"A friend of his."

"Which friend?"

"Carlos Carbonell."

"The banker? He's father's age."

"He would be a good husband to you. He's a good man, a true gentleman. He's smart and he has influential friends. He would give you financial security, and as much as you can in uncertain times such as these, he would keep you safe."

"No. Absolutely not. I won't marry someone I don't love. I won't marry someone else. I've made my choice."

Her expression hardens. "You come here speaking of your desires and your heart, but what about obeying your parents? Your father will never approve of this marriage. He will force another or send you away before he allows his daughter to marry Mateo Sandoval."

I should never have tried to reason with them. I should have just run away with Mateo when I had the chance.

"You cannot force me to marry someone else. I will not. And I would go mad in a convent. Please."

She's quiet for a moment.

"Then you need to leave now. Before your father comes home and finds out about all of this. I won't lie to him to protect you, but I won't stop you if you leave now."

I am to walk out of here with nothing but the clothes on my back if I choose Mateo.

"You need to think hard about this, Marina. You will no longer be part of this family. You'll be abandoning everything."

I swallow past the tears in my throat. "I understand."

IN THE WEEKS AFTER LUZ'S DEATH, I AM FILLED WITH A GRIEF unlike any I have ever known. With Isabella gone to my family and Mateo's whereabouts unknown, I am more alone than I have ever been.

I briefly contemplate going to the countryside to join the revolutionaries. They say there are women wielding machetes among their ranks, others like Rosa Castellanos, "La Bayamesa," providing healing to the wounded and injured. But even as I contemplate the action, I can't bear the thought of being so far from Isabella, the glimpses I sneak of her sustaining me through this difficult time. I am called more and more to ferry messages throughout the city, the network of households passing notes between them under the auspices of hiring me to do their laundering increasing steadily following the explosion of the *Maine*. Everyone is desperate to point a finger at the Spanish in order to draw the United States into war, and the intrigues carried out throughout Havana are all designed to tilt the tide of war in our favor.

Carlos Carbonell sends me a note asking me to meet him at his residence one afternoon in early March, and I hurry over there.

When I arrive, there are trunks stacked near the front door.

"Are you going on a trip?"

"I am leaving the country. The American diplomatic delegation is being recalled by Washington. They believe war is imminent. Consul General Lee is returning home to Virginia, and I am to accompany him."

"You're leaving the country? You are needed here now more than ever."

"I've done what I can. If we truly are facing a war between the United States and Spain, then the best thing I can do—the best thing we all can do—is align ourselves with the Americans."

All along he was a coconspirator in this, and our past aside, he was an ally whose commitment mirrored mine. But this—this feels a lot like he's abandoning a sinking ship in favor of firmer ground.

Am I a fool for staying? Am I a fool for believing we should continue to fight?

"I need you to do me a favor," Carlos says.

"What sort of favor?"

Done are my days of blindly diving into whatever scheme he concocts. I risked so much for my part in helping Evangelina Cisneros escape from Recogidas, and Cuba gained little, and in the end, we saved only one woman out of the hundreds of thousands that have died with no one rushing to their rescue.

A gleam enters Carlos's gaze. "I have proof that Spain blew up the *Maine*."

I HURRY THROUGH HAVANA, HOPING NO ONE WILL STOP ME, THAT the dark night will provide a measure of cover. Carlos gave me the papers, sealed letters he said proved the Spanish had orchestrated a plot to blow up the *Maine*, and asked me to deliver them to a restaurant where Karl Decker and some of the other *Journal* reporters are dining.

In their last few days in the city and with the threat of war looming, Carlos and the consulate staff have been under greater scrutiny in Havana, and he feared the odds of the letters being intercepted would be great.

I'm carrying them with another bundle of laundered clothes, a few blocks away from the restaurant, when a voice calls out:

"Stop. Who goes there?"

I turn slowly, hoping that I will somehow escape this, that they will let me go with only a couple questions.

My heart sinks.

A group of Spanish soldiers stands before me, pointing their guns at me.

Thirty-Six

GRACE

In March, our answer as to what happened to the *Maine* comes in the form of the naval court's investigation that is presented to Congress and their opinion that the *Maine* was destroyed by a submarine mine that exploded, a conclusion that in no way exonerates Spain. There have been rumors of damning evidence against the Spanish being held by the revolutionaries, but if it exists, none has materialized.

We're in Brooklyn at a fundraiser for *Maine* survivors, and Hearst has even secured Evangelina Cisneros's presence, but for once she is hardly the star attraction. The impending war is all anyone can speak of. War fever—and speculating—has ensnared the country, and Hearst could not be more in his element.

"Congress is calling for war. After everything, how can we ignore what the Spanish are doing? We look weak if we do not act," Hearst says. "Teddy Roosevelt wasn't wrong when he said that we need a war to bolster the country, to define who we are as a nation."

"Is that a reason to wage war, though?" one of the other guests asks. "What should our national identity have to do with Cuban independence?"

"It gives people something to get behind. A cause to believe in."

"And what, a distraction from the problems plaguing us at home?" I interject. "We don't want to face our society's ills, so instead, let's direct their attention elsewhere?"

"Perhaps there's a bit of that, too," Hearst concedes. "Regardless, I imagine Senator Proctor's speech in Congress last month has swayed them considerably. Our critics claim that we have invented the situation in Cuba, that we are swayed by the Junta, that we have sensationalized the news there, but the words of a man who has no such ties, no interest in exaggerating the truth, who has seen the conditions in which the Cuban people live with his own two eyes is powerful indeed. Proctor's Cuba tour confirms the stories we've run. The situation is dire. McKinley's attempts to pursue a diplomatic solution have been unsuccessful. We must act."

I remember how my father spoke of war the few times he was willing to talk of his experiences, the ghosts that lived in him frequently plaguing him. I wonder if men like Hearst would be more reluctant to call for war if they saw the havoc it has wrought. There are no easy answers here, though.

Out of the corner of my eye, I spy Evangelina standing nearby, and I excuse myself from the group and walk over to greet her.

In a way, she feels like an old friend given how much of her life she has shared with me. We've kept in touch, exchanging letters throughout the months.

"It's lovely to see you again," I say. "Although, I'd rather it be under happier circumstances."

"Yes. It is a tragic thing that happened to those men." Her gaze drifts from me to the circle of reporters where Hearst holds court. "I overheard what you were all talking about. Do you really think this will bring about the war?"

"I don't know. Hearst certainly does."

"A war between the United States and Spain is beginning to feel like the only way I will be able to go home."

I can't imagine what it must be like to be in exile, to have your entire life on hold while you wait to see what will happen to your country, while you wonder if your family is safe, if they are alive.

She spoke less of those things when I interviewed her for the book, but it was clear from her manner that she carried a great deal of worry on her shoulders. The story we told was one of triumph over Spain, a rallying cry of vindication, but as obvious as it is that she's relieved to be out of Recogidas, it's clear that for Evangelina and so many of the other Cuban exiles, there is still another battle to be won.

After the fundraiser, the war discussion rages on with everyone placing their bets on whether or not we will enter the fray. The *Journal* does its part with endless coverage of the *Maine* and congressional debate, many newspapers doing the same, until finally, McKinley addresses Congress, asking for authorization to use military force if necessary.

For a week, the government debates the merits and potential pitfalls of such an action, until ultimately, they reach the same conclusion Hearst arrived at two years ago. He announces it jubilantly from the newsroom:

"We've declared war against Spain."

I don't think I've ever seen Hearst so happy as he is when war is declared. I never thought of conflict as something to celebrate, especially after the tales my father carried about his experiences, but the *Journal* does so in its own inimitable fashion. Rockets are purchased and launched over the building. Hearst offers a thousand-dollar reward to any reader who supplies useful ideas on how to conduct the war. Of course, war means increased circulation, the need for people to stay informed. It was the Civil War that gave rise to the prominence of the newspaper in American society in the first place; people had to look somewhere to learn if their loved ones off fighting were alive or dead.

There are those who lay blame in our corner for leading the United States into war with Spain by stoking the fires and sensationalizing our coverage. One New York paper—the *Evening Post*—has gone so far as to call this the *Journal*'s war, an allegation Hearst scoffs at even as I worry that maybe we are partly responsible, that the stories I've written about Evangelina and Spanish atrocities have led us to the precipice of this point from which there is no return. Whatever our intentions, it is undeniable that we have written our articles from a certain perspective, pushing Hearst's agenda to pull the United States into the conflict.

I spend most of my days in the newsroom now, writing more stories than I ever have before. The demand for the news we provide has never been so high, and the air is electric as we produce more and more content, trying to get the scoop on all the other papers. I look up from my seat at the typewriter one afternoon and I freeze—

Rafael stands in the entryway of Hearst's office.

I haven't seen him in months, since that kiss on New Year's, and the sight of him now, when I have slept little, my hair falling out of its coiffure, ink stains on my face and arm—I barely resist the urge to duck behind my typewriter so he can't see me.

I watch him over the typewriter, his discussion with Hearst too far away for me to make out what they're saying. The two men shake hands, and Rafael turns to leave, stopping as our gazes meet across the newsroom.

I swallow, my nerves getting the best of me. When I envisioned seeing him again, I thought I'd have an opportunity to prepare, that I wouldn't be so caught off guard and too tired to properly string two words together. I also didn't anticipate the audience of journalists ready to seize on any morsel of news. Newsrooms are veritable dens of gossip, and I can only imagine what everyone else will have to say about this.

Rafael stops in front of my desk.

"What brings you to the *Journal* offices?" I ask. "We haven't seen you in some months," I add then nearly kick myself for making it sound as though I've noticed, as though I've missed him.

"I came to say good-bye to Will," Rafael answers after a beat, his usual smile gone, his manner more serious than any I've seen him adopt before. "And you."

"Good-bye? But you've been gone, haven't you? Didn't you just get back?"

He nods, his gaze not on me, but on some point over my shoulder.

"Where are you headed?" I ask, my voice low.

"Cuba."

Awareness dawns on me as a chill seeps into my bones. After all, I just wrote a story about this.

The navy was prepared for the war, but the army is a different story. They've decided to allow volunteers to join in an attempt to swell their ranks. They needed an additional fifty thousand bodies, but over two hundred and twenty thousand volunteers have been accepted. The volunteers have come from all parts of society, sons of wealthy families searching for adventure in wartime, other less well-heeled men looking for opportunity. We sounded the call of patriotic duty. One hundred thousand men joined on the night after the *Maine* exploded; an estimated million total have offered to serve in the military. They're gearing up to wage war against Spain in the Pacific and Caribbean.

"You're going to war."

"I am. It seems my connections and knowledge of Cuba along with my language skills are of some value to the military. And there's little money can't buy, including a place in the army."

I wrote some of those pieces, calling for men to serve to honor the patriots who died in the *Maine* explosion. If something happens to Rafael, will I have his blood on my hands?

"But you're not a soldier. War is a serious business. What if something—"

What if something happens to you? What if you are injured? What if you die?

He smiles now, but the emotion hardly meets his eyes. "Have a care, Grace. It seems time I fought for something other than myself. I thought you admired action, fighting for what you believe in."

"I do—but—"

"Will you worry for me?" His voice is low, and he asks the question idly, as though he couldn't care less either way.

"Of course I will."

For a moment, it looks like he might say something else, but he holds his tongue. I wish we were in a position to have an honest conversation without everyone's eyes on us, but if I ask him to go somewhere more private, I'll draw more attention to the situation than I'd like, and his reputation as a playboy is too firmly cemented, and the respect I've earned here is too tenuous.

"In that case, I will endeavor to stay alive," Rafael replies.

I desperately want to say something else, something that will keep him here, as I try to understand how in the course of a few moments so much has changed.

If I never were to see him again, if he no longer was on this earth, it would be a great blow.

I care for him.

More than I ever thought possible.

I am still reconciling this new emotion, looking at him as though he is someone I have never seen before, when he says:

"Good-bye, Grace."

I open my mouth to call him back to me, but he is already gone, his back to me, walking away, past the rows of desks filled with type-writers and keen-eyed reporters, and I am left staring after him, fear flooding me.

Thirty-Seven

EVANGELINA

For several months, I've traveled around the country, meeting with independence clubs, attempting to raise awareness and funds for the cause. Everywhere I go, I am greeted with warmth and enthusiasm, but the more I speak about my experiences, the more it feels like they happened to someone else, as though I am telling someone else's story. The story of my life, the one Grace and I worked on together, was published, although the girl spun on the pages bears little resemblance to me. Grace wrote me a letter apologizing for the changes, for the unknown authors who contributed to the book and twisted my words and life to fit their purposes. If I've learned anything from Mr. Hearst, it's to give the people what they want, so I've given them the version of me they desire, said nothing as others have published stories about my life that are more fiction than anything else.

My survival depends on the goodwill I earn.

As grateful as I am for the Americans' love and support, for getting me out of that wretched place, it feels like everyone wants something from me, as though everyone has an expectation of who they think I should be, and I live forever fearful that I will do something to disappoint them, that I won't measure up to the pedestal they've placed me on, that one day they'll realize I'm just a woman, not "the Most Beautiful Girl in Cuba," or the rest of it. Sometimes, I wish I could be myself, something apart from this spectacle we have created.

Around me, the world is changing so swiftly it feels as though I have nothing steady to hold on to.

I am surrounded by many, and yet, I am utterly and irrevocably alone.

My father was liberated by General Blanco from the Aldecoa prison hospital months ago after Weyler was recalled to Spain, but they say he is mentally and physically destroyed by the ordeal. I think of him and my sisters constantly, worry I'll never see them again.

In April, I travel to Richmond, Virginia, to the home of Consul General Lee and his wife. This trip is a welcome respite from my official duties, but the question that lingers—what happens next?—remains at the forefront of my mind. The money raised from my book sales will support me for some time, but eventually the touring will end, and I'll have to find a place to call my own. Now that the Americans have declared war, I can't help but wonder when I'll be able to return home.

Some say that it will be a quick war, that once the United States puts their military might into the conflict, Spain will have little chance of survival. Still, it's been months since the *Maine* exploded in the Havana Harbor, and considering how much is at stake in Cuba, they can't move quickly enough.

While I hope to relax a bit in the company of friends, I can't deny a desire to glean any information that I can about the Americans' position toward Cuba. As the highest-ranking American in Cuba, Consul Lee is well-informed and certainly privy to sensitive and important details.

After we have reunited and caught up on one another's lives, they lead me to the room where I'll be staying.

I rest for a few hours and then dress carefully for the evening reception they've planned in my honor, selecting one of my finest gowns, which I've routinely worn for my speaking engagements. With a moniker like "the Most Beautiful Girl in Cuba," the pressure to make sure my physical attributes shine has been great.

When I descend downstairs, I am greeted by a beaming Mrs. Lee, her husband standing beside her with a gleam in his eyes.

"We have someone who very much wishes to make your acquaintance again, as it has been some time since you last saw each other," Consul General Lee says.

They both step aside, and I hear my name in a voice I've never forgotten—

"Evangelina."

For a moment, I am too overcome with emotion to speak.

Carlos Carbonell, the man who helped rescue me from Recogidas, who sheltered me in his home for those days before I boarded the *Seneca*, stands before me.

He is as I remembered him—tall and handsome—and different still, dressed in a grand American military uniform.

He takes my hands, squeezing them, leading me a little way from the rest of the party so we are off to the side a bit, falling into Spanish between us, our conversation private from that of the rest of the room.

"I've thought of you often," I say. "I confess, I never imagined I'd see you again."

He smiles at me. "You don't know how many days I thought of you and wondered how you were faring, if you were well. You look beautiful. Happy, healthy."

The hollows in my cheeks have filled out a bit since my escape from Recogidas, my body slowly returning to normal even if it takes longer for my mind to catch up. I am still plagued by dreams, random scents or sounds taking me back to those days in Recogidas, to that night with Berriz. With each day, it grows a bit easier, but it feels like something I will carry with me always whether I wish to or not.

"General Lee has kept me abreast of your triumphs," Carlos continues. "He sent me clippings from the American newspapers who feted you like a queen. I saved them all, I confess. You made Cuba proud. You made all of us proud."

I flush now under his regard, the words so prettily slipping from his tongue. There's something so dashing about him in his uniform, and for a moment, it feels like I have gone back in time to the girl I would have been if Berriz never happened, a handsome man paying me compliments. It reminds me of how it was before when Emilio courted me on the Isle of Pines, and yet, even if the dance feels familiar, I am different now.

The man I give my heart to next will be worthy of it.

"How have you been since we last met?" Carlos asks. "Truly? It cannot be easy—all that has happened to you."

"I have been well. I miss home," I answer, feeling as though I am for once able to speak my mind considering he knew me before I boarded a ship to America and everything changed. "Miss my family. It's difficult, waiting and wondering when the Spanish will be defeated, when I'll be able to go home. If I'll be able to go home. I am building a life here while my heart is in Cuba."

"I haven't been gone as long as you have, but I understand. I miss it, too. No matter how much time I spend outside of Cuba, I am always convinced it is the most beautiful place my eyes have ever seen."

"I am surprised to find you here. Is it merely a visit, or—"

"I traveled with General Lee from Havana in March, and when he was given command of the Seventh Army Corps in April, he appointed me to his staff and commissioned me as an officer."

"So you think the Americans are the ones who will help us bring about independence?"

"I hope so. This home rule Blanco has offered isn't enough. As valiantly as we have fought, I believe it will take more to eject Spain from our shores. The Americans are our best chance."

"Is it as bad in Cuba as everyone says it is?"

He nods, his jaw clenched.

What kind of home will I return to if I ever return at all?

"How long will you stay with General Lee?" I ask.

"Until we're given orders to return to Cuba. We're waiting to see when we'll be sent over. When he told me you would be visiting, I was happy at the prospect of being able to see you again. I confess, I haven't forgotten the time we spent together at my home."

Warmth fills me at the memory of the things we said to each other, of the kindness he showed me, of the affection that developed between us in such a short time.

"I've thought of it often, too." I've wondered what would have happened between us if I'd stayed at his house longer. "I can never thank you enough for all that you did for me, for saving me. Who knows what would have happened if you hadn't intervened on my behalf. You risked your life for me, and I never will forget it."

"It was my honor. When I realized I would be traveling with Lee, I thought I might see you again. I brought something for you."

He reaches into his uniform pocket and pulls out a folded piece of paper, handing it to me.

I recognize the handwriting immediately.

It is my sister Carmen's.

Tears fill my eyes as I take the letter from his hands, as I look at the word "Evangelina" on the outside, as I unfold it, reading the words contained there.

I only make it to the first line, before I must stop, emotion over-coming me. I will read the rest of it in the privacy of my room, when I'm able to let my guard down and truly be myself.

"How—how did you—"

I can't say the rest of it for the tears clogging my throat.

"After you left Cuba, I asked after your family. An acquaintance of mine knew your sister Carmen and put us in touch. I visited her before I left the country. I told her there was a chance that I might see you since I was travelling with the Lees and I asked her if she had any message she would like me to carry to you."

"I cannot thank you enough for all you have done for me. You saved my life in Recogidas, but this—to give me a part of my sister when I have missed her so dearly, when I have felt so alone. I fear I will never be able to express how much your kindness truly means to me."

"It was my pleasure. You deserve all of it and more." He gestures toward the letter. "I can make excuses for you if you'd like to go up-stairs and read that in the privacy of your room. I imagine you are eager to hear the news from your sister."

"I am. Thank you." And then it occurs to me. "Wait. I have some-thing for you, too."

I walk up to my room and sit down on the edge of the bed. As I open the letter, I am overcome with a wave of nostalgia and homesick-ness. For all the time we spent together when my family was sepa-rated, I have always been closest to my sister Carmen.

Evangelina,

I cannot tell you the joy it brought us to hear that you have been liber-ated from that awful place, and that you are now free. When they

released me from Recogidas, I felt an unmistakable sense of relief, but
also so much worry for you. Not a day has gone by since we last saw
each other when I have not prayed for you, thought of you, and now it
seems my prayers have been answered, my brilliant, clever sister. I was
filled with pride when I saw that you had escaped their clutches, that
you bested the Spanish.

A gentleman named Carlos Carbonell came to visit me—indeed,
I believe he is carrying this letter to you himself. He spoke of your joy
at being released from prison and shared news from the American
newspapers of how you have captured the hearts of everyone in the
United States. I cannot say that I am surprised of your triumph and
successes, only that you have done our family proud.

I hope we will be reunited again soon. Everyone is as well as can
be expected, I suppose, although our father is much changed since you
last saw him. The Spanish have taken their toll on him. I believe he
holds on so he will be able to see you again, his beloved daughter. We
hope for a speedy resolution to this war and for all of us to be together
in a Cuba free from Spanish tyranny.

I love you.
Carmen

Ps. The gentleman who came to visit me seems quite fond of you and
appears to be a distinguished man of integrity and good character.

Tears spill down my cheeks as I clutch the letter to my breast,
feeling as though Carmen is sitting beside me, imparting sisterly wis-
dom and telling me all about her life. There is an ache in my chest that
I feel keenly in my family's absence. My American friends had told me

that my father wasn't doing well, but now I fear he will pass on before I am able to return to Cuba, that we may never see each other again.

After a few minutes, I rise from the bed, setting the letter on a little nightstand. I will read it again when the evening is over, before I fall asleep, and hopefully Carmen's words will bring me peace to chase the nightmares away.

I blot my cheeks, straightening my coiffure, doing the best I can to make myself look presentable after the crying jag. I can't deny that Carmen's closing words about Carlos Carbonell have stuck with me, too.

On that note, I gather a bundle from my suitcase, carrying it down to where Carlos stands near the bottom of the staircase, slightly apart from the rest of the party.

"You once did me a great kindness lending me these clothes when I needed them. I washed them and held on to them for the moment I would see you again. It is nothing compared to the gift you have given me in the note from my sister, but it is hopefully just the first step in showing you my gratitude. Thank you."

He smiles, taking the folded clothes from me.

"It is my pleasure to make you happy, Evangelina. Perhaps we could go for a walk tomorrow? Would you like that?"

"I would like nothing more," I reply.

Thirty-Eight

I spend nearly the entirety of my visit at the Lees' residence in Carlos's company. I'm more at ease with him than I am with others, perhaps because of our shared past and the bond we have of Cuba between us. When you have a common love, there is an easy understanding between you.

He always speaks of Cuba as though his return is a certainty, the idea that the Americans will win the war undisputed, whereas I am more unsure, too easily disappointed to take for granted that I will one day be able to step foot on my homeland.

Carlos is handsome, educated, honorable, and in the conversations we have, I am reminded so much of my childhood and how I used to speak to my father about all sorts of things: politics, business, Cuba's future. When I speak, Carlos listens, and it feels like he sees me not as Evangelina Cisneros, "the Most Beautiful Girl in Cuba," but as the woman I am now.

I don't feel as alone when I am with him.

Carlos meets frequently with General Lee, discussing the war effort, and on his daily visits he always finds time to see me, to bring me flowers or sweets, a beautiful silk shawl I drape around my shoulders. In the time we spend together, he keeps me abreast of all the changes, the evolving conflict between the United States and Spain, treating me as an equal, and whereas I once feared that war would never come and we would languish under Spanish rule, I now worry that Carlos will be called to fight. I don't think I can bear to have another person I care for taken from me.

One of my favorite pastimes is to go on afternoon walks with him in the garden after he has met with General Lee. It seems as though there is little we don't discuss, and I am fascinated by all of the experiences he's had, by his vast knowledge. I'm not sure that I've ever met a more interesting person.

"What do you plan to do when your visit with the Lees is over?" Carlos asks me as we take a turn about the garden. "Do you think you'll stay in Virginia?"

"I suppose I'll accompany Mrs. Logan and her daughter to Maryland."

Mrs. Logan has become my guardian over this past year. The widow and her daughter have become like family, and I am grateful for the kindness they have shown me, but I still yearn for a place of my own—a family, a home, where I do not feel as though I am a guest, dependent on another's generosity and goodwill.

"Will you be happy there with them?" Carlos asks me.

"I hope so. I imagine it will be very different from Cuba, but I must admit that I'm looking forward to taking a break from traveling the country and speaking about my experiences."

"It must be difficult to relive such difficult memories over and over again."

"It is. I am grateful for their support, and if my story can help inspire others to act for Cuba, then I am grateful for that, too, but it will also be nice to simply be myself for a while and to figure out what my future looks like."

Carlos looks away from me for a moment, his gaze drifting to the edge of the garden. "I heard a rumor that you were engaged to a revolutionary back in Cuba. That he was exiled on the Isle of Pines as well."

"I was."

I don't want to discuss Emilio Betancourt with him, don't want to admit to the foolishness that had me believing in a man who betrayed me to the Spanish to save his own skin. Emilio is firmly in my past, and while I'm not exactly sure where Carlos belongs in my life, I don't want to burden the friendship we've established with such memories.

"Is there any chance that the two of you might . . ."

His unfinished question lingers between us.

"No. None. He wasn't the man I thought he was or the sort of man I could ever love. Those days are behind me now."

"Then your affections are not spoken for?"

"Not at the moment," I reply, struggling to keep my voice light.

We don't speak for the rest of the walk.

ONE AFTERNOON A FEW DAYS LATER CARLOS ASKS TO MEET ME IN the garden, and he greets me in his military uniform.

"Are you being sent to Cuba?" I ask, my heart pounding at the serious expression on his face.

We've had less than a month together, and as it was before, it feels as though our time together is running out, and I can't help but wonder what might have bloomed between us if we'd had the time for the affection between us to grow.

"No, not yet," he replies.

Relief fills me. "You scared me. You seem so serious. I was worried something had happened."

He flashes me a rueful smile. "I suppose I am serious today. I have something important that I'd like to discuss with you. A question I'd like to ask you. Perhaps the most important question I'll ever ask anyone."

My heart pounds.

He takes my hand and leads me farther into the garden.

I've been in this position once before when it was Emilio Betancourt taking my hand, when I was little more than a young girl who knew nothing of the world, flattered by the attention being shown to me, so this time I am ready for what comes next.

It only takes me seconds to know my answer. He is an honorable man—kind, intelligent, respectful. I believe he is the sort of man who will protect the people and things he cares for. Most importantly, perhaps, with him I feel as though I am at home.

Carlos gets down on one knee in front of me, my hand in his.

"Will you marry me?" he asks.

It is fast, but then again, considering all we've been through together, we have experienced more than many couples have. Is that enough to build a life upon? I'm not entirely certain. We have a friendship between us, which seems like an important characteristic for a successful marriage. We certainly have common interests and dreams. And he is kind and intelligent. He has already proven himself to be loyal and honorable. I believe I know his character and I am growing to know his heart. I have been many people in my life so far, and I cannot help but think that I will be happy as Mrs. Carlos Carbonell, that I will be happy in the life we build together, the children we'll have. That I'll be safe.

"Yes, I'll marry you."

WE MARRY IN BALTIMORE, MARYLAND. CARLOS WEARS HIS American military uniform, my dress far less formal than the one I donned when I was presented to New York society like a bride being led to the altar. Mrs. Logan and her daughter serve as our witnesses, but our wedding is a simple affair, largely absent from the spectacle that has dogged me these past several months.

In that aspect, it is exactly as I wished it.

Despite the simplicity of the affair, and Carlos's wishes that our engagement remain private, the *Journal* publishes the news of our marriage, for the first time identifying Carlos's role in my escape, but even with that tidbit of information, the frenzy that has followed my life this past year is largely absent. The focus is on the war with Spain, and I am a private citizen once more.

I always envisioned being surrounded by my family when I married, my father walking me down the aisle, my sisters by my side. Instead, I am alone as I place my future in Carlos's hands and promise to love him for the rest of my life.

We have a short reception at the Hotel Rennert and then as a married couple we head to Florida where Carlos joins the U.S. Seventh Army Corps and works with Consul General Lee while we wait to return to Cuba.

Thirty-Nine

At the beginning of May, the United States wins its first engagement when a naval squadron defeats the Spanish fleet in Manila Bay in the Philippines. We've heard nothing yet of fighting in Cuba, and I've had no news of Rafael's whereabouts, but the newsroom is in a celebratory mood when we learn of Commodore Dewey's victory.

"Maybe it'll all be over quickly," someone shouts. "Spain doesn't stand a chance against American military might."

"Hopefully, it won't be over too quickly," another person yells. "At least, not before we can write about it."

We're putting the finishing touches on the front page, the victory in Manila the major story.

"Let's add something below the masthead," Hearst calls out, a gleam in his eye.

I look down to see what he's written for them to add.

I begin to laugh.

In true form, and in perfect rejoinder to the criticism that was so recently levied against us, Hearst has added the words, "How do you like the *Journal*'s War?"

Hearst is in his element, leading the newsroom as though he is a general commanding an army. It's clear, though, that he isn't content to sit back and watch his correspondents do the frontline reporting for him. His efforts to join the military have been unsuccessful, but shortly after we report on the success of our battle in the Philippines, Hearst calls several of us into his office with news.

"I've received permission from Secretary of War Alger to take a steamship I've chartered from the Baltimore Fruit Company—the *Sylvia*—to Cuba as a member of the press corps," Hearst announces. "The *Sylvia*'s captain and crew will be coming as well. We're going to bring a printing press on the boat so we can publish the first American newspaper in Cuba."

It's an audacious proposal, one that will likely set Hearst apart from many of his fellow newspaper publishers. While everyone is scrambling to get the scoop on the war, most are happy to delegate the task to their staff rather than take it on themselves.

"We'll call it the *Journal-Examiner*, and it'll be a good way for the soldiers to get their news," Hearst adds.

I can't help but wonder—is Rafael among those men?

If Hearst has had news of him, I haven't heard it, and I can't bear to ask for fear that he'll see me as some silly, lovesick girl rather than the respected journalist I hope to be.

"Who is going on this trip with you?" I ask, trying to keep my voice steady, the possibility contained in such an opportunity too great to be ignored. Hearst's war correspondents are legends.

"Creelman for one. One of my friends—Jack Follansbee. The Wilson sisters are going to be there, too. Several others."

I blink, convinced I've misheard him.

"The Wilson sisters?"

The Wilson sisters are infamous Florodora Girls, their presence more suited to a Broadway stage than the battlefield. They are favorites of Hearst's, rumors swirling that he is dating one or both of them, given the frequency in which he is seen out and about town with them on his arms and the extravagant gifts he has bestowed upon them.

"Should be a jolly time," Hearst adds.

It takes a moment for me to realize he is absolutely serious.

It'll be dangerous. I have no illusions about that.

When Sylvester Scovel was imprisoned over a year ago in Cuba, he was released after a month, but the threat toward journalists is still real.

Many would balk at the idea of taking a woman with them, but then again, Hearst is already taking *two*, even if their presence is designed to satisfy his needs for companionship and entertainment. And if Pulitzer was ready to send Nellie Bly to Cuba, why should I be different?

I open my mouth to ask him to allow me to accompany the party when he looks at me, a gleam in his eyes, and says—

"Care to join us?"

IF SOMEONE HAD TOLD ME MY JOURNALISTIC CAREER WOULD LEAD to me sailing around Cuba dressed in men's clothing in a convoy of chartered vessels with William Randolph Hearst and a pair of chorus girls who regularly break into song and dance, I wouldn't have believed them.

But here we are.

We traveled down to the Caribbean on Hearst's hired ship and started the last leg of our journey in Kingston, Jamaica, in mid-June where we docked and disembarked, the party checking into the luxurious Crystal Spring Hotel. Hearst went to a nearby racecourse where he bought some polo ponies to ride onto the battlefield before we embarked for Santiago, Cuba, the next morning. The American censors in Key West control the information, making it difficult to get stories out, so Jamaica has become our best option, and a convenient place to stock up on supplies.

I can't fathom the amount of money that is being spent on personnel, dispatch boats, and telegraph companies, but for all of his wealth, at the rate he's spending it, I have to think even Hearst might run out of money if this conflict continues on. He's sent an army of thirty-five correspondents to Cuba and has created his own newsroom and printing press aboard the *Sylvia*.

We sail around Cuba, rendezvousing with the American navy, waiting for the battle to start. Initially, I think Hearst was worried that he'd miss it entirely, but it's taken the United States some time to marshal our forces and prepare for war. There's been fighting in Puerto Rico, the Philippines, and Guam, but so far Cuba has been silent.

We make our way to Las Guasimas at the end of June, leaving the Wilson sisters behind on the *Sylvia* as we take the horses ashore.

The woods are dense, the ride more grueling than I had envisioned. I haven't ridden in years, since I was a young girl, and I spend as much time trying to maintain my seat as I do taking in my surroundings.

The reports we've received about the destruction of the countryside have been accurate. It is starkly barren, and I do not think I see one living animal native to the area. The war between the United States and Spain might be starting, but it's obvious the conflict has already ravaged this land.

In contrast to the destruction around us, the men riding to war do so joyously, whooping and hollering with little care for the enemy hearing their movements. It's as if there's been so much pent-up energy geared to the effort that now that the fighting is here, they are ready to greet it with gusto.

At eight in the morning, the first land engagement begins as fifteen hundred Spanish soldiers under the command of General Antero Rubin start firing their rifles. The air fills with the sounds of their short pops, followed by the heavier reports of the American guns.

Theodore Roosevelt and his Rough Riders are here, and Richard Harding Davis, Edward Marshall, and other journalists from the *Journal* throw themselves into the fray as though daring the Spanish to shoot at them alongside the American soldiers.

Is Rafael somewhere in this throng?

I hang back with some of the party, watching from a safe distance, not close enough to the direct fighting to be on the front lines. I haven't quite decided what I'm going to report on here. War doesn't fill me with the same level of excitement with which it seems to infuse the men, but after spending so much time writing about Cuba from the comfort of my newsroom in New York City, I wanted to see the real people we wrote about from a distance. There's a story here. I'm just not sure this is the one I want to be reporting on.

The air fills with smoke from the German rifles, making it difficult to see anything. The sounds emerging from the battle are ominous, yells and cries mixing with the firing of weapons. My horse dances uneasily beneath me; the polo ponies Hearst procured hardly have temperaments suited for this sort of thing.

Neither do I.

Off in the distance, men are dying and I can't help but think of all the stories we wrote about the *Maine*, the fervor we whipped up with Evangelina's case, the statements Hearst made to me when I first spoke with him in his office about using the news to shape policy.

Did we push the world to this point? Were we heroes or were we too caught up in our circulation battle?

Maybe Pulitzer was right all along. Maybe I don't have the stomach for this.

How many will be dead when the smoke clears?

One million men volunteered. When they signed up all over the country, did they envision the reality of what war would be like? Of the horror of battle? Is this what my father experienced? Were these the memories that haunted him?

When the smoke clears and the battle ends, the dead and wounded lie on the ground off in the distance. We were careful to stay out of the line of fire, but it's still close enough to smell the blood and the gun smoke, to hear the cries of the wounded. It's close enough to see death on a scale I never have before.

Hearst pulls up alongside me on his horse, and mine shies away for a moment.

"Edward Marshall was wounded," Hearst yells to our party. "Shot in the back. Stephen Crane carried him off the battlefield and then went to file his dispatch. They're saying we lost sixteen Americans. Dozens are wounded. The Spanish casualties are a bit lower. They're claiming a victory, too."

He sounds so alive, so invigorated by the conflict despite our losses. He's been waiting for this war for years, and now that it's here, it seems he wants to drink every drop of it.

"Will Marshall survive?" I ask, horrified at the thought of one of my fellow reporters lying on the battlefield wounded.

"I think so. He seemed in pretty good spirits, all things considered. Let's go back to the boat and get to work." Hearst grins at us. "We got some good material today. I don't think anyone else could have done better."

Hearst and a few reporters break off from our group to speak with some of the soldiers, and I and the others race back on our horses to board the *Sylvia* and begin writing the stories we will file. When we get back to the boat, Hearst is nowhere to be seen, but the rest of us discuss the battle before we sit down and begin writing, the air filling with the sound of typewriters.

Finally, Hearst walks into the room where we're all working.

"Look who we found," he announces. He moves aside, and another figure comes forward.

Hearst claps the man on the back, and I blink, convinced I'm hallucinating the image before me.

Rafael stares back at me.

Forty

We all dine on an elaborate feast aboard the *Sylvia*. Throughout the dinner, I try to follow the conversation, but my gaze drifts toward Rafael seated at the opposite end of the table. He borrowed evening clothes from one of the other men, and he looks as handsome as he did in New York in his impeccably tailored attire. He's quiet for most of the meal, while the rest of the diners seem to be filled with a buzz from the excitement of battle. The only explanation Hearst had provided earlier for Rafael's presence was that he had been separated from his men and we would give him a ride to meet them. Then he whisked Rafael and the rest of the men away for brandy and cigars.

Halfway through the dinner, the Wilson sisters rise from their seats and begin dancing, laughter spilling out throughout the room. Hearst is in high spirits for his journalistic triumph today, and there's no question everyone will be celebrating long into the night.

As soon as I can excuse myself from the rest of the party, I do, and I sit near the bow of the *Sylvia*, the sounds of the celebration drifting toward me, but for the most part the night is silent, the weather still.

Despite bathing, it feels like the smell of smoke and death still lingers, and I'm more than a little embarrassed by how affected I was by the battle. Everyone else seemed to greet it as a grand adventure, but I couldn't see it as anything other than a tragedy as those men died around us.

"Do you mind if I join you?" a voice asks from the darkness behind me.

My breath hitches. "No."

Rafael sits beside me on the boat, and for a moment, I struggle to come up with the right thing to say to him, afraid that I'm already wearing my emotions on my sleeve after the tumult of the day.

"I think my heart stopped when I saw you standing on the boat in front of Will," Rafael says unceremoniously.

And just like that, it seems as though he's decided to pick up exactly where we left off at New Year's, no pretense between us. Perhaps the war stripped that away from us.

My response is tangled up in my throat, and a sob escapes instead.

My shoulders shake with it, the floodgates opening. I'm not even sure why I'm crying, or where my tears are coming from, only that I feel as though I have been pushed to the brink by all I've seen today, war something I was unprepared for.

Rafael wraps his arm around me, bringing me up against his side, holding me in his embrace.

He smells like the cigars he smokes, the drink he and Hearst favor, and what I once thought to be impossible happens, and I relax inside his arms, listening to the thudding of his heart.

Neither one of us speaks as I cry in his arms, the sound of the others celebrating on the opposite side of the boat intruding on our private moment, until all my tears are gone.

I pull back slightly, wiping at my face. "I'm sorry to lose control like that. The battle today affected me more than I thought it would."

"You don't have anything to apologize for."

"The other journalists handled it better."

As one of the few women in the newsroom, I am held to a higher standard to prove that I belong here, that I can do the same reporting as a man.

"You don't know what they're doing in their private moments. Sometimes it's easier to put on a brave face than admit you are shaken," Rafael replies. "And you forget, they've been down here covering the skirmishes between the revolutionaries and the Spanish. This is the first time you've been near the battlefield. I imagine it'll get easier the more wars you cover. Or maybe not. I don't know that watching people die ever gets easier."

Weariness creeps into his voice, and I turn to study him.

The sight of him sitting so close to me is a shock to my system, as is the utter exhaustion etched across his face. The sharp edges to his personality have been sanded down, and he looks more vulnerable than I've ever seen him.

"When I thought about you in my absence, I envisioned you safe in New York," he says. "Not here. Why did you decide to come down to Cuba?"

"Because it was an opportunity to see what it was like. I've been reading the dispatches from all of Hearst's war correspondents for years now. I wanted to be in on the action—I thought—I don't know, that I could make a difference or something. That my reporting might mean something. You must think me a fool."

"Never a fool. Look at Will and the others. Everyone is down here chasing a story. Isn't that the job?"

"It is. What was it like today?" I ask him, wanting to bring him a measure of comfort as he has given me.

"It isn't what I expected. I was terrified the whole damned time. I didn't expect that."

"Why did you come to Cuba?" I ask, turning his earlier question around on him. "That day at the *Journal* offices, I was so caught off guard by you saying you were leaving, I didn't even ask why you decided to fight. There were things I wanted to say—to ask you—but we were surrounded by others, and I, well, I have to be careful in the newsroom."

He sighs. "I don't know why I came. Maybe it was a mistake."

"I thought you were conflicted about the American role in the conflict?"

"I was. I am. But it seemed time to stop talking about it and to do something. Now I'm worried I'm going to end up on the wrong side of this. You saw how much they enjoyed the battle today. They relished in victory. Are they just going to pack up and go home after all this is over? What if they want a stake in Cuba? What if we're just trading the Spanish for the Americans?"

"Is it hard for you—fighting for the country you were born in while also worrying about your people here?"

"It is. I'm American. I was born there; my father was born there. It's the country that welcomed my mother when she had to leave her home. But I am also Cuban. And I believe in their independence."

I reach out and take his hand, linking our fingers. "You're a good man," I say, trying to offer him some of the comfort he's given me. "Whatever fears you may have, however this ends up, it's clear that you love your country. Both of them. That's something to be proud of."

"Grace."

"I've been worried about you. I can't—" I take a deep breath. "I can't imagine what I would do if something happened to you."

His heart pounds against me, but he doesn't respond.

"Why did you kiss me on New Year's? Was it just the moment, or . . . ?"

"I've wanted to kiss you for a long time," he replies. "I think I've wanted to kiss you since you marched into Will's office and demanded a job."

"I didn't—I didn't realize. Not until New Year's."

"So now you know." He's silent for a beat. "You have to decide, Grace."

His voice is so low against the noises in the background—the Wilson sisters' laughter, the pop of another champagne cork, the sound of the waves against the boat—that I have to strain to hear it.

Ordinarily, I would bristle at his words, at the command there. But it's the plea in his voice, the knowledge that I've humbled him that holds me still.

"I've told you what I want," he says. "If you want me, you know where to find me."

My fingers tremble as I ball them in a fist, as I raise my hand to the heavy wood door to Rafael's cabin. The hallway is empty; the evening's revels are still ongoing.

He left me sitting on the bow, and after a few minutes I looked for him on deck, but he wasn't guzzling champagne with Hearst and his friends, or anywhere else.

It feels as though a miasma has settled over the *Sylvia*, as though the madness of the day's events, our proximity to death and the way it gripped so many others, has infected all of us. Everyone is laughing louder than normal, the alcohol flowing more freely, a manic air that suggests this feeling inside me, this desire to jump out of my own skin and don another, has seeped into everyone else on board. The revelry has taken on an edge.

It is a night for caring little of what others think.

I tried to go back to my cabin, climbed into bed and stared up at the ceiling, running through all the reasons this was a terrible idea in my mind. In the end, none of them matter.

My knuckles rap against the wood.

A muffled voice on the other side says, "Come in."

I open the door, my legs shaking beneath my dress. I can scarcely believe that I'm doing this, and at the same time, after everything, I can't imagine anywhere I'd rather be.

Rafael is seated in a chair in his cabin, in the process of removing his shoes.

He glances up as I close the door behind me, turning the lock with a resounding click.

He stills. "Grace."

He doesn't rise, and so it is up to me to cross the room to him, my gaze trained on his face, the expression in his dark eyes unreadable.

I stop in front of him, the skirt of my dress whispering against the fine fabric of his trouser leg. His collar is unbuttoned; his necktie is discarded on the arm of the chair, the first few buttons of his white shirt open.

His chest is tan, and the sight of his exposed flesh sends a thrill through me.

"You said I had to decide," I say, a shaky breath escaping my lips. "Did you?"

"It hardly feels like a night for big decisions, and as much as I wish I knew what the future held, I don't. But tonight I want you. This. Is that enough?"

He doesn't answer me, but he rises from his chair, his big body uncoiling until he reaches his full height. The pants he borrowed are a little short for his long legs, and I seize on that tiny imperfection to calm my nerves.

My heart thunders in my chest.

"No one can know," I say. "What happens between us tonight is just for us. They'll see me as one of your women, and they won't take me seriously otherwise."

Hearst can parade around the office with a showgirl on each arm, but for a woman trying to make it in a man's world, the standards are very different.

"'One of my women'?" His lips quirk. "There's only you, Grace. And I won't tell a soul."

I lean forward, unmistakably charmed by his words, just as he bends down, and we meet somewhere in the middle, his lips pressing against mine, brushing back and forth, hesitant at first, before my mouth parts and his arms tighten around me, bringing me closer to him.

It feels as though we're picking up where we left off on New Year's, and we both dive into the kiss, without the need for formalities.

He strips the layers of clothes from my body with the practiced ease of someone who knows his way around a woman's boudoir, and in this, I'm grateful for his experience where I have none. Rafael's hands are gentle as he removes each piece of clothing, teasing away my nervousness until I am left with only desire.

With each caress, I cannot help but indulge in my own curiosity to explore his body, and I reach for him, tugging at his remaining clothes, unbuttoning the rest of his shirt, fumbling with his trousers, until he is nude before me.

Rafael sweeps me up in his arms and carries me over to the bed, setting me down gently on the mattress.

He looms above me, and as he enters me, our gazes meet, and I am undone.

Forty-One

I wake early the next morning to the sight of Rafael propped up on his elbow, watching me sleep.

The intimacy of the moment catches me off guard, the sight of a naked man in bed with me momentarily startling, even if the view is more than pleasing. I explored every slope and plane of his body last night multiple times, and I have little regret over the matter.

"What time is it?" I ask, my voice husky with sleep.

"I've heard some commotion around the ship. I think everyone is readying to go to Siboney to file their stories."

"Oh no." I leap out of bed, remembering Hearst's words at the dinner table last night, his desire to take our report of the battle back to the temporary headquarters we set up at Siboney, the village in Santiago where American forces originally landed in Cuba, so we can beat the others with the scoop. The army is moving again, and Hearst planned for us to ride out from Siboney to meet them.

I can't be late.

I rummage around the ground for my clothes from the night before.

Rafael tracks my every movement, a smile on his face and a gleam in his eyes. He looks every inch the satisfied male, and after how many times we came together last night, I can hardly fault him.

"I take it you're leaving me, then," he says.

"I am. I rather thought you had business as well. Don't you have to return to the war?"

"I do, actually. Will was kind enough to give me a ride when I got separated from the rest of my men, but I should head back. Some of the other reporters are going to the front lines. I'll head out with them." He hesitates. "Tell me you'll be safe. That you'll stay out of harm's way. Will means well, but he doesn't always have the best head on his shoulders, and he isn't always as prudent as he should be."

"I'll be careful."

Rafael throws the covers back, rising from the bed entirely nude.

For a moment, I stop dressing to admire the masculine beauty before me.

"You can't keep looking at me like that and expect me to do anything other than my damnedest to get you back in bed."

My eyes widen slightly at the invitation there. Now that I've had him, known him in that way, I don't think I'll ever hear his voice and not be transported back to the intimacy of this moment, the two of us in his cabin, the sheets on the bed tangled from the night we spent together.

Even after we finally fell asleep, he didn't let me go, holding me close to the curve of his body, his strong arms wrapped around my torso.

"I could get used to waking up to you," he adds. "Though, perhaps, in a more relaxed fashion."

I'm not sure what to say to that. As much as I enjoyed myself last evening, and even though I don't regret it, things are so complicated right now.

"I'll sneak out," I say, once I've put my nightgown on, slipping on my robe and tying it tightly at the waist. "I need to go back to my cabin and get ready to ride out with everyone."

Rafael takes my hand, linking our fingers. "I want you to know that last night meant something to me. Something important. Now isn't the time to be making promises. I know that. I might not even come back from this battle. But I want you to know that I care for you. Deeply. If anything happens to me—"

I cut off his remaining words as I stand on my tiptoes, leaning up and pressing my lips to his. He groans against my mouth, tightening his grip around me, deepening the kiss.

"Whatever you have to say to me, save it until we both survive this. We have to go," I whisper.

He leans into me, resting his forehead against mine. It's the only private good-bye we'll get before we revert to the roles we must play in the company of others.

Rafael sighs. "I know."

He releases me, and I walk over to his cabin door and open it a sliver of the way, glancing out.

The hallway is empty.

I cast one last look at him before I step out into the hallway, closing the door firmly behind me.

BEFORE THE SUN IS UP, WE ALL RACE TO SIBONEY, LEAVING THE Wilson sisters and the *Sylvia* behind. Hearst's enthusiasm to scoop everyone else is infectious even as the battle wears on all of us, the effects of the evening weighing us down. Hearst's friend, Follansbee, has parted from the group, leading some soldiers to search for stray Spaniards from the battle.

Rafael joins us, set to rendezvous with the rest of his military unit when we reach Siboney.

Our headquarters in Siboney have been converted to a hospital to treat the soldiers coming back from the front lines. Clara Barton and the rest of the Red Cross workers are there when we arrive, the sounds of the wounded soldiers in pain a sobering reminder that despite last night's respite, we are at war.

As soon as we arrive, Rafael leaves us to meet up with his men, and I am left once more staring at his retreating back, wondering if I will ever see him again.

Forty-Two

I have no news from Rafael after he leaves us, but the war in Cuba occupies all of my time as we work on our stories, our efforts focused on producing the best newspaper we can.

At the beginning of July, there's another battle to cover and we once again stop at our headquarters in Siboney and pick up fresh horses to carry us the rest of the way. We find space on a veranda and try to sleep, our rest occasionally interrupted by mosquitoes swarming around us.

Despite the rough conditions, though, Hearst looks as if he could be walking down Fifth Avenue, dressed in elegant black clothes and a felt-brimmed straw hat with a red hatband and a matching tie.

We saddle up, Hearst leading our party to the battlefield.

The road from Siboney is swampy; insects and strange odors surround us as we head toward the Fifth Army's position a few miles from Santiago.

We join the American troops at El Pozo, but our appearance draws the notice of the Spanish, bullets flying disconcertingly close to us, and many of the Rough Riders tell us to dismount as we're drawing attention on horseback.

I accompany Hearst and some of the others to the village of El

Caney, east of Santiago, which has been fortified by the Spanish. Creelman can't resist the urge to thrust himself into the battle, whereas Hearst hangs back at a respectable distance, watching the whole thing unfold.

The heat is nearly unbearable.

At six thirty in the morning, the Americans open fire on El Caney.

I watch the battle, trying to make out the figures in the distance, but it's impossible to recognize anyone in the melee.

"Should we get closer?" Hearst shouts.

"Maybe best that we don't," I call back.

I understand Creelman's desire to immerse himself in the fighting, but we've already been admonished once by the military for drawing enemy fire on horseback.

"There's a spot over there." I gesture to a position several hundred yards away from us. "That looks like a good place to observe the battle. Perhaps if we dismount, we won't arouse the notice of the Spanish."

Hearst nods.

Once we're in position, I pull out my notepad and begin writing, although quickly both pen and paper are abandoned.

The impressions I had of war at the battle of Las Guasimas hardly prepared me for this.

Today is far, far worse.

When the gunfire clears, reports start coming in from our correspondents, and we meet with some of the army officers, getting updates on the wounded and deceased.

Hundreds died in battle today, hundreds wounded. Including one of our own—

"Creelman's been shot," Hearst announces, not looking particularly troubled about it.

"Will he be all right?"

"He should be. They're taking him to be cared for now."

"Was anyone else wounded?" I ask carefully, my heart in my throat.

"No one else from our party," Hearst replies.

Relief fills me, and still—it's a somber affair.

We mount our horses once more to file our stories, and as we leave El Caney we ride past refugees pouring out of the surrounding towns, women and children who look as though they've lost everything. They're sickly and thin, the toll of war etched on their faces.

Some of them appeal to the American soldiers for help along the way, but soon enough one of the commanders puts a stop to it, as though he's concerned that whatever maladies plague these people will transfer to his men, too.

The Red Cross is on the battlefield tending to the wounded, some helping the refugees as they leave their homes that have now been destroyed. Between the countryside that had already been ravaged by the revolutionaries and the Spanish, and now the destruction war has wrought to the cities and towns, it is impossible to imagine it will be an easy recovery when this is all over.

As horrifying as the battle scenes are, watching men lose their lives before our very eyes, there's another cost of war that is right in front of us and somehow even more horrific.

How much have these people endured for *years*? Is this what our push to war has wrought? Have we further destroyed their home, or have we helped them, as Hearst truly believes?

I don't know. I thought coming here would give me the answers I sought, but I'm left with more questions than anything else.

AFTER THE BATTLE AT EL CANEY, WE BOARD THE *SYLVIA* AND sail to rendezvous with the American naval ship, the *Texas*, in anticipation of an impending battle between the Spanish and American navies.

"How do you propose getting past the blockade?" I ask Hearst. "They won't let press boats through."

A gleam enters Hearst's eyes at the challenge presented. "Surely, we have something that might entice them."

In the end, our party settles on bananas as a bribe, heartily accepted even as we are warned that the bombardment on Morro Castle will begin at eight in the morning.

We leave the *Sylvia* and board a cutter. We sail outside of the battle lines and watch as eight American ships begin firing on the fortified castle from a couple thousand yards away, Spain returning fire from the shore, shells flying past. The noise is thunderous, the sky filling with smoke.

"Sail closer," Hearst calls out to his crew. "We want the cameramen to be able to get better angles."

The crew follows Hearst's command.

"They're saying we're too close to the battlefield," a crew member shouts.

"Don't worry about that. Just stay where you are."

A shell lands dangerously close to us, just a hundred feet away in the water.

"We need to get out of the way," the man shouts back. "The Americans are telling us we're directly in the line of fire."

For a moment, I almost think Hearst is going to argue with the man, but he nods, allowing us to pull back slightly.

The tide of war has firmly shifted, and the Spanish fleet races along the coast, their decks on fire as the American navy pursues them. We follow behind the navy at a greater distance than before, a flotilla of newspaper boats behind us.

We all watch in shock as sailors leap overboard from the burning Spanish ships, trying to head for the shore.

"Go after them," Hearst shouts, bending over.

When he rights himself, his trousers are rolled above the knees.

It shouldn't surprise me anymore, nothing he does should, but I gape at the sight of Hearst jumping from the cutter, brandishing a revolver in one hand.

"Surely, he isn't going to—"

"Stop," Hearst shouts at the sailors attempting to escape through the shore, and miraculously, they do.

Hearst grabs a man and pulls him onto the cutter, and then another, and another, taking the Spanish sailors prisoner as though it is the most natural thing in the world and as if we are not here to report on the war, but rather to wage it.

When the cutter is filled with sailors, we return to the *Sylvia*, where the sailors are photographed and interviewed. In all, Hearst has captured seventeen of them.

For as much as we've written about their actions in Cuba, as close as we've been to the Junta, seeing the Spanish sailors places a human face to the stories we've told, and I almost feel sorry for how dazed they look by the entire proceedings, as we explain to them that we aren't, in fact, members of the American navy, but newspaper reporters from New York City who have taken them prisoner.

Hundreds of their compatriots have died today, but their shocked expressions are also due to the blow we all watch unfold before our very eyes:

The Americans have just destroyed the Spanish fleet.

THE SIEGE ON SANTIAGO CONTINUES, BUT THE MORE TIME I SPEND here, the more I'm convinced I'm following the wrong part of the story.

I approach Hearst the next afternoon after the bombardment of Morro Castle.

"We're going to set sail for Baltimore," Hearst tells me. "We'll stop by Siboney and pick Creelman up—they say he's recovering nicely from his injuries—and then we're heading home."

Now that the Spanish fleet has been destroyed, the end of the war feels like a foregone conclusion, and it's clear Hearst's sights are already on to the next story.

"There's a cutter headed for Havana," I say. "Some journalists are going to interview the Spanish officials there. I'd like to join them. I think it's a good opportunity. I can catch a steamer back to the United States from the city."

"Why Havana?"

Ever since I have been in Cuba, my days have been filled with guns and fighting, with the men's side of the war. But war isn't just waged on the battlefield, and I want to see the other side. What role have the women played? I saw them briefly walking from El Caney, but their stories have been largely forgotten.

"When I wrote the story of Evangelina Cisneros's life, it felt like there were pieces missing. She took me inside Recogidas, she told me about the other women there, about her life there, but we showed so little of that to our readers."

He shoots me a faintly incredulous look. "You want to write about Evangelina?"

For as famous as she was for a short period of time, the papers have moved on from her story, and she's no longer the news of the day. It's as though for Hearst, he sets out to conquer a story, and once he has done so, it is no longer important to him.

"No, I don't want to write about Evangelina," I reply. "I want to go to Recogidas."

Forty-Three

MARINA

I am surrounded by forgotten women.

They rail against their jailers, beat the iron bars with their fists until their knuckles are bloody, sit in the corner of the cells and rock, soft cries from their lips, their arms wrapped tightly around their bodies.

I find myself in prison.

In the damp that escapes the stone walls, the unforgiving cold from the floor that seeps into my pores and settles in my bones. In the cries that fill the silent night, the clanging of metal, the breaking of hearts, the abandonment of hope. It is always dark, and the endless night cloaks me, and that is perhaps the greatest surprise of all, that the darkness can be a comfort. That it can allow me to disappear, to leave this place and the uncertainty of tomorrow until I am left clinging with one thread to hold on to.

I will not let them break me.

I will not let them forget me.

They call this the Casa de Recogidas. It is a place for forgetting women society does not wish to face, for punishing those who have committed perceived slights against the Spanish, for condemning those who have dared to cast off the yoke of societal expectations and become someone other than that which has been decided for them. For those who fight for Cuba's independence.

We are the abandoned women.

In the evenings, when I cannot sleep, my heart sick with all the unfinished things I have left behind, I imagine they whisper to me, all those women who lived and died here before me. Their stories become a part of me; the strength of the women who endured keeps me going.

If only I knew how to escape.

The Spanish wasted no time interrogating me about the papers I carried for Carlos Carbonell.

I denied everything, of course, said I had no idea of the contents, that I cannot read, that Carlos Carbonell hired me to do his laundering and nothing more.

I'm not sure if they believed me or not, but regardless, they threw me in Recogidas.

That was months ago.

Truthfully, besides the absence of freedom, I can't say Recogidas is that much different from the camp. Both are their own form of hell.

When I dream here, it is of Isabella, my daughter my constant companion in this miserable place. I imagine her happy and healthy at my parents' house in Havana. I dream of being reunited with her once again even as I fear I will die here. I linger over happier moments together, our life in our farm in the country, my days spent with Mateo, my memories of Luz.

I cling to hope to help me survive this unbearable place.

And then the first piece of news comes—

We learn through the prison grapevine that the Spanish fleet has been destroyed by the Americans who are currently laying siege to the fortified city of Santiago.

I can only hope that this is the final blow to Spain.

"You have a visitor," a guard announces one day.

I turn to my cellmate Rosa in surprise, not sure which one of us he's addressing. Rosa has been here far longer than I have, and she says nothing about her life before Recogidas; the only clue I've gleaned about her past is that she was once a mother, for she often cradles an invisible child in her arms, speaking and crooning to it as though it is alive and with her.

"Which one of us do they want to see?" I ask.

"You."

I have had no visitors since I came here, not that there's anyone to visit me, really. I've had no news of Mateo, and if my family knows that I'm in this wretched place, they've said nothing. I could have tried to reach them through one of the passed messages that so often fall beneath Spain's notice, but I worried that linking them to me might put them at risk, and could jeopardize Isabella's safety. These are dangerous times, the stakes high.

I follow the guard from my cell, Rosa silent behind me. Sometimes I think her body is in Recogidas but her mind is elsewhere. Maybe that's the only way to survive years of this place.

As I walk to the Salon of Justice, women cry out around me, the sounds of their wails reverberating through the stone.

When we arrive at the room, I am surprised to see an unfamiliar blonde staring back at me.

She rises from her seated position and smiles, extending her hand to me. "My name is Grace Harrington. I'm a reporter for the *New York Journal*."

Forty-Four

※

GRACE

I will never forget the women I meet in Recogidas or the stories they share with me. Some were in the reconcentration camps for a time, others fought with the revolutionaries, and some were there because society chose to condemn them, labeling them as "unruly." It was the prison Evangelina described to me in her nightmares, but I also saw a different layer to Recogidas, the women whose faces wouldn't be splashed across newspapers, whose stories wouldn't rally a nation behind them.

I spend a few days in Havana speaking to the women of Recogidas and touring some of the reconcentration camps.

And then the news comes—

There is to be an armistice. Spain has conceded. After four months, and only a few weeks of fighting, our war in Cuba is over.

Instead of returning to the United States as I planned, in the middle of July I travel with some of the *Journal* reporters to Santiago where on Sunday, July 17, Spanish forces officially surrender to the Americans under the leadership of General William Shafter.

We all watch the ceremony unfold before us from a remote distance.

Shafter has one thing in common with the Spanish—he, too, is suspicious of the press, and he's banned reporters from the city.

Despite his best efforts, there are a handful or so of us here, hiding in plain sight, trying to get the best view of the ceremony taking place in the plaza outside the governor's palace in Santiago. American and Spanish officials are present for the transfer of power, but there is no real Cuban presence here, and once again, it feels as though they've been shut out of determining the future of their own country.

We all watch as the Spanish colors come down, and just as a group of soldiers hoists up the Stars and Stripes, the *World*'s Sylvester Scovel comes up alongside them, trying to get a better view than the rest of us, flagrantly disobeying Shafter's edict against reporters.

Shafter orders Scovel to step away, and when Scovel refuses, the major general takes a swing at him. Scovel instantly strikes back, and all hell breaks loose.

I can't quite stifle the laugh that escapes.

"Why am I not surprised to find you here?" a voice asks behind me, and I turn at the familiar sound, joy filling me.

Rafael stands in front of me dressed in his American military uniform.

This time, I don't hold back as I cross the distance between us, throwing my arms around him.

For a moment, I think I've caught him off guard, and then he gathers me in his embrace, his arms tight around me.

All around us, the fallout from Scovel's interruption of the ceremony continues, and while I don't doubt we're drawing much attention, I also don't have it in me to care.

Rafael is alive, and that's all that matters.

He takes my hand and draws me a bit away from the crowd.

"I was so worried about you," I say. "I feared something had happened to you." I take a deep breath, and the words simply come out, and as I say them, I realize the truth of them—

"I love you."

He leans down, conventions be damned, and kisses me, and it feels so right it takes my breath away.

"I love you, too," Rafael whispers, before thoroughly kissing me again.

When he pulls back reluctantly, he smiles down at me and says, "I happen to have a yacht at the ready if you're looking for a ride back to New York."

I WAKE, RAFAEL SLEEPING SOUNDLY BEHIND ME. WE MADE LOVE almost immediately after we boarded his yacht, one of the many he used when he was involved with the filibusters, dining on a quick meal before reaching for each other once more.

Afterward, he fell instantly asleep, as though these past few weeks spent with the army have taken their toll on him. I stared up at the ceiling for what felt like hours, willing sleep to come, but when it's clear it won't, I sit down at the typewriter in Rafael's stateroom and begin to write . . .

In Recogidas, the woman held her arms in the perfect shape of the baby she'd lost years ago . . .

Forty-Five

When Rafael and I return to New York, I find that the city is much different from how I left it. There are celebrations in early August when some of the naval ships return from Cuba, but overall the war has left its mark on all of us.

I hop on my bicycle and ride to the *Journal* offices.

Johnny stands on his usual corner, selling the afternoon edition.

"How was Cuba?" he calls out to me.

"It was something," I reply, not sure how to explain all that has transpired since we last saw each other.

"How's the newspaper business?" I ask him.

"Can't complain, although sales have slowed down some since the war stopped. Do you think they'll go back to charging their normal prices now that the war's over?"

The newspapers raised the prices they were charging the newsboys to sell newspapers when the war started, lowering the newsboys' profit margins, but considering the volume they were selling due to the war interest, they hardly minded.

"I hope so," I answer. "They should."

Our conversation breaks off as someone comes up to buy a paper from Johnny and I head upstairs. I walk through the newsroom that has become as familiar to me as my home at Aunt Emma's and knock on the door to Hearst's office.

He shows me in, and I have a memory of that first day when I came here looking for a job.

So much has changed since.

"What can I do for you, Grace?" Hearst asks me.

"I have a story for you. My last story." I take a deep breath. "As grateful as I am for the opportunity, I don't know if I can stay on. I'm not sure this is what I was cut out for—making the news. I think we've crossed too many lines somewhere along the way."

He's silent for a moment, and I almost think he's going to try to convince me to stay, but he merely nods. "We'll be sorry to lose you, but not everyone sees the world the same way. There are many papers that would be lucky to have you."

For as much as Hearst professed me to be a valuable member of his staff, I can already tell that in his eyes I'm gone. I'm not so arrogant as to believe I am irreplaceable—in this business, no one is.

I slide the article across his desk.

THE RUMOR ON PARK ROW IS THAT PULITZER IS STRUGGLING. Circulation is down now that the war is over, but cutting the price of his newspaper isn't profitable, and if he slashes staff salaries, then there's no doubt they'll defect to Hearst's side. For a man who has built his empire on the strength of the newspaper business, it must be immensely frustrating to have his war with Hearst deal him such a devastating blow.

No one is more surprised than I am when Pulitzer sends me a note, asking for me to meet with him.

I go to Pulitzer's mansion a few days after my conversation with Hearst, and am shown into his reception room by the same butler as before.

"You once came to me and asked me for a job. Said you wanted to be the next Nellie Bly," Pulitzer says in greeting after I've been announced and shown into his study. "You weren't ready then. You are now."

I glance down at his desk, at the folded copy of the *Journal* lying there, and the article I wrote about Recogidas, my name on the byline.

"Come work for me at the *World*. Your talents are wasted where they are."

It's all I've ever wanted since I set my sights on being a journalist. And still, when I think back to the years I spent working at the *Journal*, my half-hearted attempts at pilfering information to give to Pulitzer, it's clear where my heart lies.

For as much as I wanted to work for the *World*, I've learned the fantasy and reality aren't the same. As a girl, I read the *World* and envisioned Pulitzer as a champion for the people who didn't feel like they fit in this new society we've created. But now I realize that at the end of the day, he's a businessman, driven by the same needs for profit and power as the rest of them.

"I can't."

"Can't or won't? You're going to stay with Hearst?"

I am proud of many of the stories I've covered for the *Journal*, of the journalist I've become. I'm proud, and at the same time, I am not unaware of the mistakes that have been made or of my need to do better.

"I think my stunt reporting days are behind me."

Forty-Six

EVANGELINA

I'm going home.

I can scarcely believe it.

We are in New York for a visit; Carlos has business to conduct with some of the contacts he has made in the United States before we set sail for Havana where we'll move into the house where Carlos and I spent those fateful days in hiding together.

My life has changed so much in such a short time.

On one of our last days in the city, I walk to the restaurant where I once had my grand reception—Delmonico's—to see an old friend.

She's already seated at one of the tables when I join her.

After we greet each other and I sit down, she slides a newspaper across the table at me.

The *New York Journal*.

"It didn't make the front page, but they printed it today," she says. "I went to Recogidas. I spoke with the women. I wrote an article about their stories."

I meet her gaze, and I know that for the first time, maybe, she truly understands what it was like in that place. What it did to me. How it can make you desperate to survive anything.

"I read it earlier," I confess. "It's wonderful, Grace. Truly. I've been reading the *Journal* for months now. This is one of the finest pieces I've ever read. You shone a light on that awful place, on their stories. You didn't speak for them; they spoke for themselves."

I cried when I read it, her words taking me back to the time I spent in prison. I try not to think too much of those days anymore. I'd much rather look to the future, to the family Carlos and I are going to build together, the life we'll have.

I'm ready to put Berriz and everything that has happened behind me.

"It didn't feel like enough—the article," Grace says. "I suppose it never does. I wish it could do more."

"We do what we can," I reply, because if I've learned anything in this time of infamy, it's that no matter how much attention you receive, you are merely one person—and a woman at that—in a world that's forever changing against your will.

"How was Cuba?" I ask her, because my biggest fear is that we are going home to a country I will no longer recognize.

"The people—it's clear war has taken its toll on them. We saw refugees fleeing the affected cities, in desperate straits. There was death. Disease."

It is as I feared, then.

"Let us speak of happier things, for a moment, though," Grace says as though sensing my distress. "Congratulations on your nuptials. Considering the attention that surrounded every aspect of your life, I'm surprised and impressed that you were able to keep much of it from the press. I imagine Hearst would have liked nothing more than to publish a picture of you in your wedding dress on the front page of the *Journal*."

"I fear the gown would have disappointed him. It was not nearly as grand as the one the newspaper bought for me for the reception in Madison Square."

"It would have been a fitting addition for your book—you've come full circle, marrying one of the men who rescued you. It's something out of a fairy tale."

"I think we both know by now that the fairy tale is just a pretty story you tell to make people happy. I am happy, though, and that is enough."

"Will you return home now that the war is over?"

"We will. My husband is an officer in General Lee's staff. They're sending the Seventh Army Corps to Cuba to maintain law and order and protect property interests on the island."

"Does that bother you?" she asks. "The Americans having a military presence there?"

The truth is complicated.

Much of the friendship between my husband and General Lee stems from General Lee's interest in investing in Cuba now that Americans have such a strong presence on the island. And at the same time, while I wish for autonomy, I can't ignore how gracious and welcoming the Americans have been to me. I've also learned something in all of this—how badly I want to survive.

"I don't know," I answer truthfully.

"I had heard that your husband enjoyed a friendship with General Lee," Grace replies. "The former consul presumably has many contacts in Havana. As does Carlos." She hesitates, and I can see that whatever she is going to say next, this is the real reason for her asking to see me. "I need a favor."

"Of course. After all you have done for me, I would be honored to repay your kindness."

"There is a woman in Recogidas. I believe you know her, too, as does your husband. Her name is Marina Perez. She passed messages to you from Karl Decker before you escaped."

For a moment, I am transported back to the prison, to the little area where I used to write letters for the other prisoners. To the woman with the excellent posture and the worn hands.

"Yes. She helped rescue me. I don't think I'll ever forget her."

"Months after you left Cuba, she was imprisoned by the Spanish for her part in an espionage plot. They've also accused her of other crimes. I believe she was working for your husband as a courier at the time. I promised her I'd help get her out. The Americans have control of Recogidas now. Can Carlos appeal to General Lee to get her released?"

"I will do everything in my power to make it so."

"Thank you."

Our meal passes by quickly, and we say good-bye outside of Delmonico's, leaving me to wonder if our paths will ever cross again. It seems unlikely, but then again, life has carried me in many surprising directions.

We embrace, then I turn away from her and walk along the busy New York street, and where I once couldn't walk in the city without being mobbed by people, now all is quiet and no one recognizes me. The newspapers have moved on to other scandals and intrigues, and I am forgotten.

It feels good to be free of everyone's expectations and to simply be myself.

I am no longer "the Most Beautiful Girl in Cuba."

Forty-Seven

GRACE

After my lunch with Evangelina, I walk down Park Row. The giant war signs are being dismantled by groups of men.

It's a busy day on the streets, the newsboys hawking their papers, bicycles moving in and out of traffic.

Without the war fever driving us, a strange pall has set over the city. The United States has lost five thousand military men who perished in the conflict. Hearst has returned from Cuba in a state of depression, and he is far from alone. Many are fatigued and haunted by the memories of the war, some coming back with tropical fever and other ailments, yellow fever and malaria haunting specters that loom over the victorious.

Financially, the *Journal* is in a similar state, its coffers emptied by the expense of bringing our readers the news in such an exuberant fashion. And still, Hearst satisfied his chief aim:

His circulation is unmatched, Hearst claiming that one and a quarter million people read the *Journal*.

Was it Evangelina that started all of this, the hundreds of columns we wrote about her leading to this moment? Or was it the desire to "Remember the *Maine*"? To avenge those lost voices? Or in the end, was our thirst for expansion too great to be ignored? Was this truly about the Cuban people, or was Rafael right to be cynical all along, and was this really about investment opportunities and money? I'd like to think our better angels rule us, but I'm not sure what I believe anymore.

So many point the finger at us, at the unscrupulous work of yellow journalism, but as I look back at each individual decision we made, I don't know what I would have done differently. It's easy to view events with the benefit of hindsight, but in the moment, when a young woman was being imprisoned, when a country was being destroyed, what were we to do? Who can stand by and say nothing when hundreds of thousands are massacred? It is undeniable that mistakes were made, but we did what we did with the best of intentions or so I'd like to think.

I have to hope it is enough.

I head toward the *Journal* offices for the last time to pick up my final paycheck. I'm taking a risk walking away, but between the money left to me from my father and the money I've saved since I began working here, it's enough to give me the courage to take the chance.

A lump fills my throat as I make my way up to the newsroom, to the familiar shouts and sounds of typewriters pinging away.

After I've picked up my payment for the Recogidas article, for a moment, I stop and take it all in. This is where my journalism career truly began, and even though it feels like it's time to move on, it's still hard to let go completely.

I run my fingers across my old desk, my gaze sweeping across the newsroom.

I exchange quick good-byes with the rest of the newspaper staff, Hearst nowhere to be seen, and then with one last look, I walk out of the room and make my way through the building, heading down to Park Row.

Johnny and the rest of the newsboys are out selling the afternoon editions.

"Where are you headed?" he asks me. "Chasing a hot story?"

I shake my head. "I'm leaving the *Journal*."

"We'll miss you."

I smile through the threatening tears. "I'll miss you, too."

"Will we still see you around Park Row?"

"Absolutely."

I reach out and give him a swift hug.

I try to tell myself that there will be other papers, other opportunities. This is just the beginning.

I walk farther down the street. A man stands at the end of Park Row, waiting for me.

Rafael strides forward, closing the distance between us.

We've spent every day since we reunited in Santiago together, and where I once couldn't see myself spending my life with another, now I can't imagine my life without him in it.

"I didn't think I'd see you until later," I say.

"I had a break from my meetings. I wanted to come see how you were faring. I thought today might be hard for you. Would you care to walk for a bit?"

"A walk sounds lovely."

I take his arm and we set out down the street.

"I read your piece on Recogidas," he says. "You should be proud. You brought the prison to life and you told those women's stories."

"It didn't have quite the panache of Evangelina's tale. No front-page, screaming headlines."

And still, it's the article I'm most proud of.

"Maybe not, but it was still some damned fine reporting. Not every story has to be sensational to matter. You shared the stories of the other women, the ones who were overlooked."

"I tried."

"What will you do now?" he asks.

"I still haven't decided. It was the right thing to offer Hearst the Recogidas story—after all, I went down to Cuba on the *Journal*'s dime. Besides, you said it yourself—it's an important story. I wanted it to reach the most readers possible. Right now, the *Journal* has the highest circulation."

He smiles. "Smart move."

"I like Hearst. And I appreciate the work he's given me. But I don't know that I can keep this up. The stunt reporting and all of it. We may have grown our circulation to an unmatched amount, but what have we lost in the process? The *Journal*'s name is now synonymous with more exaggeration than truth."

"Are you saying you want to stop working as a journalist for good?"

"No. I'm not sure such a thing is even possible. It's in my blood now and it's a hard thing to shake. I suppose I want to get back to the types of stories I set out to write about from the beginning. To write about pressing issues facing women, to shine a light on the stories others ignore even if they aren't the sensational ones. Did you know that the newsies haven't had their pay set back to the rate it was before the war?"

Rafael shakes his head.

"Hearst and Pulitzer charged them more money for the newspapers they sold for them because they were selling in much greater demand during the war. But now the war is over, and the demand is less, and those boys are still forced to pay more for the papers they buy to sell on the streets. And on top of it, they aren't even refunded for the unsold papers. They're children and they're desperate, and two of the wealthiest men in the city are exploiting them for profit. *Those* are the kinds of stories I want to tell."

"Then you should go for it. You're a great writer, Grace. If anyone can do it, it's you. You've built a name for yourself, hard as it is. Use it to tell the stories you want to."

I stop, turning and facing him, my hand on his arm. "Thank you. It means a lot to hear you say that."

"So now that you've figured out what you want from work, what about the rest of it?" For a moment, he looks a bit unsure. "What about us? I love you, Grace. I'm in love with your spirit, and your mind, and the way you're determined to make the world better. I've loved you for a long time."

"I love you, too. You're smart, and kind, and you challenge me, and you accept me as I am without trying to change me." I hesitate. "But I don't know that I'm cut out for marriage and the rest of it. I fear I might always wish to be dashing off somewhere chasing the next story. It's hard work and long hours. I'd likely make a terrible wife. I have no interest in hosting parties and dinners and the like. I don't even know if I want children. And I have a terrible tendency toward messiness when I'm busy with work."

"I'm not sure what sort of husband I'd make. I don't exactly have a lot of experience in the matter. I can be irritable and demanding, and I work too hard and too frequently. I take risks because I like them. But I know that I love you. Maybe we could figure it out together. Maybe it doesn't have to look like what anyone else has. Maybe it could just be something all our own."

"Is that a proposal?" I ask, torn between equal parts fear and hope.

He nods. "Grace Harrington, will you marry me?"

It feels a bit like leaping into the air, or walking across scaffolding without a safety net beneath you. But if my career in journalism has taught me anything, it's that sometimes you have to face your fears and learn as you go.

"Yes. I'll marry you."

He grins, gathering me up in his arms, as we experience our first kiss as an engaged couple.

When we are finished, we walk down Park Row, side by side as we head home, the sounds of the newsboys hawking their papers filling my ears:

"Get the Journal. *One cent. The* Journal *acts when others fail to."*

Forty-Eight

MARINA

I stand outside the entrance of the Perez mansion in Havana, waiting for the door to open.

After five months in Recogidas, I am free.

When I told the reporter from the *New York Journal* my story and she said she would do everything in her power to see me liberated from the prison, I didn't believe it possible. But in the end, I found an unlikely rescuer in Evangelina Cisneros and her new husband, our old family friend Carlos Carbonell. He saw to it that the Americans he sided with from the beginning secured my release from the prison in return for all of the work I did as a courier.

The door to my parents' house opens, and Carmela stares back at me over the threshold.

"Marina! We've been so worried about you. Wh—"

My legs give out, and the rest of her words are cut off as she gathers me in her embrace. She holds me while I cry and strokes my hair as she did when I was a little girl.

When it feels as though all of the tears have been wrung from my body, my strength returning, I wipe my face and say—

"I am here for my daughter."

Carmela leads me through the house, to the family sitting room where she brought me last time.

"Can I offer you something to drink? Something to eat?" Tears fill her eyes. "You look—"

I shake my head and speak past the lump forming in my throat. "Just my daughter, please."

"Let me get Isabella for you," she says, leaving me alone.

I sink down on the settee, my heart pounding, nerves filling me at the idea of seeing my daughter again. What will Isabella think when she sees me again? Will she want to leave all of this? I have nothing to offer her, have no idea what sort of life we'll lead going forward.

I have to hope that my love for her is enough.

At the sound of footsteps, I look up, but where I expected to see my daughter and Carmela, I am greeted by my mother instead; a small bag in her hands.

She stops mid-stride, her gaze fixed on me.

"Marina."

I am once again both the woman who left and the girl who once loved her so much, who looked up to her for some sense of security in the world, and for a moment, I want nothing more than to sink into her arms, but I stay where I am, the weight of all that has happened dragging me down. I am home, and yet, I am not.

"Thank you. Thank you for taking care of Isabella when I couldn't. Thank you for—"

She shakes her head. "No. Do not thank me. It was the least I could do. The least I could do when I could not care for my daughter." Her voice cracks, and she breaks off, her fingers drifting to the large pearl necklace around her neck.

I don't think I've ever seen her so unsettled, not even when I told her I was leaving home to marry Mateo, and it occurs to me that I am not the only one whose world has been upended even if my losses have happened on a grander scale. The world my family has thrived in has changed, and now new alliances will be made, the Americans replacing the Spanish as the ones with whom they must now curry favor.

"I never—" My mother clears her throat. "When you have a child, you want what's best for them. You imagine their future, you wish for their happiness, and you do everything you can to bring it about. There is no greater pain than watching your child suffer. When you told me you wanted to marry Mateo, I didn't want your life to be harder than it had to be. To be a woman in these times is . . . difficult. We cannot do as we please, act as we'd wish, stand up for the things we might believe in. We are defined by the men we marry, by their treatment of us. I worried for you, and in doing so, I am sorry I failed you. Your father will never change his mind. Never accept the choice you have made."

"I know. And I understand what it means to be a mother, to have to make difficult choices."

Tears fill her eyes. "I know you do. You could come home. You and Isabella could live here. Mateo could be anywhere, he could—"

"Mateo is my husband," I reply. "I do not know what has happened to him, but he will always be my husband. I cannot deny that. Not even to come home."

She holds the bag out to me. "This is for you. It will give you the start you and Isabella need."

I take the bag from her wordlessly, pulling the drawstring and staring at the contents.

She's given me jewelry—pieces that have been in the family for longer than I've been alive, pieces I've seen her wear throughout my life.

"I wish I could do more, but your father—he won't notice that

these are missing. They should be yours anyway. They are your legacy."
She offers me a sad little smile. "We women collect these currencies,
this power wherever we can."

"It's too much. I can't accept it."

"You can. You will. For Isabella and for yourself. You have always
been strong, Marina. You will need that strength to guide you through
this new part of your life. To help you start over. We all need to be
strong now."

"The food—was that you?" I ask, finally voicing the question that
I've wondered about since Carmela first handed me the bundle.

"Of course it was me. You're my daughter. I love you."

Our relationship has never been an overly affectionate one, but I
take a few steps forward, closing the distance between us and wrapping my arms around her.

"Some of the revolutionaries are coming back to the city," my
mother whispers in my ear as she embraces me. "There is to be a reception of sorts for them today. You should go look for Mateo."

We break apart at the sound of another set of footsteps in the
room, and then I see her, my daughter, and she runs toward me,
throwing her arms around me.

We walk along the edge of the sea in silence. Isabella has
spoken little since we left. I've agonized over whether this is the right
thing to do, whether I should have left her with my mother and father
where she would live in better conditions than I likely will be able to
give her.

I don't know if Isabella truly understands why I left her, or if she's
angry with me for having done so, but I hope that I will be able to
make it up to her and that she will never have to make the same

choices I've made, that she will not one day be called to fight as I have done, as her father and grandparents have done.

The Spanish are finally expelled from Cuba. Here is what we are left with:

Nearly all of the countryside has been destroyed, almost all livestock slaughtered, the crops we've relied on for sustenance, the very earth itself a barren char. No one knows exactly how many lives perished in Weyler's reconcentration camps, but the estimates are nearly a third of the island's population. The freedom we fought for as women, the blood that was shed so we could be treated as equals with men, so that we could vote or hold political office, is another dream lost to the war.

Where we were once indispensable in the war for Cuba's independence, we are now forgotten in her future.

I am surrounded by forgotten, abandoned women.

They beg throughout the streets of Havana.

The Evangelinas of the world were feted with parades and cheering crowds, whereas the women who fought on the battlefield, who lived in reconcentration camps, who worked as nurses and couriers, who raised the cry of independence and lost so much, are left without prospects, impoverished and desperate, ill and malnourished. We dreamed of a free Cuba, gave our lives and our families to her cause, and we're given nothing in return. Perhaps if we'd been younger, prettier, our skin lighter, our virtue untouched, our fortunes would have been different.

It's not Evangelina's fault, of course; even in my more bitter moments, I know that. Our lives are not defined by one thing; we are more than the events that happen to us, as Evangelina should be. But it's hard not to feel like in Evangelina the Americans saw a Cuban who needed to be protected, and after saving her they decided the whole damned island needed saving, too. That America feared this new Cuban identity we are forging. It's hard not to question my part in the whole affair and wonder what I could have done differently even as I ultimately benefited from my role in her rescue. It's hard not to feel that if we hadn't been seen as victims, we would have had a chance to be treated as equals.

It's impossible to feel victorious when the "victory" leaves your country in ruins. Rather, it's as though we helped the Americans win a war against Spain. We had no part in the negotiations that ended the war, were relegated to onlooker status when the Spanish flag was finally lowered over Havana.

Many believed that because the United States knew what it was to wage a war for their independence, they would support our right to have the same freedom. But democracy seems to mean different things throughout the world.

Under the Treaty of Paris, Spain has signed the armistice handing over Cuba, Puerto Rico, Guam, and the Philippines to the United States for the sum of twenty-five million dollars.

Isabella and I walk on, toward a ceremony that's being held by some of the revolutionaries.

I pray my husband will be there. That he is alive.

I've already had to break Isabella's heart once telling her that her grandmother Luz has passed away. I can't tell her she's lost her father, too.

As we near the gathering, it's clear that we aren't the only family hoping to be reunited today. There are other women and children who appear as desperate as I feel, searching for loved ones.

Isabella holds on tightly to me as we search the crowd, looking for Mateo.

I don't see him in any of the men who walk by us. Their expressions are haunted, their bodies gaunt, their clothes in tatters. There is talk that provisions will be made for the men who fought in Cuba's military, but for now it looks as though they've lost everything.

"Do you know Mateo Sandoval?" I ask one of the men.

He shakes his head.

I approach more of the soldiers, asking them if they know of my husband, but no one does.

Am I to be one of the widows of this war?

The sun is nearly setting, and I turn away from the crowd, leaning down so I am eye level with Isabella.

"We should go. It's getting late. We can keep searching for him. I promise."

Isabella doesn't respond, but she takes my hand, and we walk back the way we came, dusk settling over Havana.

The jewelry my mother gave me will go a long way toward giving us a new start, to rebuilding our home. In this, we are luckier than many, at least.

We walk near the water, and I am reminded of the day Isabella and I looked out onto the harbor, when I told her that our memories, our love, our hope is enough to sustain us through these difficult times.

There must be better days ahead.

It's a beautiful night in the city, others clearly taking advantage of the opportunity to be outside, enjoying the cooler air. In the distance, a man approaches, his silhouette but a speck against the sea.

I stop in my tracks, Isabella stilling beside me.

There is something in his gait, the familiar set of his shoulders, his bearing—

I'd know my husband anywhere. I've loved him nearly my whole life.

I quicken my pace until I'm running, Isabella doing the same, and then he's in front of us, looking a bit older, new lines on his face, a slight limp in his stride. In a step, his arms are wrapped around us as he holds us close to him, as he embraces his daughter for the first time in years, as my tears begin to fall.

"You're home."

I don't say the rest of it—how I feared I'd never see him again, how I feared he'd died, that all was lost, that I don't know how we have survived all that we have. Isabella has been through enough. When we are in private, we will speak of our experiences. We will tell each other our stories.

I will tell him about his mother. We will grieve.

For now, we hold on to one another.

"Where will we go?" Isabella asks us.

"Home," I reply. "We'll go home."

"And if nothing is left for us there?"

I squeeze her hand tightly in mine, my other hand linked with my husband's.

"Then we'll rebuild."

I stare up at the Havana sky, at the mighty flagpole that once heralded Spain's dominion over Cuba, the Spanish flag flapping in the breeze for all of my life.

It's been replaced by a flutter of red, white, and blue.

Not the flag we bled for, that proud Cubans died for, the blue stripes interspersed with white ones symbolizing Cuba's provinces and the purity of our cause as patriots, the red triangle of strength, the blinding white star of independence. Not the flag we raised in battle for decades, the flag we dreamed of, the future we hoped for.

Instead, different stars and stripes exercise their influence on Havana.

The American flag flies over Cuba now.

And still, we dream. That we will have a voice in this new country for which we have sacrificed so heavily.

That one day we will be free.

Viva Cuba Libre.

AUTHOR'S NOTE

In the summer of 2018, a few days before *Next Year in Havana* was announced as Reese's Book Club pick for July 2018, I was down in the Florida Keys researching the book I was writing at the time, *The Last Train to Key West*. While I was in Key West, I came across numerous references to the sinking of the USS *Maine*—an event I vaguely remembered from my history classes in school. I also visited the San Carlos Institute in Key West, a Cuban heritage center and museum honoring the fight for Cuban independence. I instantly became intrigued with the idea of writing a book set during the Cuban fight for independence from Spain and the Spanish-American War. As I began researching the book, I thought about the characters who would populate the novel. And then in my research, I came across the true story of a Cuban revolutionary named Evangelina Cisneros.

As an eighteen-year-old Cuban revolutionary exiled with her father to the Isle of Pines and later imprisoned in the horrific Recogidas prison in Havana for rejecting the advances of a Spanish colonel, her story has been largely forgotten over time, but during her life Evangelina Cisneros was an international celebrity. When her plight came to the attention of the New York newspapers who were locked in a fierce circulation battle, she instantly became famous, and nearly four hundred articles were published about her in the *New York Journal*. Her imprisonment, prison break at the hands of *Journal* reporters, and subsequent celebrity are all real-life events that were detailed in Evangelina Cisneros's autobiography, which was published by William Randolph Hearst and likely ghostwritten by members of his staff shortly after her escape from Recogidas.

There were times in telling Evangelina's story that truth felt stranger than fiction. It was important to me to follow the details of her life as accurately and faithfully as possible, and here there was no need for dramatic embellishment. That said, while I utilized over one hundred sources to research the different aspects of the novel, I used Evangelina's autobiography as my primary source for her story line, choosing to tell her story as she saw fit. At times, that made for some additional investigation. In order to protect some of the individuals who helped her escape from prison, Evangelina used code names to describe them, so it took some digging through the historical record to match those names with real-life figures. Additionally, so much of Evangelina's life was sensationalized and shaped to suit the aims of others, that it was challenging to separate between the real Evangelina, the woman who was given the moniker of "the Most Beautiful Girl in Cuba" by the American newspapers, and the woman who was vilified by the Spanish. Even her "autobiography" was written and shaped by others to fit the narrative that had been created in the American press. At times, it is difficult to grasp who the real Evangelina was.

There are also some gaps and inconsistencies in Evangelina's story. Where I could, I relied upon the words of those involved in her escape from Recogidas—Karl Decker, George Musgrave, and others—to fill in those gaps as well as looking at as many supporting documents as possible to better shape her story. The events of the night Berriz attacked her on the Isle of Pines have been contested since it occurred. At the time, Spanish officials claimed that she lured Berriz to her room so that her friends could capture him. Evangelina vehemently denied this and, reportedly, was given chances at freedom if she recanted her story, which she never did. That said, there are reports that later in life she told a friend—Fitzhugh Lee—that she had Berriz come to her room so that he could be captured by the revolutionaries. However, since this information is secondhand, there is conflicting information from Lee, and this is her story, I wrote the events of that evening as Evangelina described them. Regardless of why Berriz went to her room that night, he was the senior ranking Spanish officer of the Isle of Pines and held the welfare and lives of her and her family in his hands.

Evangelina could be a difficult character to understand. The bold woman who hatched her own plan for how to break herself out of prison and who was prepared to join her father in fighting for Cuba's future, could often come across as demure and meek in the story written about her life. Since some of the descriptions of her are more consistent with the published articles in the *Journal* rather than her actions, it seems likely that here, too, the narrative was shaped to garner public opinion and support.

As Grace expresses in the novel, out of necessity Evangelina maintained a facade of playing a caricature of herself for much of her public persona. Her life was largely co-opted by the New York press and shaped for their own purposes, including the moniker of "the Most Beautiful Girl in Cuba," which I think she really took to be a subversive name that she used to suit her own purposes (especially considering her dislike of them referring to her as a "girl"), playing the role they thrust upon her in order to gain her freedom during a dangerous time in Cuba's history. In the subsequent years, Evangelina faded from public view, so there aren't many details available about her life after her brush with fame, other than the fact that she married one of her rescuers in a whirlwind romance—Carlos Carbonell—and that they eventually returned to Cuba after the war and had a daughter together. Carlos Carbonell reportedly sought privacy for himself and Evangelina after their marriage in May 1898, which may partly contribute to the lack of available information about her life after her initial bout of celebrity.

Carlos Carbonell died in 1916 and Evangelina later remarried and had children with her next husband. In her later years, Evangelina reportedly expressed surprise at all of the fuss that was made about her life at the time. Despite her close relationship with her family and obvious love for them, she spoke little about them in her autobiography, and so at times, I had to extrapolate what her feelings would have been. There's little known about her life—and that of her family— after her period of infamy. Evangelina died in May 1970 in Cuba and was given full military honors.

The Casa de Recogidas was the main women's correctional facility in Havana until the end of 1898. When Spanish rule ended and construction on a new prison was completed, the Presidio de Mujeres in Guanabacoa replaced it. Located on Compostela Street in Havana, the Casa de Recogidas is now the site of the National Archives of Cuba.

When I began researching *The Most Beautiful Girl in Cuba*, I knew little about the circulation battle between Joseph Pulitzer and William Randolph Hearst, but I immediately found myself immersed in a larger-than-life world where newspaper magnates chartered yachts and sailed into battle. All of the outlandish behaviors in the book— the showgirls dancing on a yacht in Cuba as war rages on, the spies immersed in newsrooms, the extravagant celebrations, eccentric personalities, and more—are straight from the historical record. The Gilded Age was a time of excess, and there is no better example of that than in the newspaper business during this period. At the same time, it was an era of great insecurity. In my fictional heroine, Grace, modeled after the legendary Nellie Bly and other journalists like her, I was able to immerse myself in this fascinating world.

At the heart of all of the different story threads, I kept coming back to one place: Cuba. The war for independence from Spain is one of the darkest and most heartbreaking times in Cuban history. While there is a range of estimates, approximately one third of Cuba's population was sent to Spanish reconcentration camps. General Weyler's reconcentration camps are considered to be the first modern use of concentration camps and resulted in the death of hundreds of thousands of Cubans.

In creating Marina's character, I wanted to pay homage to the immense courage and strength of spirit of the real-life women who fought for Cuban independence and the plight of the reconcentrados. Through her character I followed my fictional Perez family through history, witnessing the beginning of Cuba's independence, and learning a great deal about my heritage researching this time period in Cuba's history.

Cuba ultimately gained its formal independence from the United States on May 20, 1902.

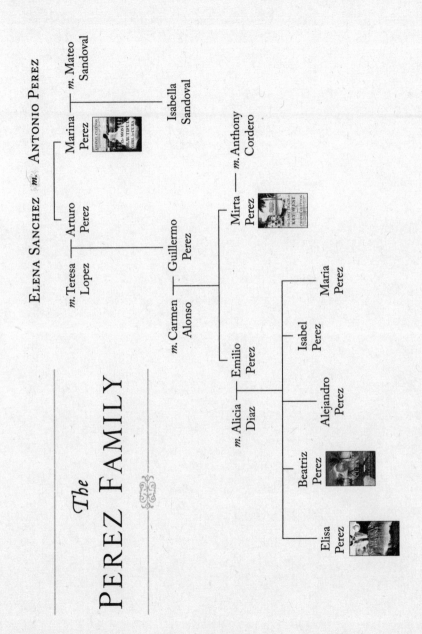

The
PEREZ FAMILY

ELENA SANCHEZ *m.* ANTONIO PEREZ

m. Teresa Lopez — Arturo Perez — Marina Perez — *m.* Mateo Sandoval

Isabella Sandoval

Guillermo Perez

m. Carmen Alonso

Mirta Perez — *m.* Anthony Cordero

Emilio Perez

m. Alicia Diaz

Elisa Perez — Beatriz Perez — Alejandro Perez — Isabel Perez — Maria Perez

ACKNOWLEDGMENTS

Publishing a book takes a village, and I could never do it without the support of all of the people who do such extraordinary work on my behalf and the friends and family who step in and offer help when I need it most along the way.

Thank you to my fabulous editor Kate Seaver and amazing agent Kevan Lyon who make all things possible. You're the best team, and I am so happy to be on this adventure with both of you.

To my wonderful publicists Erin Galloway, Tara O'Connor, and Stephanie Felty, and fabulous marketing representative Fareeda Bullert—thank you for working so tirelessly on my behalf and for sharing your talents with me. Thank you to the team at Berkley Publishing for giving me such a welcoming and supportive publishing home: Madeline McIntosh, Allison Dobson, Ivan Held, Christine Ball, Claire Zion, Jeanne-Marie Hudson, Craig Burke, Tawanna Sullivan, and Mary Geren, as well as the sales department, subrights department, and the Berkley art department, particularly Sarah Oberrender who designed the stunning cover, and all of the others who support my books. Thanks to Patricia Nelson and Marsal Lyon Literary Agency for your efforts on my behalf. Thank you to Reese's

I couldn't do this without my family and friends. Thank you for your love and for understanding when I sometimes disappear back in time even though dinner needs to be made and the laundry needs to be folded. You all jump in to help me when I need it most, and I couldn't do it without you. Thank you to my wonderful author friends—especially my fellow Lyonesses—who are always there to offer guidance and encouragement.

I am so grateful to all of the booksellers, bloggers, librarians, readers, and reviewers who read and support my books and have embraced the Perez family. Thank you for making this dream of mine a reality.

Readers guide for

THE MOST BEAUTIFUL GIRL IN CUBA

QUESTIONS FOR DISCUSSION

1. The novel alternates between the three main heroines: Grace Harrington, Evangelina Cisneros, and Marina Perez. What heroine did you identify with the most? What similarities did you discover between them? What differences?

2. Both Evangelina and Marina are involved in the fight for Cuban independence. How do they set out to achieve this aim? How are their roles similar? How are they different?

3. The three heroines in the novel struggle to find their place in society and often rebel against the limitations placed on them. What examples of this did you see throughout the book? How do the women react and adapt to these circumstances?

4. While Evangelina was an international celebrity at the time, much of her story has been forgotten. What other lesser-known women can you think of who lived extraordinary lives?

5. Grace greatly admires the writing of legendary journalist Nellie Bly, who set an important path for women in the field, and at times, Grace attempts to emulate her throughout the novel. Are there

women in your career field who you admire and who have greatly influenced you?

6. As a stunt reporter, Grace often finds herself in precarious positions in an attempt to advance her career. Did you see comparisons between the professional struggles of women during the Gilded Age and the challenges women face today? How do you think things have changed?

7. What parallels did you see about the discussion of the role of journalism in society in the 1890s and that of the role of journalism in modern times? What differences?

8. One of the major story lines in the book is the real-life rivalry between Joseph Pulitzer and William Randolph Hearst. What similarities did you find between the two men and their attitudes and strategies toward running a newspaper? What differences?

9. Grace begins her New York journalism career with a deep suspicion of William Randolph Hearst's motives and tactics. How does her attitude toward him, his newspaper, and her own journalism career evolve throughout the novel? Do you agree with her perspective or do you disagree?

10. Do you see any similarities between some of the themes and events in this novel and contemporary events? How much do you think our understanding of history informs the present?

11. Grace and Rafael are both outsiders of sorts in society. How do they relate to each other? How does this bring them closer?

12. How does war affect the characters in the book?

Photo by Chris Malpass

CHANEL CLEETON is the *New York Times* and *USA Today* bestselling author of *The Last Train to Key West*, *When We Left Cuba*, and Reese's Book Club pick *Next Year in Havana*. Originally from Florida, she grew up on stories of her family's exodus from Cuba following the events of the Cuban Revolution. Her passion for politics and history continued during her years spent studying in England where she earned a bachelor's degree in international relations from Richmond, the American International University in London, and a master's degree in global politics from the London School of Economics and Political Science. Cleeton also received her Juris Doctor from the University of South Carolina School of Law.

Ready to find
your next great read?

Let us help.

Visit prh.com/nextread